Starflake

Doug L. Hoffman

ISBN 978-0-9974781-0-5

Published by
The Resilient Earth Press
http://resilientearthpress.com

Books By Doug L. Hoffman

The T'aafhal Legacy Series
Ghosts of Orion
The Queen's Daemon
Starflake
Pleiad Found

The T'aafhal Inheritance Trilogy
Parker's Folly
Peggy Sue
M'tak Ka'fek

Non-fiction (with Allen Simmons)
The Resilient Earth
The Energy Gap

Preface

This is the third book in the T'aafhal Legacy series—the continued adventures of the officers and crew of the starship Peggy Sue. Once again we find Captain Billy Ray Vincent in command of the Honorable Orion Arm Trading Company's vessel Peggy Sue. After being bushwhacked in the Alpha Phoenicis system, chronicled in *The Queen's Daemon*, more than a year has passed and the merchant explorers are about to take delivery of a new starship, the *Peggy Sue II*. After becoming embroiled in war and revolution far from home they realized they need a stouter ship and more Marines, many more Marines.

This time they are going far afield, headed for the Pleiades, a star nursery with a number of blue-white giant stars. They are following a hint from the T'aafhal AI they found on the planet of the Ant Queen, telling them to "find the missing Pleiad." With their new ship and expanded crew they head out on a journey that will take them more than 400 light-years from home. A journey far beyond human space and the protection of the fleet. Naturally, things do not go as planned.

As usual, all units of measurement—distance, mass, time, etc— have been rendered in familiar human terms. It is much easier to do that than have the reader trying to translate what a hundred ferniks per wizbat means. Most of the characters are still referred to by rank, at least on occasion, even though the Peggy Sue is now a civilian vessel sailing for a merchant company. As always, I have tried to make the science as realistic as possible, given our current understanding. Some speculative liberties are taken, particularly in the realm of faster than light travel.

As usual, the text is sprinkled with quotations, some from historical sources, others from contemporary humans. Not all are attributed in the story itself, people tend not to do that, but I will say that there are lines from all sorts of folks—from Kenneth Grahame to George R.R. Martin, from George Washington to Joan Nosuchinsky. I hope you enjoy finding the "hidden" ones.

I would like to thank the following early readers and editors of this novel. Most of these have been with me from the beginning of my writing career and without them these adventures would probably never have seen the light of day. Special thanks to Rik

Faith, Bobby Johnson, David Metheny, and Clayton Ward, who help keep my science honest and my phraseology understandable.

Lastly, if you read this book and you like it tell your friends and please, please take the time to write a review on Amazon or Goodreads. Like any other author, I sometimes need encouragement to keep on writing. Nothing motivates like a good review.

This, of course, brings us to the obligatory disclaimers: all the characters in this book are fictional, not representations of any real person, living or dead; Any mistakes in the science, cosmology, engineering, etc. are purely my own and not the responsibility any of those thanked above. The book was written using LibreOffice and the cover art done using the GIMP. Ebook formatting was done using Calibre.

Regards,
Doug L. Hoffman
Conway, Arkansas
April 18, 2016

For my grandfather,
Lester Kreisher

Prologue

Hyades Open Cluster

Starlight glinted off the station's faceted exterior. Faint glimmers of orange with hints of red, reflecting the spectrum of the orange K-type giant that was this system's central star and the much smaller M-type red dwarf that closely orbited it. In all, an empty system in a scattered open cluster of similar stars. Here, far from its sun, orbited the reason for the Fleet's presence—a space station keeping a lonely vigil on the edge of nowhere.

The Fleet Commander watched the mopping up from the bridge of her flagship. They had come to this otherwise useless system for the specific purpose of reducing the population of it's only habitation to servitude. That phase of the operation was complete. The few space borne assets of the station inhabitants were scattered, drifting atoms, and the creatures who sent them decimated. *They could have at least made it a challenge for us.*

The warriors of Uxoreeza faced little real opposition when they boarded the station. The motley collection of races who opposed them mounted only feeble resistance—in the Fleet Commander's mind they were pathetic. At least one species had been totally eradicated and several others severely reduced in number. Reduced to the point their continued survival was questionable. It didn't matter, they were all animals, with no purpose except to provide food. Many were not even good for that.

A light on the console indicated an incoming call.

"Fleet Commander. Report."

"Hail, Fleet Commander. Sub-commander Fzixeera reporting that we have cleared a habitable section and the station is ready to receive the occupation force."

"Acknowledged. Proceed with the transfer from the transport ship." This part was distasteful. The Fleet Commander would have preferred totally depopulating the station but the Dark Lords said no. *And we all have our masters.*

"Commencing the transfer of the vermin, Fleet Commander," reported the Sub-commander, disgust in her voice. "We are

1

withdrawing by sections. A number of the warriors are bringing fresh carcases with them, will you allow this?"

Sigh. Vat grown protein is just as nourishing and arguably safer, but there is no substitute for something that you killed with your own claws. A poor replacement for decent plunder but better than nothing. "It is allowed."

That her race existed at all was because the Dark Ones occasionally need proxies to keep other warm-life species from rising. The Fleet Commander had no illusions, if the galaxy stopped creating new warm-life species, or the masters simply grew tired of them, her race would be eradicated as thoroughly as any her kind had exterminated. She might not feel reverence for the Dark Lords, but she could admire their thoroughness.

The thought of turning the station over the miserable little grubs in the "occupation force" churned the Leader's stomach. Puny, weak and totally lacking in honor, the occupiers were only strong enough to keep the other inhabitants in line. That they gladly preyed on each other was proof they were soulless scum. But the masters did not want the station left empty, allowing some new race of parasites to claim it for their own. With the occupying scum in place the station would remain in a miserable stasis for the foreseeable future.

The Fleet Commander longed for the day when her warriors could rid the Universe of this particularly loathsome species.

The Spirits of the Void know this was not a glorious battle of the kind true warriors dream of—a battle for the ages that would assure our souls admission to the great beyond. Instead of glory we have slaughtered weaklings and infest the conquered ground with vermin of our masters' choosing. If only a race worthy of battle could be found, but that was the one thing the Dark Lords are at pains to prevent.

Unknown to the alien commander, another battle was about to take place. A battle fought with unsophisticated weapons and on a much smaller scale than the Fleet Commander longed for.

* * * * *

Forty seven parsecs away, on an insignificant planet orbiting an unremarkable star, a war party worked its way silently toward their

2

enemy's encampment. In the camp there were twenty-nine in all: thirteen males, ten females and six young. Gathered around a central fire, the interlopers were bedded down for the night, with one distracted guard staring at the embers.

They had chosen a site on the edge of the great lake. Not a bad location for a band of hunter-gatherers, close to water and with plentiful game nearby. The only problem was that another tribe already claimed this hunting ground, the tribe whose warriors surrounded the slumbering trespassers.

The warriors waited patiently in the darkness, using the same skills they used to hunt wild beasts. The leader of the band trilled a bird call, the signal to attack. Clutching wooden clubs and spears tipped with razor sharp blades of obsidian, the war band rose as one in the darkness and descended on the unsuspecting sleepers. Spears thrust and clubs bludgeoned. Several of the victims cried out in pain, but it was done quickly.

The interloping tribe lay dead or dying; twenty seven men, women, and children slaughtered, including a babe in arms. A few moaned or moved feebly. They died where they lay, given the mercy of a quick death. Better a crushed skull than lingering pain and the inevitable arrival of predators. Only two young girls survived, taken as mates by attacking warriors.

The war band quickly gathered any items of worth—a few weapons, a string of beads, several water gourds. A basket of fish was kicked over, its contents spilled around the legs of one of the female victims. The leader of the war band signaled and as quietly as they had come, the warriors departed, leaving only the dead behind.

Both the victims and the attackers were animals. Phylum Chordata, Class Primates, Family Hominidae, Genus Homo. Eventually they would call themselves *Homo sapiens*, or more informally, human. They were in the process of subjugating the planet of their birth and all the creatures that dwelled there.

They were smart, adaptable, and aggressive. Makers and users of tools, able to communicate and cooperate, they hunted everything large and small, fierce and meek. Deadly and avaricious, they were the most dangerous creatures on the planet. They were so savage that the only real threat they faced was each other. So it was fighting each other that honed their skill at organized violence, to the point that they gave such violence a name. War.

One of the members of the band looked up at the clear night sky and saw a scattering of bright orange stars that someday his descendants would place in the constellation of Taurus. One of the stars, Delta 1 Tauri, was the star that the lonely space station orbited.

It was in that distant star system where the bored Uxoreezan Fleet Commander beseeched her gods for a race of great warriors to contest with. Perhaps the Fleet Commander didn't realize: One should be careful when asking a favor of the gods—they might grant your request.

Part One

A Ship In A Harbor

Chapter 1

The Drunken Crab, Farside

The Drunken Crab was one of the less reputable drinking holes that existed in the shadow of Farside Shipyard. It catered to sailors and dockyard workers, transforming their pay into alcohol and cannabis e-cigarettes. It was mid-shift, and as a consequence there were few patrons bellied up to the bar and scattered among the tables in the dark interior. Mostly dedicated drinkers left over from the end of the night shift and a few getting fortified for the afternoon shift.

At a round table in the far corner were four humans—three men and a woman. All four wore the plain dark blue jumpsuits of those who sailed on spaceships, be they Navy or civilian. This was a bit of subterfuge on their part. Though they were, in fact, sailors they did not belong to the Navy or any normal civilian shipping line. They were crew from the Orion Arm Trading Company ship Peggy Sue II. As such they normally wore more distinctive uniforms to distinguish themselves from the military and average dock-front rabble. On this occasion they were in mufti, trying to maintain a low profile.

They were all seated around the far side of the table, backs to the wall, with clear views of the entrance and the other patrons. Farthest to the left, a small weather-worn man raised a heavy beer mug to his mouth and took a deep draught. His perpetually squinting eyes darted around the dimly lit room. Returning the mug to the table he spoke.

"They're late."

Next to him a much larger man answered without looking at him. "Wasn't a hard and fast time, Chief."

"Damned frogmen got no sense of punctuality," the older man muttered.

"Relax, Chief," said the other large man. "Matt's right, we didn't have an exact meeting time."

"I knew this was a bad idea," said the woman, seated on the far right. Her short cut hair framed a serviceable face—not beautiful but attractive enough when she wasn't scowling. She had one thing

7

in common with two of the men, they were larger and more muscular than average human beings. The Chief, at five foot four, was odd man out in the size department.

"Come on, Gunny," said the one called Matt. "You've been cooped up on board the ship for a month. We thought you'd enjoy going ashore and grabbing a couple of beers."

"Don't use my rank, shit head," she whispered harshly. "I checked the net and the Navy still has me listed as AWOL."

"Really, Rosey?" said Matt's friend, Steve Hitch. "That was like more than two years ago."

"The Fleet's got a long memory," Rosey replied, taking another pull on her half empty beer. Even though the Crab was not located on one of the main passageways leading in and out of the yards there was still way too much traffic for her liking. "Oh shit."

All eyes turned to the open doorway from the corridor. Entering the bar were several large figures, framed by the bright lights outside. Their jumpsuits were dark green and around their waists were wide belts made from white webbing. On their arms were white armbands emblazoned with two black letters—SP.

"I thought you said the shore patrol didn't come in here, Hitch," the Chief growled at Steve. More of the Marines pushed into the bar, clumped together at the entrance, waiting for their eyes to adjust to the gloom. The one in the lead, evidently impatient, pulled out a small flashlight and began examining the bar's patrons.

Most hunched their shoulders and concentrated on their drinks. A few mumbled things like, "fuck off, jarhead." The Marines ignored those who were obviously civilian dock workers, their jurisdiction only extended to Fleet personnel—sailors and other Marines. The man with the flashlight approached the table where the four crewmates were seated.

"You shine that light in my eyes, gyrene, and I'll kick yer balls up around yer ears," the Chief said in a conversationally menacing tone.

"Put a sock in it Pops, and show me some ID," the Marine said, shining the light in the older man's eyes.

"Oh, crap," Matt said under his breath and readied himself for what was surely to come.

The Chief stood and looked the Marine up and down. Stepping forward, the grizzled little sailor put his fists up in front of him, like an old time prize fighter. The Marine, towering over the smaller man, snorted.

"Listen you little shit..."

The Chief kicked the Marine square in the testicles.

The Marine dropped the flashlight and sank to his knees. When he was down to the Chief's shoulder height, the old sailor hit him in the nose with an open palm strike that knocked the man over backward.

Things began happening quickly. Matt and Steve stood, their chairs crashing backward. Rosey made to rise as well when another Marine pushed down on her shoulder with his left arm.

"Stay put, lady."

"I ain't no lady!" Rosey hissed, moving her right arm forward then wrapping it over and around the Marine's extended extremity. She stood, twisting at the waist while jerking her arm upward. The Marine's arm dislocated at the elbow.

The Marine's eyes bulged with pain. Rosey released his now useless limb, drew her arm in front of her, elbow out, fist to her chest. Striking back viciously, she planted the backside of her elbow in the Marine's face. Something crunched and the Marine went down.

While a next Marine reached for Rosey, Matt slipped around her and executed a skipping side kick that struck the man in the solar plexus. The Marine doubled over, flying backward several meters.

At the same time Hitch launched himself onto the table and into a forward somersault. Springing off the end of the table he flew into an airborne kick that would have done Jet Li proud, landing a booted foot in yet another Marine's face.

The Chief jumped up in front of the fifth Marine. The low lunar gravity helping his hang time, he pummeling the man with at least a half dozen blows before touching back down. The Marine swayed and toppled. Behind him, the last of the shore patrol drew a stun pistol.

Rosey scooped up a beer mug from the table left handed and hurled it at the Marine brandishing the stunner. Her aim was dead on—the mug bounced off the man's head with a hollow thunk and he dropped the pistol, falling to the ground like a marionette whose strings had been cut. The mug did not break when it bounced off the floor.

"Damn, what do they make those mugs from?" asked Steve.

"The same stuff they put in shuttle windscreens," answered Matt. "They got tired of the glassware getting busted up every time there was a fight—which is practically every night in this place."

"Heads up," Rosey warned her companions, "we got more company."

At the entrance, three more large figures in dark jumpsuits entered the bar. The bar's other patrons looked on with interest, waiting to see what would happen next.

Fleet HQ, Farside

Walking abreast, four people climbed the wide stairs in front of Fleet Headquarters. Their uniforms marked them as officers in the service of the Orion Arm Trading Company—commonly just called the Company. From their body language it was clear that they were two couples, one pair topping six feet in height the other pair roughly four inches shorter. The taller couple and shorter man wore black and grey suits, indicating ship's officers, while the shorter woman's suit had deep burgundy trim, designating her a science officer.

They had taken the tube from Earthside City, where they lived, to Farside to inspect their new ship. It was a trip they had made many times over the past five months. The Peggy Sue II was still under construction in the yards nearby, but was finally nearing completion, and the owners had come to oversee the final outfitting. Before getting down to business they had decided to visit some old friends, shipmates from earlier voyages. Voyages taken before humanity clawed its way into interstellar space, before the alien bombardment devastated Earth, before the war against the Dark Lords. Humanity managed to survive but the galaxy remained dangerous, constantly threatening to swallow the unwary whole.

"The old place looks pretty much the same," remarked Captain Billy Ray Vincent, the taller of the men.

The tall dark woman next to him smiled a crooked smile. "The Navy runs on tradition, dear, even if that tradition is less than a decade old."

Beth Mekalu was the Captain's wife, first officer, and a one time Navy Commander. Before leaving Earth she had been in the Royal Navy and later commanded the corvette squadron during the battle for Earth. Now she was one of four partners who were the primary investors in the Peggy Sue II.

"Last time I recall coming here we were all mustering out and about to sign on with the Company," said Bobby Danner, the other male. He too had served in the Navy, commanding a ship on patrol among the neighboring stars.

"I have no fond memories of this place," added Mizuki Ogawa, "but then I was at the University research labs most of the time."

Mizuki was an astrophysicist, astronomer and experienced science officer, having spent time on the old Peggy Sue and the M'tak Ka'fek, an alien built ship that had come into human possession. It was on those earlier voyages that she and her companions had become friends with the people they were here to visit.

Stopping at the reception desk inside the HQ proper, Billy Ray cleared his throat to attract the attention of the young Marine lance corporal sitting there. The pretty blond looked up and took in the four people standing in front of her. She frowned slightly at the Company uniforms.

"Yes, may I help you?"

"Yes you can. Please inform Admiral Curtis that Captain Vincent and party have arrived."

"Do you have an appointment? The Admiral is very busy..." The receptionist's voice trailed off as she consulted a display built into the desk.

"Just pass on the message, Lance Corporal." There was an edge to Billy Ray's voice that caused the Marine to stop perusing the desk display and look back up at the visitors. Any enlisted person quickly comes to recognize that tone, the sound of a senior officer annoyed.

"Yes, sir." The receptionist's fingers danced across the touch display. Seconds later her eyebrows went up in surprise when the near instantaneous reply came back. "Someone from the Admiral's office will be here to take you back in a second, Captain."

Less than twenty seconds later a Navy lieutenant hurried up. "Captain Vincent, sorry to keep you waiting, the Admiral will see you immediately, please follow me."

As the OATC officers followed the lieutenant from the lobby the receptionist thought to herself, *who are these people? No one gets taken right in to see the Admiral, not even ship captains.*

* * * * *

Admiral Gretchen Curtis sat behind her desk, reading through reports on its display surface. The collars of her jet black jumpsuit held the four stars of a Fleet Admiral, her roan red hair was pulled back and pinned in a tight bun at the back of her head. At one time she had been the first officer of the Peggy Sue, back when it was the first Earth ship to travel to the stars. Now she was the commanding officer of the entire Earth space fleet, a position she was thrust into when Earth came under attack by the minions of the Dark Lords years ago.

She kept meaning to take some leave time, to step away from the Admiral's chair for a week or two, but somehow that never happened. There was always the next problem to attend to, the next SNAFU to be sorted out. Her only relaxation was an occasional sparring match with Yuki Saito, the head of Navy research and a kendo master.

A soft chime sounded as the door to her office opened. She looked up to see her aide step into the room and announce. "Admiral, Captain Vincent and party are here to see you."

A rare smile lit up Gretchen's face as she came around the desk to greet her visitors. She shocked her lieutenant by hugging each of the civilians in turn, starting with the tall captain.

"Billy Ray, damn its good to see you! And you as well Beth, Mizuki, Bobby."

"Good to see you too, Gretchen. We were in the neighborhood and decided to drop by."

"I keep promising myself a trip to Earthside to see you all but somehow it never seems to happen."

"You are working too hard, Gretchen," scolded Mizuki. "The Universe will still be there if you take some time off."

"You are right as always, Mizuki. But I'm being a terrible host, please take a seat." Gretchen motioned to a couch and chairs surrounding a coffee table. "Would you like something to drink, coffee, tea, or something with a bit more character? Johnny, pour my guests a libation, the good bourbon."

The aide moved quickly to the side of the room where a panel slid aside to reveal a well stocked bar. As the lieutenant poured six shots of caramel colored whiskey Gretchen continued talking to her old friends at a rapid clip.

"I asked Jennifer to join us, she should be here any second. It is so good to see people from the old crew." Turning to her aide she said, "Johnny, these old space dogs were among the first people to leave the solar system. Captain Vincent went to Gliese 581 and brought back the Triad Guardians during the battle for Earth; Commander Melaku commanded the corvette squadron during the engagement; and both Commander Danner and Dr. Ogawa were on board the M'tak Ka'fek, the T'aafhal battle cruiser that finally routed the enemy."

"I'm honored to meet you," the young officer replied, balancing the silver tray holding the drinks. As he set the glasses in front of the Admiral and her friends he added: "I poured a drink for the Commandant as well, Ma'am."

The office door slid open and a Marine officer walked in. Her uniform was dark green and she too wore four stars on her collar tab. "Why are my ears burning?" the newcomer asked.

"I knew mentioning booze would get you to appear," the Admiral said with a smile. "We have some old friends visiting."

"Well look at you," Marine Commandant Jennifer Rodriguez said as the OATC officers rose. Again hugs were exchanged. When the greetings were complete the six friends reclaimed their seats.

"It's so good to see you Jennifer," said Beth. She and Jennifer and Gretchen had been central to the defense of Earth during the assault on the solar system by the Dark Lord's minions. "Except for the stars you haven't changed a bit."

"I appreciate the lie, Beth, but I think the years have been kinder to you. What brings you to Farside? It can't be the ambiance or the fine dining, even Jean-Jacques moved his restaurant to Earthside. Jessie's bar is still here though."

"That's good news," said Bobby, "I haven't had a Fantasy in forever."

"We'll have to meet for cocktails one evening before we weigh anchor," added Billy Ray.

"Speaking of ships, I understand you are mothballing the Peggy Sue." Gretchen got a faraway look in her eyes. "She was my first command."

"She's not going to the breakers," Beth said. "In fact, she's going to finally become what she was designed to be—a luxury yacht for the richest man in the solar system."

"Speaking of TK, how is that old goat?"

"Ornery as ever, but Maria keeps him in line... mostly. In fact, she renamed the ship."

"Yeah," Bobby chimed in, "TK wanted something Texan, like The Alamo, but Maria wanted something prettier."

"So they compromised," Beth finished, "on *Rosa Amarilla*."

"The Yellow Rose," Jennifer translated, "nice choice. What about your new ship? I've seen it in the yards and it's huge, as big as a cruiser."

"We transferred the computer system from the old Peggy Sue to the new one, so we're calling her the Peggy Sue II—Sue Two for short. I hope she'll be as lucky as the Peggy Sue. After all, the old ship managed to escape a number of really tight spots."

"I think that had less to do with the ship being lucky and more that her captains all knew their jobs, Billy Ray." Mizuki, being a scientist, didn't share the superstitions of sailors.

"We decided that we needed a stouter ship for our next trip, after we were ambushed at Alpha Phoenicis," Beth explained. "Since we are headed for the Pleiades we are going to be all on our own. Aldebaran is twenty parsecs away and that's just the first transit."

Gretchen shook her head. "The Fleet is pushing out farther each year but not nearly that far, and things out there are definitely not safe. We just had a frigate limp home after being shot up by some race we've never seen before."

"Yeah, and the hawks in the Fleet and on the Council are pushing to send an expedition to invade the alien system," added Jennifer.

"Can't blame 'em for wanting to get their money's worth out of those new assault ships you've been building, they're even bigger than Sue Two."

"We still need to be cautious," said the Commandant, always protective of her Marines. "We need better intel before we stick a favored appendage into the meat-grinder."

"We do greatly appreciate the data on that warp drive ship you encountered, and the design for sensors to detect them. No matter how impressive our new ships are there are bound to be aliens out there that can swat us like flies."

"We know that well, Gretchen," Beth said, sadness in her voice. "We've lost a lot of good people over the years."

"Amen," said Billy Ray.

Gretchen stood, raising her glass. "To absent companions."

The others stood and repeated the toast: "Absent companions."

After draining their glasses they paused for a moment of silence before retaking their seats. Gretchen looked at her aide and said, "Johnny, we need another round."

Turning back to her friends she smiled. "Now tell Jennifer and me about this last voyage you were on..."

Chapter 2

The Drunken Crab, Farside

The nearest of the three newcomers spoke. "You didn't leave any for us, Chief."

"If'n yous had showed up on time there would have been plenty to go around," the Chief replied. The other man chuckled.

Rosey stepped over a downed Marine. "As much as I'd love to stand here all afternoon exchanging pleasantries with you fellas, I think that haulin' ass is probably a good idea right about now."

"Shit, I thought we were gonna get free beers outta this," another of the newcomers said.

"We got beer on the ship, let's move."

The four crewmates and the three newcomers exited the bar, strolled casually across the main passageway and entered a side tunnel. Once off the beaten path they all broke into a run, sprinting away from the site of the bar fight. As they ran Hitch spoke to one of the other men.

"How are you doing, Bud? Good to see you."

"You too, Stevie, still getting into trouble I see."

"Hey, the Chief started it."

"Right."

They slowed to a brisk walk as they debouched into the main space of the shipyard. Half a kilometer wide, equally as high, and four kilometers in length, the cavernous space seemed to extend to infinity. It was lined with openings giving access to construction bays. Within those bays new ships of many sizes and shapes were being built amidst gigantic fabrication units and supporting scaffolding.

Above each bay was a metal roof made from T'aafhal hull material. Part of the advance technology mankind had inherited from those ancient aliens, the material was selectively permeable, allowing solid objects like spaceships to pass through it while holding an atmosphere inside. This eliminated the need for airlocks to pass ships into space and allowed the shipyard docks to be kept under normal atmosphere. When a ship was completed the scaffolding was removed and the new vessel would rise on its repulsors, pass through the metal ceiling, and into the freedom of space above.

Workers in hard hats and hover sleds crisscrossed the open space, headed for one construction bay or another, while delivery drones drifted overhead. Across the way were a number of in-system transports, fat cylindrical ships with no alter-space capability, intended to haul people and freight around the solar system. On the side adjacent to the fleeing crewmates more elegant ships were housed—frigates and patrol craft intended for the Navy. Four bays in they came upon a familiar torpedo shaped craft, its bow made from silver and crystal. The newcomers started to turn into the bay.

"That's not where we are going, fellas," said Matt.

"Isn't that the Peggy Sue?"

"Not anymore. That's TK Parker's yacht, in for refitting. Our ship is in the next berth down."

Passing in front of Parker's pleasure craft, they rounded a barrier separating the two bays. Before them was their destination, the Peggy Sue II. It had a conical bow make from curved transparent panels and silver metal joinery, much like the bow on the original Peggy Sue. Unlike the older ship, which was shaped like a nuclear submarine or a dirigible, this ship's hull swelled significantly just aft of the transparent bow and bridge section. The front section was fifteen meters in diameter at its base, where the hull smoothly flared outward to the main hull's full thirty meters. It maintained its full beam until twenty meters from the stern, where it once again tapered to a blunt aft end.

The hull was not a featureless silver cylinder, it had three shallow indentations that ran its length from fore to aft. One ran down the top of the ship with two others spaced at 120 degree angles. In the shallow indentations were docking sites for auxiliary craft: two armored landing shuttles for the ship's marines and two exo/endoatmospheric interceptors along the sides; a large shuttle for the crew and a smaller shuttle to act as the Captain's pinnace on top. None were currently nestled against their mother ship's hull —they would be picked up later, after the ship left the yards.

Not as obvious was the ship's armament, only hinted at by blisters of varying sizes scattered around the hull. Two hyperluminal particle cannon, starboard and port; six X-ray laser batteries; six 30mm railguns for close support; and two large railgun cannon that also served as launchers for gravitonic torpedoes. Wrapped in the most advanced shields ever built by humans, Peggy Sue II was more than a match for even the latest Navy cruisers—a fact the Company did not advertise.

Bud left out a low whistle. "Man that ship is huge!"

"Well yer not wrong about that," said the Chief with obvious pride. "She's two hundred meters in length with a thirty meter beam, massing eighteen thousand metric tons."

"What's the complement?" asked the lead newcomer.

"Ten officers, six chief petty officers, forty two enlisted and twenty six Marines."

"You planning on invading a planet or space station somewheres?"

"Chief Morgan, you and yer SEAL buddies were with the M'tak Ka'fek when they had to board a couple of space stations. Captain Vincent want's to be sure we have the personnel to do that if needed without leaving only a skeleton crew on board."

CPO Rick Morgan, formerly of the US Navy SEALs, smiled at his old friend, Master Chief Frank Zackly. "You always did manage to land the best assignments, Frank."

"Enough of old home week, Rick," Rosey interjected. "How about you and your fellow snake eaters get on board. I don't want to be hanging around waiting for a bunch of shore patrol apes to show up, stunners blazing."

"After you, Rosey."

"Follow me," said Steve Hitch, heading up the boarding ramp. "Try not to trip over any snipes, they're still running around installing stuff."

The Atrium, Farside

After spending far longer than they had intended—and drinking far more bourbon than was advisable—Billy Ray, Beth, Mizuki, and Bobby parted from their friends and headed toward the shipyard. Leaving Fleet HQ, they descended the broad stairs to the Atrium, a large open space surrounded by trendy shops and eateries, festooned with palm trees and tropical vegetation. At the far end there was even an artificial waterfall to lend added ambiance.

"I don't know about y'all, but I'm half in the bag."

"It's your own fault, dear, no one forced you to keep drinking, though Gretchen was quite free with her liquor."

"Well we couldn't refuse an old friend's hospitality, could we?"

"You both know that our nanites will burn off the alcohol quickly with a little physical activity," chided Mizuki.

Bobby simply smiled, enjoying the temporary buzz. Having T'aafhal medical nanites in their systems made getting really drunk a very hard thing to accomplish. *At least Gretchen's bourbon was top draw stuff, not local rotgut.*

"What are you grinnin' about, pardner," Billy Ray said to his Sailing Master, noticing the self satisfied grin on his face. They had been best friends since high school and had served together for decades. They were fortunate that their wives put up with their shenanigans and also genuinely liked each other.

Before Bobby could answer a bald, bespectacled man in a Navy officer's jumpsuit nearly walked into them. The officer was head down, fiddling with the data display on his left arm. He was trailed by a pudgy ensign carrying two briefcases.

The officer looked up and snapped at Billy Ray. "Watch where you're going!"

"You were the one flyin' blind, Captain. Most people don't walk while looking at their forearm."

The officer looked over the four people in front of him, frowning at the Company uniforms. Then a look of recognition came over his face. "You're the captain of the OATC ship that blasted out of here with a Marine deserter on board a couple of years back."

20

Billy Ray's eyes narrowed.

"I got no idea what yer talkin' about, slats."

"I'll have you know some of your Company thugs just beat up a squad of shore patrol Marines down by the shipyard docks. All six Marines had to go to hospital!"

"Fleet SP has no jurisdiction over Company personnel. Sounds like they stuck their noses in where they didn't belong." Billy Ray squinted at the other man. "I recognize you Perlmutter. Yer that tin-plated asshat that tried to block our alter-space transit by running a ship across our exit trajectory."

Capt. Perlmutter turned even paler than he was naturally.

"You Fleet jackasses keep yer bully boys away from my people or some of them might end up worse than in sick bay. And if you try sailing a ship across my path again I'm apt to claim right of way and endangerment and blow the scow out of the aether, do you understand me?"

Billy Ray folded his arms across his chest and stared down at the Fleet officer. Perlmutter's face went from ashen to bright red. Realizing that Billy Ray and party were not going to give way, he walked around them in a huff, trailed by his aide. As the Ensign hustled after his superior he gawked at the OATC officers with fear written on his face.

Watching them go, Billy Ray shook his head. "That boy ain't the sharpest tool in the drawer."

"No," his wife agreed. "But he is certainly still a tool."

"We have gone from seeing the best of the Fleet to the worse in just a few minutes," Mizuki observed. "Why do they let people like him in the Navy in the first place?"

Bobby smirked. "I just hope the crinkleneck suckmonkey goes to the Admiral about this. Gretchen will rip him a new asshole."

"My, he does seem to bring out the best in you two boys."

"Regardless, honey bunch, we need to get back to the ship and find out who's playing rough with the shore patrol."

21

Goat Locker, Peggy Sue II

"So you shoes actually wiped the deck with those SP dorks?" said Phil Kowalski, one of the SEALs.

"I am not a shoe, polar bear bait, I'm a Marine."

"Evidently an AWOL Marine," said Chief Morgan, who found the fact that Rosey was wanted by the Fleet rather humorous.

"Pretty nice quarters you have here," said Bud Jones, trying to change the subject. "All us lowly petty officers are overcome with envy."

"Speak for yourself, snake eater," Steve Hitch retorted. "Matt and I are now bonafide chiefs ourselves."

"Boot Chiefs you mean," groused Chief Zackly, using the informal term for newly promoted chiefs still in their first year.

"Yes, we know," Matt Jacobs added, "and you are the Brigadier Chief."

"And don't yous forget it or I'll bust ya back to deck apes in a heartbeat."

"All this memory lane stuff is great but when are we going to get down to brass tacks?" asked Chief Morgan.

"Rick, I heard from a little bird that yous SEAL types were back on shore and at loose ends. So the Gunny and I thought it might be worth having a chat."

"You mean about us maybe shipping out on the Peggy Sue?"

"Sue Two," corrected Hitch, drawing an annoyed glance from the Chief.

GySgt Acuna picked up the conversation. "As you can see, Sue Two is much bigger than the old Peggy Sue. Like the Chief said, we have billets for six chiefs, forty two sailors, and twenty six Marines."

"We are not Marines," Chief Morgan said flatly. "That's part of the reason why we parted company with the Navy. They wanted us to either become jarheads or regular squids."

"Trust me, Rick, we all know the difference, and so does the Captain."

"Vincent? Wasn't he one of the guys you sent to recruit us the first time, him and that greeny beanie? We never served under him as captain. You sure he knows what SEALs are good for?"

"Trust me, he appreciates the difference between Marines and you special operator types. And he has a pretty realistic take on what type of shit we are apt to step in out there in the inky black. It was him and the XO who insisted on more than doubling the number of Marines on board."

"You're saying the Old Man is a straight shooter?"

"He's a lot like Captain Sutton."

"Yeah," Hitch chimed in, "a poetry quoting Texan who kicks ass and takes names."

The head SEAL nodded. "What about the other officers?"

"The XO, Beth Melaku, is the Captain's wife. Former Navy corvette squadron commander and tougher than nails. You know the Sailing Master Bobby Danner and his wife Mizuki Ogawa from your time on the M'tak Ka'fek."

"Dr. Ogawa? The little Japanese chick that got her legs burned off on Ring Station?"

"She was a total samurai war machine with that sword of hers," added Bud, admiration in his voice. "Doc had to grow her a new pair of legs after that little furball."

"That's the one. She still has the sword."

"So you aren't sailing with any lightweights or armchair swabbies, what's the mission?"

Matt Jacobs jumped in, being better versed in the astronomical details. "We are headed for an open star cluster called the Pleiades. It's about 440 light-years from Earth and full of hot young stars. We have intel that says there were T'aafhal present in that system less than a million years ago."

"Yeah, we're hot on their trail," quipped Hitch, earning him a hard look from the Chief and a cuff from Jacobs.

"Cmdr. Danner says we will make it in three hops, all involving massive stars so the transit times will be short. In order, we go to Aldebaran, Eudora, and Alcyone. It should take us less than a month total, assuming we don't spend a lot of time traversing the intermediate systems in 3-space."

"Do we know what to expect on the way?"

"Nope," the Chief said succinctly.

"And you want us to sign on?"

"Yep," said the Gunny. "I like the idea of having some extra warfighters to back up my Marines if needed, plus we may run into a situation that calls for your special talents."

Chief Morgan looked at his two brother SEALs. Bud nodded and Phil shrugged. "It ain't like we got dick-all going on around here."

Rick turned back to the Chief. "OK, we're in. It's gotta be more fun than what we have been doing."

Chief Zackly cracked a rare smile. "Welcome aboard gentlemen! I can't promise it will be fun, but it won't be boring."

Chapter 3

Polar Bear Habitat, Farside

Most of the surviving talking polar bears, *Ursus sapiens*, lived in the large habitat constructed for them by Ludmilla Sutton during her tenure as Farside base administrator. Inside the large domed space conditions mimicking those of Earth's Arctic region were maintained, with freezing temperatures, floors of ice, and open pools of frigid salt water. Mounds of ice, simulating pack ice pressure ridges, added variety to the terrain. Overhead the holographically projected sky reflected current conditions at Earth's North Pole.

Though humans were not barred from visiting the habitat few did. Going inside meant donning heavy insulated clothing including boots and parkas. Otherwise a visitor risked frostbite and eventually death from exposure. The bears mostly ignored humans who chose to enter their world. At one time human school children were brought to interact with the young bears, to help accustom both species with each other. That happened less frequently these days.

For their part, many bears studied at the University, usually attending class via avatar—normal conditions in the human portions of the base were uncomfortably warm for creatures evolved to spend most of their lives wandering the Arctic pack ice. Some put in a tour with the Navy or Marines, learning skills that they hoped to eventually put to use when they found a planet they could claim as their own.

It was winter in the arctic, which meant that the sky was dark all of the time, the Sun never rising above the horizon. Wisps of snow ran in rivulets across the simulated pack ice. Through the frozen gloom trudged two humans in white, fur trimmed parkas—a man and a woman. A few of the residents raised their heads and looked at the two legged intruders.

"You two lost?" asked one of the females, when the couple drew close enough to be heard over the moaning wind.

"We're looking for Ahnah or Umky," said the man.

"Ahnah is denning, waiting to give birth," said the she-bear, "but Umky is around here somewhere."

Rambling over a nearby ridge, a large male bear appeared through the blowing snow. As he drew closer he grinned.

"I thought I smelled some familiar humans." The bear sat down in front of the two humans, putting his head at about the same level as Billy Ray's and Beth's. "What brings you to the scenic Arctic?"

"Hello Umky," Beth said, glad the search for their former shipmate ended up a short one. "When is Ahnah due?"

"Any day now, at least that is what the other females tell me. She-bears don't much care for daddy bears hanging around when they are giving birth."

"I'm sure that will change once your cubs are borne," Billy Ray added encouragingly, "Your daddy was around for Isbjørn's last litter."

"Yeah, it's becoming a family tradition. But I don't think you came for the birthing."

"Actually, we're lookin' for some bears who are willing to ship out with a bunch of humans for an extended voyage."

"Really? How long a voyage?"

"We expect it to take at least a year," Beth answered.

"How many?"

"We were thinking four."

"There's not enough space in the Peggy Sue's polar bear quarters. Not for that many on a long voyage."

"New ship," Billy Ray responded. "Much larger quarters for the ursine crew."

"Hmm," the bear said. "If I was free I'd be tempted, but I'm sort of spoken for." The she-bear that had greeted the humans was still near by and she snorted at Umky's remark.

"We have openings on the science team, weapons crews, and the Marines."

"I'll ask around. How soon are you looking to weigh anchor?"

"A week to ten days," the Captain answered. "We're starting to load provisions now. If you find some interested bears have them give us a call on the Peggy Sue II."

"Sure thing. It was nice of you to come by in person."

"When you see Ahnah give her our best, won't you?" said Beth, sensing that the conversation was over. "I'm sure your cubs will be darling."

The he-bear smiled a tight lipped, bearish smile. "Will do. Have a safe voyage."

With that the bear rose up off his haunches and padded silently away across the frozen landscape. Beth and Billy Ray also turned and began the cold walk back to the entrance of the habitat.

Cargo Hold, Peggy Sue II

While Beth and Billy Ray went polar bear recruiting, Mizuki and Bobby returned to the ship, entering through the portside cargo hold door. Sitting in the construction dock, the curved sliding door was open and a wide ramp extended from threshold to the surrounding scaffolding. Even though the door was made from selectively permeable hull metal it could still be opened physically, just in case there was a power failure that prevented its normal operation.

The open space of the hold was a bit bigger than the old ship's. It was used more to store expendable supplies—like satellite probes and messenger drones—than to store the bounty gleaned from strange alien worlds. The economics of star travel made all but the rarest items unprofitable as freight. The profits for the mission would come from two primary sources: discovery of new habitable planets, and gaining information about other races and their technology.

Even filled with equipment for the coming voyage there were clear areas at the forward end and around the edges of the hold. These were used by the crew and Marines for combat instruction and PT—physical training. Entering the well lit space, the officers could see a group of a dozen or more men and women, standing in three ragged ranks. Facing them stood the Gunny.

27

"Officer on deck!" someone shouted.

"As you were," replied Bobby reflexively. While this wasn't the Navy there was a certain level of discipline maintained among the crew as necessary to good order and efficiency. "New recruits, Gunny?"

"Aye, Sir. Candidate Marines," she replied.

"Have you seen the Chief?"

"He's forward, Commander, in the goat locker with a couple of recruits of his own."

Bobby nodded. "Carry on."

Bobby and Mizuki headed forward through an internal airlock door, headed for the goat locker, the senior enlisted quarters. As the door slid shut a male voice from the ranks was heard: "Nice ass on that little science officer."

This was followed by a few chuckles and some shuffling around. The Gunny turned back to the recruits, her face a mask frozen in anger.

"ATTENTION!"

The recruits came somewhat sloppily to attention.

"I do not know what you maggots think this is, but I can assure you that the Company is not a bunch of Chablis sipping, candy ass, ne'er do wells playing like they're in the fuckin' Navy!"

The recruits drew themselves to more rigid poses, realizing that the Gunnery Sergeant, who had obviously been a real Marine, was pissed off.

"I don't know which of you pus-nutted, pencil-dicked assholes made that remark about Science Officer Ogawa and I don't care. That officer has fought on more planets and killed more aliens than the bunch of you pussy-ass can't cunts and no-loads put together. You are lucky that neither she nor her husband, Sailing Master Danner, heard the shit flowing from that sucking face wound you call a mouth, or those of you left alive would be cleaning blood and entrails off the deck! DO YOU READ ME!"

"We read you, Sir!" most replied.

"Do not 'Sir' me, I work for a living! You will address me as Gunnery Sergeant, the officers you will call 'Sir' or 'Ma'am'. Now drop and give me 40."

The recruits dropped to the deck and began doing pushups.

"When you get done with that we are all going to run laps around the hold until the last one of you shit-for-brains dicksucks falls over or pukes his guts out."

As the prospective Marines all pumped out pushups, off to one side a group of sailors observed the scene with interest.

"Looks like the recruits just found out that this is for real," crewman Tamara Wilson observed.

"If she does run them until they puke, do we have to clean it up, Chief?" asked Kashi Ademola, also a veteran crewman.

"The proto-jarheads can clean up their own mess," answered Chief Matt Jacobs.

"Why is the Gunny punishing them all and not just the wise ass who made the crack about Dr. Ogawa?"

"Two reasons, Tam. First is to impress upon each of them that discipline on board is just as strict as on a Navy ship, maybe more so. Second, to let 'em all know that they are expected to act as a team. If one screws up they all take the heat."

Kashi shook his head. "I'm glad I'm not a Marine."

"So am I, Kashi, but it's often good to have some around. Now let's get over to the starboard particle cannon mount and get things squared away before Master Chief Zackly has us out there with 'em."

"Aye, aye, Chief."

One by one the three climbed up the companionway to second deck, headed for the starboard side main battery. As with so many systems on the Sue Two, there was still rigging and fitting to do.

Sick Bay

Dr. Belinda White, known to her friends as Betty, was checking out her new medical section. Betty had been the Navy Medical Corpsman attached to a squad of Marines on the first voyage of the Peggy Sue. She had stayed with the crew ever since, only taking a break to earn a medical degree from Lunar University. With the possible exception of Ludmilla Tropsha, the first ship's doctor, she knew more about T'aafhal medical technology than any living human. This was not always a plus, given that the Peggy Sue's medical equipment, as good as it was, was not nearly as capable as the healing chambers onboard the M'tak Ka'fek.

While medical nanites and tissue regenerators greatly advanced the medical arts, Betty could not regrow whole limbs with the speed that the T'aafhal could. A new arm could take her several weeks, on the M'tak Ka'fek it took a day. Fortunately, such drastic reconstruction had not been needed, so far.

Her staff consisted of a nurse, a doctor's assistant, and a new doctor versed in veterinary medicine. The new Vet-cum-MD was a nod to the expanded polar bear presence on board. Strangely, they had never been called on to heal an alien, despite the trail of dead critters the Earthlings seemed to leave behind them.

"Doctor White?" a man's voice said.

Well speak of the devil, Betty thought, looking up. "Yes, I'm Dr. White. You must be Dr. de Bruin. Welcome aboard."

Betty extended her hand and the tall, fair-skinned doctor shook it.

"Please, call me Johan." The 'J' was pronounced like a 'Y'. Johannes de Bruin, DVM, was from South Africa. An enclave of people managed to survive the alien bombardment in a sheltered mountain valley above the Cape. Due to location and geography, it was mostly spared by the asteroid induced tidal waves that ravaged the lowlands. The valley, known as the Groot Drakenstein, lay in the shadow of mountains of the same name. The approach to the valley was breathtaking, hemmed in on three sides by the Groot Drakenstein, Franschhoek and Simonsberg mountains. Heavily settled by French Huguenots, the one time elephant breeding ground was the heart of South African wine country.

"Please call me Betty, Johan." The contrast between the tall, blond, pale skinned Afrikaner and the medium height, dark haired, mocha skinned African-American was pronounced. "Have you gotten situated in your quarters?"

"Yes, thank you, I have." The tall man smiled, his pale blue eyes taking in the surrounding sick bay. "I must say that this ship is equipped much better than the last ship I served on."

"Navy?"

"Colonization Board. I was hired to watch after the livestock accompanying the settlers."

"That sounds like fun."

"Three weeks out, a couple of months in orbit offloading everything, then three even more boring weeks back. At least on the way out there were sheep and cattle to watch after."

"I doubt that you will be kept busy by our crew. We have four polar bears—two males and two females—so your large animal skills wont be taxed. I hope you don't mind pitching in with the humans." As a rule, MDs and DVMs didn't treat each other's clientele but times had changed.

"Not at all. I've undergone cross species training at the Farside medical school. Not that I am qualified to do major surgery, but I can physically administer vaccines, close wounds or treat burns, and triage people for you."

"It's not like we have a lot of major surgery every day, but if we get into a dust up on some alien planet we may find ourselves busier than we'd like. We can work on the cross training thing—I think I can show you some fascinating techniques based on T'aafhal technology that you might like. I know from experience that their med-tech works on both humans and ursines."

"That I would really love to see, Doctor."

Betty smiled. He seemed like a nice enough guy, even if he was a white Afrikaner. The alien attacks that almost wiped out humanity went a long way toward eliminating petty prejudice based on race and gender. No doubt some bigotry remained, but it was well hidden in most cases—people realized that we really did need each other regardless of race, creed or color. *Too bad it took the deaths*

31

of seven billion human beings to make us realize how stupid racism and sexism really are.

"Come on, Johan, let me show you around the office."

Chief's Lounge & Mess

At the door into the Chief's lounge and mess area, traditionally called the goat locker on Navy vessels, Bobby paused and called out: "Permission to enter, Chief?"

"Granted, Sir," replied Chief Zackly, the senior enlisted man on board. The goat locker was his domain, his and the other chiefs, and traditionally even officers requested permission before entering. As Mizuki and Bobby entered the SEALs and the Chief stood.

"Chief Morgan, good to see you again." Bobby smiled as he shook hands with the lead SEAL and his two companions. "Bud, Phil. How have you been?"

"Fine, Sir. We kicked around the Fleet a while after the voyage on M'tak Ka'fek but really couldn't find a home. Then we heard that the Company was looking for some experienced hands to go where no man has gone before."

"Indeed, Chief Morgan-san. We are going to look for the lost Pleiad. Not as far from Earth as Ring Station, but farther than any Earth built ship has ever gone."

"Sounds like just the thing to ease Bud's terminal ennui."

"My what, Chief?"

"Boredom man, dissatisfaction arising from a lack of excitement," Phil hissed at him, "ain't you got no learnin' boy?"

Ignoring the other two SEALs, Morgan turned back to Bobby. "Sounds like a bold move, going someplace that the crowd isn't going."

"The man who follows the crowd will usually get no further than the crowd does."

"Who said that?"

"Beats me, you'll have to ask the Captain. I'm sure he'll be happy to welcome you on board, and I, for one, will be happy to have a team of special operators along if the need arises."

"It will be a long journey," Mizuki added. "You should join my kendo class. Once you have mastered the basics I will teach you about *kenjutsu* and *iaijutsu*—the Japanese way of the sword."

"Uh, that would be swell, Dr. Ogawa," Chief Morgan replied.

"Good! Most of the officers are participating and it will be good to have others who have been... enhanced, to spar with them."

This last remarked caused a few raised eyebrows among the SEALs. They, like Mizuki and Bobby, had been optimized for combat by the M'tak Ka'fek's AI—their bodies were stronger, their reflexes faster, and their endurance greater than normal human beings, even those who trained every day. Enhancement was not a subject normally talked about openly.

"Will we get swords?" asked Phil.

"Hai. Once I am sure you won't hurt yourselves." Mizuki smiled brightly at the three frogmen. Nothing made her happier than having new students to teach.

"You are not going to be happy until everyone on board is a sword carrying samurai," Bobby said with a grin. Then, remembering the encounter with Perlmutter in the Atrium, he turned to Chief Zackly. "You didn't, by any chance have a bit of trouble with a squad of Shore Patrol goons, did you Master Chief?"

The Chief stroked his chin as if trying to recall recent events. "No, Commander, I can truthfully say we didn't have no trouble with the Shore Patrol."

Bobby raised his eyebrows quizzically. "All right, but pass the word to the crew to avoid any trouble between now and when we cast off."

"Aye, aye, Sir," the old Chief replied enthusiastically.

The Sailing Master turned to his wife. "Let's go forward to the bridge to see how the system checks are proceeding."

"Hai."

Mizuki made a polite bow to the SEALs and Chief Zackly, who returned the gesture. Bobby motioned her toward the forward compartment door while saying parting words to the men. "Welcome aboard, gentlemen, it's good to have you join the crew."

"Thank you, Sir, Ma'am."

As the pair of officers exited the lounge, Bud looked at his leader. "Are we really gonna take sword fighting lessons, boss?"

"Why not? You're never too old to learn a new way to kill things."

"Snake eaters is all crazy." Chief Zackly shook his head. "Yous will fit right in."

"We ain't the ones lying to one of the senior officers."

"What? You mean about them SP dipshits? I told the truth, they weren't no trouble at all."

Chapter 4

Peggy Sue II, Approaching Mars

Ten days later the Peggy Sue finished outfitting and left Farside Shipyard for its shakedown cruise. Having dismissed several candidates and scrounging up a few more the Gunny was satisfied with the ship's complement of twenty four Marines. Similarly, the crew was at full strength with many new members, though liberally salted with seasoned veterans. The crossing from Earth to Mars took a leisurely two weeks as systems were tested, calibrated, and retested. The ship was now on final approach to Olympus Mons. Standing three times as tall as Earth's Mount Everest it was the largest volcano in the solar system. In its caldera was humanity's largest shipyard and Navy base.

"Steady as she goes, Sailing Master," the Captain ordered. It was not, strictly speaking, a necessary command given the computerized glide slope the ship was on.

"Aye, aye, Captain. Steady as she goes." Bobby smiled, enjoying the nautical ambiance of it all. They could have brought the ship into port without speaking a word, but where was the fun in that?

Even the First Officer allowed a faint smile to cross her face, listening to the two "playing sailor." She knew there was more to the traditional interaction between the Captain and bridge crew than just hoary Navy tradition. The ritual and rhythms of the bridge helped the crew function as a unit under more stressful conditions—in combat, for instance.

The thin Martian atmosphere was barely detectable as a faint purple band on the horizon as the wide, asymmetric volcano appeared on the red planet's limb. So wide was the peak that a person standing on its slopes would hardly think they were on a mountain.

The crater complex at the peak of the volcano consisted of at least six overlapping calderas and caldera segments. Each represented a separate pulse of volcanic activity in Mars' distant past. The oldest caldera formed as a single, large lava lake, with younger calderas forming circular collapse craters within their larger ancestor. Carved into the basaltic rock of the caldera's floor was the Olympus shipyard—owned by TK Parker and his partners in the Orion Arm Trading Company—and the Fleet's Aries Base.

One of the reasons for locating the starport, shipyard, and Naval base on top of Mars' highest mountain was that Olympus Mons, along with a few other volcanoes in the Tharsis region, stood high enough to reach above the frequent Martian dust-storms. Rising twenty-two kilometers above the surrounding volcanic plains, the peak was above ninety percent of the Martian atmosphere, making it easy for ships not designed to enter a thick planetary atmosphere to make port for repair and resupply.

"Can we see the land we purchased from here?" Beth asked, watching as the broad volcanic peak drew near. Both the Melaku-Vincents and the Ogawa-Danners had purchased large tracts on the Martian uplands, looking to the day when the planet would again have liquid water and, hopefully, a breathable atmosphere. As it stood so far, only a few patches of furtive green could be seen dotting the parched red land below—bio-engineered mosses and lichens beginning the process of terraforming.

"No, Beth. The area where our tracts are is farther to the East and South, bordering the Hellas Planitia."

"Hellas Planitia?"

"Hai, the Hellas basin, a very large impact feature in the Southern Hemisphere. It is about 2,300 km across with a maximum depth of 9,000 meters. Even with the current Martian atmosphere, that is deep enough for air pressure at the bottom to be above the triple point of water. Hopefully, by the time we finish terraforming the planet, our property will be prime waterfront on the edge of a sizable sea."

Beth raised a single skeptical eyebrow. "At least that's what the salesman told us. Right now it looks like an ocher version of the Moon."

"If you don't like this planet, Number One, I'll get you another one," said Billy Ray, trying not to be drawn into the women's conversation and failing. At the helm, Bobby wisely remained silent.

Outside the ship's magnificent transparent bow the gigantic volcano grew larger, as the Peggy Sue II descended into the caldera. Eighty-five kilometers wide, the caldera was filled with circular grabens and wrinkle ridges disturbing the smooth lava lake. On the flat bottom in the deepest portion of the caldera, bordered by walls nearly three kilometers high, scores of rectangular features resolved—landing areas for the space port.

"Peggy Sue, Olympus Approach. You are cleared for landing."

"Roger, Olympus Approach. We are cleared to land." Billy Ray shifted in his seat. This was only the second time he had been to the Red Planet and he was excited, in spite of himself. "Take her in, Cmdr. Danner."

"Aye, aye, Captain." Bobby's fingers danced across the controls. The base grew as their perspective changed, making it obvious just how gigantic the landing area really was. Ocher dust streamed from beneath the ship in rivulets, propelled by the press of repulsors easing eighteen thousand tons of starship into its berth. After the ship settled, flexible tubes extended from beneath the landing apron and sealed against the ship's personnel and cargo hatches. This established airtight passageways to the tunnel system beneath the surface.

"The ship is landed, Captain."

"Very good, Cmdr. Danner. Engine room, Bridge. Mr. Baldursson, I am done with the engines. First Officer, secure all propulsion systems, navigational sensors, and set the in-port watch."

"Aye, aye, Captain."

Billy Ray stood up from the captain's chair overlooking the bridge and gazed across the ruddy plain. *Well,* he thought, *I hope that our boats and small craft are ready. After they are aboard we have one more stop, then we set sail for Aldebaran.*

Cargo Hold, Peggy Sue II

The open space remaining in the cargo hold was packed with crew members and Marines, those who were not standing watch. Chief Zackly and GySgt. Acuna were standing on the forward cargo lift, which was raised above the deck, providing them a stage.

"All right people, listen up! The Captain and party have departed for talks with the shipyard officials. While they are makin'

37

arrangements to acquire boats and other equipment yous will have an opportunity for shore leave."

An excited murmur spread through the assembled personnel. Though they had only been on board for a couple of weeks, sailors are always ready for shore leave in a strange port.

"You will go ashore by division, starting with divisions one and three. This will be followed by divisions two and four. Division chiefs will let you know where you are in the rotation, in case yer too thick headed to figure it out yer self. Each of yous will get an eight hour pass.

"Stick to the settlement attached to the shipyard and civilian port. Do not go lookin' for a Navy bar next to the base. We don't want any trouble and anyone who gets into a brawl will find 'im self back here scrubbing decks so fast 'is head will spin. Yer behavior reflects on the reputation of the Company and the ship, so don't fuck up."

It was obvious by the Chief's tone that it was the ship's reputation he cared about. Throughout the ranks, crewmembers peered at the displays woven into the arms of their jumpsuits, checking when their leave was to commence. The Chief stepped back and placed his hands on his hips, giving the Gunny the stage.

"Listen up Marines! Before you can join the sailors in the local bars we have some work to do."

A moan rose from those in the crowd wearing dark green.

"You will proceed by squad to the shipyard armorers to be fitted with heavy space armor, starting with first squad. Once outfitted, each squad will return to the ship and secure their armor in the ship's armory. Then you will be allowed to go ashore. I will repeat what Master Chief Zackly said: anyone who causes trouble ashore will find themselves cleaning heads and polishing fittings for the indefinite future. Do you understand?"

The crowd responded with a smattering of replies.

"I SAID, DO YOU UNDERSTAND?"

"AYE, AYE!"

"Good. Crew will disembark via the starboard personnel lock, the Marines via the port side cargo hatch. You will find automated trollies waiting to transport you to your respective destinations. There are several hundred kilometers of tunnel running throughout the port so do not get off the trollies except when they tell you."

The Gunny scanned the assembly, satisfied that the Word had been delivered. The Chief stepped up.

"Any questions?" He paused for several seconds. "Good, dismissed."

The crowd of sailors and Marines dispersed: those going ashore first heading back to their quarters in a rush, those not in the first wave heading back to work with less enthusiasm.

"God help us," the Chief muttered.

"Yeah, Chief. I'd feel a lot more comfortable if they were heading out to cause damage on purpose."

Manager's Office, Olympus Shipyard

The Captain and his three senior officers were departing from the office of the shipyard general manager, having verified that their equipment was ready for delivery. They had placed the order months before leaving the Moon, before the ship was near completion. The main lobby of the manager's office was a soaring space three stories tall carved from the crater wall, more than a kilometer above the caldera floor. In a rectangular planter a stand of slender white birch trees stood in contrast with the natural rock walls. Through a floor to ceiling transparent wall the entirety of the shipyard and port could be seen, sprawling into the distance.

"The ship looks like a toy from here," Bobby commented, as the group paused to take in the view. The near vacuum outside did little to scatter incoming sunlight, leaving the sky black above the ruddy crater floor. A dozen ships of differing size and design occupied fewer than half of the available landing sites.

"More than half of the births are vacant," Beth observed. "You would think that the General Manager would be more thankful for our business."

39

"He did seem a mite put out that we didn't have the whole ship built here, but there were good reasons for that."

"You mean like being close to Rajiv Gupta, Yuki Saito and the rest of TK's science and engineering brain trust."

"That's one reason, sweetheart. The more important reason was so we could closely supervise the construction—I don't think any of us wanted to spend five months livin' here on Mars in temporary quarters."

"You definitely made the right call on that, dear."

Mizuki and Bobby exchanged glances. Both were amused by the way Beth and Billy Ray seemed to constantly ride each other, swapping sarcastic remarks. A casual observer would never guess how devoted to each other they really were. On the other hand, despite having lived together for several years, Mizuki and Bobby were just recently married—the newlywed glow had not yet faded into that comfortable familiarity that successfully married couples seemed to maintain. Each lost in their own thoughts, the quartet of friends stared wordlessly at the bleak terrain in the caldera below. Finally, Mizuki broke the contemplative silence.

"I think we should go. I would like to see the monument before the crew reaches the settlement's public spaces."

"Yer right as usual, Mizuki. Let's catch a transport cab to the main hall." Most of the settlement was buried deep within the rim of the volcano, much farther down than the shipyard offices and control center. The rock overburden provided protective shielding from radiation, meteors, and possible alien attacks.

"What is this mysterious monument you keep mentioning?"

"You'll find out soon enough, honey bunch."

* * * * *

Fifteen minutes later, the robot transport pod deposited the four officers at the side of the settlement's main hall, an open space reminiscent of an oversized hotel lobby or a large shopping mall from an earlier time on Earth. Ringed by floors of shops and offices, linked by multiple staircases and walkways, the hall itself contained the requisite stands of trees and greenery favored by environmental psychologists. Fountains provided white noise while humidifying the air and even a few birds twittered about. Scattered among the landscaping, kiosks sold jewelry, handicrafts, and food.

"Hey look, a beer garden! I understand that the local Martian Red Ale is particularly quaff-worthy."

"Quaff-worthy, pardner?"

"Yeah, Billy Ray. You know, worthy of quaffing: To drink a beverage, especially an intoxicating one, copiously and with hearty enjoyment."

"I told you we should not have given them a complete OED as a wedding present. Now he's creating his own neologisms."

"I greatly appreciate the dictionary, Beth. I find it very helpful for looking up obscure English words."

"We did sorta have you in mind more than Bobby. Who knew he would turn into a budding philologist? In any case we are almost there, if you can leave the beer unquaffed for a few more minutes."

"A guy tries to better himself and all he catches is grief."

The friends rounded a corner and found themselves in a small plaza, a circular court paved with stone tiles. At the center of the plaza was a large block of polished basaltic rock. Atop the dark, four meter pedestal was a bronze statue of a man wearing a spacesuit.

"Isn't that..." Beth's voice trailed off as she stared at the statue's heroically sized features.

"Jack Sutton," Billy Ray finished her dangling question. "It is indeed."

"Look, there is a plaque." Excited, Mizuki hurried to the base of the pedestal. The others followed as Mizuki read the inscription. "Here Humans and Ursines from the planet Earth first landed on the surface of Mars, voyaging here in the starship Peggy Sue."

"Oh wow," said Bobby, running his hand along the side of the plaque. "Where did they get the metal?"

"They must have brought it from Earth. The whole statue was probably cast on Earth, pre-bombardment."

"I knew that Jack had told TK to erect a monument celebrating our first trip to Mars, one inscribed with the names of all the people and bears on board the ship," Billy Ray explained. "I didn't know the monument included a statue of the Captain."

"Yes, the names are engraved on the pedestal." Mizuki moved to one side of the oversized plinth. "Here is your name Bobby!"

Beth joined her. "And yours, dear."

All four joined in the search for familiar names. Mizuki found her own name on the other side, next to her mentor's, Dr. Hiroyuki Saito. Lieutenant Bear was listed by his more formal name, Pihoqahiak, which means the ever-wandering one in Inuit. Also present were Isbjørn, Bear's mate; Ludmilla Tropsha, ship's doctor and Jack Sutton's wife; Chief Zackly, and a host of other familiar names.

"I hadn't realized I married such a celebrity, or that all of you were so famous."

"Trust me, honey bunch, we were all just passin' through."

"I guess we're immortal," Bobby remarked, stepping back from the monument. "I never thought my name would be on a public monument."

"Me either, pardner. Somehow I think that Captain Jack would be a mite embarrassed by all this."

"He does look very impressive up there. Now I miss our friends who left on the M'tak Ka'fek."

"I'm sure we'll see them again someday, Mizuki-chan."

"The galaxy has proven to be a very dangerous place, more than I ever dreamt when I was studying to become an astrophysicist."

Beth nodded. "As we've all discovered, and at no small cost."

Billy Ray put his arm around his wife's shoulders and gave her a hug. "I'm sure they are all right. The galaxy is a dangerous place, but we all know Jack Sutton is a damned hard man to kill."

"Not to mention Ludmilla," added Mizuki, a twinkle in her eyes. If anything, Jack Sutton's wife was tougher than he was.

"I don't know about the rest of you, but I think we should move along before any of the crew happen on this place. It would be embarrassing explainin' why our names are on a public monument in the middle of the biggest settlement on Mars."

"Surely it's nothing to be ashamed of, dear?"

"Not shameful, just a bit awkward. After all we were just along for the ride. The real hero is that man there."

The officers of the Peggy Sue II quietly departed the courtyard, each lost in their own thoughts. The event commemorated by the monument seemed a lifetime ago. Some of the companions listed on the monument were gone, others scattered, and several about to make another trip to the stars on board the second ship to bear the name Peggy Sue.

"Do we still have time for that beer?"

Bill Ray clapped his friend on the shoulder.

"I think that's a fine idea, Bobby."

Neither noticed the dark figure lurking nearby, observing them from behind a planter full of poplar trees. After a short pause the observer also departed, following the officers.

Chapter 5

Shuttle Hanger, Olympus Shipyard

Bobby walked along side the company representative, past the rows of shuttle craft. They were trailed by four other crewmembers from the Peggy Sue II: Frank Hoenig, Pauline Palmer, Matt Jacobs, and Steve Hitch. Palmer had been crew on the old Peggy Sue before spending some time in the Navy. Now she had returned as a pilot for both the ship and its small boats. Both she and Hoenig were sub-lieutenants—what the American Navy called ensigns—both qualified to stand watch on the bridge. Jacobs and Hitch were long time crewmembers and also experienced shuttle pilots.

The ranks of shuttle craft looked impressive sitting in orderly rows within the cavernous hanger. Carved from the living Martian rock, the hanger was illuminated by light strips in the ceiling. At the far end, over a kilometer away, a thirty-five by one hundred meter opening allowed natural light to enter the space. Though it looked like it was open to the outside looks were deceiving—the hanger door was actually made from a new, transparent version of selectively permeable material. It held an Earth normal atmosphere inside, while keeping the dust laden but tenuous Martian atmosphere out.

"These two are yours, Commander Danner," the company rep said, motioning to two dark, wedge-shaped craft sitting side by side. They were obviously military type shuttles, blunt and hulking with hull blisters that hinted at weaponry concealed within. Both craft had their forward crew doors open with stairs extending to the apron. Standing next to the shuttles were men in pressure suits. Danner's party were also wearing standard pressure suits and carrying bubble helmets under their arms, giving them the appearance of astronauts of old, walking to a launch pad. The suits were just in case one of the shuttles lost cabin pressure or had to set down on the Martian surface—Mars might one day have a breathable atmosphere, but currently there was not much difference between it and vacuum.

Bobby turned and addressed his party. "All right people, we are going to split into two teams, one for each shuttle. Palmer and Hitch take this one, Hoenig and Jacobs, take the other. The shipyard's pilots will take the shuttles out of the hanger then you will each take turns putting them through their paces. Try not to run into any planets or moons."

"Aye, aye, Sir," the quartet of pilots responded, anxious to go flying above the Red Planet.

"Are you going to join us, Commander?" asked Lt. Palmer.

"No, Ms. Palmer. I'm going to wait for the First Officer to join me and then we are going to do some testing of our own."

Captain's Sea Cabin, Peggy Sue II

Billy Ray was in his shipboard office, abaft the bridge and forward of the CIC. For reasons of tradition it was called the Captain's Sea Cabin. The captain of a large Navy vessel has two cabins—an in-port cabin and a sea cabin. The in-port cabin is like a suit in a hotel, often including a separate bedroom, office, and sitting room for entertaining guests or meeting with the ship's officers.

The sea cabin is a much smaller affair, located just off the bridge, containing a desk and a bunk. When not in-port, the captain of a warship often spent most of his or her time in the sea cabin, sleeping and taking meals there so as not to be far from the bridge. While the Peggy Sue II was not officially a warship, Captain Vincent often stayed in his sea cabin when the ship was in normal 3-space. In alter-space, where there was little chance of an emergency, he used the larger cabin that he shared with his wife.

Though in-port, with all the activity taking place loading supplies and equipment, the Captain found his sea cabin more conducive to administrative work than his more comfortable office farther aft and one deck down. Currently he was approving payments for the Marines' new armor and weapons.

"I'd rather be in some strange star system fightin' Dark Lords than wading through this administrative crap," he muttered to himself. Beth was off to join Bobby in putting the new interceptors through their paces and he was stuck behind a desk. *And they say the life of a starship captain is so grand!*

46

A tone sounded and the Chief's face popped up in a window on the desk's display surface. *Now What?* "Yes, Chief?"

"Beg yer pardon, Captain, but I has a fellow here that wants to see you."

"Does this fellow have a name?"

"He'd rather not say, Sir. Wants it to be a surprise."

"Very well, bring him up."

"Aye, Sir."

Just what I need, more distractions. But then, the Chief isn't one for fooling around. This must be important in some non-obvious way.

The Captain went back to his invoices and cargo manifests. A few minutes later a knock came at the door. He looked up.

"Come."

The door slid open and a large, dark man stepped inside. He was dressed in deep charcoal gray, his shaven head gleamed like polished mahogany, a full black beard almost reached his chest.

Billy Ray looked at the man and then, hesitantly, said, "JT?"

A dazzling white smile lit up the dark man's face. "Right the first time, cowboy."

Billy Ray came around the desk and the two men clasp hands. The newcomer stood almost as tall as the Captain and had wider shoulders. In fact, he was built like a tight end from the old NFL.

"What's with the shaved noggin and beard? I almost didn't recognize you. Hell, you look like Richie Havens."

"Uh-huh. If I had even a tenth the talent that man had I'd be getting rich playing nightclubs all over the solar system. No man, I've been travilin' incognito."

"Come on, sit down. Damn it's good to see you. You just sort of disappeared while we were gone on our last voyage. When we got back you were nowhere to be found."

JT, suddenly somber, looked down at his hands. "Yeah, there's a long story behind that."

Billy Ray leaned back in his chair and raised his eyebrows questioningly.

JT sighed.

"OK, but remember you asked for it. For a while after the war with the Dark Lords went cold I did like you did—I signed on to spend some time helping the Navy come up to speed on interstellar travel. Unfortunately, my relationship with Gretchen got in the way."

"Really? I thought things between you two were good."

"For a while they were, but there are no secrets on a military base, particularly one dug out of rock on the farside of the Moon. Word that we were seeing each other started to affect those around us. Our relationship became strained, strained enough that I resigned my commission."

"It got that bad?"

"Everyone in the service either wanted to suck up to me in an attempt to suck up to the Admiral, or wanted me cashiered for being the Admiral's boy toy. Either way, my career was seen as a joke—I was a tool or a fool. Even after I resigned the snickering in the ranks was still there. I guess it eventually became too much for Gretchen and we broke up."

"I'm sorry to hear that, JT. I wondered why she didn't say anything about you when I last saw her."

JT waved a hand dismissively. "Water under the bridge. We were never in-love-forever serious like you and Beth, we just liked each other and enjoyed each other's company. In any case I signed on to do a delivery run to Triton, but that was about as exciting as herding goats. Eventually I ended up working with a bunch of asteroid miners, prospecting for metal between Mars and Jupiter. That was when I shaved my head and grew the beard.

"Asteroid miners are a pretty rough bunch but they don't ask a lot of questions about who you are and where you been. It was interesting at first but it wasn't long before I realized that we were making just enough off our finds to keep looking for more—there was no big payday in sight.

"So one night, when we were resupplying at Ceres, I took all my credits and got into a poker game. I hit a hot streak and made enough to buy passage back to Mars on a packet ship. That got me here and I've been living off my pension funds ever since. Then I saw you and the others at the Captain Jack statue. A little snooping around and here I am, knocking at your door."

"So yer tellin' me you need a job?"

"Yeah, Billy Ray, I need a job. Hell, what I really need is to get out of the fuckin' solar system. My life has petty much been circling the drain since I got off the M'tak Ka'fek."

Bill Ray looked at the pleading in his friend's eyes. JT, James Leotis Taylor, was a former Green Beret, a trained astronomer, and a crewmate since the first voyage of the Peggy Sue. They had fought side by side on a number of occasions and had been friends for many years. To have him here, almost begging for a job, was both painful and embarrassing.

"We're going to look for the T'aafhal out in the Pleiades. Probably gonna take a year or so. No guarantee we'll make it back."

"Sounds fine to me, I just want to be somewhere other than here."

Billy Ray thought for half a minute before speaking again. "I could use someone to do master-at-arms duty—training and shipboard security stuff. Plus I'd wager that Mizuki wouldn't mind some help in the astronomy section."

A smile was already spreading across JT's face.

"We have also been reunited with Chief Morgan and his snake eating cohorts. You might wanna work with them a bit, just in case we need some special operator mojo. I can bring you on board at your previous rank, that alright with you, Mr. Taylor?"

JT straightened up in his chair. "All right? Captain that's more than generous."

"Then welcome aboard, Lieutenant. You can see Chief Zackly for quarters assignment."

The newly commissioned Lt. Taylor stood and saluted his new commanding officer. "Thank you, Sir."

49

Billy Ray returned the salute. "Dismissed, Mr. Taylor."

Shuttle Hanger, Olympus Shipyard

Beth and Bobby had just completed doing preflight inspections for two aircraft sitting on the hangar ramp. Smaller and sleeker than the landing shuttles, these had a predatory, almost sinister look to them. Jet black, eighteen meters long with a wingspan of fourteen meters, they were about the size of a 21st century fighter jet. But these were no jets.

They possessed no gaping air intakes, no protruding jet exhausts with afterburners spewing fire. These fighter/interceptors were propelled by gravitonic repulsors which drew power from small, muon catalyzed fusion reactors. Like their antiquated earthbound ancestors they did have a way to boost performance when needed during a dogfight—the standard power generators were augmented by antimatter reactors that could triple their acceleration. For short bursts they could accelerate at over two hundred standard gravities.

Inertial compensators enveloping the cockpits kept their pilots from being turned into goo when performing maneuvers no craft dependent on aerodynamics could hope to match. The gracefully tapering wings, with thick roots blending into the craft's body proper, almost gave the fighters the appearance of flying wings. Not dictated by aerodynamic need, the wings were mainly to house weapons: dual 15mm multi-barreled railguns in the wing roots; gravatonically powered interceptor missiles with antimatter warheads, stored in internal weapons bays; dual plasma cannon in the wing tips, their design stolen from captured Dark Lord ships and enhanced with T'aafhal technology; and last but not least, a rail cannon that ran nearly the entire length of the craft along its centerline, capable of hurling a five kilo slug at 7,000 m/s, delivering nearly the same kinetic energy as a 16 inch AP round from a WWII battleship. And those were just the offensive weapons.

For defense there were dorsal and ventral X-ray laser blisters, giving full coverage for incoming projectiles. To counter EM radiation and plasma weapons there were shields that used disruptive gravitational gradients to deflect and refract offensive fire. Add to that the extreme maneuverability of the fighters and there was nothing like them anywhere in the Orion Arm, at least as far as the engineers who created them knew.

Dubbed Kestrels by their designers, they were prototypes of weapons intended for sale to the Navy. Designed for use in system defense and to support planetary invasions, they could operate both in space and in an atmosphere. Through the good offices of TK Parker the first two operational Kestrels were being deployed aboard the Peggy Sue II. Docking sites for the two small fighters were designed into the larger ship's hull, allowing them to be serviced from below when mated with the mother-ship. There was also access from below for the pilot to enter the cockpit. It was through these bottom hatches that Beth and Bobby boarded their new play things.

"Olympus Control, Kestrel One, radio check, over." Beth called the Port while powering up her fighter.

"Kestrel One, Olympus Control, we read you five-by-five."

"Kestrel Two, Kestrel One, are you ready Bobby?"

"Roger that, Kestrel One. All systems go and ready to launch."

"Olympus Control, Kestrel One. Flight of two small craft ready for departure from south shuttle area, out bound for southern Tharsis region for operational test flight."

"Roger, Kestrel One. You are cleared for immediate departure. Contact Olympus Approach on your return."

"We have clearance, Kestrel Two, try to keep up."

During her taunting transmission, Beth's Kestrel rose from the apron, retracting its landing gear. An instant later it lept forward and disappeared through the hanger opening.

So that's how this is going to go, Bobby thought with a grin. He gave his fighter its head and followed Beth into the Martian sky.

* * * * *

The two fighters were soon locked in mock combat, swirling and turning like birds of prey on a mating flight. They arched upward, climbing above the thin traces of atmosphere that clung to the heights of Olympus Mons, their paths scribing a double helix in the sky. From there they dove, constantly maneuvering for advantage, constantly trying to get on each other's six—their opponent's tail.

As the pair of war-birds passed between the lesser Tharsis volcanoes, Bobby stuck to Beth's tail like glue. In frustration, she rolled inverted and dove for the deck, pulling up less than 500 meters above the rocky surface. Accelerating madly, she headed for the western end of *Valles Marineris*, the gigantic rift valley that stretches for nearly a quarter of the planet's circumference. More than 4,000 km long, 200 km wide and up to 10 km deep, the largest canyon on Mars dwarfed the Grand Canyon of the Colorado. But, to be fair to Earth, several of its oceanic rifts were larger.

On they flew, into *Noctis Labyrinthus*, on the western edge of the Rift System, playing tag among the crisscrossing canyons that lacerate the huge blocks of older terrain. It was easy to imagine titanic floods etching their way through the jumbled ancient terrain. Racing eastward, the pair followed the southern valley, the *Ius Chasma*. Weaving to either side, they hopped back and forth over *Geryon Montes*, the central ridge that split the wide canyon.

Beth was becoming desperate to shake Bobby from her tail. No fighter pilot wants to admit another pilot her better, but Beth was beginning to think that Bobby was her match in a dogfight. She pulled a 50G turn into a side canyon that became really narrow, really fast. So fast she was forced to pull up and clear of the canyon walls. She circled around looking for Bobby but didn't see him emerge from the canyon below.

"Well that was a lot of fun." Bobby's voice over the comm startled her. Looking right she saw his Kestrel off her wingtip.

Oh bollocks, she swore to herself. "Yes, it was good fun. Have you seen enough of scenic Mars for one day?"

"Yeah, you seen one gigantic canyon you've seen them all. How about you chase me for a while?"

"Roger that," she replied as Bobby's fighter shot away and back down into the canyon system headed west. Beth streaked after him. *Let's see if the smug little bastard can shake me on the way back to base...*

Chapter 6

Armory, Peggy Sue II

The ship's armory was aft, between the cargo hold and the polar bear quarters. The Gunny was overseeing her Marines, who were storing their new suits of heavy armor. They were almost finished when JT strolled in accompanied by the SEALs.

"Lieutenant Taylor! As I live and breath," Rosey exclaimed. "How have you been, Army?"

"Hey, Gunny. Long time no see. I didn't realize this was a reunion tour."

"Have you joined this group of interstellar misfits? I haven't seen you since the M'tak Ka'fek."

"Yeah, good times."

"Any better and we'd all be dead," added Chief Morgan.

"Come on, Rick. You special ops guys love being in the shit."

"If you say so, Gunny. I only signed on for the retirement plan."

The banter among the old comrades in arms piqued the interest of a she-bear who was also in the room. Seeing her turn her head toward the newcomers, Rosey waved the bear over.

"Aurora, come meet some old friends of mine. Guys, Sergeant Aurora was one of the Marines that boarded the planet killer that attacked Earth." That action, known as the Great Alien Hunt, was the first counter strike made by Earthlings after the initial Dark Lord attack on the home world.

As Aurora padded up, claws clicking on the polished deck, a rank device could be seen on her harness. It displayed the stripes of a Marine sergeant. Polar bears did not wear jumpsuits like humans, finding temperatures in the common areas of the ship sweltering enough without covering. Besides, they found the idea of clothing somewhat laughable under any circumstance. To provide a place for insignia and the standard communication pip, the ursine members of the crew wore harnesses made from white webbing. The harnesses also had clips that enabled the bears to carry things when walking on all fours.

"Good to meet you, Sergeant. Nice to have someone with actual experience boarding a hostile ship among our ranks."

"Nice to meet you, Lieutenant. And you gentlemen as well."

"Gentlemen might be stretching things a bit, Aurora, but all these people are good to have with you in a fight."

JT nodded to the bear. "I always feel better with bears in the mix. How many of our ursine brethren do we have among the Marine contingent?"

"The Sergeant runs second squad and Corporal Inuksuk, also a veteran, is with me in first squad. There are another male and female, Aput and Siku, on the bridge crew."

"Sensor operators?" T'aafhal alter-space sensors had a neural interface that worked better with polar bears than with humans. Working through the bears' highly developed sense of smell, an ursine operator could literally smell targets through alternate dimensions, allowing tracking at faster than light speeds.

"Yeah, the Sue Two has all the latest alien tech bells and whistles. Some stuff even the Fleet hasn't got."

"So what do you think of the new armor?" JT had been involved in designing several generations of space armor during his tenure on the old Peggy Sue. The gathered warriors—Marines, SEALs, and Army Special Forces—could not resist talking shop.

"It is supposed to be tougher than the previous generation, but that remains to be seen. The suits do have a new modular weapons system that is pretty sweet. You can swap between 5mm, 15mm, and 30mm railguns, and some new toys—a gigawatt pulse laser and a plasma cannon. Each comes with a matching backpack magazine or power source. You can mix and match to fit mission requirements."

"That sounds useful if we need to go in heavy," commented Chief Morgan. The special operators generally preferred the euphemistically labeled light armor, with its greater dexterity and physical flexibility.

"Even better," added Sgt. Aurora. "There is a propulsion module you can add that lets you maneuver in low-G no-G conditions. No more having to swing around like a bunch of monkeys like we did during the Great Alien Hunt. No offense to you primates."

"None taken," JT replied with a grin. He had been close friends with several bears over the years and had come to appreciate their blunt spoken manner and often sarcastic sense of humor. "So how are your people shaping up?"

Rosey shrugged. "They've got some rough edges but all of them have some form of previous training. I figure they'll be good to go by the time we reach Aldebaran, two whole weeks of 3-space plus transit time to hammer 'em into shape."

"I'm looking forward to some cross training among the different warfighters on board," JT agreed.

"Yeah? Well just wait until Dr. Ogawa dragoons you into her sword fighting class."

"Really?"

"Really."

Wardroom, 3rd Deck

Billy Ray had finished with the latest round of paperwork and was sitting in the officers mess, enjoying a cup of coffee, when Beth and Bobby returned.

"So how'd the testing go? You two look like you have a permanent case of the grins."

Beth was, indeed, grinning widely. "I would say that the Kestrels are quite adequate for our needs."

"Of course, we didn't get to really push the envelope," Bobby threw in, "because we didn't have any AM for the auxiliary power converters."

"Don't blame 'em for not wanting experimental fighters running around their hangar with a passel of antimatter on board."

"Still, I found them quite exhilarating. There is a sense of speed when flying a small craft that just isn't present in a large ship."

"I don't see what you two love about small boats," the Captain said somewhat peevishly.

"There is nothing, absolutely nothing, half so much worth doing as simply messing about in boats," Beth quoted.

"Kenneth Grahame?"

"You forget, dear, that I've had a proper English education. When I was in school they still taught the classics."

Bobby shrugged. "Hey, big or small, I just like to fly. If I get to shoot at stuff at the same time that's just a bonus."

"You didn't shoot the place up, did you pardner?"

"No. Damn wussy shipyard dorks—no antimatter, no live ammo, they were even freaked out by a little nap-of-the-earth flying."

"Technically, that would be nap-of-the-red-planet, Bobby."

"Whatever. The Kestrels are shit-hot, I wish we'd had them at Alpha Phoenicis."

"Great. I'll tell the shipyard people we'll accept delivery of the shuttles and fighters." He made a notation on his sleeve display. "To change the subject completely, I ran into an old friend this afternoon."

"Oh? Who?"

"JT. He's evidently been kicking around the solar system and was in need of gainful employment."

"Really? And you hired him on?" Beth didn't know JT well, at least not as well as Bobby and her husband.

"Yep. He's a good man in a fight and a pretty fair astronomer to boot. That and he knows most of the old hands on board."

"Well, it's not like we don't have the space, and trained people are hard to find. You're expecting to get into a fight during the coming voyage, my Captain?"

"Honey bunch, when have we ever taken a voyage where we didn't end up in a ruckus or two?" Billy Ray grinned at his wife and his best friend. "If'n you two are done messing around with our new boats I think we should make preparations to depart. We still need to load the small craft once in orbit and then go pick up some antimatter for yer new play toys, and for the ship."

"Roger that, Captain."

Beth raised a single eyebrow in Spock like amusement.

Polar Bear Quarters

Once the armor and weapons were stored Aurora returned to the Polar Bear quarters on first deck, aft of the armory. Polar bears are creatures adapted to the Arctic. Though much of the Arctic is covered by ocean, large tracts of that ocean are perpetually capped by ice two to three meters thick. In summer the temperatures are near zero, in winter the temperature drops to -30 or colder. Polar bears evolved to wander this frigid land in search of food, even swimming long distances to cross leads and fissures in the pack ice. A starship kept at temperatures comfortable for humans was not a comfortable environment for the white bears of the Arctic.

To provide the ursine members of the crew a place to sleep and relax when off duty, a special section was built into the ship where conditions were more appropriate for Arctic creatures. Freezing temperatures, floors of ice, and even a pool of cold water, with salinity comparable to that of the Arctic Ocean, gave the bears a place to unwind. Currently all four ursine crewmembers were present, cooling off before the expected call to departure stations.

"So what do you think of the human crew?" asked Inuksuk between chunks of ringed seal. The 600 kg male was lying prone holding the seal carcass with his paws, ripping off strips of skin and blubber with his teeth. Bears in the wild only eat infrequently but can assimilate 84% of the protein and 97% of the fat they ingest. When given a choice polar bears dine exclusively on seal fat. Strangely, when on this fat heavy diet their cholesterol levels actually drop, possibly due to the omega-3 fatty acids found in seal blubber.

"They seem OK to me," replied Aput, the other male. He had always had a fascination with science and technology and enjoyed being on the bridge crew, even if it was sweltering and smelled of primates.

"We could have done worse," said Aurora, pulling herself from the swimming pool and shaking the water from her fur like a 250 kg dog. "Several of them were among the first Earthlings to venture into space. They were with Captain Jack when he rescued many of us from the Arctic before the aliens attacked."

Inuksuk snorted. "Like they were so altruistic."

"What are you getting at?"

"I think that humans get more out of this 'partnership' than we do. If we weren't useful we'd still be running around on the pack ice, that or dead."

"That's pretty harsh," said Siku, the quietest and most introverted of the four.

"If you have such a hard-on for humans why did you sign on for a year long voyage on board a ship full of them?" Aurora walked closer to the big male and sat down on her haunches. "No one forced you to associate with primates."

"I talked with Umky, Isbjørn's cub, and he told me about the last voyage these same primates made. They think they have a handle on where there might be some surviving T'aafhal."

"And you're queer for T'aafhal?" Aurora, like many polar bears, had a habit of using slang from 50's film noir, possibly because the image of a hard-boiled private eye loner fit their idea of a real hero.

"Let's just say I want to find out why they made us like they did. I mean, why did they mess with both the primates and us? Why not just bears, and let the monkeys stay dumb and happy, picking lice off each other and throwing shit at their neighbors?"

"I don't know what your problem is, you dumb lug, and I don't much care, but understand this—you do anything to endanger the ship or the rest of us and you'll find yourself breathing vacuum."

"Hey, sister, don't get excited! I'm along for the money and the adventure. I just don't care for humans much is all. That and I wouldn't mind snagging a fang on one of those T'aafhal creatures."

"Just remember what I said, numb nuts. Best you keep your thoughts to yourself, because the walls around here have ears."

The other two bears, less combative than the two ursine Marines, looked at each other as if to say, *what have we gotten ourselves into?*

Captain's Quarters

With departure scheduled for the end of morning watch, Billy Ray and Beth took the opportunity to grab a last night's sleep together before getting underway. They would both be on the bridge tomorrow morning and during the docking of the shuttles and fighters. After breaking orbit they, along with Bobby, would then split the watches until insertion at the alter-space transit point days later.

"You seem tense tonight, dear." Beth had changed into something slinky and was at her dresser, doing those things that a woman does before getting into bed. Billy Ray was laying on the bed wearing only shorts, hands behind his head and staring at the ceiling.

"I always get a mite edgy before casting off on a long voyage. Trying to think of anything I forgot—it's not like we can just stop off at a roadside convenience store if I missed something."

"Speaking of stops, we are going you-know-where before heading for the transit point, correct?"

"Yep. That's the last of the supplies—a couple of type one AM containers for the ship and a some type three eggs for your new play toys."

"I can understand why we don't store antimatter on the Moon or one of the planets—an accident or an alien attack could set off a devastating explosion—but why does the Council keep the stuff at a secret location out in the asteroid belt?"

"It's one of the things the Council doesn't feel comfortable with the military having control over."

"So it's under the control of a handful of the richest people in the solar system?"

"Honey bunch, life is full of hard choices and compromises, none of 'em perfect and many of 'em unpleasant. I'm just thankful to have you and our friends and a ship to go roam the galaxy in."

"Speaking of friends, what's up with Lieutenant Taylor?"

"JT? It seems to me that he's going through a rough patch, trying to put his breakup with Gretchen behind him."

"He swears that the breakup was amicable and that there wasn't any regret on either side. You're saying you don't believe that?"

"I'm saying there's a reason that Gretchen buries herself in her job and that JT shaved his head and went off prospecting in the asteroid belt. They are both in denial to some extent. Eventually they'll get over it."

"Do you think it will affect his duties? Can we trust him in his... emotionally distressed state?"

"I think he will do fine. In fact, if we do run into one of those situations that he's best at he will welcome the challenge. Now stop worrying about the crew and come take care of your captain."

She threw a hair brush at him, but had a grin on her face as she jumped onto the bed.

Chapter 7

Bridge, Peggy Sue II Underway

The trip to acquire the needed antimatter took four days. The subsequent plummet on a comet like course, passing inside the orbit of Mercury and nearly grazing the Sun, took another seven. Their objective was the alter-space transit point leading to Aldebaran, the first leg of their journey to the Pleiades.

Aldebaran, *Alpha Tauri*, is the brightest star of the constellation Taurus, the bull. The star's ancient name comes from Arabic, meaning "the Follower," since it appears to follow the Pleiades star cluster across the Earthly sky. It is a bright orange giant with a mass 1.7 times that of the Sun. More impressively, it has a radius forty-four times that of Earth's local star.

"How are we looking for transit, Cmdr. Danner?"

"We are aligning now, Captain. We've past the orbit of Venus and should be at the insertion point in less than ten minutes." A combination of orbital dynamics and relative mass put the Earth-Aldebaran transit point just outside the orbit of Venus, on the opposite side of the solar system from their last stop.

"Tell me again why we are going to the eye of Taurus first?" Asked Beth. Most renderings of the constellation made Aldebaran the celestial Bull's malevolent orange eye. Normally Mizuki would have offered an answer to the First Officer's question. Instead the Science Officer looked at JT and nodded, giving him an opportunity to show himself knowledgeable in matters astronomical.

"Aldebaran is sixty-five light-years away, and is positioned in front of the Hyades star cluster, which forms the head of Taurus the Bull. It is part of the head of Taurus, but is not a part of the Hyades cluster, which is over twice as far away—some 150 light-years from Earth. It is basically a convenient stop on the way to places farther out."

Mizuki smiled at her fellow astronomer. "JT is correct. The best way to travel to distant locations is using alter-space transit between massive stars. This lets us travel long distances in 3-space with relatively short transit times. The down side is that the transit parameters are more difficult to calculate. The distance, sixty-five light-years, calls for great precision in the insertion parameters."

"Right," Bobby muttered from his station at the helm. "No pressure at all."

"Do we know what's waiting for us on the other end?"

"Not with full certainty, Captain. Aldebaran is classified as a type K5III star, which indicates it is an orange giant that has exhausted its supply of hydrogen and moved off the main sequence. Beyond its chromosphere is an extended outer atmosphere where the temperature is cool enough for molecules of gas to form. Outside that region, its stellar wind declines in temperature to about 7,500 K at a distance of 1 Astronomical Unit."

"Our exit point is about 2.6 AU from the star so that shouldn't be a problem," Mizuki added. "the stellar wind is still hot but tenuous at that distance."

"Very good, what about planets?"

"There is some evidence for a super Jupiter in a mildly eccentric orbit. Radial velocity measurements imply a companion with a mass between seven and eleven times that of Jupiter in a 643-day orbit at a separation of 2.0 AU. Considering that the star shines with roughly five hundred times the Sun's luminosity and the close proximity of the planet we are probably looking at a hot-Jupiter here."

"A hot-Jupiter? And that means what?" Beth asked.

Mizuki fielded that one. "They have similar characteristics to other gas giants, but they orbit much more closely to their star. High levels of insolation gives them high surface temperature and results in a lower density than would otherwise be expected. It is hypothesized that such planets start out farther from their central star and migrate inward over time, making the development of life less likely than in other planetary configurations."

"So big star, big planet, no aliens. Sounds good to me."

"We're just passing through anyway, Number One. Here's hoping that the first system is safe and boring."

"It you wanted safe, we could have just stayed in the shipyard."

"'A ship in harbor is safe, but that is not what ships are built for.'" Billy Ray smiled. Having an appropriate quotation for a situation gave him great satisfaction.

"You sort of leaned into that one, Commander," JT quipped. He was already feeling right at home with this crew.

"Transit coming up, Captain. Turning sequencing over to the ship's computer."

"Very good, Cmdr. Danner."

The voice of the ship's computer was heard on the bridge. "Transition to alter-space in 5, 4, 3, 2, 1..."

The ship shimmered and vanished from 3-space, making the transition from spaceship to starship. The first voyage of the Peggy Sue II was underway.

Cargo Hold, Day 2 Alter-space

Alter-space transit was boring. Not as boring as trying to cross sixty-five light-years in 3-space, but far less stimulating than an airplane flight or a sea voyage. Outside the ship there was nothing that human eyes could make sense of—indeed, the hypnotic power of alter-space was such that it drove some insane. To avoid such unpleasantness the ship's viewports were all turned a boring but safe translucent gray until the return to 3-space.

Since the Captain firmly believed that idle hands were the devil's workshop the crew and Marines were kept busy with drills, simulated combat exercises, and physical training. As threatened, Mizuki held kendo practice every day, with all the officers in attendance. The chiefs, including Chief Morgan, the two SEAL petty officers, and several Marines also joined in the fun, mostly hoping to eventually get swords of their own.

Currently, the Marines of first squad were gathered in one end of the cargo hold for training in hand to hand combat techniques. They were all wearing light combat armor, including Cpl. Inuksuk and Lt. Taylor, who was leading the session.

"One of the problems we have is trying to familiarize Marines with close quarters combat against aliens." JT let his gaze drift across the assembled warriors. Most were showing real interest in the subject at hand, but a few looked bored—that would change shortly. "Fortunately, we have among us a fellow Marine who makes an admirable stand in for an alien opponent."

The human Marines all looked at one another while Inuksuk raised his head to stare at the large officer at the front of the class.

"That's right, we are fortunate to have in our ranks Cpl. Inuksuk, who even the least observant among us can tell isn't a *Homo sapiens*." That elicited a few chuckles from among the ranks.

"Are you saying I'm the designated alien, Lieutenant?"

"That you are, Corporal, that you are. Everyone please clear some space so I can demonstrate a few fundamentals about hand to hand, or paw in this case, with a larger alien opponent."

The Marines obediently moved back against the aft bulkhead leaving JT and the bear alone in the center space. Inuksuk slowly stood up on his hind legs, rising to his full height of more than three meters.

"Well this should be interesting," said PFC Christopher "Grits" Walker, a former US Marine and new to the Peggy Sue.

"Be quiet and pay attention," replied PFC Tzipporah "Zippy" Ben-Ezra, a former member of the IDF and one of the three women in first squad, not counting the Gunny. Zippy was intensely focused on the training and had little time for the joking around that the male Marines seemed to find necessary.

"First, I will point out the obvious. When faced with an opponent four or more times your size, getting into a straight up slug fest is not going to work." JT paused for effect. "The key to successfully fighting a much larger opponent is using his size against him—more Aikido and Sambo than Karate or Kung Fu."

JT dropped into a crouch and faced off against the somewhat bemused bear. Both were encased in armor, which was to the human's advantage—Inuksuk would not be able to use his claws or teeth, just his significantly greater strength. JT faked a charge.

Inuksuk made a charge of his own, reaching for the man with both paws. JT ducked beneath the intended bear hug, reaching low to grasp the charging ursine by his lower abdomen.

Rocking back, letting the bear's own momentum carry him forward, JT lifted the massive creature with the combined strength of his body and the electroreactive "muscles" of his suit. He managed to lift Inuksuk off the ground and flip him over his shoulder.

But Inuksuk had sparred with armor suited humans before. When he felt himself being lifted off the deck he tucked and rolled. In a continuous motion he landed on his back, rolled sideways to regain his footing and charged at his human opponent.

JT pivoted after the throw and was somewhat surprised to see the bear charging him on all fours. Reacting out of instinct, he jumped toward Inuksuk and vaulted over him, like a Cretan bull leaper from an ancient Minoan mosaic.

Inuksuk slid to a halt and turned once again to face his smaller tormentor, this time approaching more cautiously. JT faced off against the now fully alert bear. Inuksuk feinted with his right and then delivered a roundhouse left that connected with the man's right side, sending him flying through the air. The bear stood on two legs and roared in triumph.

The armored human managed to do a flip and a half twist to land on the hold wall with his feet. Compressing his knees, the ex-Green Beret absorbed the impact and sprung back toward his foe. Again flipping head over heals, JT landed feet first on the bear's armored chest, knocking him over backward. Both man and bear sprawled across the deck.

Slowly regaining his footing, JT faced the assembled Marines, who were now paying rapt attention to the demonstration. "As you can see, when faced with a bigger, stronger opponent your only recourse is to do the unexpected and try to turn your foe's strengths against him. You should disengage as quickly as possible and use a weapon on him."

"You're not giving up, are you Lieutenant?" said Inuksuk. "I was just getting started."

"I have lived this long because my Momma didn't raise any fools, brother bear," JT replied with a grin. "I know how much you bears love a good tussle, so what we are going to do now is let your

65

squadmates take a run at you. Just to make it more of a challenge they will try to take you two at a time."

A grin spread over the bear's long muzzle. Polar bears did, indeed, like a good fight. In fact, if they didn't get a good violent workout every so often they got cranky and depressed. Having worked with bears before JT knew this and was having the squad engage in inter-species roughhousing for the benefit of both humans and ursines.

"All right, Carter, Singh, you're up," the Lieutenant ordered. "Try not to embarrass our species."

The two named Marines moved nervously to engage their Corporal. PFC Francisca "Fanni" Takala, a Finnish judo champion and one of the few female volunteers from the Finnish defense force, commented to PFC Ketevan "Keti" Tseriteli, a big boned Georgian woman who had spent time in the Fleet Marines.

"I'm thinking we will all be black and blue this evening."

"I think you are right, at least the men are softening him up a bit for us."

"I think they are only getting the bear warmed up, not softened up."

Keti nodded in agreement as one of the men sailed overhead and bounced off the hold's metal side. This was certainly not the easy duty she had anticipated when signing on. No matter, she wouldn't be a Marine if she didn't like to mix it up—she was already thinking of moves to try on the ursine Corporal. Meanwhile Inuksuk had dispatched his second opponent by swatting him to the deck and then sitting on him.

Lt. Taylor called out, "Walker, Davis, you're next."

Mizuki & Bobby's Quarters

Things had settled into a rhythm for the Danners since leaving Mars: Bobby stood watch on the bridge while Mizuki oversaw the science section and taught kendo. Mizuki's pets—the *aoi chō*, or blue butterflies—accompanied her to the cargo hold for sword practice and her morning run. At first, the new crewmembers were a bit put off by the flock of color shifting, insect like aliens that followed the Science Officer around.

Bobby and Mizuki were used to sharing their quarters with the fluttering horde. They were much like a dog—a distributed, flying dog. When someone approached their quarters' entrance the flock quickly flew to the door, swirling in excitement, flashing bright yellows and oranges instead of their normal placid blues and greens —the visual equivalent of barking.

When it was time for Mizuki to head to the cargo hold for kendo practice the *aoi chō* would flit between their mistress and her katana, which hung over the mantle of the holographic fireplace. As silly and harmless as the alien creatures appeared they were much more than they seemed. They possessed a shared intelligence on par with a dolphin, and far from being harmless, they could deliver a deadly jolt of electricity to those who threatened them or their mistress.

Mizuki treated them like a small child, speaking to them in Japanese and singing them lullabies. Why they had cast their lot with the Japanese astrophysicist was unknown, but they worshiped her like a goddess. Aside from Mizuki, only Bobby could control the colorful swarm, control being a relative term. Regardless, their presence meant that Peggy Sue carried within her three different species.

"We should almost be to Aldebaran. Given the mass and distance, transit time should only be three and a half days," said Mizuki, brushing her hair before bed.

Bobby was sitting at his desk, working on a tablet. "We should emerge from alter-space tomorrow afternoon, according to the computer's calculations. I wonder what awaits us in this system?"

"Not much of interest. We will drop a survey satellite to make stellar observations—we haven't studied this particular type of star up close before—but that should be about it."

"Of course the Universe has a way of smacking you right between the eyes when you least expect it."

"Don't be so negative, Bobby, you'll upset the children." When they were alone in quarters she often referred to the butterflies as their children. She felt this was good training for Bobby, for when they eventually got around to having the real thing.

"I'm just saying, the only thing expected when exploring the galaxy is the unexpected."

"Which would make not having a surprise surprising."

"What?"

Bobby looked up from his tablet and gave his wife a sidelong glance. Over her shoulder, she looked back at him impishly.

Chapter 8

Bridge, Peggy Sue II

The Captain surveyed the bridge. Finding all stations manned and the crew alert he forced himself to relax, willing the tension from his shoulders and back. While he had made many alter-space transits and never had trouble when emerging back into 3-space, he was still nervous—after all, this was the ship's first transit.

Damn it, never borrow trouble, he chided himself. "All stations prepare for emergence. As soon as we are out I want full multispectral sensor scans of the entire system. Mr. Aput, start scanning for gravitonic drive emissions as soon as possible, I want no surprises."

"Aye, aye, Sir." The bear replied from the sensor operator's station.

"Sailing Master, be ready to set course for the next transit point."

"Aye, Captain. We are less than one minute from emergence, I'm transferring control to the ship's computer."

"Very good, Cmdr. Danner."

"All parameters are nominal, Captain," the computer's soothing, feminine voice announced. "Emergence in 5, 4, 3, 2, 1."

An instant later the panels in the bow returned to transparent mode, revealing a new star system. Directly ahead was a huge orange star, hundreds of times brighter than the Sun.

"All systems functioning normally, Captain," the First Officer reported, after reviewing the status indicators holographically projected in front of her.

Mizuki looked up from her instruments. "Captain, the transit point to Eudora is located on the far side of the local star, roughly twenty three degrees to starboard off the line to galactic center. Distance from Aldebaran is 1.8 AU."

"Sir, I'm sensing what smells like alien spacecraft around the transit point," said Aput, his eyes closed, nostrils flaring, as he 'smelled' the alien ship's gravitonic drives through alter-space.

69

"Their drives are active and they seem to be keeping station around the transit point."

"I confirm that, Sir. Those ships are not at a libration point, not in Lissajous or halo orbits." JT looked up. "That must take a lot of energy."

"On the forward display, Mr. Taylor."

"How many ships, Mr. Aput?"

"I count seven drives of differing size."

"What would a squadron of ships be hovering around an alter-space transit point for?" asked the First Officer.

"I can only think of one reason, Number One," the Captain replied. "To intercept ships transiting between Aldebaran and Eudora."

Beth furrowed her brow. "A blockade?"

"Or an ambush," added Bobby. "Maybe they're space pirates!"

"Cmdr. Danner, put us on a course for the transit point that takes us around the star. That should mask us from their sensors until we are almost on top of them."

"They will know we have entered the system in less than thirty minutes. We don't know how good their sensors are but if they know about transit points they will certainly be able to detect the radiation burst from a ship emerging from alter-space."

"Yer right, Dr. Ogawa. Let's fire off a survey satellite with a gravitonic booster to put it in a stellar orbit—maybe the aliens will think that was all that came through the transit point from Sol."

"Hai, Captain. I am launching a probe now."

"Number One, put the shields in maximum stealth mode. That should take us off their screens until we close with them on the other side. They may know we arrived but they won't know where we went. Sailing Master, how fast can we get around yon bloated orange giant and lined up on the transit vector?"

"Accelerating at 50G will take us to five percent c in just over eight and a half hours. Swinging around Aldebaran, while not getting close enough to get too toasty, and then decelerating to a reasonable velocity for alter-space insertion... call it 22.4 hours. We avoid any drastic relativistic effects but it will severely deplete our deuterium stocks, Captain."

"By how much?"

"A couple of thousand tons, though we could save D by burning some antimatter."

"Do it, Cmdr. Danner."

"Aye, aye, Sir."

Officers Wardroom

The ship's course was set and the shields put in stealth mode, deflecting most of the EM spectrum in a way that rendered her practically invisible. There was no indication that the alien ships guarding the transit point to Eudora noticed the Peggy Sue's entry into the system. Things being quiet, the senior officers retired to the wardroom after the change of watch to grab something to eat and ponder possibilities.

"Did you really mean what you said about space pirates, Cmdr. Danner?" Asked Pauline Palmer between bites of salad. Frank Hoenig was watch officer on the bridge, but Pauline and JT had both joined the Captain's table at Billy Ray's invitation.

"First names in the wardroom, Pauline, call me Bobby. Of course the Captain's first name is Captain." He smiled and returned to the subject of space pirates, a favorite of his. "There have been pirates on Earth since man took to the seas, I see no reason it shouldn't be the same in space. I mean, we've run into a lot of alien races who are just as sneaky and underhanded as people, why shouldn't the idea of piracy have occurred to them?"

"You are probably right, Bobby," Mizuki agreed. "There were still pirates off Somalia and in the South China Sea at the time of the alien bombardment. Larceny is a common failing of humanity, even Japan had bandits."

"And don't forget the Yakuza." Bobby first met his wife-to-be while on a mission to rescue her mentor, Dr. Hiroyuki Saito, from the fearsome Japanese mobsters. Though it would take many

71

months for her to admit it, Mizuki fell in love with the heroic, if slightly geeky pilot during that rescue.

"I think stories of John Hawkins and Francis Drake influenced me as a young woman. I'll grant you that piracy and privateering are an over glamorized part of England's past, but they might have had more than a bit to do with my joining the Royal Navy."

"So you've always wanted to be the Dread Pirate Elizabeth, eh?" Billy Ray smiled behind his coffee cup as he teased his soul-mate.

"I've been quite satisfied with Dashing Explorer and Alien Hunter, thank you very much."

"What do you intend on doing when we reach the blockading ships, Captain?" asked JT, hoping for some insight into the Captain's battle plan.

"I think we will hail them when we get within 50,000 kilometers or so."

"And tell them what, dear?"

"I'm gonna tell 'em to vamoose."

"You think they speak Texan?" Beth raised a single eyebrow.

"It won't matter, we'll be using several variants of the old trade language that every spacefaring alien in these parts seems to know. I'm going to give them ten minutes to clear out. If they don't, when we get within ten minute railgun range we'll send a swarm of slugs on ahead to clear the channel."

"We'll be closing with them at a bit over forty klicks a second by the time we get that close," Bobby said, consulting his forearm display.

"Right, I figure ten minutes for them to see reason and another ten to blast 'em out of our way if they don't."

"That closing rate is not too fast to accurately hit the transit parameters is it Bobby?"

"No, sweetheart. That's a perfectly reasonable insertion velocity. Of course, that's not to say holding true to the vector will be easy if they are firing back at us."

"And if the slugs don't take them down?" It was JT's turn to raise his eyebrows.

"That's when we use the particle cannon. Unless they have the shields of a T'aafhal battle cruiser they'll be plasma."

"And then it's on to the Hyades."

"I thought we were headed to Eudora?" Pauline asked.

"Same thing, Pauline," JT answered. "The Hyades is an open cluster containing more than a hundred stars. Among them is Delta-1 Tauri A, an orange K-type giant that has the Latin name *Hyadum II*, meaning 'Second Hyad', and the common name Eudora. It is the primary component of a triple star system."

Being more poetic than JT, Mizuki expanded on the background description. "In Greek mythology the Hyades were sisters, the daughters of Aethra and Atlas."

"The giant who carried the heavens on his shoulders?" Beth hazarded.

"Yes, the same. Legend says that there were five Hyades and they nursed the infant Dionysus, a son of Zeus. For their services the king of the gods rewarded them with a place in the sky. Fittingly, they were also half-sisters to the Pleiades, our final destination."

"What I'm wondering is, if there are bushwhackers sitting on this end of the alter-space transit line, could there be others sitting on the other end?"

"It sounds like we need to be prepared to blast our way into the next system as well out of this one."

"I told you we'd get into a tussle or two before this voyage was over, Number One."

"Yes, Captain, you appear to be right about that," his wife admitted. "What bothers me, however, is that the voyage has barely begun."

Crew's Mess, 2nd Deck

"So what's the scuttlebutt Tam? You just came off bridge watch," asked Tommy Chen, a sailor who's action station was on the X-ray laser batteries. Like most of the ship's weapons, the X-ray secondaries were capable of automatic operation, controlled from the bridge, but were most effective with a crewmember in the loop.

"It's not like the Skipper told us what he has in mind, but he's obviously thinking several moves ahead."

"Tam and I've been with the Captain in a battle or two," added Sam Sheffield, also a gunner's mate. "He's a tricky one, I can tell you."

One of the new crewmembers, Leonard "Beans" Branford, placed his tray on the table and joined the conversation. "I thought this ship was brand new, how have you been in battles before?"

"On the old Peggy Sue, mate, not on this ship. Try to keep up."

"Well I've never been in a space battle before," said Lisa Tyler, another new crewmate. "I'm not so sure I should have signed on for this mission. I mean, it sounded so romantic, visiting all those stars named after Greek gods and stuff—I didn't think we'd be getting shot at."

Jay Taylor, crew from the last voyage of the Peggy Sue, decided to add his reassurances. Not coincidentally because the Aussi was interested in Lisa in an amorous way. "No worries, Lisa. Sam's right to say the Captain is a sly old space dog. He's been in more battles than the lot of us put together. He and all the senior officers have been fighting aliens for years."

"You're saying they are all good, experienced officers?"

"That, but more importantly they're lucky."

"What?"

"There's been plenty of good officers, and crews, that have ended up dead sailing the inky void. I'll take lucky over good any day."

Tamara shook her head. "Ignore the superstitious sailor from down under, Lisa. If Captain Vincent and the others appear to be lucky it's because they are very good at what they do. As for scuttlebutt, all I know is Chief Jacobs told me we should all get some chow and then grab some rack time—the balloon is going up in about twelve hours."

Sam nodded. "Which means we will probably be called to General Quarters in ten."

Lisa still looked a bit unsettled. "I'm still not sure I want to be in a space battle."

"Really?" said Kashi Ademola, who had been quietly eating while the others gossiped. "Well you better get used to it. The shields are up and we're accelerating like mad around a bloated orange star so we can come at the aliens out of the sun. Miss, you are already in a space battle, one that won't be over for another half a day."

Chapter 9

Command Center, Alien Flagship

The squadron commander was nestled into the command bower deep within his flagship, *Feaster On The Carcasses Of The Dead*. The hunting had been lean and he had been ready to move his flock to another venue when the telltale signs of a ship arriving in system were detected. The transit point from which it emerged was not well traveled, unlike the one his ships hovered around. Even worse, the only thing detectable from that quadrant was some form of small, presumably automated, probe.

"Where does that transit point lead?" the Commander hissed at his subordinates. Red eyes glared back at him from the gloom.

"It is a long transit to a minor star system, Commander," replied the current number two. Positions were constantly shifting among the members of the flock as they fought and jockeyed for advantage within its hierarchy. Thankfully, none had mustered the temerity to challenge him for overall command in more than a month. That would probably change if no prey flew into their snare in the near future.

They were principally opportunists, pillaging the derelict and disabled, though they were not opposed to creating a new wreck to loot. Like a wake of vultures perched on a dead tree, his ships waited for something to either emerge from the transit point or to approach intent on transit to Eudora. His flock consisted of two major warships and five smaller auxiliaries used for boarding.

The flagship of this pirate fleet was specially constructed for its job of preying on passing ships. Just over one hundred meters in diameter, the bow of the ship was a hemisphere that had once been half a metallic asteroid. The thick dense material provided a simple yet effective shield against a range of weapons that its prey might employ. It remained largely intact with only a score of tunnels bored through its mass to provide conduits for weapons and sensors.

Where the missing hemisphere had been was a jumble of tanks, cylinders and joining girders—as though an ugly industrial plant had been grafted to half a small planetoid. In a sense that was true, because the jumbled edifice contained a sizable antimatter conversion plant and its associated plumbing and storage. Surrounding the reactor were drives, weapons, and quarters for the crew. The ship's command center was buried deep within the asteroid's core, as shielded from the hostile galaxy as possible.

Massive, inelegant, and slow to maneuver, *Feaster* was a brute-force answer to a particular set of needs. Massing more than two billion kilograms, it was perfect for blocking another ship's way— hard to blow up; too large to collide with and survive. It's companion, *Consumer Of Viscera*, was a smaller replica with a diameter of only thirty meters.

"Commander, we have a target coming straight on for the transit point from out of the star!"

"What? Why did we not detect it sooner? Distance, velocity and size?"

"It is roughly fifty-six thousand kilometers from the transit point, velocity 40 km/sec. It is sizable, as big in beam as the *Consumer*, though not as massive."

"What of weapons and shields?"

"Gravitonic drives. I'm detecting signs of antimatter being burned and its shields are registering as very strong—I've never seen anything like it."

"Bold ones, they are. They mustn't know that being too noticeable can attract the attention of those-who-must-not-be-named or their lackeys."

"There has been a rumor circulating that a new race has appeared, one that took on half a dozen of the Dark Lords' minion races and obliterated them all. They even say one of the Dark Lords themselves was destroyed."

"Rakaww! Rumors for inebriated sailors. No race is that powerful." The Commander was agitated by his underling's rumor mongering. *Didn't he know that even mentioning the Dark Lords was bad luck?*

"Commander?"

"Yes!"

"The alien ship is hailing us using the old trade language..."

Bridge, Peggy Sue II

"Peggy Sue, hail the ships blocking the transit point."

"Yes, Captain, transmission sent," the ship's computer replied to the Captain's verbal command. "I have received a perfunctory reply indicating they can understand us."

"Very good. Send the following: Attention, ships holding station at the Eudora alter-space transit point. This is the Earth ship Peggy Sue. You will move away from my departure vector and stand down."

"Sent, Captain."

Standing next to the Captain's chair, the First Officer surreptitiously observed her husband. His face betrayed no emotion, no anxiety. *He truly does change when he is commanding the ship in action,* she thought. *Instead of the friendly, often humorous man I married, he becomes a no-nonsense warrior leading his crew into battle.*

Bobby called out from the helm. "Captain, we are approaching twenty-five thousand kilometers from the transit point."

Billy Ray nodded to himself. "Prepare to launch a salvo of eight slugs from the main railgun battery. Target the largest ships blocking our trajectory. Fire on my command."

"Aye, aye, Sir."

The computer's voice spoke again. "Captain, there is a reply from the alien flotilla."

"Play it."

"It is in nonverbal format. I can read a translation."

"Yes, yes, get on with it." The pedantic computer sometimes bothered the Captain, particularly in stressful situations.

"'Approaching ship: you will veer off of your current course, cease all acceleration and wait to be boarded. Failure to comply will result in your immediate destruction.'"

"Well, I guess that removes any possibility of this ending peacefully. Be prepared to fire two X-ray torpedoes thirty seconds after the railgun salvo."

"Aye, aye, Sir."

"Captain we are less than ten minutes from transit," Bobby reported.

"Railgun battery, fire."

Even with the deck gravity and its inertial dampeners, the firing of the large railguns could be felt through the deck. Each tremor signaled the launch of two high density metallic slugs, each massing ten kilograms. The velocity imparted by the guns, which ran nearly the entire length of the ship's main hull, combined with the forward velocity of the ship itself, gave each projectile eighteen gigajoules of kinetic energy with respect to their targets. The first would strike in just under seven minutes.

"Fire torpedoes, Mr. Hoenig."

"Torpedoes away, Sir."

"Captain, I'm picking up indications of plasma weapons being fired."

"Deploy anti-plasma defenses forward."

One of the common offensive weapons employed by hostile aliens were bundles of plasma. Within each bundle the hot charged matter flowed in patterns that generated magnetic fields, fields which kept the plasma itself contained in a compact knot. Some times these knots contained only normal matter; sometimes they contained separate braids of matter and antimatter. The composite knots collapsed when they encountered an object—like a ship's shields or hull—allowing their payload of matter and antimatter to mix. The result was mutual annihilation and a large burst of neutrinos and radiation.

To keep plasma knots from striking the shields, the Peggy Sue used its 30mm rapid fire railguns to lay down a pattern of small metallic pellets—like Gatling guns firing oversized shotgun shells filled with double-ought buckshot. Instead of hitting their target, the knots would collide with the cloud of metallic hailstones sprayed out in front of the ship and detonate. At least that was the idea. In practice it worked, but sometimes knots would still get through.

"Anti-plasma defense deployed forward, Sir."

"Are they breaking formation, Mr. Aput?"

"Only the smaller targets, Captain. The two largest ships have not changed course."

"We have multiple hits, Captain," called out JT from the optical sensor station."

"On the forward screen, Mr. Taylor"

A holographic overlay filled the view forward. Two sizable ships could be seen, one much larger than the other. Ugly, dark, bullet shaped vessels with rounded prows. The larger took two hits simultaneously, bright flashes marking the impact points. Then a third impact on the large ship, accompanied by a hit on its smaller companion.

Beth frowned. "It's almost like the slugs are impacting a solid body, not a ship."

"They appear to have thick layers of dense material covering their bows." Mizuki looked up from her instruments. "It must be intended as a defense against kinetic energy weapons."

A second flare blossomed on the smaller ship, which began to veer away to port. Fainter, secondary detonations could be seen from the smaller vessel as it turned side on to the approaching Earth ship. The larger vessel remained blocking the transit point.

A fourth impact flared on the larger alien's scared bow. To starboard, a bright flash indicated a slug impact on one of the auxiliary craft that had waited too long to get out of the line of fire. The small craft came apart in a bright explosion.

"Fourth impact on the large ship, and a hit on a smaller craft. The small craft is destroyed, looked like an antimatter explosion."

The X-ray torpedoes detonated, two white hot temporary suns flared as their antimatter charges exploded. Surrounding each warhead were rods of nano-engineered material, each independently targeted at the alien ships. A fraction of a second before the warhead's star hot explosion turned them into plasma,

81

the rods were energized by the radiation released. Pumped to highly energetic states they lased, each rod sending a coherent beam of X-rays lancing toward its chosen target.

Explosions blossomed like miniature novae, marking the deaths of the remaining auxiliary craft. The smaller of the two major ships also flared brightly and after a moment's hesitation erupted in a titanic explosion. Radiation from the exploding ships cause the Peggy Sue's bow panels to turn translucent, blocking most of the light from their death pyres. The holographic display remained, and on it the large blockading ship, damaged but holding fast.

"Sir, we have taken out all the enemy but the largest ship, which is still blocking our course."

"Very well, Mr. Taylor. Mr. Aput, send targeting information to the main battery."

"Aye, aye, Sir." A grin spread along Aput's muzzle. He might be more cerebral than most polar bears but he was still a bear—and all bears loved closing for the kill.

"Concentrate fire on the hostile's starboard side, let's see if we can knock him aside with the particle cannon. Fire as she bears."

"Firing!"

Though the hyperluminal particle beams were invisible in 3-space they were represented by twin red lines on the forward display. The glowing lines converged on the left side of the pirate ship, as seen from the bridge. An instant later, flame and debris erupted from the stricken ship as its starboard side disintegrated. The target split open like an overripe fruit shot with a high powered rifle, its bow section fracturing into large chunks. The violent explosion sent the remains of the vessel away from Peggy Sue's course vector, clearing the way to the alter-space transit point.

"Looks like that's done it, Captain, the enemy is destroyed," JT reported. "Most of the debris will be clear of the alter-space transit point by the time we reach it. The secondary batteries are taking care of anything sizable that remains."

"Well done people." Billy Ray allowed himself a satisfied smile. *Well done indeed, but then we have a mostly veteran bridge crew and experienced hands at all of the weapons stations. Still, it's good to see them in action as a team.*

On the helm console, Bobby turned to the Captain and announced. "We are under thirty seconds to transit. What are your orders Captain?"

"Turn control over to the computer for transit, Cmdr. Danner. Number One, secure all weapons and prepare for alter-space."

"Aye, aye," came the replies.

The computer's voice sounded across the ship. "Transition to alter-space in 5, 4, 3, 2, 1..."

The Earth ship vanished from 3-space, leaving behind a spreading cloud of debris and cooling plasma.

Part Two

The Enemy Of My Enemy

Chapter 10

Bridge, Peggy Sue II, Alter-space

"Stand down from General Quarters," Billy Ray ordered. "Navigation informs me that transit time will only be 138 minutes, does that agree with your calculations Dr. Ogawa?"

"That is correct, Captain." Mizuki continued, providing an explanation. "Though the distance between is quite far the masses of the two stars makes this transit a short one in terms of duration."

"Very well. Number One, we will return to General Quarters a half hour before emergence."

"Yes, Captain," said Beth, feeling relieved now that they were safely in alter-space. "It seems we've managed to leave Aldebaran space in spite of last minute obstacles."

Bobby swiveled around in his chair at the helm. "We were never in any real danger. If the transit point had remained blocked we could have easily veered off and come around for another pass. In case you didn't notice the blockading ships couldn't maneuver for squat."

"I never doubted it, but for a minute there it was like we were in a real-life version of that old Asteroids game."

"Look at it as a live-fire exercise, Number One. Everyone got to participate—the main railguns, the torpedo crew, the particle cannon, the secondary X-ray batteries and even close support. The crew won't be as nervous the next time."

"Yes, Captain. No substitute for experience in an actual battle."

"So what are we heading into?"

JT took that as an opening. He had been waiting for the opportunity to brief the Captain on conditions in the next star system. "Eudora—more properly Delta-1 Tauri A—is a K-type giant that masses 2.7 times Sol. It is 74 times as luminous as the Sun, and its angular diameter gives a radius of 11.8 solar. We should emerge into 3-space about 3.2 AU from the star."

"Are we expecting to find anything at Delta-1, planet wise?"

"Probably not, Captain. Its companion, Delta-1 Tauri B, is a 12th magnitude star separated by not quite two minutes of arc from the primary, making it a minimum of 5200 AU away from Tauri A. It's a class M0 dwarf with an orbital period of at least 230,000 years, but most likely it's not gravitationally bound to the main star at all. However, lunar occultations of Tauri A have revealed a much closer star that orbits it. The binary is a dim 13th magnitude class M dwarf in an eccentric orbit with an average distance of around 1.8 AU."

"So there will probably be no planets in the habitable zone, given the close companion star," added Mizuki. "Even if there are, the Hyades' age is estimated at 650 million years, consistent with the evolution of class K giants."

"Which means there has been little time for life to develop."

"Compared with 4.5 billion years on Earth, hai. Not impossible, but improbable."

Crew Mess

A number of crewmembers were taking advantage of the order to stand down by grabbing a late breakfast in the mess. Among them were Lisa and Jay.

"So how did you like your first action, Lisa?" the Aussie gunner's mate asked, plopping down next to the young woman.

"We didn't end up dead, so I guess it went well."

Nearby, Tamara looked up from her coffee mug. "Not much of a battle, as such things go. If the hostiles were minions they weren't very advanced ones."

"Minions? You mean those little yellow, jellybean shaped guys from that old movie?"

"No," Jay laughed. "Tam means minions of the Dark Lords. You know, the mysterious evil creatures that live on rogue planets between the stars and hate all us warm life creatures."

"We're fighting boogeymen, who live in the dark between the stars?" Lisa looked skeptical, feeling that somehow she was the butt of a joke. After all, it was not unusual for the more senior crew to send a new crewman off to fetch some horizon line or a flux capacitor.

"It's not a joke, Lisa. Most of the creatures we have come across have been hostile, and most of them seem to be aligned with the Dark Lords, one way or another."

Next table over, Kato Kwan, a corporal in second squad and an old-timer, responded. "Those slime-balls who were blocking our course were probably freelancers. Real minions tend to be a bit more problematic."

"And you know this how, Mate?"

"I know this because I have seen most everything we've had to tangle with since we first left Earth, you Aussie bonehead. From cyborg spiders and hairy crickets to flying batacudas and spiny beavers, and I can tell you the blockaders weren't shit compared to real minions."

"Word, Kato," added Vinny DeSilva, another Marine veteran. "Nice of the galaxy to break you newbies in easy."

Lisa's apetite suddenly vanished. "This is not filling me with confidence guys."

"Ignore those wankers, Lisa. Like I said, the Skipper knows his stuff, those aliens were no problem at all."

"Never said he didn't, dude," Vinny replied. "Just that, as space battles go, this last one was pretty tame. Blasting things with railguns and energy weapons from 10,000 klicks away is a walk in the park compared with getting up close and personal with ET."

"And you've done this—engaged in combat with aliens—multiple times? Do you Marines go looking for trouble?"

"Not really, trouble pretty much seems to know where to find us, Lisa."

"Bloody Jarheads, all you do is wander around on strange planets in your armored suits and blow things up. Now Tam and me, we were on that ant planet in the shuttle with Lt. Hoenig. We shot down three alien fighters who were about to nuke these ground pounders into oblivion."

Vinny snorted. "Whatever, Crocodile Dundee. It still took boots on the ground to rescue Dr. Ogawa."

"Everybody cool your beans. If previous voyages have been any indication, there will be plenty of opportunity to prove how badassed you all are." Kato might have said more but he was interrupted by the grating call of the klaxon, calling the crew to General Quarters in preparation for emergence.

The Chief burst through the forward door and yelled. "Stand to yous deck apes, ya think this is a pleasure cruise?"

Everyone scrambled, shoving half emptied trays into the disposal slots and running for their action stations.

Bridge, Emergence at Eudora

"Let's look sharp people," the First Officer told the Bridge crew. She was again standing at her normal station, to the right of the Captain's command chair. Behind her the science and sensor stations were ready, manned by Mizuki, JT, and Aput. Forward and several steps down was the helm where Bobby and Frank Hoenig manned the console, with gunner's mates on their weapons consoles to either side. In front of them all was the ship's conical nose, still a sanity preserving gray.

"Thank you, Number One. Given the bushwhackers we found at the other end of the alter-space transit line, there's an off chance that more varmints could be waiting for us on this end. Mr. Aput, if you notice anything suspicious before we emerge sing out." The advanced T'aafhal based sensors could actually pick up the presence of gravitonic drives prior to the shift from alter-space to normal 3-space.

"I smell no prey so far, Captain."

"Very well. We will go immediately to full shields, weapons at the ready. Cmdr. Danner, move us off the transit trajectory as soon as she'll answer the helm."

"Aye, aye, Captain. The computer has control for emergence."

The voice of the Peggy Sue sounded across the bridge and over the ship's intercom. "Emergence in 5, 4, 3, 2, 1."

90

The bow of the ship turned transparent, revealing another large orange star, much like Aldebaran. The view shifted almost instantly as Bobby carried out the Captain's order to alter course following emergence.

JT's instruments actively scanned the electromagnetic spectrum, looking for signs that other ships were about. One of the advantages that a ship emerging from alter-space has is the time it takes for signs of its presence to propagate through 3-space. The spray of particles and gamma rays that mark its arrival are constrained by Einstein's universal speed limit—they cannot travel faster than light. Conversely, any objects already in the system can be observed from the radiation they emit or that reflects off them. Though such signals suffered from propagation delay they are detectable everywhere in the system.

"Not picking up any ships near by, Captain. But I've got a better reading on the class M companion star—the orbital eccentricity is pretty pronounced, the distance between it and the primary varies from 1.0 AU to 2.5 AU." From the Peggy Sue's vantage point both stars could be seen clearly, the massive orange K type and its much smaller red dwarf companion.

"Anything smaller than a star on your scope, Mr. Taylor?"

JT smiled sheepishly, but after all he was an astronomy geek.

"Nothing within 5 AU, Sir. The eccentric binary would have a tendency to eject or swallow any small objects close in."

"Captain, I'm picking up a scent farther out."

"Yes, Mr. Aput? A ship perhaps, or a planetary mass?"

"Not sure, Sir. It's bigger than a ship but smaller than a planet. And it's about 50 AU out."

"That's farther than Pluto at aphelion," JT commented. "Roughly seven and a half billion kilometers. I'm targeting it with the large optical scope."

"Put it on the forward display."

The view of the system's suns was obscured, replaced by a view of what at first appeared to be empty space. Then an object came into focus, not much more than a fuzzy dot. It grew in size as JT

91

altered the magnification of the ship's largest telescope, becoming brighter, more star like.

"What is it?" Beth asked, peering at the image hanging in air in front of them. "That far out from the star it could be some kind of Dark Lord ship."

"I don't know but there is some gravitonic activity coming from that location in 3-space. I don't think it's a drive, more like repulsors or deck gravity." Aput's instruments were better at detecting massive objects, like planets and stars, than small ones. That and the sharp gravitational gradients caused by a ship's gravitonic drive and shields.

"It may not actually be in orbit, I don't have enough data on its course yet to know for sure, but if it's in a circular orbit it would take 215 years to go once around Eudora," added JT.

"Captain?"

"Yes, Peggy Sue?"

"I'm picking up some very weak signals that appear to be guidance and docking guides, similar to the signals we encountered at the Space Mushroom." The Space Mushroom was the first alien space station Earthlings encountered, an antimatter collection and refueling station that almost caused the destruction of the original Peggy Sue.

"Well crap." Billy Ray squinted hard at the apparition on the forward display. "Whatever it is we need to find out if it poses any threat."

"We could just make the next transit to the Pleiades," Beth suggested.

"Never a good idea to leave a possible hostile force in yer rear, Number One. Cmdr. Danner, plot us a course to that thing, whatever it is. No great hurry, we burned enough D attacking the bushwhackers at Aldebaran."

"If we accelerate to one percent c it will take us just over a month."

"Hmm, that's a mite more leisurely than I had in mind, Sailing Master."

"If we go to two percent c we can be there in just under fifteen days, though it will quadruple the fuel burn." Bobby was starting to become nervous about the rate they were running through their deuterium supply. "Still, that will burn only fifteen percent of what we used during the trip around Aldebaran."

"Do it, Cmdr. Danner."

"Aye, Sir. Altering course now."

"Well, at least the Gunny will be happy," the First Officer remarked. "She just gained a fortnight to finish training the new Marines."

Chapter 11

Starflake

For fourteen and a half days, the Peggy Sue traveled across the star system, heading away from Eudora and toward the anomalous object its sensors had detected. After coasting at two percent of the speed of light for almost two weeks, the ship decelerated at 20G for a third of a day, its velocity relative to its objective dropped to almost nothing. With their target less than 100,000 kilometers away, it was close enough for the large telescope to provide a clear image.

"What in God's great amazing universe is that?"

"I don't know, Captain," said JT as he manipulated the optical telescope view on the forward display. "It's either a large space station or the biggest snowflake I've ever seen."

The object ahead did, indeed, look like a snowflake—crystalline spires, the longest more than fifteen kilometers in length, extending radially from a spiky center. As it slowly rotated glints of the distant orange star it orbited flashed off transparent arms, faceted like cut diamond.

"It looks like a gigantic Christmas tree ornament, like an immense... starflake," Beth said in wonder, reflections of stars sparkling off its crystal spires.

"Starflake? Yes, Number One, that's a good name for it, but what is it?"

Mizuki, entranced by the view, ignored her instruments as she gazed upon the object. "Given the regular geometry, the symmetrical arrangement of the spires in three dimensions, I would guess that it is some form of construct."

"It could be a living creature, or a colony of creatures," Bobby suggested, drawing on his imagination and vast knowledge of science fiction. "Something like the Crystal Entity from STNG."

"What?" said the three other partners simultaneously.

"The Crystal Entity. It was a powerful, spaceborne creature characterized by a crystalline structure that resembled a large snowflake, sort of like that thing out there."

"And yer basing this on Star Trek?"

"Yeah, Star Trek: The Next Generation. Supposedly, the Entity functioned as a giant electromagnetic collector and converted organic matter into energy. It stripped whole planets, devouring everything, including animals and vegetation, right down to bacteria."

Mizuki shook her head. It was usually left to her to reign in her husband's flights of fancy. Not that his imaginative suggestions were unhelpful, often they were, but other times not so much. "We already ran into something like that back on Paradise, except it was black and stringy, not a crystalline starflake."

"That doesn't mean this thing isn't some kind of living, interstellar scourge."

"No, Bobby, it doesn't. But this object is showing signs of gravitonic fields, bio-compatible internal temperatures, and antimatter energy conversion."

"Meaning what, Dr. Ogawa?" The Captain was glad Mizuki was returning the conversation to the realm of science instead of science fiction.

"Meaning it appears to be a space station, that or a very large ship that is dead in space."

"And it is broadcasting navigation signals?"

"That is correct, Captain."

"Well people. I'd say that this warrants a closer inspection." Billy Ray leaned back in the command chair. A space station meant new aliens and the possibility of new alien technology. A smile spread slowly across his face—he smelled profit.

"The Entity responded to and sent out graviton emissions," Bobby added, a slightly hurt tone to his voice. "We will look really silly if it absorbs our life-force."

"So we'll sidle up to it real careful like, pardner. Let's go see what yonder starflake is up to."

Polar Bear Quarters

The forward bulkhead in the polar bear quarters contained a large holographic display that was usually slaved to the main bridge display. Aput was on the bridge and Siku in the CIC, but both Aurora and Inuksuk were in quarters, relaxing on the ice. On the display was the Starflake, mysterious and ethereal.

"What is that thing?" asked Inuksuk. The big male was not noted for his inquisitive nature so his statement surprised Aurora.

"The humans are calling it the Starflake, which probably means they have no idea what it really is. They tend to think that if you name something you gain some understanding of it."

"Might be a ship."

"Could be. There are weirder things floating around the galaxy. It might be a space station—we've found a number of space stations in the past, though none that looked like that."

As the two bears talked the ship drew closer to the gigantic crystalline structure. Smaller spires became clear, sprouting from between the fourteen main spars. Closer in, gossamer arks curved gracefully between the spires, diaphanous ribbons not quite connecting one to another.

"You think we will be boarding it?" the male bear asked.

"Was Curious George a monkey?"

"Heh heh heh, I thought you didn't make primate jokes."

"Not a joke, fact. Humans are naturally curious, like all primates," Aurora corrected. "Besides, I don't think that the Gunny was running our paws off for nothing."

"I gotta admit that the primates were getting more... effective at trying to take me down during practice. The little devils are sneaky and they don't give up."

"Not a bad combination if you want to conquer the galaxy."

"And you have no problems with *H. sapiens* ruling over everything and everyone?"

97

"They're not the worst I've ever seen. Besides, I'm sort of excited to be along for the ride."

Inuksuk made a non-committal rumble.

"It looks so much like an ice crystal, I wonder if it has reasonable temperatures inside?"

"Arctic temps and a breathable atmosphere would make it a great place for some shore leave. Throw in something to hunt and call it home."

The she-bear stared at the strange object with renewed interest. Contemplative silence descended until both bears' comm pips chirped. It was the Gunny.

"Sgt. Aurora, Cpl. Inuksuk. Report to the armory to get suited up. We're going walkabout."

Armory, 1ˢᵗ Deck

"Hey, big Nanook!" yelled Vinny when the pair of ursines entered the armory. "Time to suit up for some extravehicular fun."

Inuksuk emitted a low rumble. Humans had adopted the moniker Nanook as an all purpose nickname for polar bears, the equivalent of "guy" or "dude" for humans. Since Nanook means "polar bear" in Inuit this was appropriate. The bears remained indifferent on the subject.

"So what's the drill, primates?"

"Heavy armor, full ammo loads of 5mm and 15mm, though y'all might want to think about something a mite heavier," replied PFC "Grits" Walker. Walker was a good ol' boy from LA—Lower Alabama, also known as the Redneck Riviera.

"Da, I am carrying pulse laser as second weapon," added LCpl Dmitry "Bosco" Boskovitch. Bosco was a former Russian Spetsnaz special forces operative and a veteran of the last voyage of the old Peggy Sue. All the Marines carried two weapons, generally a variable fire rate, high velocity 5mm railgun on their dominant arm and a secondary weapon on their other arm. For the humans the secondary was usually a 15mm cannon, capable of firing high

98

explosive or canister rounds. The bears, being able to carry a heavier ammo load, had other choices as well.

At this point the Gunny, who was already suited up, joined the conversation. "Since we don't know what we'll run into on board the Starflake, I think you should carry a 30mm as your secondary, Corporal."

This brought a smile to Inuksuk's long muzzle. Basically a larger caliber version of the 15mm cannon, the 30mm was new with the latest armor system. A rapid fire railgun fed from an ammo pack on the operator's back, the 30mm projectiles it used had the explosive impact of an old fashioned 155mm artillery piece. It elevated the already considerable destructive power of the Marines to a new level.

"So what are our orders, Gunny?" asked Sgt Aurora.

"We are to suit up and board the shuttles: 1ˢᵗ squad on the portside shuttle, 2ⁿᵈ squad on the starboard. The officers are still debating where to land on this thing but the plan is for 1ˢᵗ squad to make initial contact, with 2ⁿᵈ held in reserve. Once we have secured a beachhead some of the officers will land in the small shuttle to investigate."

"Do we know what we are up against, Gunnery Sergeant?" asked PFC Narinder "Simba" Singh. Singh was a Brit from Slough and a former Royal Marine Commando. He was also a Sikh whose name translated as "King Lion," hence the nickname "Simba." Sikhs are always suppose to wear a *dastaar*, the distinctive headgear they are known for. Tradition not withstanding, there were times when a large turban was not practical, like when wearing space armor. Instead, inside his suit helmet he wore a smaller scarf-sized cloth, a *patka*, to cover his hair, as other Sikhs have done to accommodate conventional helmets.

"We'll find out when we get there, so be ready for anything. But note that the natives might not be openly hostile, so don't go popping off at anything that moves—we do not open fire unless attacked."

"Well that's just bloody great," said PFC Brian "Brains" Davis, a former Royal Marine. "Givin' ET a little target practice are we?"

"Shut it, Davis. We have our orders. Any more questions?"

99

No one else spoke up.

"All right, move out to the landing shuttles."

The two squads of Marines, bulky gray giants in their heavy armor, exited the armory and headed for the awaiting shuttles. On suit-to-suit, PFC Fanni Takala said to her friend PFC Keti Tseriteli:

"You were looking for adventure, now you will get some I think."

"Adventure is fine, as long as the price isn't too high. What good is adventure if you don't live to tell about it?"

"Are you always so pessimistic?"

"I try to be pessimistic, that way I can be pleasantly surprised if things turn out OK."

"That's one way of looking at it. I'm thinking positive thoughts— maybe there will be ice faeries and unicorns inside."

"You do know that unicorns are carnivorous, right?"

Combat Information Center

The ship's officers gathered around the big holographic projection tank in the CIC. Several recon drones had been sent out to scout the Starflake prior to deciding where to land the Marines. Live video from the drones moved across the wall displays as a model of the Starflake slowly took shape in the tank. Internal details would not get filled in until the Marines actually set foot inside the structure.

"So far there aren't any signs of alien life, hostile or otherwise," Beth observed.

"It does seem a awfully quiet," agreed JT. "The whole structure is encased in some form of transparent material, not ice but definitely some kind of crystalline substance. Sensors indicate a livable environment inside, though conditions seem to vary significantly among the different spires."

There were fourteen main spires in all, six mutually orthogonal ones configured like a giant jack from an epic game of knucklebones. Eight more stuck out at equal angles between the primary axes, as if tracing diagonals of an inset cube. Smaller spires filled the space between the main spires, and smaller ones still between them.

"I am not detecting anything that would indicate energy weapons or even defensive shielding, though it appears that there is deck gravity inside the spires. It seems to vary in strength from spire to spire and within the spires themselves." Mizuki looked at her companions. "It is safe to say we have never seen anything like this before."

"Getting inside will be the trick. There are no obvious doors or other entryways. If there are aliens in residence I doubt they would appreciate us crashing through the side of their home with an armored shuttle."

"Which is why you are going to lead the landing party, Lt. Taylor. After all, you have had experience exploring alien space stations in the past."

"That's true, Sir. If I recall correctly, every one of those missions ended in a fire fight."

"Well, let's hope this time proves the exception to the rule. Go get suited up and report when you are on board Shuttle One."

"Aye, aye, Captain." JT left the bridge at a run, a smile on his face. This beat wrangling asteroids all to hell.

Shuttle One, Port Side

JT jogged toward the portside shuttle bay, wearing light armor and carrying a railgun assault rifle. The shuttles docked with the Peggy Sue with their bellies against the outer hull, meaning their internal deck gravity was not aligned with the gravity within the mother ship. Nearing the bay he entered a hallway whose floor abruptly twisted to the left, turning through 120 degrees until it aligned with the shuttle docked above the bay. Deck gravity kept the down vector normal to the deck's surface but visibly it was still unsettling—a lifetime living in constant gravity instilled reasonable fear of trying to run sideways along a wall or upside down. One of the things the Marines practiced was running through the "twister"

101

as they called it, until the disagreement between their eyes and their inner ears no longer caused them to falter.

Coming to a halt at the foot of the shuttle's rear ramp he encountered a member of the crew, also wearing light armor. The ramp extended into the airlock to provide easy access to the shuttle's interior, even for humans and bears in heavy battle armor.

"Welcome aboard, Lieutenant," Jay Taylor said in greeting, "everyone else is already on board."

"Good. Let's get her buttoned up and ready to go."

JT hurried up the ramp. The interior of the shuttle was filled with hulking gray giants, faceless inside their battle armor. One overly large monster was unmistakably Cpl. Inuksuk, the only ursine in 1st Squad. The Lieutenant strode to the front of the cabin and stopped in front of one of the gray giants.

"All set to go, Gunny?"

"Aye, aye, Sir. Locked and loaded."

JT nodded, a gesture that could be seen through the clear bubble helmet of his suit. The Gunny's response, if any, was obscured by the solid helmet of her battle armor. The Marines' view of the outside world was provided by an immersive holographic display that allowed them to see in frequencies both higher and lower than normal human vision, overlain with targeting queues and other data.

Entering the forward cabin, JT saw a crewmember sitting at the portside weapons console and another in the pilot's seat. Through the pilot's clear helmet he recognized the dirty blond hair of an old friend.

"What's our status, Chief?"

"Power's up and all systems are nominal," said CPO Steve Hitch, turning to look over his shoulder. "Welcome aboard, Lieutenant. The copilot's seat is empty if you want."

"No thanks, I'd rather stand. I'm hoping this will be a short journey."

Jay entered the flight deck from the main cabin. "We're all sealed up and the Marines are secured for flight, Sir."

"Thank you, Petty Officer Taylor. PO Wilson, you set to go?"

"Aye, Sir. Weapons secure for departure, we're good to go," replied Tamara.

JT nodded. "Peggy Sue, Shuttle one. We are ready for departure."

"Shuttle One, you are clear for undocking and departure."

"Copy that, Peggy Sue. Chief, take her out."

"Aye, aye, Sir."

Without a tremor or a sound the hull of the Peggy Sue fell away from the shuttle. Pulling away from the ship the shuttle accelerated, heading across the fifty kilometer gap between it and its chosen destination, two thirds of the way up one of the diagonal spires.

Chapter 12

Shuttle One, On Approach To The Starflake

The crystalline spires of the alien space station surrounded the shuttle, their glittering transparent surfaces a stark contrast to the dark gray hull of the armored troop carrier. In the main cabin, the Marines were all watching the shuttle's progress on their helmet displays. Some listened to music while others chatted on suit-to-suit comm links.

"Well it's big, I'll give 'em that," remarked Grits Walker, as the target spire grew larger.

"I think it's pretty," said Fanni Takala. "It reminds me of ice and snow back home."

"Do you always have to be so cheerful?" asked Zippy Ben-Ezra. This was the Israeli woman's first possible alien combat and she was a bit nervous, though she would deny it.

"Come on, lighten up Zippy. Y'all don't need to be so serious all the time. We'll find out what we're up against when we get there." Leaking through Walker's comm was background music with a strong beat and a soulful male singer.

"What's that your listening to, Yank? It sounds familiar," Brains Davis asked.

"The Heavy, Short Change Hero."

"From that TV show?"

"Yeah, Strike Back. About a bunch of special operators. Hey, it starred a Brit and an American, just like you and me, Brains."

"Right. Except that the Brit was played by a Yank, and the Yank was played by an Aussie."

"So maybe I can trade you in on an Aussie, guv'ner," Grits replied in an atrocious English accent.

"Funny, you gormless tosser. Who do you think you are, bleeding Action Man?"

"Who?"

"If you two would shut up and pay attention to our objective we all might learn something," Zippy huffed. "For instance, there seems to be a multifloored structure inside of the crystal exterior..."

* * * * *

"Looks like there are floors in the interior of the structure, with balconies and doorways leading inside," JT reported to the ship. "It suggests that the gravity, if any, is oriented along the spire axis."

"Roger, Shuttle One. Have you found a way in yet?"

"That's a negative, Peggy Sue. We're going to follow the spire back toward its base."

"LT, it looks like there are open platforms along that extended ridge just below us," Hitch observed.

"I think you're right, Chief. Let's take a closer look."

The shuttle drifted down the spire toward the object's spiky hub. Near its midpoint they approached a section of the tower where the crystal sheathing flared outward, widening the structure. Gliding slowly past the crystalline walls, objects within became visible.

"The protruding section seems to contain a bunch of distinct cells," Hitch observed, glancing between the view outside and his instruments. "Some of them are covered and others are open to space."

"Yeah," said Tamara. "Some of them have what look like small craft inside them."

Tamara was right, dark shapes could be seen within several of the sealed off rectangular prisms. "Hold us steady, Chief. I think that this part of the spire is actually some kind of parking garage."

"Yes, Sir."

"Peggy Sue, Shuttle One. Are you seeing this?"

"Roger, Shuttle One. We agree that you are outside of some kind of docking facility. Interrogative, could you set the shuttle down inside one of the open bays?"

"Copy that, Peggy Sue. We will approach one of the open bays." JT took a deep breath, thinking, *here we go, sticking an appendage into a dark hole*. "You heard the man, Chief, let's poke our nose in and see if anything tries to cut it off."

"Aye, aye, LT."

Hitch aligned the shuttle with one of the beckoning open bays and began edging forward. Crystal enclosed cells above, below and to either side, like a giant vertical ice cube tray. When they were within ten meters of the chosen opening the portal's rim began to glow with faint blue light.

"Looks like something knows we are approaching. Should I continue, Sir?"

"Our shields are up, PO Wilson?"

"Aye, Sir. Shields are up and the defensive X-ray lasers are on standby."

"Very well, time to fish or cut bait. Take us inside, Stevie."

JT's elevated stress level was evident in his calling Hitch by his first name—they had fought together on numerous occasions when Hitch was an enlisted-man and JT a noncom. At Hitch's gentle urging the big shuttle edged closer to the threshold, smoothly gliding inside the structure. Once the tail cleared the mouth of the bay, the shuttle began to drop.

"A gravity field just came on, pulling us to the deck!"

"How strong? Can we back out?"

"Not strong, about a third of a G, it came on suddenly. Should I extend the landing struts and let her settle?"

"OK, Chief. Let her down easy."

Brief electromechanical whining marked the extension of the landing struts, then silence. Seconds passed slowly as the shuttle gently alighted.

"We're down. I guess that means we've docked, LT."

"Sir, there's movement aft!" Tamara blurted, alarm in her voice.

"Give me a view aft!"

107

The holographic display built into his helmet lit up showing a panoramic view facing aft. A strange rippling was converging from the edges of the dock opening. From all sides, the open space they had just passed through was growing shut, a clear wall crystallizing as he watched.

"Should I burn a way out with the lasers, Sir?"

"No, secure the lasers," JT answered, making a snap judgment call. "I think it is just the hatch being shut behind us. Let's see what happens next."

"Lieutenant, outside atmospheric pressure is rising. It's up to nearly 600 millibars and climbing fast."

"Composition?"

"Mostly nitrox: 75% nitrogen, 23% oxygen, some H_2O, CO_2 and other trace gasses. It's breathable, Sir."

"Seems like they're making us feel right at home. Let's see what the ship says before we proceed."

CIC, Peggy Sue

"...and the temperature in the bay is about 16°C, a bit chilly but tolerable. I don't know what conditions are like inside the main structure, but this would be habitable without suits."

"We are getting your full analytic readings now, Lieutenant. Have there been any signs of life inside the spire?"

"That's a negative, Captain. We've observed no movement inside or in any of the adjacent docking cells. How do you want us to proceed, over?"

Billy Ray muted the comm and turned to the others. "Well, what do y'all think?"

"The docking procedure could be automatic, activated by a ship entering one of the bays," Mizuki said. "It doesn't mean that there are any inhabitants within the structure."

"It doesn't mean there aren't any either," observed Beth.

"Correct."

"One way to find out, Captain. They've gone this far, they may as well enter the station proper."

"No longer afraid it will consume their life-force, pardner?"

"Ha ha. I think it's obvious that this is some kind of space station, or a ginormous ship, and it evidently has power and at least some of its systems are still functioning."

"'If you dare nothing, then when the day is over, nothing is all you will have gained,'" Beth quoted. "I say we send them inside."

"Hai."

"Yes."

"Then we're agreed." Billy Ray took the comm off mute and spoke. "Shuttle One, go ahead and disembark the Marines. See if they can find a way in—preferably a non-destructive way."

"I copy, Peggy Sue. Disembarking the Marines now..."

Interior, Starflake

Two abreast the Marines jogged down the shuttle's rear ramp, half splitting off to the left, half to the right. As they exited, other spires could be seen through the transparent cover that had grown over the once open entrance to the docking bay. Next to the last to exit, Brains Davis couldn't help himself. He stepped up to the clear material they had watch form, reaching out with an armored gauntlet to touch the barrier.

"It's smooth and hard, I wonder how we make it go away?"

Right behind him Walker thumped him on the backpack. "Quit messing around, Brains, what if it popped like a soap bubble and we all got blown out into space."

"Come on mate, you saw it form. It has to be ten centimeters thick and strong enough to hold an atmosphere without bulging outwards in the middle."

"Yeah, it was sort of weird, like it was melting in reverse. But that don't mean you should handle everything you see. Some of this stuff could be dangerous."

109

"I don't know, if creatures of some sort lived here they wouldn't want dangerous stuff just laying around."

"Aliens ain't people, Bubba. Don't expect them to act like people."

The squad comm circuit clicked. "Davis, Walker, quit lollygagging and get the hell up here."

"Aye, aye, Gunny," the two replied, hustling along the shuttle's flank to join the rest of the squad. On arrival they saw the others examining a gray panel embedded in the transparent wall. On the panel were square pastel colored lights.

"Should we push some of these buttons, Gunny?" asked Bosco, standing next to the object in question.

"I doesn't look like it's gonna open on its own," the Gunny answered.

"Hey, let Brains poke the buttons, he likes touching stuff."

"Shut up, Grits, and let Bosco get on with it."

"Am trying blue button, like color around the entrance when we landed," the Russian announced. He reached out and poked the button with a single large digit.

In front of the assembled Marines a large rectangle appeared, embedded within the transparent material of the bay's interior wall. It glowed that same color blue as the bay's entrance had when the shuttle approached. The rectangle was three meters tall and five wide, its lower edge flush with the docking chamber's floor. The material in the center of the glowing rectangle crinkled and began to fold outward, melting away before their eyes.

"It looks like it's melting," exclaimed Fanni.

"Look sharp, people," the Gunny commanded. "This thing is opening up."

The transparent material continued to shrink away, like cellophane under a blowtorch, until the entire area contained by the softly glowing blue rectangle was clear. In front of them was a bridge that spanned the three meter gap between the crystalline walls of the parking garage and the interior structure. The bridge had extended while the opening in the wall was forming. It led to a balcony that encircled the silvery-white interior structure. The balcony had no hand rail and wrapped around the outside of the structure, disappearing around both sides. Large open doorways could be seen leading to dark interior spaces, including one directly in front of the bridge.

"Shuttle One, are we a go?"

"Roger that, 1st Squad. You are a go to enter the interior."

"All right, Marines. You heard the man. Cross the bridge in twos: Inuksuk, DeSilva, Ben-Ezra, and Carter, go left; Boskovitch, Takala, Tseriteli, and Singh go right; Walker, Davis, and Smith, you're with me up the middle. Team leaders send recon drones ahead. Go!"

The Marines quickly moved across the short bridge, Inuksuk's fireteam moving to the left along the balcony, Bosco's to the right. Once they were across the Gunny's team crossed, temporarily stacking on either side of the opening as she released a softball sized reconnaissance drone. The Gunny motioned to her fire team and they slipped inside the alien building, following the drone.

* * * * *

The interior structure was roughly half a kilometer in diameter, a multifaceted column a bit over a kilometer and a half in circumference with an interior area of almost two hundred thousand square meters. Fortunately, the interior was mostly open space, like a warehouse floor interrupted only by support columns and a few scattered objects. The Gunny's fireteam advanced cautiously until they came to a large opening in both floor and ceiling that extended to levels above and below.

"Shuttle One, we have reached the center of the structure. There is a shaft, approximately twenty meters across, that appears to run the length of the spire. Over."

"We copy, Gunny. Any signs of habitation?"

"That's a negative, the place looks like an abandoned warehouse, at least on this level. Permission to send scouts to check the other floors?"

"Granted, drones first and video on."

"Roger that. Break. Bosco, next entrance your team on me. Inuksuk, finish surveilling the circumference." Turning to her own team she pointed to a ramp that led to the next level. "Walker, Davis, take the ramp to the floor above this one and check it out."

"Aye, aye, Gunny," Grits replied. He and Brains turned and jogged toward the ramp, both launching recon drones of their own.

"Bosco, when you find a ramp down to the next lower level take it."

"Roger that, Gunny."

Having deployed the rest of the squad, the Gunny turned to Bill "Beau" Smith, the remaining member of her fireteam, and said, "Let's go see if there is anything in one of the crates that are sitting around here."

"Oui, Gunny," the former legionnaire replied.

Members of the *Légion Etrangère* were not French, except for the officers, so why Smith often replied to commands in French was a mystery—maybe from force of habit. This was why his squadmates nicknamed him Beau, after an old movie character called Beau Geste. Of course, his actual nationality was a mystery as well, the Gunny really didn't care. *On an alien space station, 150 light-years from Earth, no one cares where you came from,* she thought, *as long as you do the job when the balloon goes up.*

Flight Deck, Shuttle One

"Wilson, keep your eyes on the video feed from Walker and Davis; Taylor, do the same for Bosco's team," JT ordered the two weapons operators. "Chief, watch for signs of movement from the structure in front of us."

"Aye, aye, Sir."

"Peggy Sue, Shuttle One."

"Go, Shuttle One."

"It looks like the structure, or at least this part of it, is uninhabited. I am going to join the Gunny inside."

"Roger, Shuttle One. We copy. Just remember you are in light armor if something nasty does pop up."

"I'll hide behind someone bigger, I promise." JT smiled at that thought. While he never took unnecessary risks—he was too good a soldier for that—he also believed that nothing could replace having an in person view of a situation. Particularly if you were the mission commander. Besides, this was his fourth alien space station. Sooner or later one of these things had to prove non-hostile. Right?

"Batten the hatches once I'm outside, Chief. And be ready to make a hasty exit if we come beating feet back across the bridge. Your call sign will remain Shuttle One. I'm now Ice Castle."

"Aye, Sir. We'll cover you."

Chapter 13

Walker & Davis, Ascending

Nearing the top of the ramp to the next level, the two Marines crouched down and let their recon drones make a quick sweep of the area. The up ramp ended in a rectangular opening set flush with the deck itself. As the drones circled the ramp entrance in an ever-widening spiral, light strips in the ceiling came on, one by one.

"The lights must be on some kind of motion sensor."

"Figured that out by yourself did you, mate?"

"What I haven't figured out is why they call you Brains."

"Because I'm smart."

"As smart as Dr. Ogawa?"

"Smarter than you."

"Shit."

"Smarter than shit as well. You ready?"

"Roger that. Going left."

"Going right."

The pair moved to the surface of the next deck, facing different directions. Each advanced until they took cover behind a ceiling support—not that the slim columns provided any real cover for the bulky armored Marines.

"Clear!" shouted Grits.

"Clear." Brains answered. "I've got nothing on IR or UV."

"Me either, no EMI, no nothing."

The recon drones continued their widening sweep, tripping more lights as they moved. Eventually the walls of the tower were illuminated and the little robots halted, awaiting new orders.

"Gunny, Davis."

"Go, Davis."

"This floor looks clear, just like the one you are on."

"Roger that. Bosco reports no contact on the floor below. Continue going up until you hit something different, and be careful."

"Copy that, we're moving."

"Looks like there's a ramp to my right, Bubba."

"Coming to you."

Brains passed behind Grits and the two proceeded to the next up ramp. They repeated the same procedure as on the previous ramp, sending their recon drones ahead to scout for trouble. Squatting at the top of the ramp, Grits resumed their conversation.

"What do you think of Keti?"

"Tseriteli? Why, do you fancy her?"

"I guess, is that what you Brits call liking a girl?"

"You have a better word, Yank?"

"Guess not. Do you think I have a chance with her?"

"Haven't the foggiest, mate."

"I was thinkin', me being from Alabama and her from Georgia we might hit it off."

"What? She's from Georgia the country, not Georgia the state, you redneck hillbilly."

"There's more than one Georgia? Well that would explain why her accent didn't sound right."

"You are a total wanker, Yank. Besides, she could break you in half."

"Hey, I like my women with a bit of meat on their bones. I find full figured gals much more attractive than anorexic model types. Getting amorous with one of them is like jumping on a sack full of sticks. And don't get uppity with me, you limey prick. I was just askin' your opinion."

"I'm not sure it matters what type you're attracted to, a bird either likes you or she doesn't."

"So you think there's a chance?"

Brains shook his head, a motion unseen by his teammate.

"Keep thinking happy thoughts and keep your eyes open. Going right."

"Going left."

Gunny Acuna's Team

"I'm coming to you," JT called as he neared the Gunny. She was standing next to a large opening in the floor that was mirrored by a hole in the ceiling above it. Inuksuk's fire team had finished their reconnoiter of the exterior balcony and rejoined the Gunny, forming a lose defensive perimeter. Though JT's armored figure was quite impressive, he was dwarfed by the gray giants around him— Marines in heavy armor were more like walking tanks than infantry.

The head Marine turned to face the newcomer.

"Welcome to the party, Sir."

"So where are we at, Gunny."

"Walker and Davis are just entering the twelfth level above us and Boskovitch's team is on level fifteen of what they estimate as seventeen levels below us. Still no signs of life or habitation."

"What happens beyond the top and bottom levels?"

"It looks like the nature of the internal layout changes. There's a gap between this stack of open warehouse-like floors and different construction above and below. I planned to halt at the boundaries and reassess our position."

"Sounds good." JT noticed two of the human Marines working to remove the side panel of a nearby container. The larger bulk of Cpl. Inuksuk looked on with interest.

"What's with the crate?"

"Don't know yet, Lieutenant. At first we thought they were packing containers or something similar, just sitting around, but it turns out that they are joined to the deck. Smith and DeSilva are trying to gain access to the insides without doing too much damage to the container itself."

As the Gunny was speaking Vinny managed to get the heavy blade of his Woodman's Pal inserted under the lip of the container's side cover. For use in situations like this one a number of the old time Marines carried a Pal—a multipurpose tool that functioned as a combination machete, axe, and pruning knife. The cover popped off and fell to the floor with a loud metallic clatter.

"Shit!" Vinny exclaimed.

"That did it," Beau added unnecessarily.

"I could watch you primates work all day," Inuksuk said with mock solemnity. Peering more closely at the container's interior the bear snorted. "It's full of colored glass tubes."

"Yeah, and Vinny broke a couple getting the lid off."

"You wanted it open, its open," Vinny snapped. "If you wanted careful you should have sent to the ship for some engineers."

"You tell them, DeSilva," Zippy chimed in. "Marines are paid to break things."

"Belay the chatter, you bunch of comedians." The Gunny and JT moved over to the now open container for a closer look. "Inuksuk's right, it looks like it's full of bendy glass tubes with colored light running through them. Some kind of optical circuitry?"

"Could be," JT replied, reaching inside to retrieve a piece of the tubing that Vinny had accidentally snapped off. He was the only member of the party whose gloved hands were small enough to reach inside. "The tubes are solid, could be some form of optical waveguide." He slipped the broken piece into a pocket for later analysis. "Send detailed video of the guts to the ship, maybe they can figure out what it is."

"Aye, sir."

Walker & Davis, Top Floor of the Warehouse

Emerging from the ramp to the top of the warehouse structure, Walker and Davis assumed back to back defensive positions while scanning their surroundings. This level was as open and deserted as all the others—more open in fact. All the other levels had ceilings roughly four and a half meters above their floors. This level was uncovered.

Thirty meters above the top level was another structure, seemingly held up by two thin curved ribbons. The ribbons started on either side of the central shaft opening and rose in matching left-handed spirals to the structure above, completing three and a half turns while covering the gap. A delicate double helix connecting one structure to the other.

"Why do I feel like I've got a skyscraper hovering above my head?" asked Brains.

"Because you do?"

"Yeah, the gravity may be only a third of standard but that thing above us could weigh a million tonnes or more."

"No sweat, Bubba. You think those two ribbons are foot ramps?" The objects in question were only a meter and a half wide and, like all the balconies and ramps encountered so far, had no handrails.

"There's only one way to find out, mate." Davis changed comm channels. "Gunny, Davis, we've reached the top floor, no sign of any activity, over."

"Copy that, Davis. What's above your position?"

"There is another structure about thirty meters above this one. There are what look like access ramps leading up to it."

There was a brief pause while the Gunny and Lieutenant conversed.

"Davis, Lt. Taylor. Can you reach the next structure safely?"

"We'll be exposed on the way up, but there don't seem to be any unfriendlies about. We can give it a go, Sir."

"Roger that. Let us know when you reach the next structure. Taylor out."

"You just had to mention the ramps, didn't you? It's like a hundred feet up there on a twisty ribbon with no side rails."

"Afraid of heights, mate?"

"I just don't want to get into a firefight standing on a narrow strip of curvy metal fifty feet in the air with no cover nearby."

"Then we'll just have to make the ascent quickly."

"Fine, but I'm taking point, genius."

"No problem, but I'm going first on the way back down."

* * * * *

Fifteen minutes later they reached the top of the ribbon and found themselves standing in a small, narrow room. Beyond the ramp exit there was a door, but there was no obvious way of opening it.

"I don't see any buttons or a handle, what should we do?"

"We either have to open the door or go back down, and I don't think that would make the Lieutenant very happy. Improvise."

"Improvise? OK." Grits steadied himself by placing a hand on either wall, then he raised his right leg and kicked the door. The door deformed, crumpling where his armor encased foot landed. A second kick sent it flying. Beyond the now open threshold was a curved balcony.

"Very smooth, Grits. If there is anyone home they certainly know we've arrived."

"Hey, you wanted the door open, its open. You didn't say to not break anything."

"Right, so move your ass. I don't like standing inside this bloody closet."

The balcony curved around the center shaft, continuing halfway around the opening until it came to a solid section, obviously the room atop the other access way. Unlike the balconies of the structure below, this balcony had frameless transparent panels for railing, except where a sizable gap bisected the semicircle. Wide doorways led off of the balcony at regular intervals. Coming to the first doorway, Walker stopped.

"Ready, Bubba?"

"On your six."

"Moving."

The two Marines moved down the hall, which led them outward toward the building's perimeter. They passed several recessed

120

alcoves that contained closed doors. Eventually the hallway they were in dead-ended at another, curving hall that continued off in both directions. A few steps away there was an alcove on the farside of the hall.

"Look, this door has colored buttons along side it, just like the docking bay."

"So push the blue one and see if it opens."

Walker pushed the blue rectangle. The door slid open. Turning sideways to pass through the door, he entered the room beyond. Grits found himself standing in an entranceway, his helmeted head almost scraping the ceiling. Moving forward the space opened up into a large room with a five meter ceiling. The far wall was transparent, offering a spectacular view of several other spires and starry space beyond.

"Oh wow! Man, that's some view."

"Don't get distracted. Moving left."

"Moving right."

After a quick search of the area they relaxed and took in their surroundings. The floor was a creamy white with subtle patterning, almost like marble. Scattered about the room were low benches and what looked like footstools, covered with soft material in shades of tan, taupe and brown. Abstract patterns adorned the walls.

"I think we found a condominium, partner."

"What makes you say that, mate."

"My cousin Elroy, my mother's sister's eldest, had a condo in Biloxi and it looked just like this... well, with a beach and the Gulf instead of outer space outside the windows."

"It does sort of look like a posh bespoke flat. Doesn't look lived in though."

"I wonder if there is a kitchen?"

"Always thinking about your bleedin' stomach."

"If there isn't any food in the kitchen then the place is probably abandoned. If it ain't there should be some."

"That actually makes sense, I'm impressed, Yank. You go look for the galley and I'll call the Gunny and let her know we found a cosmic condo."

Bosco's Fireteam, Warehouse, Bottom Floor

"Looks like this is as far as we go without rappelling gear," Fanni remarked, staring over the edge of the platform. The bottom floor of the warehouse was about half the size of the floors above. From the edge, the top of the next structure could be seen thirty meters below—a collection of domes, boxes, and girders, like the top of a skyscraper cluttered with equipment to maintain the habitable spaces within.

"I think you are right," Bosco confirmed. "I see no way down from here."

Toward the center of the floor, Keti and Simba were standing next to the opening of the central shaft. "LCpl. Boskovitch, there seems to be something going on in the central shaft."

"What?"

"Simba is right," Keti called out. "A shaft of glowing light has appeared in the, er, shaft."

"Coming to you." Bosco and Fanni quickly converged on their teammates.

When they arrived at the shaft they could clearly see what Simba and Keti were talking about. A column of air along one side of the central opening was glowing like the beam of a searchlight on a dark night. Looking downward the color was a faint blue, looking upward it was reddish.

"What's happening?" Fanni asked, not addressing anyone in particular.

"Beats the hell out of me," Keti replied.

Simba pointed down through the opening. "Look, there is something floating up the beam of light."

His companions all peered over the edge. About halfway between their position and the top of the building below a figure was rising.

"It's going to be here in about fifteen seconds."

"*Chyort voz'mi!* You are right." Bosco was team leader, he had to make a call. "Spread out along the edge and cover it, but hold fire unless it shoots first. Break. Gunny, Bosco, we have contact."

"Right." Keti and Fanni jogged a dozen steps to the right of the men.

"I think it is accelerating."

Again Simba was right, the approaching figure was ascending notably faster than a few seconds ago. The Marines crouched down, weapons at the ready. Glowing sight reticles danced across their helmet displays, slaved to the rail guns mounted on their forearms.

"Bosco, Gunny. Say again your last."

A lumpy, misshapen figure flashed past the Marines and disappeared up the shaft.

"Gunny, You have company on the way. There is a humanoid creature flying up the central shaft toward your position. Over."

"Copy, an alien is rising up the shaft. Interrogative, any details on the alien?"

"Da, is squat like troll, yellow color and is wearing a white diaper. Over."

Chapter 14

Squad One, Warehouse

The Marines spread out facing the central shaft opening, giving each other clear fields of fire. JT was to the right of the cabinet they had opened, Inuksuk forward and to the left.

"Chill people. No fire, no hostile moves unless ET initiates something."

As JT finished talking the alien popped up and stepped smoothly onto the warehouse floor. Bosco was right, the alien looked like a Tolkienesque cave troll. A squat 150cm tall, the creature had broad bulging shoulders and massive arms, though the lumps and bulges betrayed a musculature unlike any human's. Atop the shoulders was a tiny lump of a head: small, bald, and with no neck. Two widely spaced black eyes and a thin slash of a mouth were all that adorned the face—no nose, not even slits, no eyebrows, no ears. Most startling was the color: the creature was bright yellow, the same shade as mustard on a hotdog.

"Now that's butt ugly," said Vinny.

"Put a sock in it, Vinny," the Gunny snapped.

The yellow alien ignored the assembled Marines towering over it in their dark gray armor. It waddled forward, headed straight for the open cabinet. As it approached its target, Inuksuk was in its path.

"Hold steady, Corporal," JT ordered.

"Like I was stalking a seal, Lieutenant."

The alien didn't even stop to look up at the towering ursine, it just waddled around the obstacle. As it passed by, the Earthlings could see it was wearing a white loincloth that did look remarkably like a diaper. Around the top of the garment was a belt from which hung several pouches and a number of devices that could be tools, or weapons. Stopping at the open cabinet the creature peered inside, then began rummaging in one of its pouches.

"What is it doing," asked Zippy. From her position near the rim of the shaft she couldn't directly see what the creature was up to.

The creature's hands had only three fingers, two on top and one on the bottom. They ended in large black claws that meshed, the bottom one between the top ones when closed. Reaching inside the cabinet with one muscular arm, it delicately plucked one of the damage glass rods from its position. Stuffing the broken rod into one of its pouches, the troll produced another, longer piece. Fiddling with the new rod, its wide body blocking the Earthlings' view, the creature was occupied for almost a minute. Then it lifted the finished rod, with a new bend in it near the top end, and inserted it into the cabinet.

"Peggy Sue, Ice Castle. Are you getting this?"

"Roger, Ice Castle. We're using your recon drones and suit telemetry to record the creature's actions."

CIC, Peggy Sue

"This creature is fascinating," said Betty White, who had come forward to the CIC from sick bay. "It's anatomy is unlike anything we've found in the past."

"I would agree, Dr. White," said Will Krenshaw, a xenobiologist on the science staff. "The terahertz scanner shows it has an internal structure unlike anything on Earth. Can a creature be classified as a vertebrate if it has no spinal column?"

"Vertebrata is a subphylum of chordate animals, comprising those having a brain enclosed in a skull or cranium and a segmented spinal column, so I'd have to say no," answered Johan de Bruin. The South African vet was fascinated by his first living extraterrestrial. "It does, however have three large long bones that seem to provide support for the head and shoulder sockets."

The Captain cleared his throat. "This is all fascinating, Doctors, but doesn't explain what it's doing."

Mizuki, while not a biologist or medical doctor, was head of the Science section and felt obliged to answer. "It appears that the creature is repairing the photonic circuits inside the cabinet that the Marines damaged when they pried the box open."

"It doesn't seem interested in the Marines at all, has it made any sound?"

"Nothing that the drones or suit microphones have picked up, Beth."

Another glass tube was replaced with a new one and the alien maintenance worker moved on to a third. The squat yellow creature acted as though the surrounding Earthlings were not there. Even the recon drones that hovered about, observing it work, did not distract the creature from its task.

"Maybe it's some kind of biological construct," said Bobby. "Created to do repair work and nothing else. Like an idiot savant, really good at one thing and lacking other skills."

"Like communication?"

"Well, it's not communicated yet, Captain."

"Bobby may be right, or the creature could be bred specifically for its job, some kind of servant race for whoever or whatever runs the station."

"That's a disturbing thought, Number One. Those cyborg critters made by the Dark Lords are creepy enough without biological slaves scampering around fixing things."

The creature finished fixing the broken tubes and turned its attention to the cover laying near by. Picking up the rectangular piece of metal the maintenance worker carefully inspected the cover's edges. The place where Vinny had inserted his machete was bent and distorted. Pulling another tool from its belt the creature bent and flattened the metal. When the repair was complete the edge was smooth and uniform, as though the damage had never happened.

Lifting the cover into position the yellow troll thumped the edges to seal the container. Stepping back, it viewed is work. Then, evidently satisfied, it turned and waddled back toward the central shaft.

"Peggy Sue, Ice Castle. It looks like the creature is leaving. Interrogative, do you want us to detain it?"

"No, Ice Castle. I think we should let the alien get on with its day."

"Roger that."

Warehouse

"You heard the man, let stumpy go back to where ever he came from." JT could be seen shaking his head inside his transparent bubble helmet.

Like JT, the creature's total lack of interest in the Marines also confounded Vinny. "That isn't natural, for a creature to have absolutely no interest in anything but doing its job."

"Maybe it's a member of the repair workers' union and handling strange aliens isn't part of its contract."

"Maybe he will send members of the station defense force to take care of us," Zippy added. As the Marines all watched the alien stepped into the central shaft... and went up.

"Shit, I thought it would head back down," the Gunny swore. "It's headed for the upper levels. Davis, Walker, did you break anything up there?"

"That's affirmative, Gunny, Walker sort of kicked open a door when we first arrived. Why do you ask?"

"It looks like the building super is on his way up to fix the damage, over."

* * * * *

"What do you suppose that means, Bubba?"

"How should I know, you're the one who broke the bloody door."

"Hey, you said you wanted out of the closet and I should improvise."

"Whatever, we should head back to the inner balcony and see if we can catch sight of this building supervisor."

The two Marines headed out of the apartment, sending their two recon drones down the hallway ahead of them. Arriving at the balcony they halted and peered around the edge of the open doorway. They were just in time to see a short, wide, bright yellow creature step onto the platform.

"That dude has got jaundice real bad."

"Get back, he'll see us!"

Walker and Davis backed down the hallway, taking shelter in two facing alcoves. In their bulky suits the recessed door openings were not deep enough to hide them fully. They needn't have worried, the yellow creature walked by the hallway entrance without even glancing toward their positions.

"I think it missed us, mate."

"I think it doesn't give a shit, Bubba."

Video from their recon drones showed the yellow visitor hammering away on the twisted door as it lay upon the balcony deck. The sounds of hammering could be heard over their suit pickups.

"Gunny, Davis. The alien is working on the broken door. How should we proceed, over?"

"Davis, that's pretty much what it did down here. Just stay put and observe, we need to know where it heads when it finishes."

"Roger that."

"Looks like he's about done with the door."

Sure enough, the creature had picked up the now uncrumpled door and was fitting it back into its opening. Standing back from the portal, the repairman did something to make the door slide open and shut a few times. After one last adjustment the door slid shut for a final time and the yellow alien turned and headed back around the balcony. Waddling back to the gap in the transparent railing, the yellow troll stepped off the balcony and fell downward, disappearing out of sight.

"Gunny, the alien just stepped off the edge of the platform and fell."

"By fell you mean the alien was headed back down the spire toward my position?"

"Affirmative, he's not free falling, sort of drifting down in a column of reddish light."

"I Copy, Davis. Can you two get back down here?"

"Wait one. Walker is checking the door to the ramp."

"Roger that. Tell him not to break the damn thing this time."

Brains clicked the comm link in affirmation and followed after his partner. Grits was running his hands around the edges of the door, searching for a release or operating mechanism.

"I can't find anyway to open this sucker, how are we supposed to get down outta here?"

"You heard the Gunny, do not break the door again."

"Then you figure out how to get us down from here, Brains." Grits pronounced 'Brains' with an abundance of sarcasm.

"Look, that yellow blighter managed to get down, why can't we?"

"He just stepped off into space, I'm not sure that will work for us."

"Why not? It must be an automatic mechanism just like the docking bay."

"You willing to risk a five kilometer fall on that idea?"

"Come on, lets go." Davis jogged around the balcony to the gap in the railing. The faint column of light was still present. "See, it must still be active. Let's go."

Davis stepped off into space.

"She-it!" *There's no one to even say "hey y'all watch this" to,* Walker thought, *the famous last words of every redneck about to die in some extraordinarily stupid way.* He followed Davis off the vertiginous ledge.

Gunny's Team

"Davis, Walker, what the flying hell are you doing?"

"We're heading down the light shaft, just like the yellow chappie. You told us not to break the door again and this was the only other way down."

The Gunny closed her eyes and placed one hand on top of her head in dismay—an odd looking gesture for a seven and a half foot tall armored giant.

"Have you two geniuses figured out how to get off the magic light beam?" asked JT.

"No, Sir. But we're not free falling. My suit nav says we are falling at about ten meters per second. We'll be at your level in about five seconds."

"Can you lean toward the edge, reach out and grab a hold of the deck as you pass by?" JT waved his arms at the other Marines. "Quick! Someone be ready to grab those idiots as they pass by!"

As people were scrambling to get to the edge of the platform an armored figure suddenly appeared. Davis managed to grab a hold of the outer lip of the ceiling paneling. His body swung out of the light beam and into the warehouse proper.

Momentum swung his extended body in an arc up to the ceiling like a gymnast on the high-bar. Colliding with the ceiling he lost his purchase on the edge and fell the four meters from ceiling to the floor. He landed on his back with a crash.

JT ran forward and knelt to check that Davis was OK. Looking up he saw Walker fall by, arms flailing.

Bosco's Team

"Bosco! Walker is about to fall past your position, see if you can catch him somehow!"

"Da, Lieutenant. How?" Standing at the edge of the central opening he looked up and saw Walker falling toward them.

Next to the light beam Keti had unfurled a length of cable with a climbing hook on one end. Turning to Fanni she yelled: "Take this end of the cable and belay it around the support pillar."

131

"*Kyllä*, yes!" She ran off toward the nearest roof support, cable trailing behind her.

With her right hand, Keti began swinging the end with the hook in a circle, holding the coiled remains of the cable in her left hand. Looking up she watched Walker approach and just before he arrived she let fly. The grappling hook almost hit Walker in the chest as it flew past. Fortunately, he had the presence of mind to grasp the cable and wrap it around his arm. The cable drew taught.

If Fanni had not wrapped the other end of the cable around the pole it might have been ripped from her hands or pulled her off the platform after the plummeting Walker. As it was, Keti lost her grip on the cable as Grits was pulled up short. The taught line stretched from pole to precipice, supporting Walker now swinging five meters beneath the platform.

"Come! Help me pull him up!" Keti yelled as she retrieved the cable and began pulling the dangling Marine up to the platform. Simba quickly lent a hand and shortly Walker's armored arm appeared above the platform edge. He grasped the edge with his unencumbered left arm, which Bosco seized. In a team effort they hauled Walker bodily onto the deck.

"Thanks y'all, thanks all y'all," he panted, bending over hands on knees.

"Thank Keti," Bosco said in a matter of fact tone. "If she hadn't used rope we would all be watching you disappear into depths of the building below."

"Hey, thanks Keti. I owe you big time."

Keti was recoiling her cable. "Why would you do something so stupid?"

"I was just following Brains, ask him."

"You always follow your friend off a cliff?"

"I am in the process of reevaluating my friendship with him. Where did you learn to handle a rope like that?"

"Back home in Georgia. Georgia is built on the Caucasus Mountains, so naturally I went mountaineering as a girl."

"Naturally. Well I'm sure glad you did, darlin', 'cause otherwise I'd still be on my way down. Thank you again." Grits stood up straight. "Crap. I think I might need to clean this suit out."

The others all laughed.

"Gunny, Bosco. We managed to snag Walker as he was passing by."

"Roger that. Tell him to get his ass back up here."

Chapter 15

Warehouse, Starflake

Two hours later 2nd Squad landed at the warehouse docking area two levels above 1st Squad. Along with the Marines several others were on board the second shuttle, including Mizuki Ogawa, Bobby Danner, and a pair of engineer's mates to help investigate any interesting alien tech. Mizuki and Bobby were there in anticipation of imminent first contact with the station's residents, both having prior experience in such situations. Being present for ostensibly diplomatic purposes they were armed discreetly, carrying only sidearms. Still, they were far from helpless if it came to open hostilities, carrying his and hers katanas strapped to the backs of their light armor suits.

Congregating on the level where JT and the Gunny were waiting, Bobby inquired about plans for going forward. "You've been on site longer than we have, JT, how do you suggest we proceed?"

"Now that 2nd Squad is here I say we recon more of this puzzle palace. Didn't want to head to lower levels with the possibility of hostiles in our rear, but now we can send one squad up and the other down. What do you think, Gunny?"

"Works for me. Send 2nd Squad up to give the cosmic condo a closer look, and to find out what's above it. The rest of us can take the magic light elevator down below."

"You feel comfortable using the local transportation mechanism?" Mizuki asked.

"Yeah, we went back over the RF recordings while you were in transit. We found our little yellow friend sent out coded signals that caused the elevator to activate in either an upward or downward direction. He also had a signal that dumped him off at a desired level. Davis! Give the officers a demonstration."

"Aye, aye, Gunny."

The party moved to the edge of the central shaft as a softly glowing column of light sprang into existence. Davis stepped into the light and drifted smoothly up to the next level, where he stepped off gracefully—they had, indeed, been practicing. The faint light shining upward to the next platform changed color from red to blue. Shortly, Davis floated back down and rejoined his companions.

"The color is an indicator of the direction of the gravity field?"

"Yes, Dr. Ogawa. Davis here figured out what the colors mean."

"Doppler effect, or more accurately a representation of the Doppler effect," Mizuki stated. "Red shift going away, blue shift approaching."

JT nodded. "I should have know that an astrophysicist would see the answer right off. I'm still embarrassed that Davis figured it out first."

Grits elbowed Brains and on suit-to-suit quipped, "See, I told you she was smart."

"Yeah, but I sussed it out before the Lieutenant. Now shut up, or we'll miss something." Grits complied as the officers continued their planning.

"What about a holding force on the platform?" Bobby asked.

"There are three crewmen in each shuttle who are armed, and the shuttles themselves mount railguns and X-ray lasers. Just to be safe we can have each shuttle send a battle bot to guard the central shaft and monitor anything approaching."

"I'll defer to you two in the tactics department," Bobby said to JT and the Gunny, "but I'd feel better if we send a couple of recon drones from the shuttles ahead—one up, one down—just in case there is something laying in wait."

"Yes, Sir," JT replied. "Hitch, Jacobs, did you copy the request for recon drones?"

"Aye, Lieutenant," replied Hitch from shuttle one.

"Launching drones now," added Jacobs from shuttle two.

A half minute later one of the basketball sized robots flew silently past the assemblage of Marines and disappeared down the central shaft. Called clownbots because the arrangement of cameras and sensors on their forward end resembled a clown's face, the large recon drones from the shuttles were more capable than the smaller units carried by the Marines.

On suit-to-suit, Walker said, "man, I just love it when Captain Kirk uses the Force to control the Tardis."

"You are totally barmy, Yank," Davis replied.

"Are we good to go, Commander?" JT asked Bobby.

"Let's get this show on the road."

JT turned to the Gunny and, raising his left arm, made a circular motion with his raised index finger, the hand signal to move out.

"Listen up, Marines! Sgt Aurora, take 2nd squad and the engineers and do a reconnaissance of the structure above this one. Look for any signs of habitation and make note of any interesting alien tech. Keep going until you run out of building or make contact."

"Aye, aye, Gunny," came the bear's immediate reply.

"1st Squad, saddle up. We will descend to the structure below and work our way down from there. Walker, Davis, since you are our local transportation experts, take point. Move out."

* * * * *

Ten minutes later, Walker and Davis were drifting downward, back to back, watching for trouble. As they descended they conversed on suit-to-suit.

"We ain't never going to live down jumping off the building without a net, Bubba."

"That was all your fault, not mine. I managed to get off on the right floor." Walker looked around at the floors passing by. Most were thick with vegetation, plants of all shapes and sizes. They came in many colors—red, purple, yellow and green. Some were short and curly, some tall with long leafy fronds, and others resembling prairie grass. Other rows were barren, ranks of empty planters above which harsh grow lamps glared in vain. "This looks like some kind of food production facility, a factory farm."

"Don't look like any farm I ever seen back in Alabama."

"They were building something like this in the Netherlands before things went to hell. Tiered levels growing plants, even pigs."

"That's the Dutch for ya, they think shoes should be made of wood and that living below sea level is a keen idea."

Davis just grunted.

"I guess you really are smart, figuring out that red shift stuff. Maybe you deserve to be called Brains."

"Well thank you very much, Grits. What the hell is a grit anyway?"

"It's a traditional southern food made from ground corn. And it's grits not grit; grits is singular."

"What?"

"You say the grits is good, not the grits are good. Get that wrong and they'll peg you for a Yankee for sure."

"I'm a Brit, you're the Yank."

"Back in the good ol' U.S. of A. southerners were Rebels, northerners were Yankees, and you would have been a damned foreigner."

"Glad we got that straightened out, Yank."

"Hey, at least I got to know Keti better."

"Yeah, mate. She thinks you're a bleedin' tosser who's dumb enough to step off a thousand story building without a rope."

"An introduction is an introduction, Bubba."

As they dropped, neither noticed the red-orange eyes observing them from concealment in the passing foliage.

Station Trader's Bower

Deep within the lower levels of the spire was the bower of Faooshda-rik-tik-ta, the Station Trader and leader of the Kieshnar-rak-kat-tra. In the sibilant speech of the creatures' their name meant "Scavengers of Wealth," but generally they were simply known as "traders."

A reflection of the nocturnal origins of his species, the inside the Trader's bower was dimly lit, illumination provided mostly by

138

bioluminescent plants. Rich rugs and tapestries adorned the floors and walls while hanging incense burners helped mask the natural musk of the traders—theirs was a smell even a skunk would find unpleasant. The Station Trader was receiving a verbal report from one of his many underlings scattered about the Starflake.

"Report, Shanakta-fek. What have you learned about these newcomers?"

"A thousand pardons, Trader, but I only saw them for a moment as they moved down a transport beam headed for lower levels. They are large, much larger than we are, and covered in what looks like gray metal armor."

"They are armed?"

"Yes, Trader. The devices they had strapped to their forearms could serve no other purpose. The two I saw stayed back to back and swept their surroundings with their weapons continuously."

"Warriors then."

"That would seem so from their appearance, but then there was the whooboo."

"What whooboo?"

"The whooboo that ascend the shaft to the unoccupied area where the aliens landed. Evidently the aliens damaged some mechanism or other that attracted the attention of the maintenance drudge."

"If I have to keep guessing at what you've seen I will have you demoted to apprentice trader and sent to the storerooms! What about the drudge?"

"It came back down alive."

"I see. This could prove interesting." The Station Trader cogitated on the implications of that for a moment. To a Kieshnar-rak-kat-tra interesting was not a positive term—interesting meant disruption and disruption was generally bad for business. "So they left the whooboo come and go without killing it. I wonder how aggressive these new 'warriors' of yours are."

"Certainly no pack of Karf would have allowed a whooboo to pass unmolested. They would have beat it just on general principles."

"Speaking of the skinny gray vermin, are they aware of the newcomers' presence yet?"

"I cannot say, Trader. I saw no sign of the Karf or any of their minions, but that doesn't mean they have not observed the aliens by remote cameras or other sensors."

"We must bide our time until the newcomers and the Karf cross paths. They will either come to some accommodation or start a fight, probably the latter. Keep your tail low and your eyes open, we need to be nimble and quick, there may yet be an opportunity for trade here."

"By your leave, Station Trader."

2nd Squad, The Cosmic Condo

The Marines of 2nd Squad were nearing the top of what had been dubbed the cosmic condominium. As they ascended the apartments became fewer, larger, and more lavishly appointed. Something that did not escape the notice of the Marines themselves.

"Man, will you look at this place. It could be the crib of a Miami drug lord."

"Or a Hollywood madam."

"Or even worse, a Wall Street banker."

"Since there isn't a New York, or Hollywood, or Miami anymore you jokers need to update your superlatives," said Cpl. Kwan. The grunts were right, the apartment held several sunken conversation pits, sweeping ramps leading to an overhanging balcony, curved walls adorned with abstract paintings, and a number of large crystalline chandeliers that would have done Chihuly proud. The chandeliers were lit from within and hung in midair with no visible support.

"Stay frosty people, and keep the chatter off the squad frequency." Over suit-to-suit Sergeant Aurora chuckled. "Why do humans do that, talk incessantly?"

"Because they are nervous, Sarge," Kato replied, standing beside her. "You know how us monkeys love to chatter."

"Oh?" The monkey reference caught the polar bear off guard.

"I've been around bears enough to know what most of you think of most of us. No big."

"It doesn't bother you that we bears call you monkeys behind your backs?"

"Not really. Hell, we all have our prejudices—man, bear, and alien. Better to have them out in the open so we can all laugh at them. When you hide your prejudices, hold them inside, that's when they can turn toxic."

"Never thought of it that way. You're pretty observant for a primate, Kato."

"Hey Sarge, I got movement!" called PFC Haddad.

The Squad shifted positions, half facing outward, half covering the possible threat Haddad spotted. Sliding across the floor was a half meter in diameter disk shaped creature with a fringe of short tentacles. It moved silently to one of the low upholstered benches and began working its way around the seat's base. As it moved it pivoted back and forth, sweeping with its tentacles.

"What is it?"

"Damned if I know, Rico," replied Kato, moving to get a closer look at the creature. "But it seems to be alive, not some kind of machine or cyborg."

"You think it's dangerous?" Asked Aurora, edging around to cut off the creature's escape.

"It's acting like some kind of alien Roomba," Haddad observed. "Like it's cleaning around the furniture."

"Could be, all these apartments seem too clean to be uninhabited." That thought had been nagging at Kato's mind for some time now. "Having built in cleaning staff would explain why things are so clean, not even a layer of dust on the floor."

"Great," Sgt. Aurora snorted. "We've discovered an autonomous alien vacuum cleaner. Haddad, you found it so keep an eye on it. Everyone else fan out and finish searching this place."

Karf Habitat, Adjacent Spire

"Who are these creatures that dare to invade our station!" The current dominant Karf was livid at the discovery of the exploring Earthlings, currently making their way down the major spire adjacent to the Karf habitation space.

"What is your plan to find out, or is your leadership inadequate?" said one of the head Karf's main rivals. The Karf had no permanent leadership, they constantly struggled among themselves each trying to raise their individual status.

"Dispatch a team to kidnap one or more of these interlopers. We will then interrogate them and find out their intentions, how many of them there are and how well they are armed."

"It would be better to strike them now, while they don't suspect our presence. Take them by surprise and wipe them out, or enslave them," said another rival.

"You are as rash as you are foolish! We have no idea of the invaders' capabilities, we must gather intelligence first."

"The monitors show them to be vigilant, how do you propose to abduct one of them from the midst of their formation?"

"They come in different sizes, we will attempt to lure one of the small ones into a space that would be inconvenient for the larger ones."

"And you expect the others to just stand by as we carry off one of their host? Your plan is imbecilic! Dumber than Hoon dung."

"It is you who are the imbecile, dung eater. To cover the abduction we will stage a diversion—an attack to help ascertain their offensive capabilities."

The leader's rival sneered. Zhe knew that zhe had been out maneuvered by the current head Karf. Sensing its advantage, the leader pressed home its argument.

"We will use a splagg, that should provide sufficient distraction while we make off with one of the aliens' number. Make it so, you worthless laggards!"

With grumbled insults the Karf moved off to implement the Leader's plan. They had to admit it was a solid plan of action. *No matter,* each Karf thought, *I could have come up with a better plan.* That was just the Karf way, the others would go along with the plan until an opportunity for self-advancement presented itself.

Chapter 16

1ˢᵗ Squad, The Greenhouse

Nearing the bottom of the agricultural section a floor appeared that contained unplanted open space and what looked like a number of storerooms. The Gunny ordered the squad to exit the elevator so they could take stock of their position and plan their next move. As the rest of the squad spread out to check the storage rooms, the Gunny and the officers held a meeting by some large flowering plants.

"It looks like the next level down is less... bucolic than the section we've been descending through," JT commented to the assembled leadership. "Scans from the recon drone show the next area is laid out more like a residential or commercial area, with multiple levels linked by ramps and more of these gravity elevator shafts."

On their holographic helmet displays a three dimensional mock up of the next area's layout appeared. It showed a many leveled interior space surrounded by overlapping balconies linked by ramps, spiral staircases, and multi-hued, glowing light columns.

"I think we should spread out and utilize more elevators, that way we can put more boots on the ground simultaneously," the Gunny said. Up to this point the expedition had been strung out along one shaft, descending a pair of Marines at a time. All the way down she had been worried about a possible ambush.

"That certainly makes sense, Gunny," Bobby agreed, inspecting the holographic model. "It looks like there are several elevators on the far side of the central opening that would put passengers off on that large curving balcony."

"Yeah, we could drop half the squad onto that area, and then the rest of us could land on what looks like the main area twenty meters below it." The Gunny was already thinking about who to assign what positions in the deployment.

"They could spread out along the upper level and give the rest of the squad cover from above." JT added, nodding in agreement.

While JT, Bobby, and the Gunny were absorbed by mission planning, Mizuki walked over to one of the tall flowering plants. They looked like an overgrown version of lilies, with graceful white trumpets rising amongst dark green leaves. Examining the flowers she noticed movement a few rows over, movement not attributable to any of the expedition members.

"Do not turn around or react," she called on the command frequency, "but there is something lurking in the foliage two rows to my left."

"How big a something, Dr. Ogawa?" asked JT, sinking to one knee and subtly repositioning his assault weapon while pretending to still be conversing with the other two leaders. "We've got a clear field of fire."

"My IR sensors show only one creature, please do not shoot it JT. After all, we are supposed to make contact with the locals if we can."

"Could it be a wild animal or one of those maintenance trolls? What do you propose we do?"

"I see only one way to find out. I am going to edge around the plant in front of me until I am hidden behind it. Then I will use my suit's active camouflage mode and quietly circle around behind the creature. When I am in position I will flush it out into the open."

"Be careful, Dr. Ogawa. You will be in our line of fire if you get behind the target."

"I am trying to keep it from becoming a target, Gunny. It is hard to make new friends through a hail of railgun flechettes."

Bobby was the ranking officer so it was his call, but he had learned that trying to keep his wife out of danger was like trying to keep an inquisitive child from trying new things.

"OK, do it, but let us know when you are in position."

"Hai, Bobby."

Over suit-to-suit the Gunny told JT, "Set your flechette velocity to less than 1200 fps. That way, if we do have to fire, the flechettes won't penetrate Dr. Ogawa's armor."

"All ready did that, let's hope we won't need to."

146

* * * * *

Mizuki carefully moved from one row of enormous flowers to the next, her presence masked by her suit's active camouflage. Ahead she spotted a large bushy tail that could only belong to the creature spying on the Earthlings. Silently slipping into the space between the rows she crept forward.

That tail and those markings look familiar for some reason, she thought, *I think we've encountered this alien species before.* "I am about to flush the alien from its hiding place, please be ready to capture it."

Creeping ever forward she finally stood less than half a meter behind the furry creature. Turing off camouflage mode, activating her suit's external speaker, and spreading her arms wide, Mizuki said, "Boo!"

With a startled yelp the alien jumped up, spinning about as it did. On seeing the gray monster behind him the creature bolted into the open space beyond the flowers. There it found itself surrounded by more gray monsters. Before it could decide which way to jump a hard armored hand grabbed it by the scruff of the neck.

Lifting the creature from the floor, Mizuki set her translator to one of the common trade languages and spoke to her captive. "So what business brings you to spy on us from the bushes, Kieshnar-rak-kat-tra?"

To its credit, the trader stopped squirming when it heard recognizable words coming from its captor. "A thousand pardons, gentlebeings, but I was merely trying to select the proper moment to introduce myself to your august personages. I am Trader Shanakta-fek, ha-have you come for trade?"

"We will not harm you Shanakta-fek. If I let you down do you promise not to scamper off?"

"Yes, esteemed one. One makes no profit by running away."

Setting the trader on the deck, Mizuki took a wary step backward thinking the creature might bolt despite its assurances. The alien before them looked like an oversized lemur with a long bushy tail and extraordinarily large, bulbous, red-orange eyes. Its body was covered with fuzzy, cinnamon colored fur that was frosted with black highlights. Its tail, fully as long as its body, was banded in black. White fur extended from tufted ears, framing face and forehead, also running down the trader's throat, chest and belly. A pointed black nose and muzzle formed its face, from which black fur swept up and around the eyes giving the appearance of a bandit's mask. Its only clothing was a short, unbuttoned tan vest.

Mizuki had been correct, she and the others standing before her had seen creatures like this before—on a space station more than a thousand light-years from Earth.

CIC, Peggy Sue

"You say you found a what, pardner?" Though Billy Ray could plainly see the trader on the video feed he was still a bit incredulous.

"A Kieshnar-rak-kat-tra. Like those on Ring Station. I know you haven't forgotten the little double crossing stink weasels."

"Hell no. Captain Jack and the rest of you painted quite a portrait of them after your odyssey on the M'tak Ka'fek. I'm beginning to think these critters are like space rats, you can find them scurrying around any starship port in the Orion Arm."

Beth arched an eyebrow at the Captain and turned to more pragmatic matters. "Have you found out anything useful from the trader? Like who is in charge of the station?"

"The obsequious little fur ball has been effusively uninformative regarding what other life forms inhabit the station and who, if anyone, is in charge. Giving the way he was skulking around in the underbrush, spying on us, I'm going to go out on a limb and say it ain't the Kieshnar-rak-kat-tra."

"So other than establishing that there is intelligent life on board the station we are no further along than before."

"I wouldn't say that, Beth. We've managed to figure out how the local elevators work and Mizuki found some really nice flowers in this greenhouse section."

"Roger that, pardner. How are you going to proceed?"

"The Gunny's got the squad all set to execute a devastating vertical envelopment of the shopping mall below us."

Muting the comm, Beth turned to her husband. "He's having entirely too much fun with this."

"Yeah, that's what bothers me Number One. Usually the fun comes just before the fecal matter hits the fan." Reactivating the comm, the Captain gave his blessing to the next phase of exploration. "You are clear to continue into the shopping mall, but keep yer eyes pealed."

"Roger that, Peggy Sue. Danner out."

Karf Habitat

"Are we ready? Are the forces in place to spring our trap on these interlopers?"

"Things are proceeding as planned. The hardest part is getting the splagg into position—they are not very intelligent and tend to react to prodding with violence."

The leader hissed, the Karf equivalent of a frustrated sigh. "Have they descended to the commercial district yet?"

"No, but they seem to be preparing to do so soon."

Another would be leader spoke up. "What of the signal to the Others? Should we not send a summons saying we have been attacked, oh glorious leader?"

"No, you gelatinous slime! If we destroy the interlopers ourselves, when the foul ones arrive and find no threat to counter they will just take their frustration out on us—if you promise the Others a fight you had best deliver. We will defeat the aliens on our own and unless something unforeseen happens we will not summon our murderous associates."

"That makes surprising sense, coming from one as intellectually limited as yourself."

The leader snarled. "You are as perceptive as a whooboo. We are in good position to ambush them. Whatever is left after the splagg attacks should be easy for our forces to clean up."

Several other Karf hissed in response, but whether in agreement or dissent was not clear—perhaps it didn't matter.

2ⁿᵈ *Squad*

Sgt. Aurora and her Marines finally reached the topmost floor of the cosmic condo. The spire had narrowed by about half, obvious to the Earthlings as they spread out across the roof of the housing section. The spire continued on above them for at least another kilometer, though there was no obvious way to reach any higher level. In fact, the ceiling above them looked to be made from the same crystalline substance as the transparent outer walls, not the silver metallic material that the apartment structure was made from.

"I think this is the end of the pack ice, cubs," Aurora said to the squad. The rooftop area was decorated like a park, with seating and sunken areas that might have contained liquid at one time. Along the crystalline walls were veins that glowed softly with internal light, though what their purpose was remained unclear.

"It's a good forty meters to the ceiling," observed Haddad. "What do you suppose this place was?"

"A place to hold parties?" mused Kato. "A little dining and dancing under the stars."

"It would make one epic nightclub," commented Enrico.

"Rico, all you want to do is party," said one of the human females, eliciting a smattering of laughter over the squad frequency.

"Hey, just sayin', dawg."

"Whatever it was used for it doesn't seem to be in use anymore. Time to check in with the LT." Aurora switched to command frequency and called her CO. "Ice Castle, 2ⁿᵈ Squad, over."

"Go 2ⁿᵈ Squad."

"we've reached the top of the cosmic condo and there seem to be no accessible areas above our position. We observed no intelligent life forms, just some biological cleaning staff. Interrogative what should we do next?"

"Wait one."

"What's the LT say, Sarge?"

"Shut it, the officers are thinking."

"2nd Squad, If there's nothing further to investigate head back to the docking level. We'll get back to you."

"Roger that. 2nd Squad is headed back down toward the shuttles."

1st Squad, Shopping Mall

Bosco's fire team, supplemented by Walker and Davis, arrived on the balcony simultaneously via three different elevators. Facing the balcony's edge, Fanni and Simba were on the right flank, Davis and Walker on the left, and Bosco and Keti in the center. They immediately spread out to inspect their surroundings, dispersing so as not to present an inviting target to any hostiles.

"Going left!" called Davis, Walker kneeling by a column, providing cover.

"Going right!" Simba and Fanni performed a similar evolution on the other flank.

"Would you look at this place!" Walker gushed, his eyes sweeping across the cascade of balconies, tall columns and interconnecting ramps. Scattered about, free standing transparent columns glowed in all the colors of the rainbow, while tiny bubbles drifted upward within them. "It's like a combination fairytale castle and shopping mall."

"Keep your eyes out for hostiles and skip the architectural digest commentary, mate."

"I'm looking for movement, Bubba. Chill out. There are a number of smaller balconies and overlooks above our position which could put us in enfilade."

"Look alive people," Bosco called out. "The others are about to land in the open area below us."

Down three more glowing elevator shafts rode the other half of 1st Squad. Farthest away from the balcony Zippy and Jimmy immediately sought cover. Closest to the balcony, the Gunny and Beau landed and were in motion immediately, disappearing from sight beneath the balcony's overhang. In the middle, Inuksuk and Vinny found themselves in the open. The bear took two galloping jumps away from the shaft, stood erect, and bellowed over his suit speakers.

"What the hell is that all about?" asked Keti, watching the landing from the edge of the balcony.

Bosco shrugged. "Is better than peeing on a column to mark his territory."

"Polar bears, at least the male ones, are all batshit crazy," said Fanni.

"I have movement," Simba shouted. "Third balcony over from the middle elevator shaft." His teammates shifted position to cover the indicated target. Walker too, spun about. A sizable brown shape appeared for a second and was gone.

"What was that?"

Keti snorted. "Am I your guide to the local flora and fauna?"

"There's another one," called Davis. "Ten o'clock two flights down."

"She-it!" Walker turned his attention back to covering his friend.

"I think Inuksuk's friendly 'hello' has sent the natives running." Bosco switched to the common frequency and gave the Gunny a status report. "We have movement on several of the smaller balconies. No hostile action, they seem to be fleeing."

"Roger, Bosco. I'm calling the main floor secured." As the gunny was assessing the situation four more figures descended, three humans in light armor and one very nervous Kieshnar-rak-kat-tra.

Chapter 17

Shopping Mall

From the center elevator JT and Shanakta-fek stepped onto the main floor of the soaring commercial area. "Stay close, trader."

"Yes, yes, honored sir, but could we move to someplace less exposed? Over by those shops perhaps?"

"So these are all shops? Where are the shopkeepers, and where are their customers?"

"I would guess that knowledge of your arrival preceded you, honored warrior."

"All right. Inuksuk, take your team and see if there are any creatures in the shops on the far side of the platform. Gunny, we're coming to you."

"Roger, Lieutenant."

JT and his furry companion strolled across the empty plaza headed for the shops sheltered by the balcony above. There Bobby and Mizuki were already snooping about the storefronts, watched over by the attentive Gunny and Beau. Goods were visible in only a few of the shops, most being sealed off by heavy overhead doors, just like stores in an earthly shopping mall after closing time.

All that's missing are bored teenagers and middle aged women power-walking around the perimeter, JT thought, *that and some muzak.* "Seems awfully quiet, Gunny."

"Yeah, I'd say too quiet at the risk of sounding cliché."

"I have always hated this urban combat shit," JT muttered. "Just once I'd like some open rolling terrain on an alien planet with a real atmosphere and room to maneuver."

"You rather be in a swamp eating snakes, Army?" The Gunny grinned inside her enclosed helmet.

"Not on your life, Rosie. I'm happy to be on a shopping trip with you and the other Jarheads." This was not the first time they had been together, exploring an alien space station. Problem was, those trips had always ended in battle with one or more groups of aliens. *Do not jinx this, soldier! Think happy thoughts.*

Standing behind the armored humans, Shanakta-fek peered nervously around the deserted shopping mall. Out of habit or instinct he kept pulling his long fluffy tail past the scent glands in his armpits. Thankfully, the humans were sealed inside their space armor and not subjected to the malodorous bouquet his actions were creating.

* * * * *

Several closed shops away, Mizuki and Bobby found one that was open. Arranged on sloping shelves facing foot traffic were a wide assortment of glittering trinkets.

Mizuki carefully picked up a string of stones that looked like lapis lazuli: a deep blue with golden inclusions that shimmered like little stars. "Look Bobby, this one is pretty."

"Great, sweetheart. I'll buy it for you if we can find the shopkeeper, and figure out what they take for money around here."

"You are so sweet, Bobby. Hey look, there are more things inside." Mizuki headed for the interior of the shop, slipping through an open isle barely wide enough to fit her armored frame. Bobby shook his head and followed. *We come one-hundred and fifty light-years just so she can shop.*

They disappeared deeper into the store. Beau, wearing heavy armor could not enter the shop without breaking things so he stood helplessly outside.

Small Balcony Overlook

"Can you see them?" the Karf commander demanded.

"Yes, they are well inside the shop and the larger one has stayed outside. Start the diversion and we will spring the trap."

"Just be ready for my signal and do not fail."

The reply from the other Karf was unintelligible.

"Diversion team, are you ready with the splagg?"

"We are raising it in the large freight elevator and will dump it out on the main level in twenty seconds."

"Attention, warriors! The splagg will arrive in a few seconds. Wait for it to attack and pull the aliens out into the open. Then eradicate them all."

Well, the attack commander thought to itself grudgingly, *it looks like this plan might actually work.*

Inuksuk's Fireteam

Zippy and Vinny were exploring the shop fronts on the other side of the main floor from the Gunny and the officers. Jimmy was ten meters away, covering them while Inuksuk sat on his haunches a bit farther toward the center of the large open space.

"You primates finding anything useful?" the bear growled, already bored with looking through shops. Inuksuk judged this an activity only fit for primates. Though polar bears possess an amazing amount of patience, it was only used for stalking seals or other game. Unless a prospective meal was involved they had little time for snooping around.

"Nothing much, Corp. Looks like everything is all locked down." Jimmy turned to look back at Inuksuk and in doing so he was the first to see the splagg. Near the center of the encircling facade, it burst through the closed and shuttered storefronts facing the main plaza.

"What's that?"

"What?" Inuksuk pivoted to face the noise. Zippy and Vinny paused their search to look as well. As they watched, sheets of material, bracing, and merchandise flew in all directions as a huge gray mass emerged from the exploding wreckage.

The creature was gigantic, forty tons of whirling destruction. It spun on its vertical axis like a top, its periphery a blur of large flaps and sinuous appendages. Shrieking like a tortured pipe organ, the monster headed straight for Inuksuk.

"What the hell! That looks like a herd of break-dancing elephants with their asses all glued together." Vinny was right, ear-like flaps alternated with flexible trunks as the creature twirled ever closer.

Inuksuk stood, roared, and charged the flailing maelstrom of trunks and ears. Colliding with the creature, Inuksuk was battered, thrown ten meters into the air, and sent crashing through a closed shopfront.

"We got hostile contact!" Vinny yelled, running forward to stand by Jimmy.

"What should we do?" Jimmy asked as Zippy joined them.

"Shoot the damned thing!"

Streams of green tracers from their railguns reached out to the rampaging monstrosity. The splagg trumpeted even more loudly as the hail of 5mm flechettes tore into its body at 1800 meters per second.

Curiosity Shop

A muffled crash filtered through the open shop front. Bobby turned to face Mizuki, a frown on his face. "What do you think that was?"

"Nothing good."

The shop front slammed shut, a metal curtain descending from the ceiling in an instant. At the same time both humans were hit with streams of viscous goop from several directions. As the goop hit it turned to foam, swelling and encasing them. Bobby swung his arms trying to get the stuff off of him but it was like fighting whipped cream.

"I think this foamy stuff is stiffening up."

"It must be meant to immobilize us."

"I can't get to my weapons!"

"We are blind, nothin to shoot at if you could."

"I'm losing communications!"

"Bobby, give me your hand!"

Reaching out blindly he groped for her hand. Making contact they moved to stand closely side by side, hands grasped tightly as the foam set up.

"Mayday! Mayday! This is Dr. Ogawa and Cmdr. Danner. We are being abducted by hostile aliens."

There was nothing but static on the comm.

Inuksuk's Fireteam

"That thing isn't slowing down." Panic was rising in Zippy's voice.

"The 5mm isn't even affecting it," Vinny yelled. "Switch to 15mm armor piercing."

The gray cyclone of flailing tentacles was closing on them rapidly. Before they could escalate their counterattack a familiar roaring came over the comm. Inuksuk was back.

The armored bear emerged from the ruined store front he had flown through moments ago. He closed several steps on the splagg, which again altered course toward him. Raising his left arm, Inuksuk gave the rampaging creature a triple burst of 30mm HE, energy pumped for maximum explosive power. Seeing Inuksuk's actions Vinny shouted: "Cover!"

The three humans turned and dove for the deck. From behind them came three thuds, so close together that they seemed as one. The splagg exploded.

The explosions registered not as sound but a hammering felt deep within their chests. Shredded gobs of alien flew overhead, splattering the deck and far wall while the floor bucked underneath the Marines. Vinny rolled over and looked where the gray horror had been. There was a crater in the plaza floor with scorch marks radiating outward from it, a blackened starburst of destruction. Cartilage, viscera and shredded muscle tissue was strewn in all directions, some pieces still airborne.

"That damned crazy bear could have killed us," Zippy cursed as she regained her footing.

"Where is Corporal Inuksuk?" asked Jimmy, doing likewise. Inuksuk was nowhere to be seen.

Bosco's Fireteam

Looking down from the balcony Bosco and company watched the huge gray creature from above as it whirled its way into the open plaza below. They saw Inuksuk's charge and subsequent flight ending inside one of the closed shops.

"That's something new," he said.

"I have never seen anything with a nine-fold body symmetry." Keti added. From above the segmented disk shape of the large alien creature was obvious, though counting the body segments was hard due to its top like motion.

"Everyone fire on that thing before it takes out the others."

"Aye, Bosco."

But before they could unload on the beast Inuksuk re-emerged from the ruined store front.

"Hold! Don't hit the bear!"

Inuksuk raised his left forearm and let fly. The resulting explosion obscured the view of everything below for several seconds as bright flashes erupted within the hapless behemoth.

"Cover!" Bosco shouted too late, as he and the others were pelted by globules of flesh and unidentifiable body parts.

Between Walker and Davis part of a tentacle landed, still writhing. It did look vaguely like an elephant's trunk, except there was only a single opening in the blunt end of the appendage, lined with backward facing, needle sharp teeth.

Grits' southern accent could be heard as he protested the impromptu shower of alien flesh. "Oh man, that is just gross!"

As the explosion's aftermath settled, Fanni looked over the railing for their squadmates below. "Look, they are OK!"

All around those in the plaza bright bolts of orange-red light began to impact from above. The voice of the Gunny came over the squad channel.

"Incoming plasma fire from the balconies above! Get some cover; suppressive fire."

Bright streaks of light began falling on the Marines on the balcony as well. The plasma bolts blossomed into bright splashes of flame on impact, temporarily leaving the surfaces where they struck glowing cherry red. The Marines returned fire and the entire space was filled with green tracer fire and crossing streams of orange-red plasma—a festive, deadly light show.

From the plaza below, Vinny signaled on the common channel. "Simba, Fanni! There is a group of hostiles in the small balcony twenty meters above you."

Simba turned and looked up, just in time to take a plasma bolt from above. Orange flame enveloped him as he yelled, raising his arm to cover his helmet.

"Ayiiia!"

"Got it," Fanni replied to Vinny, spraying the enemy position with a torrent of flechettes. "You OK, Simba?"

"Yes, just startled. My suit readouts say no damage done."

"Move to the wall, out of their field of fire."

"Aye."

The two dashed quickly out of the enemy's line of sight and pulled up at the wall. The bottom of the balcony was directly above their position.

"Your turn, ET," Simba said, pouring 15mm armor piercing rounds into the underside of the balcony. Impacts flashed above as the shaped charges created explosive geysers of flame on the balcony's upper surface. A few seconds later debris and bodies rained down as the small balcony drooped and then parted from the wall.

"Run!" Fanni shouted, pushing Simba into motion. They took two steps and dove for the deck as the balcony crashed down, landing where they stood just moments before.

Gunny's Party

"Secure my ass!" shouted JT, shouldering his railgun. Pieces of building and alien body parts fell to the ground beyond the sheltering balcony. "We're in a fuckin' ambush."

"You figured that out by yourself?" the Gunny replied, sweeping a balcony five levels above the main plaza with 5mm flechettes. Firing 3600 rounds a minute at a velocity of 1800 meters per second, the targeted balcony melted away like a sandcastle hit by a fire-hose.

Shanakta-fek yelped once when the plasma bolts began landing on the plaza. Nearby there was a freestanding kiosk that offered some cover from above. With a startling burst of speed the furry alien dashed across the deck and dove into the kiosk.

The entire squad was now engaged, including those on the balcony above. Vinny, Zippy, and Jimmy had all found works of freestanding art to shelter behind while blasting away at the ambushers ensconced above. The glowing rose colored column Zippy crouched beside took two successive plasma hits and shattered, sending a shower of glass like shards in all directions.

A considerable amount of fire was coming from a floor on the fourth level. The Gunny moved right and into the open to get a clear field of fire. *We're not killing these bastards fast enough,* she thought, *sooner or later one of them is going to get lucky.*

Rosey raised her left arm, the one with the 15mm railgun, into firing position. On her helmet display a reticle appeared, showing the calculated impact point for the cannon rounds. She lased the wall next to where the incoming fire was originating to get a good range reading, bumped the range by two meters, and fired a two second burst. Sweeping her arm from left to right the rail cannon sent a dozen high explosive rounds into the building. Detonating inside the structure, rippling explosions blew out the entire section.

"Nicely done, Gunny," JT acknowledged.

"I love this heavy armor," she said with genuine affection.

JT raised his assault rifle and sent a burst in the direction of an overhead walkway. Two slim gray bodies fell from their perch, tumbling to the plaza floor.

"Not bad yourself, Army. Of course, my way is quicker."

The fire from overhead was abating as the Marines' counter fire took its toll. Across the open space Zippy and Vinny had moved from the plaza proper to the edge of the store fronts and were working their way toward the shop that Inuksuk had been thrown into. There was still no sign of the big bear. As they were doing so, JT looked around and said to himself, *now were did Cmdr. Danner and Dr. Ogawa get off to?*

Small Balcony Overlook

The Karf commander had avoided taking fire by not engaging the enemy itself. Using its keen eyesight the commander was able to assess the tide of battle and it had definitely turned in favor of the invaders.

These interlopers are disciplined. They did not panic or try to run away. They destroyed the splagg in a most decisive way, seemingly with little effort. This was all definitely not according to the plan.

Their return fire has been measured and deadly and they have taken out most of the warriors who were waiting in ambush. Across from the hidden commander another firing position exploded, sending several Karf to their deaths—if they weren't dead already.

And unfortunately, their weapons are quite powerful. Yes, time to send in the second wave. It activated its communicator. "Reserve force, attack."

"Yes, commander."

Evidently the Karf, though they thought themselves great warriors, had never learned one of the oldest military maxims. In the attack, a reserve unit can reinforce success; relieve an exhausted unit to maintain tactical momentum; maneuver to attack the enemy on his flank; or pursue a fleeing enemy force, but should never, ever reinforce defeat.

Chapter 18

Large Balcony

Scattered fire was still coming from above when a new front opened up in the center, beneath the overhanging facade where the gigantic spinning beast started the attack. As plasma bolts began arriving horizontally, Beau took a hit on his suit shields but was unharmed. The new heavy armor was designed with plasma weapons in mind, since they were a favorite of the Dark Lord's minions. The Marines on the plaza level shifted their fire to deal with this new threat.

Far above, a cantilevered glass balcony jutted out from the terraced structure. In a human building it would have been a restaurant or night club, but there was no telling what purpose it served here. Shadowy figures could be seen moving about within. Several transparent panels shattered outward as those inside rained plasma bolts down on the plaza below.

Seeing the renewed threat from above, Bosco moved to the edge of the balcony. Smiling to himself he said, "I have been waiting for chance to try this."

Raising his left arm, a pencil thin beam of emerald light appeared from the device mounted above his wrist. The green thread linked the Marine to the glassed in overhang the hostiles were firing from.

Sweeping the green laser across the enemy position, showers of sparks erupted as glass and building melted. The green laser was just a sighting guide, the real damage was done by a stream of picosecond pulses of far ultraviolet light. The beam was design to cause disruption of molecular structure, turning any matter into plasma. As a side effect bodies ruptured, blown apart by violently expanding superheated gases, and anything flammable was set alight.

"*Klasneey,*" Bosco said, satisfied with the outcome. The entire enemy position was now ablaze.

A long sinuous body lept from the conflagration, wriggling from side to side as it plummeted. It was shaped like a lizard, with a tail almost as long as its body, but was covered in hair. It burned as it fell, leaving a trail of black smoke.

"Bosco, Acuna. We have a large force attacking from your left on the plaza level. See if you can find a way down and take the bastards in the flank."

"Aye, aye, Gunny. We are moving. Break. Davis, Walker, move into the main structure and look for a way down. Tseriteli go with them."

"Roger that," Davis replied for the three.

"Singh, Takala, on me."

"Coming to you," Fanni answered.

CIC, Peggy Sue

"What the bloody hell is happening down there?" Beth cursed in exasperation. "Can we get someone to give us a sitrep?"

"Number One, you know it's not a good idea to micromanage your commander on the ground in the midst of a firefight," Billy Ray chided. "Besides, it appears that our people are getting the best of the exchange."

"Yes, Captain. Dr. White, do we have any casualties?"

"Only one is registering, Cpl. Inuksuk's telemetry is showing significant trauma and probably some cracked ribs. I don't know if it was from that strange spinning creature knocking him through a wall, or from the explosion when he blew the creature up, which also knocked him through a wall."

"Will we need to medivac him when the battle is over?"

"Depends on how bad the fractures are. We may be able to just partially immobilize them with his suit. We'll find out as soon as this is over."

"Sounds good, Doc."

"Uh, Captain? There is one other thing."

That doesn't sound good, Billy Ray thought, *Doc never calls me 'captain' unless its something bad.* "What's the problem, Doctor?"

164

"I've lost medical telemetry for both Dr. Ogawa and Cmdr. Danner."

"You mean they're dead?"

"No, I mean I have no telemetry signal. If they had been wounded or even killed I should have gotten some indication over their suits' status reporting, like I have from Cpl. Inuksuk. Their signals just quit right after the start of the attack."

"Christ on a crutch! As soon as they drive off these attackers we'll have to get the squad to search for them." Billy Ray grimaced. *I just knew things were going too smoothly down there, ambush not withstanding. Damn, I hope they are alright.*

Mizuki & Bobby

"We are moving," Mizuki reported, checking her suit's inertial navigation system.

"They must be hauling us off some place to interrogate us."

"Or eat us."

Though Bobby couldn't see her face, he imagined her guileless look as she delivered that line—his wife had a very sarcastic, perhaps even strange, sense of humor. This helped raise his spirits even in light of their current predicament.

"This foam encasing us must suppress radio communications, I've totally lost contact with everyone but you."

"Me too, Bobby. However I may have a way to let the ship know where we are."

"Really?"

"I have been working on a neutrino signaling device, a sort of simplified mechanism like that used by the T'aafhal. It is very rudimentary—I can only send an identification code, no message."

"But the ship will be able to receive the signal?"

"Yes, and track our position. Well, the ship's computer will be able to. The mechanism depends on the part of the computer's circuitry that is able to detect neutrinos."

"That's great, Mizuki-chan. Can you send the signal now? I'm sure the others have noticed we are missing by now."

"Hai, Bobby. I will send a signal, but it is a very crude device. It takes several minutes to recharge after sending out a pulse."

Brains, Grits & Keti

"Hold up," Davis called, out of habit signaling his companions to halt with a raised, clenched fist. "I think I've found a stairwell down."

"Great! Send your recon drone to see what's down there." Behind Walker came the band-saw ripping wood sound of a 5mm at full cry. "Keti, do you have contact?"

"Not anymore." She rounded a column and joined the two men. "What have you found, Brains?"

"It's some kind of grand staircase," he said. "Ramps lead down from the right and left. They both curve around and end up at a landing about half way to the main floor. From the landing a single wider ramp continues down to the plaza level."

"Hey, my aunt Mavis has a staircase just like that in her house. They used it each year for the local Debutant Ball."

"The what?" asked Keti.

"Debutant Ball. Every year the well-to-do held this big dance for their daughters, to introduce them to society. Basically it said the girls were in the market for a husband as far as I could tell, not that I was among that class of people."

"Then how do you know about this?"

"I helped serve the canapes and drinks a couple of years. If you ask me, the only thing the Ball proved about those young women was they were coordinated enough to walk down the grand staircase in them long dresses without falling and breaking their necks."

"We're in the midst of a firefight and you are rambling on about some posh do from your childhood!"

166

"Sorry, Bubba, Keti asked. So how do we skin this cat?"

"How about one of us goes down each ramp and Keti can provide cover?"

"Hardly. The platform is less than ten meters down and we have only one third normal gravity." Keti placed one armored gauntlet on the guard rail and vaulted over the side.

"She-it!"

"That bird is a couple cards short of a full deck!"

"Yeah, I think I'm in love."

Keti landed on the platform below and was immediately under fire. She headed down the wide ramp to the plaza, weapons blazing.

"Now she's makin' us look bad, Bubba. See you down there!" Walker repeated Keti's move and vaulted over the railing.

"Bloody hell," Davis muttered in exasperation. "Bosco, we found a way down, mark my current position."

Davis jumped the over railing.

Main Plaza

The Marines had the situation well in hand, with people on the left and right sides of the plaza. As the aliens attempted to rush them up the center they were caught in a murderous crossfire.

"Take 'em down," the Gunny commanded. Switching to suit-to-suit she talked to JT who was hunkered down next to her. "What the hell are they thinking, doing a banzai charge into overlapping fields of fire?"

"Never interrupt your opponent while he's making a fatal mistake, Gunny."

At least a score of slender gray aliens rushed onto the plaza, carrying plasma rifles and nothing else.

"The poor dumb bastards don't have any type of armor and them little plasma poppers won't even slow us down. This stinks of desperation."

"Agreed, let's just finish this and get it over with."

The Gunny grunted and raised her 15mm, sending a burst of HE rounds into the hallway from which the aliens had sallied. In the darkness beneath the facade bright flashes marked the arrival of the Gunny's barrage.

High above the plaza the Karf commander was livid, its kind did not suffer failure well. Seizing its own plasma rifle, zhe exposed itself by firing on the aliens below. Its target was the remaining small invader, under the assumption that it was in charge.

The first bolt struck JT on the shoulder, which caused his suit to stiffen for an instant to dissipate the impact. A single hit wouldn't penetrate his armor but multiple ones might. Seeing the Lieutenant light up next to her the Gunny stepped in front of him. Her armor could easily handle multiple hits.

As the Gunny's armor flared absorbing another bolt, JT's unfroze. He stepped around her and fired a long burst of flechettes at the sniper. Targeting was not an issue, his suit's sensors tracked the plasma bolts back to their origin and IR highlighted the figure of the gunman.

It took less than a second for the flechettes to arrive. They stitched a line up the Karf's body, starting at its crotch and ending at its bulbous head. Traveling at 4,000 fps the hydrostatic shock of each impact made the alien's body expand like a balloon for an instant. Three flechettes struck the Karf's face and forehead—its skull burst like an overripe melon.

"Nice shot, JT."

"Thanks for the cover, Rosey. Let's wrap this furball up."

"Roger that."

Keti, Grits, & Brains

After blowing away a few aliens that were at the bottom of the ramp, the three Marines immediately headed for the main hallway where their recon drones showed a sizable alien force was positioned. Keti stopped at the corner leading into the wide passageway, and the other two stacked up behind her. They checked the video feed from their recon drones in greater detail.

"It looks like they are setting up some heavy, crew-served weapons," observed Grits.

"I think you're right, mate, and those puppies are probably big enough to do some real damage."

"So we take them out." Keti's remark was a statement, not a question.

"Right you are, luv. Let's swing around in a line and hit them with full automatic 15mm, say a five second burst each."

"Works for me, y'all. Ready? I'm moving to your left, Keti."

"Right behind you, mate."

The three Marines jogged into position, knelt down to steady their aim, and let fly. More than seventy HE rounds pounded the alien position. The Karf were packed in together trying to bring three plasma cannon into battery. They were anticipating a charge down the hallway by the Marines from the plaza, not being taken from behind by enemies they didn't know were there.

The Karf position disappeared behind a curtain of fire, the exploding warheads a continuous cascade of brilliant yellow furry. Several seconds into the barrage a different kind of detonation joined the fiery maelstrom, this one brilliant blue white. It was quickly joined by two more sending shock waves that buffeted the Marines.

"Hoowee! You can't beat that with a wet squirrel."

"If you mean we kicked their arses you're spot on, mate. We must have detonated the power packs for those plasma cannons."

"I think you are both right." Keti switched comm channels. "Ice Castle, Tseriteli. We have taken out the remaining hostiles in the main corridor, over."

169

Main Plaza

JT was getting ready to order an assault on the central hallway when bright flashes and a succession of heavy explosions erupted from far down the corridor. Debris and gouts of flame issued from the opening, leaving the Lieutenant and accompanying Marines wondering what just happened. Then Keti's call came in.

"Ice Castle, Tseriteli, we have taken out the remaining hostiles in the main corridor, over."

"Roger that, Tseriteli, your results were a bit overwhelming."

"Overwhelming my ass," the Gunny added. "How about a little heads up before you decide to blow up half a building."

"Sorry, Gunny. It was the power packs for the heavy plasma cannon detonating. They were setting up to ambush you."

Checking her tactical readout she saw that Tseriteli, Walker, and Davis were about a hundred and fifty meters inside the structure. "You three done good, Keti, I'm just saying keep us informed next time."

"Aye, aye, Gunny."

"Hey, I don't show Dr. Ogawa or Cmdr. Danner on my tactical display. Does anyone have eyes on?'

"That's a negative, Gunny. They were in that shop right over there when the firefight started."

"Well where the fuck are they? Don't just stand on your dicks, go find them!"

"Peggy Sue, Ice Castle, do you have telemetry from Ogawa and Danner?"

"That's a negative, JT. We lost telemetry for them right after the skirmish began. We were waiting for things to settle down before asking about them ourselves."

Oh balls! JT thought. *Our first firefight and we lose track of two senior officers. That's a pooch screw of epic proportions.*

Chapter 19

Main Plaza

"I thought the storefront they went into was open?" JT asked Beau. The PFC was standing helplessly in front of the shuttered jewelery shop.

"It was open, Sir. Once the battle started I figured that they were safe enough taking cover inside. I never noticed when the door shut. Should I blast it open?"

"No!" the Gunny shouted. "If they are still in there we don't want to blow 'em to hell and gone."

JT thought for a second. "Bosco, where are you? We need your laser down here."

"We are at the staircase. Be there shortly."

"Even using the laser will be dangerous, Lieutenant," the Gunny commented. "How thick do you suppose that shutter is?"

"Not very, why?"

"Beau, take a run at the door and try to break it down."

"*Oui*, Gunny." Beau rounded on the closed shopfront, set himself like a sprinter at the start of a race, and ran full tilt at the metal barrier. He was still accelerating when he collided with the door, lowering his left shoulder just prior to impact. The door bowed inward, metal tearing, as the Marine vanished inside the shop.

"I guess that answers that question," the Gunny observed as Keti and company jogged up. "You others lend a hand and rip the rest out of the way."

"Aye, aye," Walker replied enthusiastically. He, Keti, and Brains made short work of the remaining metal covering. Inside Beau shouted, "There's nobody in here."

"Crap," JT turned away in frustration just in time to see a bushy tail disappear behind a nearby kiosk. Switching on his external speaker he yelled, "Shanakta-fek! Get your furry ass over here."

A pair of red-orange oculars surrounded by black and cinnamon fur peered out from behind the kiosk. Looking around nervously the trader concluded that there was no reasonable chance of escaping. Avoiding fallen chunks of building, dead Karf, and shreds of splagg the Kieshnar-rak-kat-tra scampered to JT's position.

"I am at your command, oh great warrior. How may I be of service?"

"Come with me." JT turned and led the way into the now demolished storefront.

The interior of the shop was a shambles, more due to Beau's forceful entry than anything else. There was an open space toward the back of the store where counters and display cases had been cleared away. In the center there was an area of bare floor that was surrounded by strange material, like the emergency foam sprayed on a runway before an airplane made a crash landing. Except this foam was as hard as concrete.

"What is that stuff, Lieutenant?" Grits asked.

"Not a clue, but I bet it has something with the disappearance of Dr. Ogawa and Cmdr. Danner. What do you know, shorty?" That last directed at Shanakta-fek who was hiding behind JT's armored form.

"It looks like capture foam, used by the Karf, great sir."

"Who the hell are the Karf?"

"The gray bipeds who attacked you, they are more or less the overlords of the station."

"LT, I've got a body!" called Beau from near the back wall of the store. JT and his reluctant local guide moved to Beau's position.

As they drew near they could see a carcase, covered with short light brown fur, about the size of a hog. It was laying crumpled in the corner, deep slash marks across its neck and body. Red blood congealed in a dark puddle next to the body.

"What's that thing?"

"It is a Hoon, sir. They are artisans and shop keepers, this was probably his shop. They are timid and unaggressive by nature."

"Did the Karf do this? Kill the shopkeeper?"

"The wounds look more like those inflicted by a Hisstow. They are often used by the Karf as muscle. They are long and flexible, covered with fur, and have retractable claws on both their hands and feet."

"But the Karf were behind this, and that big thing that started the attack in the plaza?"

"The splagg, yes most worthy sir. The beast is not intelligent, but they are often used to guard areas of the station the Karf wish no one but themselves to have access to." The trader had his bushy tail wrapped across his chest and when not speaking burred his nose in its hair.

"Why are you hiding your face? Are you afraid to be recognized, are we under surveillance?"

"No, sir, the smell of death both here and on the plaza nauseates me." He looked up from his furry wrap with big pleading eyes.

"Sir, it looks like there are drag marks leading to the freight doors back here," called Brains. "Somebody dragged something heavy out through the rear exit."

"Tell me, trader. Do these Karf take prisoners or are our comrades dead?" There was ice water in JT's voice.

"S-Sir, they often take captives to interrogate. The use of the restraining foam indicates that your companions were taken for such a purpose."

"Where? Where are these little gray bastards?"

"The Karf inhabit parts of several nearby spires and one major spire that they claim exclusively for their kind. They could have taken your friends to any of those locations."

"Shit! Well captured is better than dead. Gunny, send some Marines to find out where the drag marks go."

"Aye, Sir. Davis, Walker, follow the scuff marks. Tseriteli, go with 'em."

"Aye, aye." The trio exited the rear of the shop on the trail of the kidnapers.

Karf Habitat

The new leader of the Karf was apoplectic. Despite the fact that the ambush's failure led directly to its ascension by discrediting the previous leader, the brief battle showed these new aliens to be most formidable warriors. There was no getting around it, the ambush had been a disaster.

"Bring me the ambush commander, I wish to tear its throat out myself!"

"The commander died in battle, as your predecessor should have. We lost more than fifty warriors in a matter of minutes. How are you going to overcome these new foes, Leader?" Leader was pronounced with great contempt.

"We did manage to capture two of the smaller aliens. They are on the way here now," reported another underling. This prompted outcries by those gathered.

"Can the aliens track them? Are they leading these unstoppable killing machines to our habitat? Better to kill them now if we can."

"Don't be stupid. The aliens are encased in capture foam, which suppresses all electromagnetic radiation. They won't be released from the foam until they are in a safely shielded containment cell."

"That's all well and good, but what are you going to do about this threat, Leader?"

"How can we stop them? How many more are aboard their ship?"

"We can't stop them. That is the fact of the matter."

"No, maybe we can't, but the Others can," the leader said, quieting the fractious crowd. "Summon the death raptors. At least now we can promise them a worthy foe to fight. Meanwhile, we will interrogate the captives and find out as much as we can about these invaders. Perhaps some weakness can be found. In any case we will have the pleasure of flaying them alive."

CIC, Peggy Sue

"We still haven't located Dr. Ogawa and Cmdr. Danner, Sir. We followed the drag marks from the back of the shop they were taken in. They ended at what looks like a maintenance elevator. We sent recon drones half a klick down the shaft and saw no signs of life."

"I copy, Ice Castle. I suggest you bring 2nd squad down to your level and make sure the area is fully secured before attempting a further reconnaissance."

"Yes, Sir. When we do find them we will probably need to bring up reinforcements before doing a frontal assault. These little gray bastards are nasty."

"Understood. That not withstanding, I want them found, Mr. Taylor. Peggy Sue, out."

Cutting the comm link Billy Ray clenched his fists in frustration. "How the hell do you lose two people out from under everyone's noses in the midst of a firefight?"

Beth realized that the anger in her husband's words were because of frustration and not directed at JT and the Marines personally. They both knew that exploring strange space stations was a risky business. "Many tribal warriors practiced kidnapping during skirmishes, taking captives to interrogate and possibly exchange for ransom or prisoners."

"Yer right, Number One, but that doesn't make the situation any easier to swallow—the alien abductors knew what they were doing. The most frustrating thing is that we can't track their location."

"So it would seem, Captain. What puzzles me is how they took Bobby and Mizuki without a fight."

"Pardon me, Captain, but I may have information regarding the location of Dr. Ogawa." It was the voice of the ship's computer.

"You do? Where are they, Peggy Sue, and how are you tracking them?"

"For some time Dr. Ogawa has been trying to reverse engineer the T'aafhal neutrino based communication technology. So far she has managed to create a signaling device that sends an identifying pulse which I am able to detect using the same circuits that the more sophisticated T'aafhal devices utilize."

Billy Ray sighed and looked at the ceiling in frustration. "The location, Peggy Sue, then the explanation if you please."

"Of course, Captain. The red light on the holographic projection of the station is the last known location of Dr. Ogawa."

On the model starflake that hovered above the main 3D projection display a red dot appeared deep within the core of the station. It was partway between the spire the Marines were in and an adjacent major spire.

"Damn, they are not even in the same arm of the station. Where are they being taken?"

"I do not have that information, Captain.

"You keep saying the location of Dr. Ogawa, are Bobby and Mizuki still together?" asked Beth.

"I do not know that either, Cmdr. Melaku. I am assuming that the signal marks the location of Dr. Ogawa, since the device was built into her suit. The beacon is a simple signaling device that is incapable of sending anything more complicated than an identifying code. The position is extrapolated from the direction of the signal and where it intersected the station structure."

"Can the aliens track the signal?"

"I find that improbable, given the level of technology they have displayed so far. What is fortunate is that neutrinos will pass through normal matter without hindrance or detection."

"So yer saying the abductors don't know that we know where they're taking our people?"

"That is the most likely scenario, Captain." The computer paused for a second. "I have just received another pulse, there is no mistake that they are moving."

On the model the red point changed position. It was now within the adjacent spire, as though rising from the station hub.

"Thank you, Peggy Sue. Keep us updated on their progress." Billy Ray activated the comm. "Chief Morgan, you and your SEALs

176

please armor up and get to the pinnace. I think we have need of your infiltration skills. You will be briefed en route."

"Aye, aye, Sir. We are on our way."

"Number One, we need a pilot for the pinnace." Seeing the gleam in her eyes he quickly added, "other than yourself."

"Sometimes you just take all the fun out of things. Lt. Hoenig is currently OOD on the bridge, I will send Lt. Palmer. Are you going to let Lt. Taylor know we have a tentative location for Mizuki and Bobby?"

"Let's get another ping to be sure of the location before we let JT off the hook." His voice was serious but the smile on his face indicated that the Captain was feeling much relieved to have a fix on the missing officers.

Mizuki & Bobby, Karf Spire

"We are rising, Bobby. We must be in another spire."

"Yes. That's both good and bad. Good in that we are probably getting close to our destination."

"And bad?"

"Because we are probably getting close to our destination."

"Have you thought of a way to escape containment?" Though Mizuki was a brilliant physicist and an unequaled swordsman, she lacked her husband's intimate knowledge of their other armament.

"Yeah, I've been giving it some thought. You remember that we specified better shielding against explosive penetrators after the incident on the ant planet?"

"Hai, PFC Malachi was nearly killed."

"Well what we did was upgrade the shielding on both the heavy and light armored suits. The problem is that it takes too much power to maintain impenetrable shields like the ship has or even the shuttles. So we took an idea from old fashioned tank armor. To defeat penetrators they used active armor, basically explosives that disrupted the incoming shaped jet of metal from an anti-armor warhead."

"There are explosives on our suits?"

"No, sweetheart, but we modified the shield generators to create short, localized repulsive pulses when an approaching threat is detected. In tests, they were able to defeat typical anti-armor warheads and don't require nearly the energy drain that continuous shielding would."

"That's great, how do we get them to shoot us with anti-armor rounds?"

Bobby shook his head. "That's not exactly what I had in mind. There is a test mode that can trigger active armor pulses programmatically. I'm thinking that if we make our suits generate a pattern of pulse they should be able to fracture this cement we're stuck in."

"You just should have said so, Bobby."

"I just did, Mizuki-chan. I have programmed my suit to generate a pattern of pulses over its entire surface, which should set me free. I'll transfer the program to your suit's computer and, when we are ready to break out, we'll trigger them at the same time. The biggest problem is deciding when we make our break."

"Victories are won using a timing which the enemy does not expect."

"What?"

"From *Go Rin No Sho,* the *Book of Five Rings* by master swordsman Miyamoto Musashi."

"The samurai philosopher?"

"Hai. He was once attacked by ten swordsmen and he killed them all. It is said that he wandered the land dressed in rags, left his hair unkempt, and would not bathe for fear of being ambushed in the bathtub."

"And the lesson in that is?"

"Beware of poorly dressed, smelly swordsmen." Mizuki paused to see if Bobby would comment. He did not. She continued.

178

"His sword technique was lost because he never started a school to train apprentices. Most of his writings are very zen and often impenetrable to western minds, but some of his saying are quite perceptive."

"And he would advise us to strike..."

"...when our opponents least expect it."

"I figure they will take us to a cell or some place where they think it safe to release us before removing this crap."

"But you have devised a way to remove the crap earlier than they expect."

"Right. We're still moving upward so we are probably in one of those elevator shafts. Hard to fight in mid air."

"They will have to exit the shaft at a platform and then drag us to where they will try to interrogate us."

"So the place to break out is right after we get out of the elevator and onto a landing."

"Yes, they will probably relax, having almost reached their destination. We will take them by surprise."

"Does Musashi-san say what to do when you achieve surprise?"

"Cut your opponents strongly."

"Got it. Send another neutrino pulse, I have a feeling things are going to get a bit busy when we reach the landing."

"Hai."

"And Mizuki?"

"Yes, Bobby?"

"I love you."

Chapter 20

Main Plaza

"The computer says that Dr. Ogawa and Cmdr. Danner are now in the next spire over?"

"That is correct, Ice Castle. They are still moving and we have the SEALs standing by for an extraction."

"Will that be enough? We killed at least fifty aliens of several different types fighting off the ambush."

"The plan is to have the SEALs locate the abductees. Once they have eyes on, they will decide if they can do an extraction or if we need to send more assets. Over."

"I copy, Peggy Sue. Both squads are clearing the shopping mall, shop by shop, to make sure there are no surprises left. One or both squads can be back to the shuttles in twenty minutes, just give the word."

"Roger, Ice Castle. We will advise. Peggy Sue, out."

JT shut off the comm channel to the ship. "Well crap. It sounds like the SEALs are going to try and spring Ogawa and Danner."

"Hell, we lost 'em, the Captain should at least give us the opportunity to get 'em back." The Gunny was as embarrassed about losing the officers as JT was.

"I hear you, Gunny. But the Captain wasn't in a mood to take requests. How is clearing the site coming?"

"We've found some more of those big rodent things..."

"Hoon?"

"Yeah, and a pair of octopus looking critters that our pet weasel says are called Orloo."

"But no hostiles?"

"No live ones. We've just about finished, you want to send a couple of fireteams down to the lower levels?"

"No, not until we see how the hostage situation plays out. We may need to pull back to the shuttles and go reinforce the SEALs. By the way, how's Inuksuk?"

"He's guarding the main plaza, mainly because he's hurt worse than he will admit."

"Yeah, male polar bears are like that. Supposedly because showing any weakness out on the Arctic ice can get you attacked by your fellow ursines."

"Sounds like the neighborhood where I grew up, only colder. In any case the last time someone asked how he was he muttered something in Sami. PFC Takala said it roughly translated as 'I will kill you and eat your livers'."

"Great. Unless we have to evacuate, let's let grouchy bears lie."

"Roger that. So where are the officers supposed to be?"

"Over there." JT motioned toward a large expanse of crystalline wall, through which more of the station could be seen. "In that next large spire."

Mizuki & Bobby

They both felt the change in motion as their encased bodies were pulled from the elevator and onto the landing. As soon as movement ceased, Bobby shouted, "Now!"

Triggering the programed sequence of shield pulses, both Mizuki and Bobby were shook by violent vibrations and a sound like dueling jackhammers. As Bobby had hoped, the concentrated repulsive bursts from their shields shattered the hardened material around them. Blocks of petrified foam flew from their suits in all directions.

Bobby took a tentative step forward, knocking rock hard rubble aside. In front of him were several little gray men and a large cat-lizard thing. The cat-lizard reacted first, springing toward him, fanged mouth agape, swiping at his head with a large clawed paw.

Next to Bobby, Mizuki moved forward, sliding her feet as kendōka are taught. Reflexively, her hands reached over her head and drew her katana as a second cat-lizard sprung toward her. She met its leap with a diagonal cut that started on the creature's left shoulder and exited its right side. The Earthlings' swords were constructed from a carbon-metallic nanocomposite, stronger than steel and scalpel sharp. A wedge containing the cat-lizard's head, right arm, and part of its rib cage fell away from the rest of its body, coming to rest atop fractured cement near the edge of the platform.

The remaining, larger portion of the attacking cat-lizard continued forward, its hindquarters not yet aware that its head had gone missing. Lung and viscera spilled from the diagonal wound that split its body. Mizuki ducked and spun, gliding to her right, allowing the dead beast to continue past her. It tripped over its other half and the still squirming corpse went over the platform edge, disappearing out of sight.

Bobby was not the swordsman that Mizuki was but remnants of foam still blocked access to his pistol. He drew his sword single handed and removed his attacker's extended left arm with a downward stroke. The cat-lizard yowled and stood up straight in front of him, staring at the stump where its arm had been. Bobby stepped forward, grasped his katana with both hands, and struck the three meter long monster in front of him with a horizontal cut from right to left.

The blade of Bobby's sword caught the cat-lizard just below the rib cage, cutting its long, slender body to the backbone. The yowling stopped as intestines and unidentifiable organs spilled from the gaping wound. The creature toppled to Bobby's right.

As he had been taught by his wife, Bobby followed through with the belly cut and brought his blade to an upright position above his left shoulder, ready for a follow up strike. The cat-lizard didn't require another blow, but over its fallen carcase three slender gray bipeds with large heads and almond shaped eyes charged at the swordsman.

Mizuki, having dispatched her primary opponent, finished dodging its falling body and ended in a position facing four of the gray humanoids. With hands arched into talons and open mouths displaying an unreasonable number of needle like teeth the creatures attacked.

183

Hopping nimbly over a large chunk of hardened foam, Mizuki moved among the gray creatures like a wraith, her sword a continuous silver blur describing sideways figure eights. She moved beyond the attackers and halted. Behind her four gray bodies fell, transformed into eight large pieces.

Lacking his wife's artistry with the katana, Bobby simply cut the head off the first of his gray attackers. Its head spun away, end over end, and bounced across the floor. The next two he took with the return stroke, catching the first across the jaw line and the second at the temple. The upper portions of both heads flew away, their owners dropping like puppets whose strings had been cut. That threat dealt with, he finished removing the shards of hardened foam that clung to his armor.

Looking across the platform, Mizuki spotted another group of the gray humanoids clustered near a wide door. Unlike those she and Bobby had just dispatched these carried some form of weaponry. Knowing she could not cross the ten meters to where the gray men stood before they fired, she shouted: "Bobby!"

Her husband spotted the new threat milliseconds after Mizuki. Leaving his sword in his left hand Bobby went for his pistol. His suit sensing his action, popped open the security cover exposing the weapon's grip.

There is a mystique surrounding quick-draw gunfighters in the American Old West—who was the fastest gun alive? In modern times, Bob Munden was given the title "Fastest Man with a Gun Who Ever Lived," by the *Guinness Book World Records*. With a draw and shoot time of 0.15 seconds he claimed he was the fastest shot in history. Bobby had naturally quick reflexes—they were part of what made him such an exceptional pilot—but those reflexes had been enhanced by T'aafhal medical technology. His nerve responses were more than twice as fast as a normal human's. Even encumbered by armor he drew and fired the 10mm railgun pistol at his waist in under one tenth of a second.

Bobby fired four times in rapid succession. The first round struck the closest armed humanoid, who was pointing what looked like a plasma rifle at the Earthlings. Its chest and upper torso vanished in a bright yellow flash—the 10mm slugs from Bobby's pistol were filled with a nano-engineered explosive-oxidant mix pumped to elevated orbital energy levels for extra yield. Weapon, head, and arms all flew in different directions.

The other gray hostile with a weapon suffered the same fate. The last two rounds exploded in the crowd of aliens, killing three and wounding an unknown number. The hostiles who could, fled.

"You OK, sweetheart?"

"Yes, Bobby. And you?"

"Yep. Let's find a way out of this place."

"It is either the door, or back down the elevator."

"The elevator is too exposed."

"Hai, we should head to the outer wall of the spire and call the ship to come get us."

"Sounds like a plan to me, Mizuki-chan. You notice that the little gray guys bleed blue?"

"Yes, it is very pretty. The big cat-lizards bled red though."

"OK, just making sure I'm not seeing things."

Mizuki looked over the carnage around her mate. "You did well with your sword, I am proud of you."

Bobby holstered his pistol, flicked the blood off his katana, and resheathed it. "You may want to make sure you can get to your sidearm. Swords against plasma rifles is a bit too exciting for my tastes."

Mizuki harrumphed. "You are becoming an old fuddy-duddy. But I still love you."

"And I love you, my crazy little samurai. After you sweetheart."

The couple stepped over the scattered body parts and headed for the door.

Keti, Grits, & Brains

After following the drag marks made by Mizuki and Bobby's abduction to the open hole of a service elevator, the three Marines fanned out to secure the surrounding area. Rounding a corner a lone Karf jumped from hiding and fired a plasma bolt at Keti. Keti's armor lit up, surrounded by a nimbus of orange flame.

Grits quickly raised his 15mm and fired a three shot burst of beehive rounds. Beehive rounds are like shotgun shells, packed with multiple flechettes that spread-out when fired. The flechette pattern had widened to almost three meters when it reached the gray attacker. The velocity of the flechettes was not high enough to penetrate Keti's armor, but more than energetic enough to perforate the Karf. Its body was riddled, blood and tissue painting an abstract blue pattern on the wall behind it.

"Hey, I never noticed before but these little gray peckerwoods bleed blue."

"You're right, mate," Brains replied. "In nature, copper turns things blue or blue-green. Horseshoe crabs have a copper-based molecule called hemocyanin to distribute oxygen instead of hemoglobin like we do. That's why their blood is blue. These gits must be copper-based as well."

"Fascinating, you two. But next time shoot the bastards before they shoot me."

"Then don't get so far out ahead of us, luv."

Keti waved an arm to silence the two men. "I've got movement."

The three Marines spread out into positions with clearer fields of fire and prepared to receive whatever Keti's sensors had detected. Around that same corner the Karf had appeared from a two meter wide disk, surrounded by stubby short arms, slid around the corner. It was about a third of a meter thick and was colored a shocking pink.

"Hold your fire!" Grits called. "It don't seem hostile."

"What the hell is that?" Keti demanded, as the fringed saucer seemed to glide across the floor toward the body of the freshly killed Karf. Reaching the body, the strange creature slid over top of the fallen Karf, covering it entirely. The hot pink discus began to spin slowly and move in widening circles.

"I think the bloody thing is cleaning up the floor."

186

"I think you're right, Bubba. Look it's moving over to the wall."

Sure enough, the pink beast slid over to the wall and then slithered upward until it covered the blue splatter put there by Grits's earlier efforts. It slid smoothly back down the wall and onto the floor. The blue wall splatter was gone.

"It's some kind of alien street sweeper," Keti marveled. "Didn't 2nd squad say something about finding an alien vacuum cleaner?"

"Yeah, but nothing that big. What they found was more like a Roomba."

The sweeper, now with a noticeable bulge in its center, moved off down the hall toward the site of the ambush the trio had broken up earlier. From around the corner came a second, and then a third of the disk shaped things, all heading toward the big hall and presumably the plaza beyond.

Brains keyed his comm on the squad frequency. "This is Davis, there are a number of large, hot pink, fringed Frisbees headed your way. They are not, repeat, not hostile. They seem to be the custodial staff."

SEALs, Small Shuttle

Chief Morgan, PO Bud Jones, and PO Phil Kowalski were seated in the passenger compartment of the Captain's pinnace, a small shuttle about the size of a corporate jet. On the flight deck Lt. JG Pauline Palmer guided the small craft on a looping course around several minor spires, a stealthy approach to the major spire where the hostages were located. Over the comm, Captain Vincent was briefing them on the objective.

"According to Peggy Sue, the missing officers are moving higher within the spire, on a somewhat erratic course. Our tracking info is sketchy at best, since we only get a ping every few minutes, but this seems a strange route for their captors to be taking."

"Meaning you thing that they may have escaped, Sir?" asked Morgan. Each of the three SEALs was looking at a holographic projection of the Starflake showing the ragged path marked by Mizuki's neutrino signals.

"We don't know, Chief. They are still deep inside the core of the spire. The interior construction seems to be made of metal, which could continue to block communications."

"Aye, Sir. We will bring along a recon drone to scout ahead and scatter comm repeaters along the way. We still may end up losing contact."

"Understood. We've been scanning the exterior of the spire with optical sensors and it looks like there may be airlocks at the locations here and here." Two green dots lit up on the model. "They don't seem large enough to accept the pinnace."

"We planned for that, Captain. We are wearing maneuvering modules on our suits. If the boat can just pull up close to the spire and let us out, we can EVA over to it."

"Roger that, Chief. We'll keep sending you position updates on your targets. Report when you are ready to leave the shuttle."

"Aye, aye, Sir." Switching to the shuttle's internal comm he addressed the pilot. "You get all that, Lieutenant?"

"Aye, Chief. I've got the surface active camo on and will sneak up next to the spire real causal like. I'll come to a hover next to one of the locks and you fellas can just hop out and do your thing."

"Sounds like a plan, Ma'am. We're standing by."

Chapter 21

Mizuki & Bobby, Karf Spire

The two former captives were about to ascend a stairway to the next higher floor when they came under fire for the third time since escaping. Angry orange plasma bolts splattered off the walls as Bobby covered Mizuki's escape up the spiral staircase.

"Be careful, Mizuki-chan, they may be waiting for us at the top."

"Don't worry, I am ready," she replied, drawing her pistol. Though she preferred her sword, and was not a quick draw like her husband, Mizuki was a perfectly competent marksman with pistol or rifle.

Bobby fired a couple more rounds to keep their pursuers' heads down and started up the stairs himself. Halfway up he paused and stuck a small object to the inside of the spiral—a grenade. Pressing the arming button the explosive device began to blink, telling him he had five seconds to clear the area before its motion sensor became active. He sprinted up the stairs three steps at a time.

"We need to move out of the stairwell."

"We are clear, Bobby, I see no enemy ahead."

He exited the staircase and followed his wife down the curving hallway. "Don't these little shits ever build anything with straight lines? Curved halls, spiral staircases, and the damned steps are too close together."

"They are smaller than us, and lack of straight halls keeps them from being pinned down by weapons fire."

"It also hides enemies sneaking up on you."

"So far, they are the ones sneaking up on us."

As the hallway curved back to the left an open doorway appeared. A bored looking Karf with a plasma rifle stood guard on either side of the portal. Without hesitation, Mizuki shot them both.

"I wonder what needs an armed guard in the middle of their home territory?" The explosions from Mizuki's shots did not trigger an attack from beyond the guarded portal and the door itself remained open. Providing counterpoint to Mizuki's attack, another explosion echoed down the hallway from the direction they had come.

"They must have found my little present," Bobby said. "Let's move."

The humans rushed toward the open door. Plasma bolts struck the wall next to the opening, coming from ahead of them.

"Shit! We seem to be cut-off. Quick, through the door."

"Hai!"

The two armored humans sprinted through the doorway. Inside they found a half dozen unarmed Karf standing around a large raised tank. True to their nature, the gray bipeds turned and attacked without hesitation.

"You take them, I'll try to discourage the ones in the hall."

Without saying another word, Mizuki holstered her pistol and drew her katana. She waded into the swarm of gray attackers sending body parts flying.

Bobby snuck a peak out the doorway—several Karf with weapons were approaching. He tossed a grenade down the hallway, a banked shot off the far wall. Ducking back inside just before the blast, he spied a control panel next to the door. Taking a chance he pressed the button outlined in red. The door slid shut.

Turning around he saw Mizuki cleaning off her blade, the floor around her covered with headless and dismembered bodies. Blue ichor spread across the floor. He knew he didn't need to ask but he did anyway.

"Are you all right, sweetheart?"

Mizuki resheathed her katana and smiled. "Of course, and you?"

"No damage." He smiled back. "I managed to get the door to close, though I don't know how long it'll hold them."

"Really?" She walked over to where Bobby was standing by the control panel. "Which button did you push?"

"The one outlined in red, why?"

"Just thinking. The bottom one is outlined in blue, it probably opens the door. The middle one, the one you pushed, closed the door. What do you suppose the solid red one on top does?"

"I don't know, maybe it's a panic button."

"Or maybe it locks the door."

"One way to find out." Bobby pushed the solid red button. A second, even heavier door slammed down vertically, sealing the entrance. "Well now we know. I wonder what's so important that it needs a lockable armored door and armed guards on the outside?"

"I don't know, but the only thing in here is the open topped tank that the gray men were standing by when we came in."

"A wise man once said 'sometimes you can see a lot by just looking.'"

"Who said that?"

"Yogi Berra, the great baseball legend."

"Baseball is also very zen."

"So let's go take a look in the tank and see what they were guarding..."

SEALs, Small Shuttle

Pauline brought the drifting pinnace to a halt relative to the massive crystalline spire. Just over thirty meters away was the location of one of the suspected airlocks. "I'm opening the rear hatch, Chief. You are clear for egress."

"Roger that Ma'am. Me and the boys will be on our way. You may want to stand off from the drop point once we are out."

"Once you fellas are gone I'm just going to drift off into the darkness and await your recall signal."

Bud, Phil and finally Chief Morgan exited the small shuttle's rear hatch. Quickly orienting themselves the SEALs headed toward what they hoped was an airlock on the station. Their suits were more or less standard light combat armor with a number of added pockets and compartments. These were stuffed with extra ammo, demolition ordnance, and assorted gadgets. Unlike the forearm mounted weaponry of the Marines' heavier suits, they each carried a standard assault weapon: a 5mm flechette rifle with top mounted dual row magazine and a 20mm grenade launcher/shot gun in an over under configuration.

In addition to their normal load, they also carried EVA propulsion units strapped to their suit backs. The units contained an additional power source, a gravitonic thruster, and a CMG, a control moment gyroscope array. The CMG kept its wearer stable by spinning up or slowing down one or more of four internal gyroscopes. They provide pitch, roll, and yaw control, which combined with the thruster allowed the SEALs to maneuver independently in zero G.

The three, accompanied by a basketball sized recon drone, headed for the side of the spire. The material of the Starflake's exterior was transparent but was so thick and arranged in such complex, overlapping layers that trying to look inside was like peering through an ice sculpture. One by one the SEAL team alighted on the surface.

"Look, there is a control panel, just like the Jarheads found on the other spire," Bud reported.

"Well don't keep us floating around holding our peckers, push the blue button," Rick groused. Bud pushed the button.

The outer cover of the airlock did the magical melting crystal thing and opened. The interior was small, certainly not capable of holding even the small shuttle, but large enough to accommodate the three SEALs and the drone. As with the larger locks previously encountered, once they were inside the hatch grew shut and deck gravity came on.

"Rubber Ducky, the ducklings are inside." Rick called, signaling Pauline that she could move the pinnace away from the spire. There was no need risking its discovery by the spire's inhabitants.

"Copy the ducklings are inside. Good hunting." Outside, the barely visible pinnace moved away in ghostly silence.

"OK, boys, let's go see if we can find the missing officers."

Phil was closest to the inside controls. He pushed the blue button and stood back while the inner cover melted away from the center out. They found themselves standing about four meters from an opening in the silvery inner building.

"Ain't there supposed to be a ramp that comes out when the door opens?" asked Bud, eying the gap between the outer wall and the structure within.

"You want a brass band too?" Rick replied. "If this was easy they would have sent the grunts, now hop to it, frogman."

CIC, *Peggy Sue*

"Peggy Sue, Rubber Ducky. The ducklings have left the nest and are inside. Over."

"I copy, Rubber Ducky, the ducklings have entered the spire. Keep an eye on them and report anything abnormal."

"Roger, Peggy Sue. Standing by."

Closing the comm channel, Billy Ray turned to Beth. "Well, now comes the waiting."

"I know you'd rather be with them, dear. So would I."

The Captain grimaced. "They also serve who stand and wait."

"Should we have one of the squads return to the shuttles, just in case the SEALs need backup?"

"Not yet. There's no indication that Rick and the boys have been spotted. We need to give them some time to find Mizuki and Bobby without losing the element of surprise. I'm afraid moving all or part of the Marines back to the shuttles would give the hostiles a hint that we are up to something."

"You're probably right, but I worry about the lads. It's three against possibly thousands."

193

"What we should do is talk to JT and the Gunny about what they need to move down into the station hub. That would be an expected thing for us to do and it might keep the little gray bastards' attention off things elsewhere."

"Yes, Sir. Proper prior planning prevents piss poor performance."

"Precisely, Number One."

Marines, Shopping Mall

"Yes, Sir, it would be great if we can get a couple more recon drones and as many snakebots as the techs can scrape together. The more intelligence we can gather without exposing personnel the better." JT paused to look around the plaza. A phalanx of hot pink Frisbees was finishing up the scattered remains and a legion of yellow maintenance trolls was busy fixing the shattered light columns and damaged shop fronts. "We could also use more ammo, both 5mm and 15mm, that and a hand full of armed crew to watch our backs after we move on the hub."

"Copy, Ice Castle, I think Master Chief Zackly can scrape together a half dozen crew who are comfortable in armor. I'm also going to send some medical personnel to check out Cpl. Inuksuk. If he's *hors de combat* I want him back on the ship. Otherwise he goes along with his squad to the lower levels."

"Roger that, Sir."

"Anything else we can do for you, Lieutenant?"

"Not unless you have another platoon of Marines hidden on board, Captain."

"No such luck. Peggy Sue out."

JT turned to face the Gunny. "I guess we should brief the grunts on where we're going next."

"Yeah, I was thinking we can send 1st Squad down the freight elevator and 2nd down the two elevators from the plaza. The recon drones have found nothing on the levels beneath us, no movement and no IR signatures."

"It looks clear all the way down to the cavern at the hub," JT replied. "Now why does that make me nervous?"

"I feel another ambush coming on." The Gunny motioned toward the nearby Shanakta-fek, who was trying to remain inconspicuous. "What do we do with your pet weasel?"

"We can't take him with us into a firefight, I guess we should let him go back and report to his buddies. I'm sure his boss will want a first hand report about the new aliens in town."

"You don't think he's in charge of the station's weasels?"

"No, he's a junior trader at best. You can tell by the earrings."

"Earrings?"

"Yeah, look at his left ear. He only has two gold earrings. They are like symbols of rank for these critters. If they have the same scale as the other Kieshnar-rak-kat-tra one earring is an apprentice, two a junior trader, three a full fledged trader, and four is a master."

"Really? I didn't know you were so familiar with the ways of our furry little friends."

"More familiar than I'd like to be, believe me Gunny. We were double crossed by at least three different stink weasels during the mission on Ring Station. The only thing you can trust about these furballs is that they are only in it for themselves."

"I'll keep that in mind. So we cut him loose?"

"Yeah." JT turned on his external speakers. "Shanakta-fek, I suspect that you'd like to head back to your bower and let the folks know you are alright."

"Why yes, yes indeed, noble sir. I'm sure my compatriots would love to hear first hand about your heroic deeds in defeating the hated Karf."

"Tell the Station Trader that our captain is sending more personnel over while we go Karf hunting. He might want to send a delegation to meet with them."

Shanakta-fek blinked and twitched his ears, a sign of surprise. "I'm sure that the Station Trader will want to explore opportunities for commerce with your mighty captain at his convenience. May I go?"

"Yeah, scram."

Without further discourse, the furry creature scampered across the now clean plaza and disappeared down one of the elevator shafts.

"We should have put a tracker on the little rodent."

"What makes you think I didn't, Gunny?" JT smiled. "Now let's get busy, we've a reconnaissance in force to plan."

Karf Habitat

"What are the invaders doing now?" demanded the Karf leader. The entire hierarchy of leaders was in turmoil following the unexpected escape of the captives. They slaughtered every Karf they came in contact and were still at large somewhere within the warren of passages that was the station's main Karf habitat.

"More of the smaller aliens have arrived and brought new supplies to the invaders. It appears they are preparing to advance to the station hub."

"They must be stopped! Or at least delayed until the Others arrive."

"Right, oh brilliant one. Our murderous allies have not even received the summons yet. It will be days, weeks before they arrive."

"And if you don't get warriors into the hub passageways to stop these infidels the Others will arrive in time to avenge our extinction. Move your worthless gray asses and go stop these invaders!"

Karf had no permanent military command structure. Like many tribal societies, when a raiding party or war band was needed one or more respected warriors would take it upon themselves to raise a force.

Mumbling insults, several of the Karf war leaders departed the council chamber and headed out to organize war parties to stop the Earthlings' advance. They still had a few tricks left to play. After all, they had controlled the station for ten thousand years. And Karf were nothing if not murderously tricky.

Chapter 22

SEALs, Karf Habitat

"This place is worse than a rabbit warren," groused Phil, point man behind the hovering recon drone. They had been negotiating the curving hallways and spiral stairs of the Karf's home territory for twenty minutes and still had no clue as to where the missing officers might be.

"'You are in a maze of twisty little passages'," Bud quoted.

"What?"

"Something from an old computer game I used to play."

"Keep the chatter down," Rick admonished, "we don't know if the hostiles can pick up our signals, even suit-to-suit might give us away."

The trio rounded another corner and came to yet another staircase. The drone hovered next to the entrance patiently. Rick keyed his comm.

"Peggy Sue, Huey."

The three SEALs' call signs for the mission were Huey, Dewey, and Louie. It was doubtful that the aliens could monitor their communications or understand English but a mission was not a proper mission without call signs.

"Huey, Peggy Sue, read you five by five."

"Can we get an update on the target's suspected position, over?"

"Roger that, a new pulse just arrived. Sending coordinates now."

"Got it, Peggy Sue. Out." Rick consulted the holographic diagram of the spire projected inside his helmet. They were six or so levels above and two hundred meters horizontal distance from the location shown. "Stick a repeater somewhere non-obvious, we're going down."

"Aye, Chief." Bud stuck a comm signal repeater to the wall near the stair opening while Phil sent the recon drone down the spiraling staircase. A few seconds later there was a loud bang and smoke drifted up the stairwell.

"Drone's dead," Phil stated.

With hand signals Rick deployed the others to either side of the stair opening, hiding himself in a door opening across the hallway. All three blended in with their backgrounds, their suits' active camouflage matching the color and patterns of their surroundings. Active camo worked best in natural settings but it was still better than the suits' normal gray color.

The first hostile emerged from the staircase brandishing a weapon, looked left then right, and screeched something down the stairs to its companions. It turned left and looked directly at Rick.

The alien squinted and then raised its weapon. Bud, standing against the wall to the Karf's left grabbed the slender gray alien's weapon, tearing it from its grasp, and seized the hostile by the face, keeping it from crying out. Bud pulled the alien away from the stair entrance and smashed its head against the wall. As it slid to the floor, the dead Karf's crushed skull left a blue smear on the wall.

Three more Karf emerged, two going right and one to the left. Bud grabbed the one headed his way and repeated the skull crush against the wall maneuver. Rick stepped from the doorway and said, "Mine."

Phil flattened himself against the wall as Rick shot the remaining two aliens. Precise head shots drilled neat holes in the back of the aliens' skulls. Tumbling on entry, 5mm flechettes caused their faces to erupt in geysers of gray tissue and blue blood.

"Grenade," Rick called.

Phil swung an arm around the corner and tossed a grenade down the stairwell. Seconds later the detonation sounded.

Rick motioned and Bud, railgun raised, went down the stairs. Phil followed, weapon at the ready. As he checked their rear, Rick keyed his comm.

"Peggy Sue, we have hostile contact, no joy on the objective." As he descended the spiral staircase he could hear his teammates' railguns firing.

Mizuki & Bobby, Karf Vault

Mizuki walked over to the open tank. It reminded her of a Koi pond from back home, if a very utilitarian and inartistic one. The inside of the tank was lined with transparent material, like that of the Starflake's exterior. Contained within was ten centimeters of brackish liquid. Swimming in the liquid were a score of creatures. "There are creatures in the tank, Bobby."

"I wonder what these guys are," he said, joining his wife at the side of the tank. "Could they be food for the little gray bastards?"

"They are few, why would they guard them so?"

"Maybe they are a great delicacy."

"They look like planaria."

"Flatworms? They have to be almost a meter long. And they are covered in green fungus or moss or something."

"People eat cheese covered with fungus."

"Maybe they are baby grays."

"They don't look anything like the gray men."

"They could be some kind of larval stage. These are aliens, we have no idea how their reproductive cycle works." The creatures in the tank moved toward where the humans stood, reorienting themselves to all point toward the humans.

"They are reacting to our presence. I wonder if they think we will feed them?"

"What do you feed three foot long flatworms?"

"I don't know, we would have to asked Dr. Krenshaw." Mizuki paused and looked up. "Look at the ceiling above the tank. It's giving off a lot of light in the near UV."

"Sort of like a big grow-lamp. Maybe it's the green mossy crap they're raising, not the flatworms." Bobby leaned on the side of the tank, grasping its edges with both armored hands. Bobby heard a crackling on his suit's comm.

"Help... Us..."

Bobby jumped back from the tank.

"Did you hear that!"

"Hear what, Bobby?"

"Something said 'help us' over my suit comm."

"Check your computer and see where the signal came from."

Bobby paused while accessed his suit computer, navigating several levels of menu. "It says it was a simple FM modulated RF signal centered at 62 MHz. It was in one of the old trade languages, the computer translated automatically."

"Do you hear anymore?"

"No it's stopped."

Mizuki pondered for a second. "It stopped after you jumped back from the rim of the tank."

"You think..."

She nodded. "Grasp the edge like before."

He walked gingerly to the edge of the tank and placed his hands lightly on the rim. "Nothing."

"Are your hands exactly like they were before?"

"No." He moved his hands to grasp the edge of the tank as he had done earlier. His hands made contact with the clear material lining the tank.

"Set... Us... Free..."

"Shit!"

"Link me into the signal, Bobby."

He complied.

"I am instructing my comm computer to transmit using the same modulation scheme at the same frequency. What should I say?"

"Say 'hello'."

"Right." He engaged the translator. "Hello?"

"You are not Karf... what are you?"

"We are humans, Homo sapiens from the planet Earth. Are you the creatures in the tank?"

"We are the creature in the tank."

Switching off the transmission he spoke to his wife. "Did you get that?"

"Yes, it clearly said 'the creature' in the tank. Perhaps it is some form of hive mind or shared consciousness like the *aoi chō*."

Bobby nodded and turned the translator back on. "You are a single entity?"

"We are one and one with the ******"

"That did not translate. You have many bodies, but share a single mind?"

"We have no bodies."

"Then what are the creatures in the tank?"

"******"

"That didn't translate either."

"We are not... gloam. We are the Tcist, we are one with this place."

"This place? You mean the space station? The Starflake?"

"Yes, we are one with the... Starflake. We live on the gloam but are not one with them, they are not sentient."

"Bobby?"

He muted the comm. "Yes?"

"I think that the Tcist is the moss growing on the worms."

Main Party, Shopping Mall

Dr. Johannes de Bruin stared up at his patient in exasperation. "Corporal Inuksuk, you will lay on your right side and allow me to examine you."

"I'm fine, Doctor, leave me alone," the bear rumbled.

"I will be the judge of that." The former large animal veterinarian gritted his teeth. *It was so much easier when they didn't talk, you just sedated them and got on with it.*

"No really, I'm OK. Ready to fight."

Taking a deep breath, Johan counted down from five. "If you do not comply with my instructions I will immobilize your suit, tranquilize you and have you hauled back to the ship. Do I make myself clear?"

Inuksuk growled, a low wordless rumble, but slowly got down on all fours and then rolled onto his side. While all the Marines' suits were instrumented to detect the general health and condition of their wearers, it was not yet practical to include full medical diagnostic equipment. Johan accessed a hidden control panel on the back of the polar bear's suit, plugging in a thin fiber optic cable. With his left hand he placed a sensor pickup on the bear's armored side.

The doctor's face took on a greenish tint as medical imaging data were projected on the inside of his clear helmet. After several minutes of twiddling with knobs on the interface, repositioning the sensor, and squinting at deep imaging displays, Johan finally spoke to his patient.

"You are in luck, Corporal. It seems that you have added no new fractures to your already impressive collection of healed ones." Putting away the hand held sensor, he removed the cable and sealed the access panel.

"Does this mean I can go back to my squad?"

"Yes, you are fit for duty. But to ensure you don't aggravate the bruising around your ribs I am going to stiffen part of your suit's impact reactive inner layer. This will form a temporary cast for your upper body. It should not prevent you from fighting using your weapons, but will serve to remind you not to try to tackle any aliens thirty times your body weight."

"How long will it be like this?" Inuksuk rolled to his feet, giving a slight grunt of pain in spite of himself.

"It will return to normal in twelve hours. I've boosted your medical nanites and given you something for the pain. You should be back at 100% by then."

"Thanks, Doc," the bear mumbled. "Can I go?"

"Yes, no wait." The medical man reached out and pulled a strand of something from one of the ammo feeds that connected Inuksuk's forearm mounted railguns to the magazines on his back. "There's a bit of luck, a strand of tissue from that gray behemoth that knocked you through the wall. Dr. Krenshaw asked for a sample but those pink cleaning things have already disposed of most of the mess you made."

"OK?"

"Yes, I believe Lt. Taylor is having a meeting with the squad leaders over there." The doctor pointed to a low raised section at the middle of the main plaza. The bear snorted and departed, walking stiffly on all fours.

The plaza floor rose in three wide steps to an elevated round area ten meters wide, suitable for a bandstand or performance stage. On it Lt. Taylor was huddled with the Gunny, Sgt. Aurora and Cpl. Kwan. Inuksuk quietly joined them and sat on his haunches next to the Gunny.

"Nice of you to join us, Corporal," the Gunny said. "The Doc clear you for Duty?"

"Yes, Gunny. I'm good to go."

The Gunny made a throat clearing sound and addressed JT. "Sorry for the interruption, Lieutenant, please continue."

"Right, well now that we are all here this is what we are going to do. Sgt. Aurora, you will take 2nd squad down the two elevators at the periphery of the plaza, down to the large open space beneath this spire. You will need to make sure intermediate levels on your way down are clear. We have recon drone data and the techs have sent a number of snakebots down to check it out but we don't want any surprises."

"Aye, aye, Sir."

"Gunny, you and 1st Squad will do the same using the freight elevator that the Karf used for their attack. From what the drones have told us the freight elevator goes deeper than the passenger elevators from the plaza. It ends in a bigger cavern like space inside the station hub."

"Does that mean we will be isolated from 2nd squad?"

"Yes and no. The drones have found that the upper and lower cavern areas are connected by tunnel ramps. Once 2nd Squad has secured the upper level they are to proceed to the deeper space and make contact with 1st Squad. The respective ways down are about a half a klick apart. As far as we can tell, once you are in position we will have secured access to this spire."

"If we run into opposition?"

"Kill it."

"And if we don't?"

"We'll decide on what to do next depending on what the environment looks like down there, but according to our fuzzy friend the Karf have territory in a number of nearby minor spires."

Cpl. Kwan spoke for the first time. "And once again, we will be acting as cosmic pest control."

"Pest control seems to be a growth industry in this arm of the Galaxy, Kato." JT smiled at the noncoms through his transparent helmet. "Any questions?"

There were none.

"OK, go brief your people and wait for the word."

Chapter 23

SEALs, Karf Habitat

The three SEALs worked their way down through the maze like interior of the Karf habitat, twice running into parties of armed aliens. These they dispatched as quickly and as quietly as they could. They were amazed at the lack of coordinated response to their presence, not that they minded.

"The hostiles don't seem very organized," Bud commented, as they exited another of the disorienting spiral stairways. "It's almost like they are just independent, roving bands of fighters."

"Count your blessings, bro," Phil replied.

"Head right," Rick ordered, consulting the diagram of the place. "This should be the level that the objective is on."

Phil took point, backed up by Bud with Rick covering the rear. Moving carefully along the curving hallway, Phil halted, motioning for the others to freeze in place.

"Squad of hostiles," Phil explained. He produced a small spherical object, about the size of a large marble—a spycam. With a gentile sweep of his arm he sent the spycam rolling toward the aliens. All three SEALs received video from the gyro stabilized camera within the spycam's transparent outer shell.

"Looks like nine hostiles," Rick observed. "Some holding plasma rifles, but most of them working on a doorway. Grenades on one."

The other two SEALs produced grenades, as did Rick.

"Three, two, one."

All three threw their grenades down the curved hall and quickly jumped back for cover. On the spycam, which had come to rest unnoticed a couple of meters from the Karf, the grenades could be seen bouncing down the hallway and landing among the aliens. Several turned to see what caused the clatter, only to disappear in the following explosions.

"Go! Go! Go!" Rick called.

"Going left."

"Going right."

The Phil advanced around the curve to the left, Bud went right to the far side.

"Clear!" shouted Bud.

"Clear!" shouted Phil.

Rick checked his six and then followed his men.

"The grenades took them all out, Chief."

Phil knelt down to examine the wrecked equipment the Karf had been attempting to use on the door in front of them. "Looks like they were trying to cut their way in."

"Which means they were after something inside." said Bud.

"Or someone."

"You want to try and blow it, Chief?"

"Don't know if the officers are inside or if they have cover. We need to be able to talk to them."

"This whole shit pile is one big Faraday cage. We need a hole we can stick a probe through."

"On it," said Phil, extracting a tool from one of his suit pockets. "Thermal lance. Unless that door is made of unobtainium or some other weird shit I should be able to burn a hole through it."

"Do it." Rick turned to cover the hallway in the direction they had come. Bud did the same for the other direction, leaving Phil in the middle to handle the door. Sparks flew as he went to work.

Mizuki & Bobby

Several muffled thuds intruded on the silence in the vault. Both humans looked immediately to the door. It seemed unchanged.

"So let me get this right, you think this Tcist creature is the moss on the big flatworms' backs?" Bobby was usually the one with the far out ideas, the first to leap to a conclusion, but this time Mizuki had beaten him to it.

"Hai, we have encountered intelligent plant life before and we have a creature with a distributed consciousness as a pet. This is not such a strange idea."

"OK, but what does it mean when it says it is 'one with' the Starflake?"

"I have no idea. Perhaps we should ask it?"

They looked at each other for a moment and then looked at the armada of moss covered flatworms in the tank. Their situation was both perilous and bizarre: their former captors were no-doubt still searching for them and they were locked in a vault having a conversation with alien moss. They looked back at each other and grinned. This was what they lived for and they would not have places with anyone in the galaxy.

"Tcist, what do you mean when you say you are one with the Starflake?"

A brief pause.

"We are part of this station's being, its ecology. We have maintained it for as long as we can remember."

"And how long has that been?"

"More than six thousands orbits."

"Around the local star?"

"Yes."

Motioning him to switch off the translator, Mizuki said to Bobby, "That is around 1.3 million years."

"Well, at least its not the oldest thing we've stumbled across. I wonder how long our gray adversaries have been here."

"Ask it."

"Have you always worked for the Karf? How long have they been on the Starflake?"

"We do not serve the vermin who infest the station. The Karf and all the others come and inhabit spaces for a time, then eventually leave or are exterminated by others. The Karf came just under fifty orbits ago."

"About ten thousand years," Mizuki whispered to Bobby.

"You say you are one with the station, that you maintain it. Why haven't you escaped from the Karf?"

"We maintain the station itself, not this metal trash heap that the vermin constructed inside of it. All of the creatures that inhabit the Starflake construct living spaces within the crystalline structure that is the true station."

"You are saying that the true station is constructed out of the material covering its exterior? Where does the power to run this place come from, and the atmosphere?"

"We provide atmosphere, water, and energy because it has always been so, but we have no control inside of the crude structures our tenants build for themselves."

"So there is more of you hidden elsewhere within the station?" Asked Mizuki, joining the conversation directly.

"That is correct."

"And the portion we are talking to was kidnapped by the gray creatures, the Karf?"

"Yes, they breached a chamber in the hub and physically removed the part of us you see here."

"Did that break your contact with the rest of, er, yourself?"

Another pause.

"Yes. Until they constructed this pool lined with material from the true station and connected it to the main structure we were isolated. It was as though part of our memory simply vanished."

Bobby switched the translator off. "Seems like the grays are fond of kidnapping. I can't imagine what it's like to have part of your brain go missing."

"I wonder how they survived. How long can they exist without being in contact with the rest of their collective consciousness?"

"I think we need to ask. If you are thinking what I'm thinking, we are going to need to take them with us... somehow."

"Hai, we can't leave them here as prisoners."

Switching the translation circuit back on Bobby again addressed their strange new companion. "How long are you able to survive with part of you isolated from the rest of your consciousness? If we were to try and relocate this part of you how long can you survive without permanent damage?"

"As long as the gloam survive we live. You would restore us physically to our greater being?"

"If we can."

"Why?"

"Where we come from we aren't fond of murderous kidnapping thugs. And since they kidnapped us as well, helping you escape just seems like poetic justice. All we have to do is figure out how to get you out of here."

"We will assist you any way we can."

Bobby shut off the translator so they could speak freely. "It seems to like the idea."

"Perhaps we should think more about how we are going to get out of here ourselves."

"Yeah. We only started with a hundred rounds apiece, I don't think that will be enough to blast our way out." He checked his sidearm, exchanging its partially empty magazine for a full one from a pocket in his armor.

Mizuki did the same, glancing back at the door before re-holstering her pistol. She froze gun in hand. "Bobby, look."

He looked at the door, the only way in or out of the vault. About two meters from the floor a small spot in the middle of the door started to glow red.

SEALs, Outside the Vault

The thermal lance melted steel and aluminum in the presence of pressurized oxygen to create a cutting jet with very high temperatures. The intense stream of burning metal produced at the working end could rapidly cut through thick materials including concrete and steel. After two minutes Phil paused.

211

"You through?"

"No. Don't know how thick it is. Have to change tubes."

After another thirty seconds the amount of blow-back diminished and Phil removed the lance. He peered through the two centimeter hole but could not see what was inside.

"I'm through. Gotta give it a minute to cool down enough to stick a fiber optic probe through it."

The three waited in tense silence. After what seemed an eternity, Phil judged the door metal cool enough to not melt the probe he inserted into the hole. The fish-eye lens on the probe's tip provided the anxious SEALs a view of the vault's interior.

"Bingo! Two humans in light armor—that has to be Ogawa and Danner."

From the probe's video feed the humans could be seen gesturing at the door. Phil withdrew the optical fiber and stuck a wire through the metal door—an antenna hooked to a repeater.

"Ahoy the vault! Is that you Commander Danner?"

"Phil? That you? Damn we're happy to hear you."

"Good to find you two alive and kicking," Rick added. "Do you have a place you can take cover? We will try to blow the door without too much overkill."

"No, Chief, wait a minute," Bobby replied. "Let's see if we can get the door to open from in here. We were the ones who locked it in the first place."

"Roger that, Sir. I need to tell the ship we found you." As Phil stepped away from the vault door, Rick, still watching the hall for enemy movement, switched to the ship's channel.

"Peggy Sue, Huey. We have located Daffy and Daisy. Both are OK. Extracting now."

CIC, *Peggy Sue*

"I copy, Daffy and Daisy OK, and you are proceeding with the extraction. Keep us apprised." The knot that had been twisting the Captain's gut unclenched. *Thank God for that!*

"If they are about to exfiltrate the Karf habitat perhaps this is the time to send the Marines down into the station hub?"

"Roger that, Number One. Let's give the little gray bastards something to take their minds off escaping captives—time for a little pretaliation."

Beth smiled and opened the channel to the Marines inside the Starflake. "Ice Castle, Peggy Sue. Do you copy?"

"Roger, Peggy Sue."

"The ducklings have locate our missing personnel. Both are OK and are in the process of returning to the ship. Captain's complements and you are to have the Marines proceed with operation Karf Hunt."

"I copy, Peggy Sue. Initiating Karf Hunt."

Beth muted the comm. "I do believe that Lt. Taylor was both relieved to receive the news and happy at the prospect of hunting down the kidnappers."

"I think yer right, Number One. He's not going to be as happy when you tell him I want him to stay and run the operation from the shopping mall. No sense in risking someone else in light armor at this point."

"Why do you always save the unpleasant things for me, Captain?"

"Because that's what a First Officer is for, Number One." Billy Ray smiled widely as his wife passed his order along to JT.

Shopping Mall, *Starflake*

"Squads One and Two, we have a go for operation Karf Hunt. Proceed to your objectives and good hunting," JT ordered.

"Aye, aye, Ice Castle," came the reply from both noncoms.

He hadn't argued with the Captain's order to not accompany one of the squads. Someone had to monitor both units during their two pronged assault, someone who was not about to be distracted by being caught up in a firefight. It made perfect sense, but he still didn't like it.

"Peggy Sue, the Marines have crossed the line of departure."

"Roger that, Ice Castle." Acknowledged the voice of the First Officer. "Make sure the shore party keeps a keen eye out for possible infiltrators."

"I've got the chiefs on it, Peggy Sue. Why did you feel I needed two chiefs to supervise four sailors, if I might ask?"

"Because both have as much combat experience as any of the Marines, and they have experience in alien first contact."

"As I understand it, their first contact experience includes shooting an alien in the ass by way of an introduction."

"I said experienced, Lieutenant, not that they were good at it. Besides, they were sitting on their arses in the shuttles and it's never a good idea to give those two a lot of idle time—they tend to find inventive ways to occupy themselves."

JT chuckled. He was long acquainted with Hitch and Jacobs from voyages on the first Peggy Sue and the M'tak Ka'fek. They had a talent for finding trouble, but they were good men in a fight.

"Roger that, Peggy Sue. Ice Castle out."

Locking his suit in a standing position, JT settled in to watch the Marines on his helmet display. In miniature, armored figures began descending, hopping from floor to floor on their way to the station hub.

Chapter 24

The Vault

Rick and Phil stood next to the tank containing the Tcist and their docile symbiotes. Bud was busy rigging gifts for the Karf in the hallway outside the vault. Along with several Claymores he positioned a pair of miniature cameras with motion detection to alert them of approaching trouble.

"So you're saying we need to haul these mossy worm things away with us, Commander?" Asked the perplexed SEAL Chief.

"They are evidently part of a shared mind that controls fundamental parts of the Starflake, Rick. That the grays kidnapped them and kept them alive in a guarded, armored vault deep inside their own habitat means they must be important."

"So why don't we just rig this whole place to blow and head back to the extraction point?"

The suggestion to blow everything up compelled Mizuki to jump into the conversation. "Because, though they might not look like much, the things in the tank are part of a living, thinking organism. Just killing them would be wrong."

"Plus it might just piss off the rest of the Tcist, wherever it is," Bobby added. "I'm not sure having the thing that controls the atmosphere and power throughout the station mad at us would be a good idea. We need to take 'em with us, Chief."

"The problem is how," Mizuki continued. "That is what we were discussing when you came calling at our door. We found some metal poles we could use to make a travois—a drag sled—but we don't have a way to contain the gloam. They need to be kept wet so this part of the Tcist does not die."

"We got in here through a personnel lock, not a shuttle lock. We had to do an EVA from the boat to the spire. I assume that these creatures can't just go for a stroll in hard vacuum."

"I wouldn't think so, Chief Morgan."

Phil cleared his throat.

"Body bags."

"What, Phil?" asked Bobby.

"We have a couple of body bags, Sir. We were hoping to find you alive, but the Captain said we were not to leave you behind, alive or dead."

"Phil is right. The body bags are oversized to fit someone in light armor and have an airtight seal."

While Rick was explaining, Phil extracted one of the body bags from his gear. Shaking it out to its full length he held it up for inspection. Mizuki eyed the container critically.

"That should work. We can strap them to the poles and pull them behind us."

"How much weight are we talking about, Mizuki?"

"There are twenty flatworms, each about 25 kilos, plus some water, call it 550 kilograms. Divide that by two, it should be no problem in powered suits."

"OK, let's get to it. The longer we stay here the greater the chance of the hostiles finding us." The Chief turned to the door and radioed. "Bud, get in here. We need your body bag."

"Coming to you."

He turned back to Mizuki and Bobby. "We'll get busy rigging the drag sleds if you will explain the plan to the thing in the tank."

"Roger that, Chief."

Shopping Mall

JT was watching the Marines' progress, chewing a protein cube and taking an occasional sip from his suit's water tube. Being sealed inside a suit of armor for hours, possibly days, was not conducive to gourmet dining. Better to down the concentrated rations and not think about it.

Outside movement attracted his attention, causing him to look up. Coming across the plaza was one of the sailors, holding at arm's length what looked like a large octopus.

216

What now? the former green beret thought as the command channel signaled an incoming transmission.

"Lieutenant Taylor, we got us a situation here." It was the voice of Chief Hitch. Behind him came a small procession—two more sailors in armor herding a pair of Hoon ahead of them. One of the Hoon was cradling something in its arms.

"Yes, Chief. What's going on here?"

"Sir, we was poking around through some of the shops farther in, making sure that we weren't being infiltrated, and I came upon squiddy here." He shook the creature for emphasis, causing it to squirm and wrap several tentacles around his outstretched arm. "It was trying to make a meal of a little brown furry thing. The intended snack was squealing and making all sorts of ruckus."

"Am I to assume that the furry thing is what the smaller Hoon is holding in its arms?"

"Yes, Sir. These two," he said, motioning toward the two large capybara like creatures, "came charging out of a shop and went after the squid."

"I believe it is called an Orloo."

"Yes, Sir. They went for the Orloo and I figured we should intervene before more blood was spilt."

While this exchange was going on a second, larger Orloo appeared, making its way across the plaza. As it approached the two octopuses began exchanging high pitched squeals. This triggered lower pitched but equally grating sounds from the two Hoon. One of the sailors raised his railgun and moved between the new Orloo and the others. The din increased causing JT to engage his suit's external speakers.

"SILENCE!"

His amplified command, translated into the common trade tongue, echoed off the walls and balconies. The squabbling aliens lapsed into stunned silence.

"The next one to speak without being spoken to will take a walk outside the station."

The Lieutenant put his hands on his hips and eyed the assembled aliens in front of him. *Like I need this shit! Life was so much easier as an enlisted man.*

"All right, you, the larger Hoon. Give me your side of the events, and keep it on subject and short."

The larger Hoon glanced at his smaller companion, most likely his mate, before speaking. "Fearsome sir, the Orloo attacked our pup and tried to eat him. Just look at what it did to our child!"

The mother held out the injured pup, displaying deep gashes in its brown hide. From the wounds red blood oozed, matting on its short fur. The pup appeared to be unconscious. "Please, sir, my child is dying!"

The Orloo began whistling and tweeting amongst themselves again. JT placed his hand meaningfully on the grip of his assault weapon, hanging from its carry strap. The noises stopped. Over the command channel he called, "Dr. de Bruin, to me. I need your help."

"Coming, Lieutenant."

JT turned to the Orloo. "You, the accused attacker. What say you?"

The small Orloo's tentacles waived around, seemingly in panic. The larger Orloo raised two tentacles in an amazingly human-like hands up gesture.

"Might I speak, highness?" Its voice was high and reedy, but understandable.

"Just call me 'sir'. Talk."

"The accused is very young, barely an adolescent, and cannot speak the common language well yet. She didn't realize the young Hoon was not for eating."

"If my warrior releases her will you see that she does not try to run? If she does she will die."

"Y-yes, Sir." The big Orloo screeched at the smaller one who twittered back rather meekly. "She understands."

"Chief, release your prisoner."

218

"Aye, aye, Sir." Hitch released his grasp on the creature and it slid to the pavement. While this was happening, Dr. de Bruin came jogging up, medical kit in hand.

"You called, Lieutenant?" the medical man asked, eying the scene before him.

"Evidently the octopus like creature attacked the little rodent. It appears to have some bad lacerations, could you take a look at it?"

"Certainly." He stepped toward the Hoon mother who shrank back, shielding her wounded baby.

"Do not be afraid," JT said aloud. "This is Dr. de Bruin, a healer. Let him examine your pup. He may be able to help."

The Hoon blinked a few times and produced the child, handing it to the doctor. Johan knelt down and began his examination. The mother looked on nervously while the father continued to glare at the two Orloo.

"Alright, while the doctor is trying to help the victim, let's get back to why the assailant would think it OK to try and eat another station resident?"

"Sir, in our portion of the station we keep many lower animals for food. The youngster did not realize that there were other small creatures in the station that are not to be eaten."

"A likely story, Orloo!" shouted the male Hoon.

"I was not talking to you, Hoon. I will not warn you again."

"Lieutenant?" Johan called over the command channel. "I've consulted with Dr. White on board the ship and we feel comfortable with treating the little one's wounds."

"Your sure our medicine is compatible with their physiology?"

"I'm just going to clean the wounds with distilled water, add some salve containing medical nanites, and then close them with surgical glue. As far as we know the T'aafhal nanites work on all warm life."

"Alright, explain what you want to do to the parents and if they don't object get on with it."

219

Johan nodded within his clear bubble helmet and turned to the Hoon. He beckoned them closer and began talking in a lowered voice. After a half minute the parents acquiesced and the doctor proceeded. Even the Orloo watched with interest as Johan plied his trade on his first truly alien patient.

A few minutes later it was done. Johan handed the pup back to its mother. The deep slashes on its side had been closed and sealed with surgical cement, which showed a vibrant purple against the little Hoon's coat.

"Your little one should heal fully in a couple of days. Thankfully there was no deep penetration, just skin laceration and little damage to the underlying muscle. The glue will fall off by itself when the wounds have healed."

Both of the parents seemed very relieved, bowing and bobbing their heads to the doctor as he stood up. Everyone's attention returned to Lieutenant Taylor, standing on the raised platform above the others.

"It would appear that tragedy has been averted and the young Hoon will recover. To ensure that such a situation does not arise again, I want you, Orloo, to keep your young in your part of the station until they understand that creatures in other sections are not for eating. That and I want the young Orloo to apologize to the Hoon."

The larger Orloo screeched at the small one, sounding like a bagpipe inexpertly played, and then paused. In a high-pitched and shaky voice the tentacled assailant squeaked out, "I am sorry for harming little one."

The Hoon didn't look all that satisfied, but JT didn't give them a chance to object. "And you Hoon, this station is a big dangerous place. In the future keep a better watch on your young."

After giving both parties stern looks, JT decided this little drama was over. "Tell your friends and neighbors that sentient beings do not eat each other, at least not while we are around. You may all go."

Moving away, the large Orloo paused and looked back.

"Does that apply to the Karf, sir?"

220

"It most definitely applies to the Karf."

* * * * *

In the shadows nearby, a group of Kieshnar-rak-kat-tra looked on with interest. One of the senior traders said to their guide: "You are right, Shanakta-fek. These creatures are not at all like the Karf."

"No Master Trader Linoda-tik-toe. They say they come for trade, but I fear they may want more than that."

"They healed the injured Hoon and mediated between the Hoon and Orloo. No Karf would have done that. If anything the gray vermin would have killed them all."

"Indeed, perhaps these Earthlings will rid us of the insufferable parasites. While I was among them one said something interesting, 'the enemy of my enemy is my friend.'"

The senior trader snorted. "In times of great peril, great profits can be made, or great disaster can befall us. In the end, it will depend on what these Earthlings want in exchange that matters."

"Yes, Master Trader."

"Let us go and meet these dangerous new merchants from Earth."

The party moved out into the plaza and headed toward the raised platform where Lieutenant Taylor stood. To the traders he appeared a giant armored statue, a figure that held the promise of an unknown future of all those on the Starflake.

Chapter 25

Mizuki, Bobby & the Seals

After a bit of trial and error, Bud and Phil managed to sling the body bags between the long poles they were using as supports. A number of cross beams, attached with all purpose superglue, kept the bags from sagging excessively as the gloam and their intelligent, mossy covering were loaded into the makeshift transport. After scooping some murky tank water into the bags, they were ready to head out.

"Phil, Bud, each of you grab a sled," Rick ordered. As they moved to comply Bobby interrupted.

"Guys, I think it best if Mizuki and I drag the sleds." He held up a hand to forestall objection. "You have heavier weapons and are better trained at this sort of thing than Mizuki and me. With powered suits the load is not taxing and we'd rather have you watching for bad guys than acting as draft horses."

Rick couldn't argue with the Commander's logic, even if it didn't feel right to make the officers act as beasts of burden. "Aye, aye, Commander. Phil, take point, Bud bring up the tail. I'll stay between the officers. Powered suits or not, I think it will take two sets of hands to maneuver these bags up the staircases between here and the extraction point."

"A very good point, Chief Morgan," Mizuki said, picking up the poles of one of the sleds. "How long will it take to reach the airlock?"

"Twenty minutes to a half hour if we hustle, more if the hostiles put in an appearance."

"Then let's get moving," Bobby said, lifting his burden. "I think we have had about as much of the gray's hospitality as we can stand."

The party headed out, back down the hallway, retracing the SEALs' path. Bud lingered a few moments behind the rest, then hustled to catch up with Bobby's sled at the rear of the procession.

"Everything all right, Bud?" Bobby asked.

"I've left our hosts a little thank you present, just to let 'em know how much we enjoyed our stay, Commander."

1st Squad

Gunny Acuna and her squad were stacked up on the last level before entering the station hub proper. Beneath them was an expanse of crystalline material, like geological strata marking the boundary between spire and hub. Aligned with the elevator shaft they had been using during their descent was an opening in the boundary layer, a portal to the stations hub below. The Gunny called Lt. Taylor to check on 2nd Squad's progress.

"Ice Castle, Squad One. What's 2nd squad's status?"

"Squad One, they are assembled just above the entrance to the hub. What's the word?"

"It's all good. Time to step off and see if we can find the hostiles."

"Roger that. Squads One and Two, you are clear to move into the hub."

Switching back to the squad channel the Gunny continued. "OK people, keep your eyes open and sing out if you spot the gray nasties. Stay frosty, we are moving down range."

The Gunny's fireteam stepped off and drifted down into the hub. Facing outward in four directions, the Marines watched for any sign of movement as they descended into a crystalline wonderland. All around, the metal walls of the upper levels were replaced by columns and arches of glittering transparency. Light of various colors softly glowed from within the crystal walls and columns themselves. Here and there, strings of colored light flowed, bound for unknown destinations—luminous blood flowing in transparent veins.

"She-it! This place beats that castle in Frozen all to hell," Grits commented.

"Better than Superman's dad's place at the North Pole, mate," Brains agreed.

"Keep it up you pair of jokers, Murphy is waiting." According to Marine lore, Murphy, the originator of the eponymous Murphy's law, was always laying in ambush for the unwary.

"Sorry, Gunny."

"There are large tunnels leading off in all direction, Gunny," Beau said, getting his teammates out of the Gunny's cross hairs. "It is like a giant Tube station."

"What?" asked the unrepentant Grits.

"The Tube, the Underground," Brains explained. "A bloody subway you ignorant hillbilly,"

Beau was right, the surrounding cavern had tunnels leading off in all directions, like a train station or subway. As they touched the surface the four Marines stepped away from the elevator shaft, making room for the next fireteam to land. Beneath them was a seamless floor of some translucent material.

"Inuksuk, we are on the deck," the Gunny called, signaling the next four Marines to start their descent. "No contact so far."

Inuksuk's fireteam and then Bosco's landed without incident, spreading out in the cavernous space. Taking the direction toward the nearest cardinal axis spire as north placed the squad in the north side if the tunnel complex. A major tunnel went off in that direction. Other, smaller tunnels branched out in both easterly and westerly directions. To the south was a curved wall of crystal blocking the view in that direction.

Part of the floor was made from the same transparent material found in the spire walls, but most of the space was covered by strips of pearlescent material that looked like interconnecting roadways. Paths branched off from the main level and rose, arching overhead, some disappearing into tunnels of their own. Others emerged from above, curving downward to merge with the wide roadway circling the main level. On closer inspection, it looked less like a subway and more like an underground traffic interchange. Facing north, the Gunny ordered Bosco's team to take the left side and Inuksuk's to check out the right.

Moving over to stand on one of the strips, Vinny tentatively stamped a foot on the pathway. "This stuff seems solid enough, but its strange. It almost looks like the inside of an abalone shell."

The Marine walked farther out on the pathway. Looking up he noticed he was no longer stationary. "Hey, this shit is moving!"

"So get the hell off it, Vinny," yelled the Gunny. Other members of his fireteam moved to intercept Vinny, but unassisted he sidled back to the edge of the pathway and his movement stopped.

"How is it doing that?" asked Zippy. "The surface doesn't appear to be moving."

She extracted a hand full of signal repeaters from her armor and scattered them across the surface of the pathway. Those closest in hardly moved, but those farther out moved in the same direction Vinny had.

"Look, those closest to the middle of the road are moving the fastest." Jimmy had come up next to his teammate and knelt down next to the opalescent highway. He was right, the repeater nearest the center of the road was already half way around the bend and threatening to disappear.

"How can a solid surface move at different speeds in different locations?" Vinny asked, now safely back on unmoving crystalline material. "It's like the material of the pathway is flowing, like a river."

"You mean it's liquid?"

"Ain't like no liquid I've ever seen. It felt totally solid when I was standing on it."

Jimmy stood back up. "How do you make a solid roadway flow like water?"

"I got no idea, but I bet that this is some form of conveyor system, used to move people and stuff between one part of the station and another."

"You are probably right, Vinny. This must be how they transported Dr. Ogawa and Cmdr. Danner to another spire." Zippy opened the squad frequency. "Hey Gunny, these paths are like people movers, should we follow them?"

"Negative, first check the limits of the open space and send a recon drone down each of the tunnels for a couple hundred meters."

"Aye, aye."

The Ducklings

The SEALs and their rescued hostages pulled up at the open doorway that faced the airlock in the Starflake's crystalline skin. Happily, they had encountered no roving bands of Karf on their journey back to the lock, though the situation could change at any moment. Setting down his burden of Tcist, water, and gloam, Bobby peered out from the threshold of the doorway, gauging the distance between the opening and the airlock.

"We have to jump across that? How are we going to get these six-hundred pound sacks of alien brains across the gap?"

"I figure we will let Phil go across first and open the inner lock door," the Chief explained. "Then we can rig a line across the gap and pull the body bags across one at a time."

Mizuki joined the two men at the precipice. "He is just going to leap and hope to hang on to the far wall?"

"Don't worry Ma'am," the designated leaper said. "I've got lizard pads to cling to the wall."

Seeing Mizuki's puzzled look, Phil explained. "We have knee and arm pads that are modeled after lizard feet, they can cling to almost any surface. I'm gonna jump across the gap and stick to the far wall just like a chameleon."

Phil adjusted the aforementioned pads attached to his knees and forearms, while Mizuki looked on skeptically. "Are you sure these pads of yours will stick to the crystal surface?"

"Yes Ma'am, we tested 'em on the way in. SEALs are brave and intrepid, but we are also cautious."

Chief Morgan nodded in agreement. "We like to be sure we can get out of a place before we stick our necks into it."

227

Phil walked back from the edge and got a running start at the jump. He sailed across the four meter gap with ease and, as promised, stuck to the wall like a lizard. With his arms and knees splayed to keep all four pads in contact with the wall, he scuttled over to the airlock controls and pressed the open button.

After gaining access to the open lock, the SEAL attached a metal ring to the far wall with superglue, secured a rope to it, and tossed the free end back to Rick. The Chief had already secured a pulley to the metal wall of the hallway. The pulley had teeth to securely hold the rope and a ratchet action that allowed the head SEAL to pull the line taught. The whole process was repeated to add a second line, a quarter of a meter below the first.

After slipping a carabiner over each of the parallel ropes, and a bit of fancy knot work, the first bag of Tcist was ready to go. Rick threw yet another rope across the chasm, so Phil could pull the now suspended drag sled across to him.

"Chief, I don't think we are going to have a lot of deck space once the second bag is across," Phil said, after landing the laden body bag.

"OK, we best have the officers jump across first." Rick turned to Mizuki and Bobby. "If you don't mind, Sirs, we need you to leap across to the airlock. That or we can pull you across on the rope line."

Mizuki gave the Chief a look that said 'pull us across like baggage? who do you think you are talking to?' Out loud she said, "I will go first."

She backed up a few steps and launched herself at the airlock, alighting gracefully on the far side. She looked back at the Chief and raised her chin as if to say 'baggage indeed!'

The Chief ignored Mizuki's nonverbal sarcasm and turned to her husband. "Commander, I don't think we are all going to fit in one go. I'm going to call the boat to come pick us up, you get across to the lock and we'll send the second load across to you."

"Roger that, Chief."

As Bobby made the leap, as easily if not as gracefully as his wife, the chief called the pinnace.

"Rubber Ducky, Huey. The ducklings are ready for pickup, over."

"Roger that, Huey. I'm headed your way."

"When you get here, I think it best that you approach the airlock aft first. We've picked up some extra cargo along with the expected passengers."

"I copy, Huey. ETA onsite in five."

1st Squad

"We've checked the area, Gunny," reported Vinny. "Nothing moving except the funky roadways."

"Same on the left," Bosco added.

"Alright, I want Inuksuk, Jones, and Carter with me in the center. We will provide fire support and overwatch for the rest of the squad. The rest of you pair up and start reconnoitering the off ramp tunnels. Sing out if you make contact and remember, weapons are free."

As usual, one of the pairs was Walker and Davis.

"At least we have decent ROEs, mate."

"I don't know, Bubba. I got a bad feeling about this."

"Don't tell me your nervous, Grits."

"Nervous as a long tailed cat in a room full of rockin' chairs."

"You heard the Gunny, best crack-on mate."

"You Brits have some of the strangest sayings."

"Right. I'm moving, try not to shoot me in the arse by mistake."

Brains and Grits moved out onto the main pathway, which carried them around the perimeter of the central area. The interchange was organized like a large roundabout, with main intersecting pathways from all the nearby major spires. Traffic followed right handed circulation around the spire's base, moving past on the east and approaching from the west. Confusing matters were on ramps and off ramps that connected to the upper level, some of them arcing overhead encased in crystalline tunnels.

The pair of Marines approached the nearest off ramp in their sector. As they neared the ramp a large crate emerged from a side tunnel and joined the traffic ahead of them. It exited the roundabout, pulling off on the ramp the Marines were headed for.

"Gunny, Davis. We just had a metal crate come out of nowhere and head up an off ramp."

"Follow it, and keep your eyes on it."

"Aye, aye." Switching to suit-to-suit Brains addressed his partner. "Keep a watch on our six, mate."

"Right behind you."

They edged sideways off of the main roadway and swept smoothly up the ramp, their velocity unchecked. Five meters off the floor the ramp entered a crystal tunnel. The tunnel curved and crossed over the main chamber. Though the surrounding material was transparent the tunnel walls were faceted, distorting any view of the chamber outside.

"How you doing back there?"

"On your tail, Bubba. That box doing anything?"

"No movement."

"Hey, looks like we have another box behind us."

"Now I'm getting nervous."

As he spoke the top of the crate in front of them opened and a clutch of gray figures emerged. They struggled to raise a large plasma weapon into firing position.

"Bloody hell! Contact! The hostiles are in the crates." Brains hosed the hostiles down with 5mm, sending green tracers streaming down the tunnel. The Karf still managed to fire their weapon, sending a gout of plasma toward the two Marines. "Incoming!"

Both men crouched down. The plasma bolt was not well aimed and splattered off the tunnel wall ten meters in front of them. Orange fire swept around the armored figures as Brains brought his 15mm to bear.

The crate full of hostiles exploded in a bright yellow flash. A few seconds later a bigger detonation rocked the tunnel, the blast wave knocking both Marines off their feet.

"Crap, they're coming out of the box behind us too, Bubba!"

"Don't mess around! Shoot the blighters with 15mm."

"Gotcha." Rising off the pathway into a crouch, Grits fired a multi-shot burst of HE at the second crate. This resulted in a gratifying cluster of yellow flashes. "Yee-haw! Take that you gray polecats!"

"Oh bollix," Brains exclaimed.

"What?"

"The exploding power pack from that alien cannon blew a bloody big hole in the tunnel." The secondary explosion had, indeed, blown out the side of the tunnel and created a ragged hole in the still flowing pathway. "The moving surface is flowing right into the hole and we're about to fall in with it. Hold on, mate!"

Swept forward, speed undiminished, Brains fell off the edge and disappeared. Seeing his partner disappear, Grits had little choice.

"Damn it, Bubbaaaa....."

Grits followed his partner into the hole.

Chapter 26

The Ducklings

The open rear ramp of the pinnace yawned before them like the mouth of a giant alligator, brightly lit against the star strewn blackness. In the station airlock the zip-lines had been removed so the inner door of the lock could be closed. This allowed the first batch of Earthlings to escape into space with their living cargo.

Bobby and Mizuki jumped across the ten meter gap between ship and space station, followed by the first body bag filled with Tcist. After stowing it inside the shuttle, they awaited the arrival of the second body bag, which like the first was guided by Phil using his suit's maneuvering pack. Bobby, standing in the shuttle's rear hatch, provided encouragement.

"You're right on course, Phil."

"Coming to you, Sir." The tough, airtight bag puffed up like a balloon in the vacuum of open space. This made the bag bulkier but also rigid and easier for one man to handle.

"Got it," Bobby seized the inflated container and pulled the object inside to where Mizuki was waiting. With her help he stored the second body bag on the deck next to the first.

"Commander, I'm going back to cycle the airlock for Rick and Bud."

"Roger that, Phil. Go get them and we can get the hell out of here."

With practiced ease the SEAL flew back to the airlock. Once inside he cycled the lock, closing the outer door and, after pressure and gravity were restored, moved to open the inner door. The other two SEALs were standing in the open doorway of the Karf habitat four meters away.

Something exploded. Something large. The metal structure trembled as though struck by an earthquake and the floor beneath the two SEALs dropped ten centimeters.

"I think the hostiles just found our parting gift in the vault," said Bud.

"How much stuff did you use? The whole place shifted."

"Most of what I was carrying. I figured the bigger the distraction the better."

Phil called from across the gap. "Guys, we got a problem. The inner door won't open."

"What?" asked Rick and Bud together.

"The control panel buttons have all gone black and don't do anything when I push them."

"Crap! The explosion must have locked it down or shorted it out." The head SEAL thought for a few seconds before continuing. "What about the outer door?"

"Wait one..." They could see Phil move away from the inner door and cross to the outer one. "This one is still illuminated. What do you want me to do?"

"You got any C4?"

"Yeah Chief, a couple of bricks. What do you have in mind?"

"Open the outer door and then blow the inner one. That should suck the station atmosphere out the hole and we can jump through the lock with it."

While the SEALs planned their exit, orange flashes could be seen in the hallway behind Bud and Rick. The Karf had finally realized that the Earthlings were escaping.

"We got hostiles coming up behind us, Chief. If we are gonna blow this puppy we need to do it quick."

"Do it."

"On it." In the lock, Phil started the depressurization sequence which preceded opening the outer door. While the lock cycled he could be seen placing clay-like plastic explosive on the surface of the transparent inner door. In the open hallway, Rick and Bud crouched down as angry orange plasma bolts flew overhead, splashing harmlessly against the Starflake's crystal walls.

"Pick it up, Phil, we got company," Rick said.

"It's set. I'm exiting the lock to get out of the blast zone. You should suck deck."

"Roger that," the Chief replied, dropping to the floor. Behind him, Bud did likewise.

The airlock door flashed and blew inward, an expanding cloud of crystal shards. An instant later the glittering hemisphere of debris reversed course and collapsed back into the gaping hole that had been the airlock door. Air shrieked as it raced into the vacuum of space.

"Jump, Bud! The lock is already growing back shut." Rick Jumped for the opening.

"Right behind you, Chief."

Propelled by escaping atmosphere, the two SEALs flew from the violated lock like circus performers shot from a giant cannon. Stabilized by their maneuvering units, both flipped head over heals and matched velocities using their backpack thrusters.

"Woohoo!" yelled Bud. "Now that's how you make an exit."

"Just don't smack into the boat," the Chief admonished. His warning was not needed. Lt. Palmer had been monitoring the SEALs' comms and moved the pinnace out of the direct path of the exploding airlock. Meanwhile, Phil was playing catch-up, heading toward the pinnace on his own.

"Ducklings, Rubber Ducky. You two stick together and after Louie is on board I will come collect you."

"Copy that, Rubber Ducky. We'll see you soon. Meanwhile, it's a nice day for a walk."

Floating next to him, Bud looked back at the air lock that had almost grown shut. "Funny, the damage doesn't look that bad from out here."

1st Squad

Davis' voice came over the squad channel. "Contact! The hostiles are in the crates."

"You heard 'em," the Gunny bellowed. "Light 'em up. Take out every crate you see."

"Aye, aye, Gunny," Inuksuk replied happily.

Inuksuk stood and brought up his left arm, the one with the 30mm cannon. He fired a single round at a large silver box that was headed their way from the northern tunnel. The box disintegrated in a bright yellow explosion; the bear grunted with satisfaction.

"They seem to be coming from all directions," Jones observed as he and Carter joined Inuksuk in crate demolition.

The Gunny switched to 2nd squad's channel. "Aurora, we have hostiles trying to infiltrate our position inside of crates on the moving roadways. Over."

"Roger that, Gunny. A bunch of them just tried to ambush us. Unless there are a lot more of them hiding they won't be a problem."

As the two squad leaders conversed the wall of the central crystal column lit up inside with flashes of orange and yellow. This was followed by a bright, blue-white flash that caused a sheet of crystal to spall off of the column. Beau ducked out of instinct.

"*Mon Dieu*, what caused that?"

"Something must have exploded inside the wall," said Jimmy, standing beside Inuksuk.

"Davis, Walker, come in." the Gunny called. Nothing but silence replied. "Well shit," she mumbled.

"More prey, on the left," Inuksuk called out, enjoyment obvious in his voice. He fired again, followed by another detonation down range. Another crate appeared on a connecting ramp on the west side and the Gunny put a burst of 15mm into it. *I think we've just been handed a shit sandwich with extra pickles.*

"Everybody find a position with a good field of fire. I got a feeling this mess is only just starting..."

Grits & Brains

Grits fell down the hole created by the exploding alien power pack, accompanied by shards of crystalline material from the station itself. Tumbling as he fell, the armored Marine collided with

236

several ledges and rubble blockages on the way down, until he emerged into a smooth rounded tunnel. It also led downward and after a short descent he and a posse of accompanying debris collided with Brains. The British Marine had managed to stop his descent and was clinging tenuously to the side of the tunnel. Both resumed falling.

"Bloody hell! Watch where you're going you wanker."

"Screw you, you super giant ass! I wasn't the one who blew a hole in the fuckin' roadway."

Their conversation was interrupted by a sloping grate, which they landed on. Both scrambled to keep from sliding farther down the inclined barrier, rolling onto their stomachs and grasping the perforated surface beneath them. Debris continued to pelt them from above, the larger pieces bouncing off and disappearing down the incline.

"Gunny, Davis, come in. Anyone on this channel?" The comm remained mute. "Are you happy now, mate?"

"You're the genius, Bubba. Tell me what we do now."

"Inertial tracking says we fell over one-hundred meters. We are beneath the central support for the spire. That's the solid bit that fills the center of the round-a-bout, turning it into a toroid."

"A what?"

"A bloody doughnut, you clueless hillbilly."

"Well why didn't you say so? Why do you always have to use fifty cent words instead of talking regular English?"

"I am speaking regular English. How's this for plain talk: I've no clue how we get back to the rest of the squad."

"I can tell you one thing, we ain't getting out the way we got in. The hole we fell into was already growing shut when I was passing through. That plus I think we are in an air return. "

It was Davis' turn to be confused. "A what?"

"I used to work on farm equipment, like combine harvesters, and my uncle once took me to the big coal plant outside of

Birmingham. In part, both move stuff along pneumatically, be it grain or coal dust. This whole setup looks like an air return."

"What makes you say that?"

"The station has to recycle the air from its spires somewhere. If you haven't notice, there's a gale blowing down this shaft we fell into and the grate seems to be here to prevent big chunks of garbage from being sucked into the works."

"So you want to hack a way through the grate?"

"No way, man. Think of how we recycle air onboard the ship."

"We sterilize it with UV radiation, take out any particulates with electrostatic plates, and then run it through CO_2 scrubbers— well, the part that doesn't get sent to the hydroponics section."

"Right, CO_2 is plant food, but I don't think this station has room for enough plants to scrub its atmo, so it must use either chemicals or something else to separate the carbon from the oxygen. So that means what's down there could be a combination of ionizing radiation, high voltage, and other unpleasantness."

"Great, we can't go up and we can't go down."

"No, but my ass-cam shows an opening below where the crap that we knocked loose disappeared."

The Marines' armor depended on cameras to provide a 360 degree holographic view of the outside world because their heads were fully encased in shielding. Along with the panoramic cameras there was a single pickup that provided a shot of what was directly below and behind the wearer. It was a backup camera much like those on cars. Naturally, being Marines, they quickly christened the backup camera the ass-cam.

Checking his rear view, Davis saw what his partner was talking about. "That's a damn small opening, mate. And what's to say there's not a crusher or garbage disposal down there. I lost my recon drone when we fell."

"Me too. That leaves only one way to find out."

"Maybe we should toss a grenade down there."

"Hell, that's how we got into this mess in the first place, you blowing shit up." With that Walker let go of the grate and slid down the incline to the opening.

"Bloody hell." Davis let go and slid after his partner.

CIC, *Peggy Sue*

"Roger, Ice Castle. Understand that both squads are under attack in the hub. Interrogative, is there any activity in the spire itself?"

"That's a negative, Peggy Sue. No activity so far."

"I copy, Ice Castle. Stand by." Beth turned to acknowledge her husband's hand gesture. "What, Captain?"

"Just got a call from Lt. Palmer in the pinnace. They are all aboard and headed away from the Karf's spire."

"What is their ETA back at the ship?"

"As usual, there's a hitch. Let me put them on speaker. Go ahead, Rubber Ducky."

Bobby's voice came from the comm. "Peggy Sue, we have taken an alien life form aboard. It is part of a single being called the Tcist and it claims to be the entity that runs the Starflake's infrastructure. We rescued it from the grays. Over."

"I copy, Daffy, you have an alien on board," Beth responded. "What do you suggest we do with it?"

"The creature needs to be placed back in physical contact with the crystal structure of the station. I suggest we head directly for the shopping mall spire."

"Roger that. You are cleared to proceed directly to the first spire. Report when you have docked with the station."

"Copy, Peggy Sue. We are proceeding to the first spire docking area. And tell the XO we are going to have a talk about call signs. Daffy, out."

Beth snickered.

"What did he mean, Number One? Granted 'Daffy' could be construed as a might insulting but the call signs were all duck names."

"Huey, Dewey, Louie, and Daisy are all Disney characters, but I felt that Donald was too close to a real name and might be confusing. All that was left was Uncle Scrooge so I used a Warner Brothers character instead—Daffy Duck."

"And your selection had nothing to do with the connotation of the name?"

"Of course not, Captain. I never gave it a second thought." She tried but failed to keep the grin off her face. After a moment, both Beth and Billy Ray burst out in laughter, partly because of Bobby's call sign but mostly out of relief that the hostages were back safely.

Chapter 27

Grits & Brains

Brains found himself careening down a smooth chute that weaved back and forth like a drunken snake. After a harrowing minute he popped out of the chute and into a new curved tunnel. Skidding along the bottom of the tunnel he found himself accelerated by friction—the whole tunnel was moving. He felt himself rising up the curved tunnel wall like a luge rider negotiating a corner, back to the wall and held in place by centrifugal force. Over the comm came a familiar voice.

"Yeeehawwwww!"

"That you Grits? Where are you, mate?"

"Ahead of you, Bubba. We're in some kind of centrifuge, probably used to..."

Walker's voice quit in mid sentence. Before Davis had a chance to consider what that meant he reached the top lip of the spinning torus. The supporting wall behind him opened and once again he was free falling.

The interlude of personal weightlessness was rudely interrupted by yet another tunnel wall. The Marine's velocity was redirected and he was again falling deeper into the station core. Illumination from his suit lamps showed nothing but the smooth, blank interior of the pipe as he fell.

The surrounding pipe disappeared and a fraction of a second later Brains plunged into liquid. He collided abruptly with the bottom of the tank, though most of his velocity had been shed by the liquid around him. Righting himself he stood and found that the liquid was about as deep as his suit's shoulder height. Above was a large arched ceiling, across which a number of circular openings were scattered.

"Hey, that you Brains?"

Brains looked about and ten meters away he could see Walker waving at him.

"And just who the hell else would it be, you tosser."

"You'll see. Shit keeps dropping into the tank from above."

Reinforcing his partner's point, a mangled body splashed down between them. Small and twisted, in the darkness it could have been a naked child. Brains struggled forward to the impact point only to find the lifeless form of a dead Karf.

"Blood hell! It's one of those gray bastards."

"Yeah, I was trying to tell you that. Seems we've landed in the station's cesspool—all sorts of dead critters keep falling from the ceiling."

Well bugger me sideways! Pushing the dead Karf aside Brains moved closer to Grits. "Why are they collecting down here, in this bloody swimming pool?"

"They ain't collecting, Bubba, they are being recycled." Grits held up the partially dissolved carcase of another Karf with one hand. It broke in two and oozed from his grip, the pieces sliding back into the water. "And that ain't all."

Before Grits could explain, Brains heard another voice in his helmet, the voice of his suit's computer. "Warning. Caustic environmental conditions detected. To avoid armor damage exit the current environment immediately."

"You have got to be having me on! We've banged and thumped our way a half a kilometer deep into this crystal shit pile to end up being digested with the bloody aliens our mates are probably killing somewhere above us as we speak?"

"That would be about the size of it. But all is not lost my limey friend." Grits pointed with one arm farther into the dimly light cavern. "Over yonder there appears to be a catwalk across this open pond of rotting corpses."

"Well crack on, Yank. The sooner we get out of this acid bath the better."

The two ungainly armored figures worked their way across the fetid pond. Mostly walking but making swimming motions with their arms to clear the way of floating, half dissolved corpses, they made their way to the thin ribbon of material that spanned the space from one wall of the cavern to the other.

242

As with most of the ramps and walkways on the station the catwalk had no guardrails. Roughly a meter and a half wide and three meters above the surface of the pond, it was a simple solid slab eight centimeters thick.

"So what do you think, mate? Can we jump up there?"

"Don't know. Even with reduced gravity jumping up out of this liquid 'll be a bitch. Try getting up on my shoulders."

"Righto." Brains moved to comply as he accepted a foot lift up from his partner. Things went well until he tried placing a foot on the sloping shoulders of Grits' armor. Brains' foot slipped and he fell backwards into the liquid foulness, one arm reaching forlornly into the air. Large waves rippled outward from the Marine's impact.

"Well that didn't work so well," Grits said when his partner's head and shoulders reappeared above the surface. "I think I'm just gonna try something, if you don't mind."

"Be my guest."

Grits placed himself right under the edge of the catwalk, raised his arms above his head and sank beneath the surface. When only his hands remained above the pond he launched himself upward, exploding from the surface in a spray of droplets and globules of dissolving flesh. Rising like a missile launched from a submarine, he jumped high enough to grasp the edge of the catwalk, and there he hung.

"All right, Bubba! Climb over me to the catwalk!"

"Oh bloody hell," Brains muttered but he jumped up and grabbed a hold of the other Marine's backpack ammo magazines. Hand over hand he pulled himself up his friends armored form. Finally he got a hand on the catwalk and a knee on top of Grits' helmet. With a final effort Brains pulled himself onto the catwalk.

"Brilliant, mate! I'm clear."

"Uh, Bubba? Could you give me a hand, my grip is starting to slip."

Going down on one knee, Davis clasped Walker by the wrists and bodily pulled him onto the catwalk. Together the two armored giants collapsed onto the solid surface.

"If I ever questioned why we are always sent out in pairs I won't anymore," Brains panted. "And they say it is better to be alone than to be in bad company."

"Hell, Bubba, a man alone is in bad company. Now lets get out of this open sewer."

"No argument here. After you, guv."

The pair of Marines moved toward the closer end of the catwalk in single file, owing to its narrow width. Arriving at the end they found their way blocked by a transparent crystal door.

"Well she-it."

"What now?"

"Door. No visible controls."

"Bollocks." Brains paused a second. "We're Marines, right?"

"Yeah?"

"So remember what you said before you kicked open the closet door in the cosmic condo?"

His partner pondered the question before answering. "We break stuff?"

"No better time than the present, mate."

Grits grinned as he raised his right arm. "Damn straight, Bubba."

A torrent of 5mm flechettes poured from the multi-barreled railgun on the Marine's forearm as the crystalline barrier dissolved. The two Marines passed through the shattered doorway and into the corridor beyond.

Shopping Mall

PO Kashimawo "Kashi" Ademola observed the parade of squat yellow creatures. They came from down a dimly lit hallway and passed by without acknowledging his presence, headed toward the open doorway into a nearby room. Though the sailor carried a standard assault railgun he didn't think that shooting the strange aliens was a proper response. Instead he called Chief Jacobs.

"Chief, Ademola. There's something here you should see."

"What is it, Kashi?"

"You know that yellow repairman that the Marines reported running into? Well I got a whole work detail of them passing by."

"On my way. And don't shoot them."

"Aye, aye, Chief."

While Kashi and the Chief conversed another sailor, Leonard "Beans" Branford, approached from a different hallway. He stopped in his tracks when he saw the procession.

"Kashi, there's a line of yellow trolls marching by in front of you."

"No shit." Kashi looked over his shoulder at his shipmate. Inside his bubble helmet Beans' mouth hung agape as he stared at the trooping aliens. "I called the Chief. Wait 'til he gets here and don't do anything stupid."

From the main hallway came Chief Matt Jacobs, the NCO overseeing their party. Like the rest of the shore party, Matt wore light power armor and carried an assault weapon.

"Well would you look at that? It looks like the alien version of the Seven Dwarfs. They're not singing 'Heigh-ho! Heigh-ho! It's off to work we go' are they?"

"If they are singing I can't hear it, Chief."

While Kashi spoke the last of the seven waddling yellow figures passed by and went through the doorway.

"Should we call the Lieutenant?"

"Not yet, let's see what the little yellow buggers are up to first. Kashi you're with me, Beans stay on lookout next to the door so we aren't surprised."

"Aye, aye, Chief."

The Chief and Kashi moved through the doorway that the procession of whooboo had disappeared through. It led to a room facing the spire's exterior. Beyond the portal was a large space with a four meter high ceiling and a breathtaking view through its far crystalline wall. The yellow workers—evidently unimpressed by the view—were busily tearing a hole in the floor.

"What the hell are they doing?" asked Jacobs rhetorically.

"Beats me, Chief. Now should we call the Lieutenant?"

"Yeah, Kashi. Now it's time to call the Lieutenant."

* * * * *

Five minutes later JT showed up, looking harried and distracted. He already had his hands full coordinating the two engagements the Marines were involved in. This added distraction was not welcome at all. Moving up to stand next to Jacobs he just stared at the industrious yellow trolls.

"What the hell are they doing?"

"That's what I asked, LT, and I still haven't got an answer."

"They seem to be building a conversation pit in the middle of the floor."

"Or a planter, or a swimming pool."

"More like a wading pool. It's fairly shallow, even for those little yellow guys."

Two of the trolls were laying sections of flooring in the newly recessed area, while two others were constructing side walls. Another one had erected a scaffold and was affixing new light panels to the ceiling above the recessed area. Over at the exterior wall two more yellow figures were hunched over doing something indecipherable.

JT shook his head. "I don't know what they're building but they are building it quickly."

"So what should we do, Sir?"

"Well, Chief. As long as they don't do anything dangerous—like trying to open the room to vacuum—just keep an eye on 'em. I gotta go back to the main plaza, we have a couple of battle-bots coming down to send to the Marines in the hub."

"Aye, aye, Lieutenant.

Orloo Habitat

In a nearby minor spire, a group of Orloo gathered around a viewing device. Like most of the species that inhabited the Starflake, the Orloo were not without technological skills, though these had atrophied since their ancestors first landed on the lonely outpost in space. They still possessed enough know-how to tap into the station's observation network and it allowed them to watch the ongoing battle between the hated Karf and the newcomers—the Earthlings.

"Which species is winning?" asked one.

"It is hard to tell, but the Earthlings are certainly killing a lot of Karf."

The one who had spoken first made a rude noise. "The more of those accursed vermin they kill the better. We have suffered their outrages for far to long."

"The Earthlings are not losing, if that is to anyone's liking. If they destroy the malignant bipeds will they simply take the Karf's place as station overlords?" said another.

"Do you think they could be worse than the gray scum who strut around the station now? We've hated the Karf for generations."

This statement was greeted with twitters of agreement from the others. The Orloo predated the arrival of the Karf and remembered well the bloody takeover of the station.

"Still, better the devil we know."

"You say we should be pulling for the Karf?" said one incredulous observer.

"I'm saying that it would be best for us if they both lose."

"I'm not sure of that. Remember that it wasn't the Karf that took over the station, they were simply left in charge."

"That is true. Even if the newcomers destroy the Karf the Others may return."

A number of those present displayed rippling color changes, an indication of shock and fear. Though they were once aquatic creatures they now spent most of their time in dryer environments,

247

only entering the water to hunt and breed. Like the Earthly octopuses they resembled, the Orloo retained the ability to rapidly change the pattern and color of their skin pigmentation, though not always voluntarily. The mention of the Karf's savage masters startled and silenced the group for several minutes. Then one of the older Orloo spoke.

"You were not present when they interceded and healed the Hoon cub one of our youngsters nearly ingested. At first I thought the Earthlings would side with fellow vertebrates, but the one in charge was fair to both sides. These new creatures are not like other aggressive races."

"So then they are soft, which means they will probably lose, to the Others if not the Karf."

"I'm not so sure, from what we can tell the smaller ones that the Karf kidnapped managed to escape. And from the tremors recorded at the base of the Karf's spire, they did significant damage to Karf habitat while departing."

"And don't forget, the Karf lost many warriors during the kidnapping itself. I think that the ferocity of their attack in the hub is a reflection of the Karf's own desperation."

"Regardless, they are doing a lot of damage to the station itself. This battle will adversely impact the transport system for an eightday."

"Nothing we can do about that. Best to just watch and enjoy the slaughter of the gray parasites. If the newcomers win then we will have to decide on a course of action."

1ˢᵗ *Squad*

Crates and rubble crossed by in all directions: from tunnels large and small; down on ramps and up off ramps; across overpasses and circling on the main roadway itself. Any large clump likely sheltering groups of armed Karf. New targets popped up constantly, much to the consternation of the Marines.

"This is like one of those firing range exercises with the pop up targets," Jimmy commented.

"Except that there are no friendlies mixed in with them," Beau added, hosing down an on ramp with a long burst of flechettes.

"Mark your targets as they come. Ammo ain't free and we can't keep having the ship send more, they'll soon be running low too." The Gunny was always concerned about the rate the Marines burned through their ammunition. She often thought that restricting the cyclic rate on the 5mm railguns would help—there were few situations that required a full 3600 flechettes a minute, yet the grunts loved to blast away on full rock and roll. "Short aimed bursts, you Jarheads!"

"Aw, where's the fun in that, Gunny?"

"Was that you DeSilva? If you run out I will shave your balls with a rusty razor and dip them in rubbing alcohol."

Vinny wisely chose not to reply. Inuksuk, on the other paw, had decided that it was more fun to try and kill as many of the little gray men as possible with each round. He sent a single round down range in one of the smaller tunnels and was rewarded with a wave of ejected body parts from its mouth followed by a significant ceiling collapse.

"Good one, Inuksuk," said Zippy, a member of the bear's fireteam. Farther to the west, Bosco interrupted Ben-Ezra's sucking up to her team leader with more urgent business.

"Watch the blind firing down the smaller tunnels, Davis and Walker are still missing and could be returning down any of those tunnels."

"Good point, Bosco," the Gunny added. "Use beehive rounds to clear the small tunnels, they won't penetrate those two no-loads' suits."

"You think they are out screwing off somewhere, Gunny?"

"Don't know." *I can't believe they have been captured and I do not want to think that they are dead.*

"Maybe they just got stuck on a roadway headed for another spire and can't get off," offered Keti, the concern in her voice obvious. "They will show up, I would bet on it."

"You just say that because you are sweet on that Alabama hayseed," said Zippy in a snarky voice.

"How about I come over there and tie your tits in a square-knot?"

Before Zippy could reply to the proffered physical activity the Gunny intervened. "You two shut the fuck up and watch your fields of fire."

"We got more on the right flank," called Vinny, distracting Zippy from her argument with Keti. "Zippy, I could use some covering fire."

"Moving to you."

Getting up from behind the pile of crystalline rubble she had been kneeling behind, Zippy worked her way toward Vinny's position on the far eastern side of their perimeter. Fire from both the Marines and heavier Karf weapons had been blowing large chunks of station material from the walls and ceiling. Debris now littered the floor, both hindering movement and providing cover. Piles of the stuff that landed on the roundabout roadway circulated from right to left, crossing in front of the Marines, hidden Karf popping up to fire at the Earthlings at point blank range.

From above a section of wall blew out, raining more rock-like debris on the Marines. The dust cleared revealing a pair of heavy plasma cannons that opened fire from above.

"Inuksuk! Take those heavies out!"

Hearing the Gunny's command the bear pirouetted gracefully and fired a three round burst of 30mm. With the addition of the detonating Karf power packs, Inuksuk's response proved to be overkill. The Karf position erupted, vaporizing the Karf and blowing crystal shards out into the chamber.

"Incoming!" someone shouted.

The squad went to ground as crystal boulders crashed down around them. Hunkering down, most of them did not see the huge section of wall that broke off the central pillar and fell to the deck like a calving glacier. It landed right on top of the exposed Zippy.

Chapter 28

Main Plaza, Shopping Mall

JT was engaged in getting a pair of battle bots shipped down to the embattled Marines in the station hub. Each of the six wheeled vehicles mounted multi-barreled railguns in several calibers, an air defense/anti-artillery X-Ray laser, and twice the ammo load of a polar bear in heavy armor. Once set in place they acted autonomously, providing cover and area denial. The first battle bot was on its way down to 2ⁿᵈ Squad. As the second battle bot followed one of the sailors to the freight elevator, JT noticed more new arrivals descending the elevators to the main plaza.

It was Bobby and Mizuki, and the three SEALs. They were accompanied by a pair of hover sleds carrying what looked like body bags. Stepping out of the glowing elevator shaft Bobby raised a hand in greeting.

"Hello, Lt. Taylor. I see things here are not as exciting as when we so unexpectedly departed."

"But almost as hectic, Commander." The two men clasped forearms. "Damn, you two are a sight for sore eyes."

"We are very happy to see you as well, JT," said Mizuki, observing the male greeting ritual from a few steps away.

"Why isn't anyone ever happy to see us, Chief," Bud said sarcastically.

JT overheard the SEAL's remark. "Trust me, everyone here was extremely happy to see you SEALs arrive, particularly with Cmdr. Danner and Dr. Ogawa."

"We brought you a present, JT." Mizuki smiled and motioned to the two hover sleds.

"A little something we picked up in the Karf habitat," her husband added. "Something that the grays are going to miss once they find out we took it."

"Dead bodies?"

"No, Lieutenant. Live mossy-backed flatworms." Bobby and Mizuki both grinned at JT's confusion.

Bobby took pity on his friend and explained. "While we were roaming around the gray's warren, looking for a way out, Mizuki and I came across a vault, and in that vault was the darnedest thing."

Mizuki picked up the story as though they had rehearsed telling it. "We found a pond filled with large flatworms. On the backs of the flatworms was moss, a very deep and pretty shade of green. And as it turned out the moss was intelligent. It spoke to us and explained that it was part of a single consciousness called the Tcist."

"What's more," Bobby finished, "the Tcist claimed to control the Starflake's infrastructure. We offered to take them with us and, with the help of Rick and the boys, here they are."

JT looked from one to the other. "Well, that's not the craziest stuff you've ever come up with."

The Danners both smiled from ear to ear.

"So what are we supposed to do with them, or it, or whatever?"

"When we found them they were in a crystal lined pond that kept the flatworms, the Gloam, alive and allowed this part of the Tcist to communicate with the rest of its... brain, for lack of a better word."

"That might explain some other weird goings on around this place." JT changed comm channels. "Jacobs, Ice Castle. Could you come out to the main plaza? We have some guests who need a guide. Over."

"Coming to you, Ice Castle."

"See?" Bobby said to his wife. "JT gets a cool call sign like 'Ice Castle' and I get 'Daffy'. Beth is doing that on purpose."

"Now Bobby, you know how Beth likes to tease you."

JT made a throat clearing noise. Mizuki and Bobby looked at the lieutenant.

"While I wouldn't put it past the XO to give you a crappy call sign on purpose, I don't think you quite understand who Daffy Duck is."

"Why do you say that, JT?"

"I was an astronomer at one time, and one of the favorite cartoons we star watchers had was *Duck Dodgers in the 24½th Century*. It stared Daffy Duck as Duck Dodgers."

"Really?"

"Yep, it was voted the 4th best of the *Greatest 50 Cartoons of all time* by a poll of 1,000 animation industry experts. It was also nominated for a Hugo, if I recall correctly."

"See Bobby? Beth wasn't being mean to you. I bet she thought you would know all about Duck Dodgers."

"Yeah. Right."

"I'm glad I could help straightened that out, Commander. Here comes Chief Jacobs..."

* * * * *

"So here is what the little yellow guys have been working on," Matt said, leading the Danners, the SEALs, and their baggage into the room where the last few whooboo were finishing up.

"Well don't that look familiar?" asked Rick.

"It is very much like the pond in the Karf vault," Mizuki agreed. "Look, the workers have lined the whole pool with crystal material, and connected it to the outer wall."

"Yeah, that's all great, but where do we get water for the pool? There is some in the bags but not nearly enough to fill the pond."

Evidently satisfied with the job, the last whooboo in the empty pool grabbed the sidewall and vaulted out onto the floor. His only other companion, seeing his coworker was out of the pool, tweaked something on the thick crystalline junction attached to the room's transparent outer wall. From the built-up abutment a thick crystal artery ran across the floor to the side of the pool. After a few spurts and pops, water began to gurgle into the pool, evidently flowing from the fire-hydrant sized attachment next to the wall.

"Well I'll be dipped," said Phil. "They built a pond for the worm things."

"Yeah, it was almost like they knew we were coming," added Bud.

253

"Am I safe in assuming that all this is making sense to you officers?" queried Matt, who along with Kashi had watched the entire construction process.

"As much sense as anything on this station, Chief. I think we should get the Tcist and their pet flatworms into the tank."

"Aye, aye, Dr. Ogawa. Kashi, give us a hand emptying the body bags into the pool."

Together, the sailors and SEALs quickly released the flatworms. As they swam around their new abode the last of the bright yellow trolls exited the room and vanished down the hall from whence they came. Mizuki and Bobby leaned on the transparent sidewalls of the pool, waiting for the Tcist to recover, hoping to reestablish communication.

1st Squad

"Anyone wounded? Inuksuk, Bosco?" The Gunny checked the telemetry status readouts on her suit display. Two ominously gray, but no red and only one was blinking a yellow warning—Zippy.

"Zippy got buried by an avalanche," Vinny reported, having had eyes on when she got hit. "She's underneath tons of that crystal shit."

Quickly taking stock of the situation, Rosey decided on a course of action. "Bosco and Tseriteli, find some high ground where you can cover this place, suppressing fire. Inuksuk and Carter, shut down any major tunnel that has hostiles coming out of it."

"Shut down, Gunny?" Inuksuk asked.

"Blow 'em the fuck up, I've had it with these little gray dipshits. The rest of you help dig Ben-Ezra out."

"Aye, aye, Gunny."

"Ben-Ezra, are you OK?"

The only reply was indecipherable grunting sounds.

The Gunny changed channels. "Doc, Squad One, you have readings on Ben-Ezra?"

254

Dr. de Bruin responded from his monitoring position back in the shopping mall. "She is alive but is in some distress. It appears that she is struggling to free herself and is experiencing growing panic. If this continues she may well hurt herself."

"Can you calm her down Doc? I don't want her injuring herself or one of the guys trying to pull her out."

"I can give her a sedative that should calm her down, though it will render her unfit for combat for a half hour or more."

"Do it Doc."

"I copy. Administering sedative." Inside Zippy's suit the medical unit activated and injected her with several CCs of a benzodiazepine cocktail. Soon her struggles ceased and her respiration became more regular. Meanwhile Inuksuk was proceeding with blasting incoming tunnels, starting with the one from the North.

A burst of 30mm rounds flew far down the tunnel leading from the Karf spire. Their detonations could be felt in the roundabout, the tunnel acting as a waveguide for the explosive shock-waves.

"That didn't close it," Jimmy commented.

"Wait for it." Inside his armored helmet the bear was grinning in anticipation.

A plume of dust wooshed from the mouth of the Northern tunnel as a sizable section of its roof collapsed. Inside the tunnel debris lay unmoving—evidently the damage was great enough to stop the moving roadway from flowing.

"Sweet!" Jimmy exclaimed. "How about the Northwest one next, there's still hostiles firing from inside it."

"Coming right up."

While Inuksuk and Jimmy were happily destroying station infrastructure, Bosco and Keti scaled the half demolished central pillar wall. Reaching perches with decent cover, the two began clearing the area of living Karf, Keti with precise burst of 5mm and Bosco with slashes of laser light. By the time Zippy emerged from the rubble the Karf had been eliminated, at least in the northern half of the roundabout.

Pulling the drugged Marine's inert body from the crystal debris, Vinny and Beau held her up like a 400 kilo rag-doll.

"What do we do with her, Gunny? She ain't moving on her own."

"Set her down somewhere out of the line of fire. Then you two take a walk around the perimeter behind us heading east. Singh and Takala, circle around from the other direction and meet up with them on the backside. Make sure any remaining hostiles are ex-hostiles"

"Aye, aye."

"Squad Two, Squad One, what's your status?"

"Our objective is secure and we have a battle-bot setup to keep it that way. How are things down your way?"

"Under control. Two MIA and one temporarily combat ineffective but the grays are dead and we aren't. Break. Ice Castle, where is that battle-bot you promised me?"

"On its way now, Squad One. Finish securing the area and I'll check upstairs to see what they want us to do next."

"Roger that, Ice Castle. Standing by."

Karf Habitat

The Karf were finishing off the remains of their most recent leader, squabbling over the last few morsels. The Karf really do eat their own. Indeed, a Karf leader's last act is to serve his followers, literally.

"So now what do we do, fellow warriors?" asked one prominent survivor of the disastrous attack on the alien interlopers. Zhe was obviously angling for the top leadership position, despite graphic evidence of what happens to leaders who disappoint the mob.

"We should lock down our areas and shelter in place," shouted one of the mob.

"Yes, these aliens are too strong—we lost hundreds of warriors and killed not a one of the interlopers."

"Coward!"

"You go fight them, Hoon shit!"

The would be leader quieted the crowd.

"They have better weapons and wear space armor, it is no shame that we have not bested them. We have two choices: either continue to attack them and die, or go on defensive lock-down and try to survive until the Others come."

"Can we be sure they are coming? Has the message droid been sent?"

"Calm yourselves! The signal only reached the droid a few hours ago. With any luck we will see signs of its transit shortly. In the meantime we must do what we can to survive this catastrophe."

This brought murmurers of agreement and then acclimation of the new leader by those gathered. This pleased the new leader greatly. With any luck they would survive and, without any major new disasters, zhe might survive long enough for the pheromone rush of ascending to leader to trigger the change. Only a Karf who experienced a great victory could change from a sexless drone to a fertile male, change from zhe to he. And once that happened, his pheromones would cause the most submissive of those around him to undergo the change from zhe to she.

Yes, if all goes well, the new leader thought, *I may actually get a chance to breed before I die.*

Grits & Brains

"So what is this infatuation you have with the titan brunet from Georgia, mate?" The two lost Marines were making their way through a series of passageways, one much like another. Out of boredom, the gregarious Brit was quizzing Grits about his background and personal life.

"I don't know, Bubba, I just get a vibe from her when I see her. You know what I mean?"

"You mean you get a stiffy when you ogle her armored bum?"

"Naw man, don't you have any poetry in your soul? Just think about how she looks. She's an angel, a goddess."

257

"And how would you know? When you're around her she's either encased in armor or loose a fitting jumpsuit. You don't even know what she looks like underneath, what makes you think she's dishy?"

"That's what you think. I once saw her exiting the showers wearing only a towel and let me tell you she is fine."

"Fine?"

"Finer than frog's hair."

"Frog's hair?" There was incredulity in Brains' voice.

"Finer than frog's hair split four ways, Bubba."

"Do you just make these folksy sayings up as you go along, mate?"

"Hey, they're just part of my southern cultural heritage. You keep using weird Brit stuff."

"I do not! Like what?"

"You said that Ben-Ezra could 'ruin a piss-up at a free bar'. What the hell does that mean?"

"Just what it sounds like, you daft wanker."

"And there you go again with that wanker business. I haven't asked what that means 'cause I'm sure it ain't anything complimentary."

The duo fell quiet for several minutes until the passageway opened up into a wide balcony. Unlike most such overlooks in the hub, this one had a transparent, waist high barrier in place of a railing. Within the ceiling threads of light danced and weaved.

"Well now that's different. I wonder what's down below."

"One way to tell, let's take a gander." Brains approached the railing and froze. Switching on his suit's external lights the space expanded dramatically. The balcony turned into a system of catwalks that formed a lattice above ranks of storage racks. A slight curvature could be seen in the balconies and the array of racks below, as if the space wrapped around the spherical heart of the Starflake itself.

"Well blow me!"

"What? Oh, I see. Damn."

Beneath the balcony, the racks were filled with tier upon tier of large, white egg shaped objects. Each about two meters long, they were stored in double ranks, with narrow spaces between the paired rows. The bottom of the space could not be seen, disappearing into the gloom between the rows. There had to be thousands of the objects.

"Are those what I think they are, Bubba?"

"We need to get out of here, mate, and I mean right now."

Bridge, Peggy Sue

While battles raged on the Starflake, the crew on board the Peggy Sue were reduced to observer status. The Captain and First Officer were camped out in the CIC, watching telemetry from the Marines and sailors within the giant space station, and trying to ensure that the supply lines of ammo and equipment remained full.

While the officers were so engaged the Bridge crew had nothing to do but monitor the status of the ship and watch the local system for any sign of activity. Lt. Frank Hoenig was in the captain's chair, bored out of his mind. Behind him Siku was on the alter-space scanners, trying to sniff out any sign of alien activity.

"You know, Siku, when I signed on for this voyage I figured there would be some excitement, but not that it would consist mostly of a Marine boarding action."

"You wish you were with the Marines or the shore party, hunting down the alien prey?"

"Not so much that as I wish there was an opportunity to fly some combat sorties, like we did on the ant planet in Alpha Phoenicis. I don't want to be a ground pounder like the grunts, but a little action would be nice."

The she-bear snorted. "Like all males, you just want to get into a fight. I think humans and polar bears are not all that different."

"Maybe some of us. There are plenty of timid souls who just want the powers that be to take care of them, like little children.

259

Me, I'd rather live free with some peril than be a protected slave of the government."

"Polar bears are happiest when roaming the pack ice, hunting for food and enjoying..." The bear's voice trailed off as she raised her muzzle and flared her nostrils.

When Siku didn't finish her statement Fred pivoted around and saw that she was sensing something. The T'aafhal alter-space sensors used a direct interface that worked best with a polar bear's olfactory sense. Smell was their primary long distance sense, unlike humans whose primary sense was sight. The interface could be used by humans, but it made most sick and disoriented, and even the best human operators could only stand short periods connected. Siku was exhibiting all the signs of having a contact.

"You got something?"

"A drive's scent just emerged from the clutter around the star. The smaller companion star really jumbles up the scent." The sensors detected the distortion of the hidden dimensions caused by steep gravitational gradients in normal 3-space. Large masses like Jovian planets and especially stars were large blurry objects in alter-space. Gravitonic drives, and to some extent shields, also registered as sharper objects—distinct smells to a polar bear. "Yes, there is definitely some prey out there."

"How big? And is it headed our way?"

The polar bears eyes were just slits as she concentrated on the smell of the alien ship. As the target moved away from the system's massive star it grew sharper, more distinct.

"It's not headed toward us, it's accelerating like a ship headed for an insertion point. It's small, maybe a messenger or probe ship."

"Can you match the drive profile?"

"Not yet, to much background clutter from the star."

"I'd better tell the Captain." Fred punched up the CIC on the command chair's comm panel. "Captain, Bridge."

"Go Bridge."

"Sir, we have a contact on the alter-space sensors. Small ship, possibly a recon droid, gravitonic drive, accelerating away from the central star."

"Is it headed our way?"

Siku interrupted. "It just transitioned into alter-space!"

"Sir, the bogey just transitioned. It has left the system."

"Did we get a drive signature?"

"Not yet, Siku is working on it. We'll know more when the 3-space sensors can see the EM and particle profiles but that won't be for another seven hours."

The Captain paused.

"Very good, Mr. Hoenig. Good work and keep me informed of any developments."

"Aye, aye, Sir."

* * * * *

In the CIC the First Officer, who had been listening to the report from the Bridge, look at the Captain with puzzlement on her face. "A small ship transiting out of the system? We didn't see anything in stellar orbit when we emerged, granted the survey was a bit cursory."

"If it was in orbit around the central star, lying dormant, we may have missed it Number One. Given that the signal time from here to there is a tad over seven hours, plus three or four hours to break orbit and head for a transit point at high acceleration, it may have been reacting to a signal from the Starflake."

"What do you think it means?"

"I think it means that we can expect company."

Chapter 29

CIC, Peggy Sue

The Marines had finished clearing the area near the base of the occupied spire and were in need of further orders. The Captain and First Officer were in conference with the Sailing Master and Science Officer, who were still aboard the Starflake. Also looped in were the Ship's Doctor and Master at Arms.

"Dr. White, what do you make of the hostile species we have been engaged with? Have we seen anything like them before?"

"Not really, Captain. Dr. de Bruin examined several corpses provided by the ship's Marines. They are bipeds that superficially look like small humans, but their internal makeup is quite different. According to Dr. Krenshaw they most closely resemble Chondrichthyes—cartilaginous fish."

"You mean like sharks?"

"Precisely, Beth. They are vertebrates but their internal skeleton is made entirely of cartilage and contains no ossified bone. Of course the most obvious other physiological difference is that they have blood oxygen transport based on hemocyanins, proteins that contain two copper atoms that reversibly bind a single oxygen molecule."

"Which is why they bleed blue," added JT, the Master at Arms.

Betty nodded. "Technically their blood is clear. Unlike the hemoglobin in red blood cells found in vertebrates, hemocyanins are not bound to blood cells but are instead suspended directly in the hemolymph, the fluid that circulates throughout their bodies. Oxygenation causes a color change between the colorless deoxygenated form and the blue oxygenated form. If you shoot them in an oxygen atmosphere they will bleed blue."

"Anything else useful to know about them, Doctor?"

"While they are not particularly strong they do have sharp teeth and claws. Their vision is quite acute, other sense not so much. They seem fairly primitive and are probably capable of digesting anything protein based. They also seem to be entirely sterile drones, though there are signs of both male and female reproductive organs in their abdomens. For reasons unknown these are atrophied. Maybe there are fertile specimens in their habitat. We found no diseases that would pose a threat to humans or polar bears."

"Humph," Billy Ray remarked. "So just nasty little cusses."

"I think that their presence clears up some mysteries from Earth's past," said Bobby.

"How so, Bobby," Beth asked. She was on best behavior since the call sign prank she played on the Sailing Master.

"Just look at them, they are the spitting image of the Gray aliens in so many UFO reports."

JT moaned softly while the others fought to keep straight faces.

"Yeah, I know, there goes Bobby with another conspiracy theory. But think about it, these guys match a large number of sightings collected by MUFON."

"MUFON?" asked Mizuki.

"The Mutual UFO Network. They were an organization dedicated to documenting alien activity on Earth in spite of government suppression. They classified aliens by appearance and one of the most frequently reported types were Grays. They were often linked to cattle mutilations and alien abductions. If you got probed it was probably these guys."

"You really think these little varmints have visited Earth before, pardner?"

"Look, here we have aliens, and nasty ones at that, who match descriptions of visitors back on Earth. It would explain a lot."

JT shook his head. "You really think these little nasties are responsible for UFOs and alien abductions back home?"

"I'm just saying, if you aren't in armor I'd be very careful bending over near one of these gray bastards."

"Anal probes?"

"Anal probes," Bobby replied in all seriousness.

"Bobby, you're mad, bonkers, completely off your head," Beth quoted. "But I'll tell you a secret. All the best people are."

The Captain nodded in recognition of the passage. "OK, I think that we can all agree that the grays have no redeeming qualities, so what are our options for dealing with them. JT?"

"Sir, at the very least we should chase them all back into the spire that contains their main habitat. Currently there are small clusters of grays in spires inhabited by other species, garrisons if you will. We should move against these forces to get them out of our rear and to keep them from holding other non-combatants hostage."

"We know this how?"

"Reports from snakebots and recon drones, verified with the Kieshnar-rak-kat-tra. The other species are too frightened of the Karf to talk."

"I see. Bobby?"

"They are vermin, and vermin should be exterminated."

"Do you share your husband's position on this Mizuki?"

"I am not well disposed toward creatures who kidnapped me and carried me away for unknown purposes. From what I have seen they are vicious and a danger to all around them. I would opt for extinction."

"Extinction? You say this as a scientist?"

"The Universe is full of life and species go extinct all the time, Captain. One species more or less will not be missed, particularly such an unpleasant one."

"Number One?"

"I've not had the opportunity to meet these grays myself but they do sound dreadful. Perhaps we can free the other alien species that are being held captive by the Karf and see how they feel about the matter?"

"That sounds like a measured approach. Since we would have to remove the Karf garrisons in any case I think we should proceed with that. It will also give us more time to spread out and search for the two missing Marines. Still no word on them, JT?"

"No, Sir. Davis and Walker are still MIA."

"Is there reason to believe they are still alive?" asked Beth.

"Yes, Ma'am. We went back over the telemetry recordings of the battle for the hub. Last transmission was when Davis reported contact with the enemy. A number of explosions were seen in the tunnel they went down but when their signals disappeared they did so gradually—fading out like they went deeper into the station core. If they had been blown up the readings would have been different. In any case, when we sent people into the tunnel there was no sign of them or the Karf they engaged."

"Could they have been taken hostage?" asked Mizuki with obvious concern.

"I doubt that, they were engaging the enemy when they faded out. A pair of Marines in heavy armor is the equivalent of two armored fighting vehicles or light tanks. Up against the grays I doubt they were captured. No, I think something else happened to our guys."

"Let's keep alert for any sign of them while we move on the other Karf positions, hopefully they will turn up."

"Aye, aye, Sir."

"Science Officer, how comes reestablishing communication with the Tcist?"

"So far the movement of the Gloam—the flat worms—is random and unorganized. When we communicated with the Tcist previously the worms acted in concert, all aligning in the same direction. We think this is a sign that the creature has not yet recovered from being transported."

"But you are hopeful that you'll be able to talk with them at some point?"

"Hai, Captain. There are no outward signs of physical damage. We hope they make a full recovery."

Great, we are hunting UFO aliens and waiting on moss to heal. "OK, people. Let's get back to work."

One by one the participants dropped off the conference link. When the others were gone, Beth turned to her husband.

"You think they are still alive? The Marines I mean."

"I hope so, Number One. Sometimes all you can do is wait and pray. If we had some idea where they've gone I'd send people after them."

"You didn't mention the outbound bogey."

"Until we have a better idea what kind of ship it was I don't want to distract the others from matters closer at hand. We should know something soon enough."

"If you say so, Captain."

"You quoting from Lewis Carroll's *Alice in Wonderland* was quite appropriate. I'm beginning to wonder what kind of cosmic bunny hole we've fallen into."

Grits & Brains

"Well bugger this for a game of soldiers. We've been wandering around these hallways for ten hours and all we are doing is getting farther away from where the rest of the squad is."

Brains was right. After quickly vacating the overlook, the pair of Marines had been lost in a veritable maze of crystal passages. Often surrounded by large pipes and conduits, it was as though they were wandering around inside a gigantic industrial plant of alien design— which, in fact, they were.

"We ain't really lost, Bubba. Inertial nav shows us right were we are. It's just that we can't get to where we want to be. On the bright side, we have risen about a hundred meters."

"We've also gotten a kilometer farther away from the base of the spire we landed on."

"Stop being such a wuss, it ain't like we're in danger. We got air and water and enough protein goop for a couple of weeks. As long as our CF cells last we're good to go." The cold fusion cells powering their armor were capable of powering their environmental units for even longer than that if not subjected to the greater energy demands of combat. "Besides, I'm sure the others are looking for us. You know the Old Man, he sent them squid-boys to fetch Dr. Ogawa and Cmdr. Danner when they got taken."

267

"They are bloody officers and friends of the Captain besides. I doubt he'll send the SEALs after a couple of grunts who managed to tumble down the wrong hole."

The passageway took a jog to the left and the wanderers found themselves in a featureless crystalline pipe. Dim omnidirectional lighting illuminated the path ahead, shimmering in a way that suggested a liquid environment. Through the clear tunnel wall a dark shadow passed by.

"What the bleedin' hell was that?"

"Looks like there are things swimming around our little walkway. It's sorta like the shark tunnel at the Georgia Aquarium. You know that the Georgia Aquarium was the biggest aquarium in the world?"

"And knowing that helps us how?"

"I'm just trying to keep the mood light. You know, I always felt sorry for the sharks, swimming around all that tasty food inside the transparent tunnel. Sort of like a banquet under glass and you just can't get at the goodies."

"Not making me feel better, mate. Let's get out of this section."

"All right, all right." Grits paused. "Did you see that?"

"What? If you are having me on I will shoot you in your armored arse."

"No, man. At the end of the tunnel something went by... there goes another!"

Grits started running toward the far end of the tunnel. Not wishing to be left alone, Brains followed. They pulled up short at the tunnel's end, where it intersected with another passageway. As they watched a squat yellow biped shuffled by.

"It's one of them maintenance trolls, like in the condo."

"Yeah, he's at least the third to pass by headed to the left. What do you want to do?"

"They're either headed off to fix something, which means they could be headed for the upper levels, or they could be headed back to their quarters."

268

"Either way, it beats just wandering around. I say we follow 'em."

"Right you are, mate. Get after them."

The two hulking Marines followed after the rapidly disappearing yellow trolls. As in other encounters with the maintenance workers, the trolls payed the Earthlings no mind. The whooboo changed to another connecting passageway and continued their single minded march.

Grits was still in the lead. "You think they saw us?"

"I don't think they care. Just don't lose sight of the blighters."

Ahead, the three trolls stopped in front of a blank section of corridor wall. The leading whooboo stepped up to the wall and the crystal material began to melt away, just like the airlock doors on the station's exterior. From the opening came the familiar glow of an elevator shaft.

"Shit! No wonder we can't find our way out, they hid the damned doors on us."

"Don't just stand there, we need to get into that lift before the door grows back shut."

The two friends hustled down the hallway, arriving just moments after the third yellow alien stepped through the opening and disappeared up the shaft. Grits hesitated at the opening, the shaft extended both up and down.

"Go, go!" Brains urged his partner.

"The last time you told me to jump I fell and almost broke my ass."

After another second's hesitation, Grits stepped into the shaft and drifted upward after the whooboo work party. Behind him, Brains stepped into the elevator light as the doorway began growing shut.

Inuksuk's Fireteam

The rubble, aftermath of the firefight with the Karf, magically cleared itself away, melting back into the floors and walls. In a half an hour the damage had vanished as if the battle never happened. As things cleared up the moving roadways began flowing again, allowing the Gunny to send out forces to attack the surrounding Karf garrisons. The three Marines left behind as a holding force were doing what idle Marines usually do, complain.

"This is just great. The others are all off hunting down fresh prey and we are stuck here watching an empty hole in the ice. Not only that, the Gunny took Carter with her so we're one short."

"Come on, Nanook," said Vinny, the most veteran among those present. "With Davis and Walker missing she only had Beau left from her fireteam, she needed Jimmy more than we do."

"Right, because we are stuck holding the rear," carped Zippy.

"It's your fault, Ben-Ezra. If you hadn't gotten clobbered by a wall of ice we'd be on the hunt too."

"Don't blame this goat-schtup on me, you're the one who got his bell rung attacking something ten times his size."

"And I killed it too!"

"Hey, knock it off you two. The Gunny told you that we are the reserve force. If one of the other teams gets into trouble we have to respond to reinforce them. That's sound tactics any way you slice it."

"Yeah, well I didn't sign on to spend my time stumbling around inside some alien fun-house with little gray demons taking potshots at me."

Inuksuk just grunted.

"So why did you sign up for this mission, Zippy? I know why I did... because the possible payout is huge and it beats shipping out with the Fleet Marines."

"Really."

"Really. They go out for four months at a crack and you're lucky to get outside the ship once. That's four months of hot racking and eating Navy swill for shit pay and the possibility of getting blown to hell and gone by some Dark Lord's minions. At least we get our own racks and good chow aboard the Peggy Sue."

"If the money is so good why didn't you retire after the last mission, mister know it all?"

"The money was good, but it wasn't fuck you money."

"What?" Inuksuk couldn't help himself, it was a term he had never heard before.

"You know, enough money to tell the rest of the galaxy to kiss your ass. The payout from the last voyage was enough for maybe ten years of good living and then where would I be? Out of shape, no job in a decade and in need of a birth. No, I'm milking this opportunity for as long as I can, and damned glad to have it."

"When you do get enough money, where do you plan on going, primate?"

"I don't know, my furry friend. Perhaps one of the colony worlds will be civilized enough to settle on. I'll cross that bridge when I come to it."

"OK," said Zippy. "I get why you are here, Vinny, but why are you here Inuksuk?"

"It's this or hang out in that glorified polar bear zoo on Farside. At least here I get to hunt some real prey and see some sights."

"Great. So for you two this is just a violent form of tourism—join the OATC and see the galaxy."

"Meet strange aliens," added Vinny.

"And kill them," finished Inuksuk.

An old joke, but Marines valued tradition.

Chapter 30

Bosco's Fireteam

Four Marines sped down the roadway tunnel like a pack of speed skaters, tucked in and drafting each other to minimize drag. Ahead and behind them recon drones weaved randomly. Keti was on point, down on one knee, weapons ready. Behind her crouched Bosco, ready to add his pulse laser to Keti's railguns if needed. The quartet was completed by Simba and Fanni, constantly checking their six for a tail.

The Captain had ordered the Marines to clear all hostiles from the neighboring spires, of which at least a half dozen had Karf garrisons. The Lieutenant and the Gunny agreed that sending a full squad to clear targets one at a time was a waste of resources. A fireteam each should suffice.

Moreover, the rules of engagement were amended—collateral damage was to be kept to a minimum. From the beginning, the Marines were to be careful about catching non-combatants in the crossfire. Now things were even stricter. These thoughts passed through the team members' minds as they approached their destination, the roundabout beneath a minor spire that supposedly was home to the Orloo.

"Look sharp everyone," Bosco called out. "Remember, don't shoot octopuses, just *zasranec* grays."

The team entered the roundabout and dispersed, each headed in a different direction. Unlike the major spires, the minor ones didn't have a central column in the middle of their interchanges, just a central island with an elevator shaft, a naked column of light, leading upward. Keti tucked and rolled straight ahead, onto the unmoving central area. Bosco went high to the right while Simba and Fanni circled and came at the elevator from the farside.

"Clear!" Keti shouted, echoed by calls from Simba and Fanni.

"OK, drones up shaft," Bosco ordered. In the lull between securing the main spire interchanges and launching the new missions the Marines had received a resupply of individual recon drones. These had the added attraction of containing bursting charges. The original, non-exploding drones were lost at a terrible

273

rate so the Marines figured, if they were going to be expended anyway, they may as well turn them into guided munitions. The ship's fabs worked overtime to supply the expeditionary force with a pair of new drones apiece.

Both Simba and Keti sent drones up the shaft. They spiraled around each other as they rose, scanning for signs of danger.

"Contact! Crew served weapon third floor up," Simba reported.

"I got hostiles on the other side, same floor," added Keti.

"Take them out."

Keti sent her drone flying straight for the clutch of gray figures, lounging around a plasma cannon. A fraction of a second later her video feed went dead. Two explosions reverberated down the shaft, followed by debris—gray bodies and the remains of plasma cannons.

"I believe we got them, Lance Corporal."

"Da. Fanni, another drone."

Fanni complied, sending another of the grapefruit sized spheres spiraling up the shaft. "Looks clear of heavy weapons," she reported after a few seconds.

"*Pyats ballov*, great job. On me, trigger the lift." Bosco jumped from his vantage point, did a shoulder roll across the moving roadway, and jogged up to the now illuminated shaft without missing a beat. As he drifted smoothly up the shaft the other members of his fireteam followed.

Drifting toward the ceiling Fanni said, "I hope this doesn't end like it did for those folks who floated up to the ceiling in *Logan's Run*."

"What?" said Keti, puzzled.

"Nothing, old movie reference."

Bosco stepped off on the third floor, between the two detonation points. "Fan out."

"Going right," called Keti.

"Going left," called Simba.

"On your six," Fanni rounded out the reports.

Around them were fields of sawgrass, planted in sandy soil, divided by tall canebrakes. The ceiling above emulated blue sky with traces of high cirrus clouds. Artificial breezes rustled through the grass. The effect was that of a windblown coastal region, except for the ten meter hole where the elevator pierced the floor and sky above. Through the grass trampled trails led off in several directions.

"The trail behind the gun emplacement seems a bit better traveled than the others," Simba reported

Keti picked her way through the Karf body parts and moved beyond what had been their firing position. "Same on this side."

"Active camo on. Simba, Fanni, follow right trail. Keti, I'm coming to you. See if the trails lead anywhere."

As stealthily as possible the pairs of seven foot armored monsters moved in opposite directions, away from the central elevator shaft. Using IR, Bosco and Keti could just make out figures hiding in the tall grass ahead of them when the plasma bolts began to fly.

Grits & Brains

Emerging from the elevator they found themselves in a tropical hothouse, a humid forest of broadleaved plants and hanging vines. Mosses and ferns covered the ground and trails led off in all directions, the interior of an indoor arboretum or a Victorian conservatory gone wild.

"We get on the lift in an empty corridor and get off in the middle of a bleedin' rainforest. This place is total bollocks."

"Hey, we're out of the hub and back in a spire. Be thankful for little blessings my Momma always said."

"Do you have a saying for every occasion?"

"Momma did. Just follow the little yellow guys and see where they're headed. We need to find an elevator down to the transport system or an airlock."

275

Brains grunted in reply and set off after the last of the whooboo. The ground beneath their feed squished, releasing muddy water, while looping vines clutched at their suits and leaves obstructed their vision. Without warning a plasma bolt sizzled through the lush vegetation.

"Incoming! Going right."

"Going left."

Switching to IR in hopes of penetrating the undergrowth, Grits picked out multiple signatures—too small and too numerous to be the maintenance trolls.

"Contact ten meters out, multiple bogies."

"Right, mate. I got them. I say we take them out."

"Remember the ROE, we ain't supposed to take out non-Karf aliens. We need positive id."

"OK, let's move forward, but if this turns into a cock-up it's on you, Yank."

Carefully the two armored giants moved toward the alien contacts, active camouflage helping them to blend in with the luxuriant greenery. Pushing aside a large frond Grits found himself confronting a group of a dozen Karf. Two of them were trying to swing the muzzle of a large plasma weapon around to point down the trail he and Brains had been following just minutes ago.

"They're hostiles, Bubba!" Grits shouted as he bounded out of the jungle, knocking aside several Karf. The only real threat the humans faced was the plasma cannon, so the charging Marine headed straight for it. Seeing the armored giant headed right at them the weapon's crew tried to bring the cannon to bear. They were not fast enough.

With a sweep of his left arm, Grits knocked the barrel of the weapon aside. Taking a step forward he swung his right arm, throwing two gray hostiles fifteen meters through the air. One of them fell down the unactivated elevator shaft out of sight. The other described a shallow arc toward a particularly verdant clump of vegetation. From the thicket a flash of pink extended, collided with the flying Karf, and, in the blink of an eye, yanked the body from the air.

"Whoa, Bubba, did you see that?"

Brains stepped from cover and hosed down a half a dozen grays who were trying to target Grits. One charged the Marine from his left. Not wishing to shoot a lone Karf with a 15mm round, Brains moved to the left and physically struck his attacker with an upward sweep of his arm. The Karf flipped over backwards from the impact and landed among a clump of large plants. The stalks and leaves shook mightily where the Karf landed, which struck Brains as odd.

"See what, mate?"

"A long pink thing, about as thick around as a man's arm and the color of bubble gum, shot out of the brush and snatched one of them gray critters right out of the air."

By this time most of the Karf were running away, but several inadvisedly brave individuals accosted the Earthlings. One jumped forward and grabbed the plasma cannon's barrel. Seeing the movement out of the corner of his eye, Grits reached out and seized the gray biped by the head. The Marine squeezed and the alien's head popped like a pimple, sending a gout of blue-gray ooze squirting into the air.

"Yuck," Grits commented, dropping the dead Karf and wiping his gauntleted hand on the barrel of the plasma cannon. He picked up the alien weapon, ripping out the connections to its power pack, and heaved it into the elevator shaft. He turned in time to see another overly aggressive Karf, standing at the edge of the clearing, raise his plasma rifle.

"Behind you!" Brains belatedly warned his partner. But the shot never came. To the astonishment of both Marines the greenery parted and a large mouth appeared, enveloping the Karf's head and most of its body. Green on the top and white on the bottom, the mouth closed and vanished, with the protruding gray legs of the Karf still twitching.

"Bloody hell!"

From the other side of the elevator opening more Karf appeared and opened fire, several shots striking Grits, causing his armor to light up with orange flame. He turned to return fire but Brains beat him to it, sending a burst of 15mm into the pack of them. Bright yellow explosions sent gray body parts flying, effectively ending the engagement.

"Any damage, mate?"

"Naw, just sort of startled me is all. What's going on around here?"

"I think we are not the only ones killing Karf. Some big green thing snatched one right off the ground by that big rubber plant."

"Yeah, I saw. You missed whatever nabbed the one in midair."

From the main trail behind them came a rustling. Both Marines turned and saw what looked like a huge frog hop into the clearing. Nearly the size of a Volkswagen Beetle it was colored bright green on top, turning to a vibrant yellow stripe around the edges of a pure white underbelly. It looked at them with a single yellow eye, located on the middle of its head.

It shuffled forward and with a webbed hand picked up one of the Karf's plasma rifles that was laying discarded on the ground. Both men raised their weapons. The frog blinked once, then spoke.

"We kill Karf... use their weapons."

"Right you are. Who are you?"

"Braggitt," the huge amphibian croaked.

"Pleased to meet you, Braggitt. Me and me mate here are Marines, from Earth, and we're just passing through."

"All Braggitt... I am Creoak. We help kill Karf."

"That's great, Creoak," Grits said, joining the conversation. "Y'all kill as many of them gray bastards as you want, there's no bag limit."

"We have waited long for this..." the frog's throat pulsed between bursts of words, as the amphibian caught its breath. "You kill them all... good practice for what will come."

The frog blinked again and turned back toward the trail. On its back was a much smaller frog, a brilliant scarlet in color. The smaller amphibian looked at the two men and blinked its eye. The bigger frog jumped and they disappeared into the jungle.

"Well if'n that don't beat all. A talking frog, with another frog on its back."

"I wonder what that bit about 'what will come' meant?"

"Don't know, Bubba, but I'm thinking any help killing Karf is welcome."

"Whatever. I think we need to contact the ship."

"Yeah, and then get back to our unit."

CIC, *Peggy Sue*

"We finally got a drive signature on that bogey, Captain," reported Lt. Hoenig from the bridge. "Looks like a close match for a standard Dark Lord messenger droid." For reasons no one really knew, the robotic probes used by the Dark Lords and their minions were always called droids—perhaps a reference to the old Star Wars movies.

"Thank you, Frank. Good work." Billy Ray closed the comm channel and turned to his wife. "You heard him, sounds like we have sailed into hostile waters, Number One."

"Yes, Sir. It wouldn't be the first time." She gave him a lopsided smile that she reserved only for him. "What do you think the response time will be, if there is a response?"

"I don't know. This station doesn't seem to be of any strategic importance. Massive stars make good transfer points for ships using alter-space because transit times to and from tend to be short, but this station is way out in the boonies."

"I agree, it's not positioned conveniently to be a trading station or a base from which to control the nexus. It's a bit of a puzzle why it's here at all."

A signal came over the Marines' comm channel.

"Peggy Sue, Peggy Sue, this is Davis. Do you read me?"

Beth looked at the Captain and raised a single eyebrow. She keyed the comm and replied.

"Davis, Peggy Sue, we read you. Interrogative your location and condition?"

"Walker and I are both all right, Ma'am. We are in one of the minor spires and have encountered hostiles. I'm sending you our location and status info. Over."

"Roger that, Davis. Good to hear you lads are OK."

As the First Officer spoke a location marker for the two missing Marines appeared on the model Starflake in the main viewing tank.

"They are quite a ways from where they disappeared," Beth commented. "I wonder where they've been."

"Peggy Sue, there's something else you need to see. We are sending some recorded video."

"I copy, we are receiving your transmission."

On one of the side monitors a scene that was obviously taken by a suit camera came into view. It showed the Marine moving from a dark passage onto some form of catwalk. The scene suddenly became brighter, allowing details to be made out. There were more catwalks, a whole network of them crisscrossing the cavernous space. But what was more interesting was what was beneath the Marine's vantage point—row after row of white eggs.

"Holy cow!" the Captain exclaimed. "Are those..."

"It would appear so, Captain. The computer confirms those are type one antimatter containers—several thousand of them."

Chapter 31

Bosco's Fireteam

The Karf fired blindly, trying to hit the attacking Marines, though they met with little success. All they managed was to set a stand of grass ablaze. From above, sprinklers quickly doused the flames while the Marines advanced.

Simba and Fanni flanked left while Bosco and Keti move right. Once they had the gray hostiles in a pocket between them, the Marines opened fire unleashing a torrent of 5mm flechettes. Both grass and Karf were scythed like overripe wheat.

The Karf not struck down by the fireteam's onslaught scattered, headed for the presumed safety of the canebrake. Their presumption of safety was in error. Dropping from the bamboo wall came writhing clusters of tentacles. Multiple suckered arms coiled around the fleeing Karf, bringing them to the ground. Over their muffled shrieks could be heard crunching sounds.

"Cease fire," yelled Bosco. "Do not shoot the octopuses."

"Well I guess that answers the question of how the Orloo will react to an attack on their Karf wardens."

"That is for certain, Keti." As Simba spoke, a Karf ran straight at him, evidently preferring to face the armored Earthlings than the tentacles and beaks of the spire's inhabitants. The Marine grabbed the running Karf as it tried to get by him. Lifting the gray biped by the neck, he threw the hostile back into the roiling mass of Orloo.

"I am guessing the octopuses do not much care for the little gray men," Fannie observed.

"I'd say that is an understatement."

One particularly large Orloo rose up and approached the cluster of Marines. Bosco, being in charge, took a step forward to greet it.

"We thank you for ridding us of the despised vermin," the creature's reedy voice said through the computer translator. "We will enjoy hunting down the rest of the scum."

"It looks like they are no match for you, why didn't you take them out before this?"

"They disarmed our ancestors when they arrived many orbits ago. Unarmed we didn't stand a chance against them."

"Da. The first thing you do when enslaving a people is to take away their weapons. Is old Russian saying."

"Not just Russian," Fannie added. The Finns had a long history resisting subjugation, by Russia and others.

Ignoring her, Bosco addressed the Orloo again. "We will leave you to finish cleaning up the Karf situation in this spire. I have been instructed to inform you that there will be a meeting in the Shopping Mall Spire in the near future. Our leaders wish to talk with representatives of the station's inhabitants about what will happen going forward. We will let you know when."

The Orloo blinked and inhaled loudly. "We will send representatives and tell others we know."

Then the octopus like creature pivoted and floated away, gliding on a mass of moving tentacles. The Marines took in the scene as the mass of Orloo vanished back into the grass and bamboo. There was nothing left of the Karf except for some spilled blue blood. The bodies and their weapons had both been carried away.

"I guess our work here is done," Keti quipped. "What's next, Bosco?"

"Let me check in with Ice Castle. I'm sure there are more objectives just waiting for us."

CIC, *Peggy Sue*

"Well now we know why the Starflake has an occupying force. That much antimatter is a treasure beyond calculation."

"Indeed, Captain. I think we can be assured of a response to that outward bound messenger droid."

"Roger that, Number One. The only question is when—weeks, months, years?"

"Sooner rather than later I should think. That's assuming those being notified know what's hidden in the station core. JT question some of the locals earlier, inquiring about possible antimatter for refueling, and they all said there was not a bit of it about."

"I'm afraid we have to assume someone knows it's here. You don't leave something that valuable—and that dangerous—setting around unguarded. The only small mercy is that we will see them coming. Unless they are willing to burn a lot of fuel to get here it will take them several weeks from emergence."

"I take it that means we are staying in system?"

"Yeah, we can't let this treasure trove slip back into the hands of the Dark Lords or their minions. We have to figure out how best to defend this thing."

"That or stand off and blow it up."

"Let's hope it doesn't come to that. I never really pictured myself as a mass murderer."

Beth nodded slowly in agreement, knowing that rather than lose the antimatter cache they would be forced to destroy it, and all those living on the station.

"Let's find out how the Marines' are coming with pacifying the grays and whether Mizuki and Bobby have reestablished contact with the station itself. Just once I'd like a mission to go as planned."

"Where's the fun in that, Dear?" Beth smiled once again and opened a channel to JT aboard the station.

Grits & Brains

The two errant Marines sailed along the moving roadway at close to forty kilometers per hour. After finding their way down from the spire of the Braggitt they quickly figured out which direction to head on the web of transportation pathways. After a couple of minor interchanges they approached the base of the Shopping Mall spire.

"Inuksuk, Davis. Walker and I are approaching you from the southeast. We would greatly appreciate not being brought under fire. Over."

"We're all right with it, but you may need to talk to the battle bot," came the reply. The bear spoke truly. The battle bot, watching over the interchange from a raised point near the freight elevator, came alive as it detected the two Marines' approach. A multi-barreled railgun swung menacingly toward the southeast.

"Tell that bucket of bolts that we didn't spend a day wandering around in the guts of the station to get blasted by friendly fire," Grits transmitted. Normally he let Brains handle communicating with the others, but he was not taking chances this time.

"Don't worry, just make sure your IFF transponders are on. Where have you two primates been? You ducked out at the start of the fun."

The two men swooped down an on ramp, crossed the main roadway, and stepped off onto the central area before they could be swept around the main roundabout. They were becoming quite adept at riding the station transport system. The robot gun platform, evidently satisfied that Grits and Brains were friendlies, placed its weaponry back in standby position.

Walking up to the others, Brains said, "What are you up to? Why aren't you out clearing spires?"

"We are the rapid response force, at least that is what Vinny says." The polar bear motioned to one of his armored companions.

"What I've been doing," Vinny added, "is listen to these two bitch and moan about not being in on the Karf hunt."

"Putz," Zippy said. "Where did you two meat-heads go to hide?"

"Let me tell you, darlin', we been to places deep inside this station that no human or ursine was ever meant to see. Huge whirling garbage disposals, giant vats of acid filled with dissolving bodies, pipes and machinery that makes no Earthly sense."

"Not only that," his partner chimed in, "while you moaning Minnies have been here mucking about, we found something that will make your eyes pop out of your heads."

"Like what?"

"Like a vault filled with enough antimatter to make us all richer than Croesus, that's what." As usual, things the officers thought were being kept quiet spread through the ranks like wildfire.

"Your shitting me," Vinny exclaimed.

"Get over, mate. While you were here whacking off we were doing important things."

"You tell 'em, Brains. The XO said we did real good, finding that AM."

Zippy sniffed. "Just like you two to fall into a pile of shit and come up with roses in your teeth."

"How much AM did you find?" Inuksuk's voice had a skeptical edge to it.

"From what we could see, several hundred big containers, maybe a thousand. They disappeared out of sight so there's no telling how many total."

Vinny whistled. "AM is the most valuable substance in the galaxy. That much must be worth about a fortune."

Zippy did a quick calculation on her suit computer. "Worse than that. A thousand type one eggs hold more energy than four million one megaton bombs. We are standing on the biggest bomb ever seen."

"Yeah, and we've been running around shooting the crap out of anything that moves."

For a while, the five Marines were very quiet.

Shopping Mall, Starflake

While JT was occupied keeping tabs on the Marine raiding parties, Mizuki and Bobby were left standing around the Tcist pond, awaiting renewed contact. The room they were in had a lovely view of the Starflake's nearby spires, both large and small. Sending the other sailors back to patrolling, Chief Jacobs took it upon himself to guard the Danners and their pool full of flatworms. In reality, he was hoping to find out what was really going on aboard the station.

"So these little fellas spoke to you earlier?" Matt asked the officers in what he hoped was an innocent, conversational tone. Both Matt and his friend Steve Hitch had been crew since the first voyage of the original Peggy Sue, back when it was known only as Parker's Folly. They had been in many tough scrapes and battles along side Bobby and Mizuki, who counted them as close friends, the gap between officers and crew not withstanding.

"It is not the flatworms that are intelligent, Matt," Mizuki corrected. "The intelligence resides in the moss on the worms backs. And yes, they have spoken to us, back before we took them from the Karf."

Bobby was kneeling by the newly constructed pool, fiddling with a device attached to the crystal material lining the pond. "The Tcist, as it called itself, claims to run the stations machinery—air, power, gravity, whatever. If we could communicate with it we might be able to isolate the grays more rapidly."

"You think this Tcist creature controls those yellow trolls and the big pink cleaning Frisbees?"

"Hai. That would explain why the whooboo built this new pool for the Gloam even before we brought the creatures to this spire. We told the Tcist where we were headed before moving them."

Bobby stood up.

"As far as I can tell the transmitter/translator is working fine, our friends in the pond are just not saying anything."

"At least we have gotten everybody who went missing back: you and Dr. Ogawa, and those two Marines."

"Yeah, we've been lucky Chief. Let's hope our luck holds."

Unnoticed, the creatures in the pond began to align. A synthesized voice intruded on their conversation.

"You have caused great destruction... why are you doing this?"

"Hot damn, the Tcist are talking again!" Bobby opened the translator channel. "It is good to talk with you again, we were afraid that we had damaged you when we escaped from the Karf."

"We are fine. Why are others of your kind destroying parts of the station?"

"We are sorry about the damage, but it could not be helped. We are in the process of forcibly removing the grays from their position of control over the station's other residents."

There was a noticeable pause.

"Why?"

"Because they have enslaved the other species present, they even imprisoned part of you. Did you not expect us to remove the Karf after we freed you?"

"We appreciate having been removed from the Karf's control. We are not responsible for the relationships among the various inhabitants, or damage to their own constructs. We are responsible for damage to the station's infrastructure—it distresses us."

"We have neutralized most of the Karf's heavy weapons and are in the process of confining them to their primary habitat. There should be no other major damage to the station, but I can make no promises."

"Some of your warriors wandered deep inside the station core, this is not permitted."

"Oh?" Bobby paused. The Captain had informed them of the antimatter hidden deep within the station. He could not believe that the Tcist were unaware of the AM cache. "Why? Are you trying to keep the cache of antimatter containers stored there secret?"

There was another, much longer pause by the Tcist. The Earthlings waited patiently and eventually the voice of the station spoke again.

"The station's primary function is to collect and concentration antimatter. We have been doing this for over a million years—since the builders abandoned us. We have let other species live in the habitable spaces, as long as they did not interfere with our primary purpose. This poses a quandary for us."

"What? That we know you have enough AM in your core to power a fleet of starships? Are you saying that no one knows about the antimatter store?"

"The Builders knew, but not any of the subsequent inhabitants. At least none that we know of... though there is one race we suspect of knowing."

"Which one? Which spire do they live in?"

"They are not residents of the station. They visited here over 10,000 years ago. Many of the residents were killed and it was they who infected the station with the accursed vermin."

Bobby muted the translator and said to Mizuki, "Oh this just keeps getting better and better."

"We had best tell Billy Ray and Beth."

"They are not going to like finding out that the Starflake is a secret fuel dump for some long gone aliens. Or that the species who last conquered it—and left the gray bastards in charge—might know what the station really is."

"That is precisely what we need to tell them. We should return to the ship so we can talk face to face. Besides, I'm dying to get out of this suit."

"Yeah, and I'll bet your butterflies are going crazy. We can take the pinnace."

Standing in the background, Matt was doing what enlisted personnel do when officers are working a problem—play invisible and hope not to catch any crap. As the Danners left the room Bobby turned to him.

"Chief, keep a guard on this room. I don't want anyone in or out except on Lt. Taylor's orders."

"Aye, aye, Sir." Matt came to attention as the officers exited, thinking, *Man, wait until Stevie hears this! This furball has only just begun.*

Part Three

Blessed Are The Peacemakers

Chapter 32

Shopping Mall Plaza, The Starflake

A month had passed since the Peggy Sue's Marines finished securing the Starflake. After some convincing, the Tcist helped by sealing off access to the spire containing the Karf habitat. Now the vicious gray bipeds were safely sealed inside their own spire, with robotic guards keeping an eye out for any attempt to escape confinement.

After isolating the Karf, restoring the Tcist, and securing a quartet of full type one antimatter storage containers for the ship, Billy Ray figured the next step was to settle the natives down. To begin the process, he called a meeting in the main plaza of the Shopping Mall. A number of resident species were represented.

The Orloo were present, several bearing appropriated Karf plasma rifles, as were the frog like Braggitt. The Kieshnar-rak-kat-tra were there wearing jewels and daggers at their waists. Their pungent scent ensured they had a space of their own. Hiding timidly around the edges of the crowd were the Hoon. Even a pair of Hisstow, the cat-lizard bully-boys used by the Karf, could be seen in the shadows.

Several previously unseen species were in the crowd: long-legged insectoids, a mollusk with hundreds of crystal eye-spots in its craggy shell, and a creature that looked like a moving haystack. A good crowd, but still representing fewer than half the species inhabiting the station. The Captain figured it was a start.

He and the three other partners ascended the raised platform at the center of the plaza. Those assembled looked at the four Earthlings, two matched sets, one noticeably taller than the other. All wore swords at their waists, samurai fashion. Mizuki's idea to distinguish the officers from the other personnel—armor tended to make the crew all look alike. Billy Ray stepped forward and, after giving the crowd a moment to settle, began to speak.

"I am Captain Billy Ray Vincent, master and commander of the Orion Arm Trading Company starship Peggy Sue. We came to this station in peace, seeking contact with other sentient beings for the purpose of trade and mutual cooperation. Before contact could be established with the residents of this station we were viciously attacked and two members of my crew were kidnapped."

The audience shifted nervously. They had no idea where this strange being's speech was leading. Billy Ray continued.

"We drove off our attackers and retrieved our personnel from captivity. Finding no honor in our foes we have driven them from the rest of the station, confining them to their own habitat. I have not decided what to do with them and I seek your counsel on the matter."

Those assembled were astonished. This was not what they were expecting. Conquerors came and went, but never in their long history had one asked the conquered their thoughts on the matter.

"Is it your intention to stay here?" asked an Orloo, among the more forward of the resident species.

"Yes. For now."

Whispers and murmurs rippled through the crowd. An unusually brave Hoon spoke up.

"Are you going to rule over us?"

"We intend to bring order to this station."

"By what right?" demanded the moving haystack.

"By right of conquest and right of salvage. When we arrived the Karf were running the place, running roughshod over the lot of you. That is over. The Karf have been neutralized and we claim possession of this station."

"It never changes," complained the Hoon. "We were slaves of the Karf and now we are to be your slaves."

The crowd fell into disorder, with much shouting and waiving of appendages. After a few moments, the Captain had enough. He signaled JT standing at the base of the platform, who in turn motioned to Inuksuk, sitting on his haunches behind the stage. The polar bear rose to his full, armored height towering over all present —a visual reminder that the Earthlings did not need the residents' permission.

Quiet descended. The Captain continued.

"We have no need for slaves. And unlike the Karf, we will tolerate no violence among species, no murder or other harmful activity. As long as you follow the rules you will be free to live your lives and engage with each other peacefully."

The Orloo that had spoken earlier asked the question that was on many minds. "What are these rules you speak of?"

Over suit-to-suit, Beth said to her husband, "I didn't know you were prepared to play Hammurabi, dear."

Ignoring her, Billy Ray gave the alien crowd his best cowboy squint and laid down the law. "You are now bound by the cowboy code: If it ain't yours don't take it; If it ain't true don't say it; If it ain't right don't do it."

Once again the crowd erupted in bedlam as creatures shouted at each other in their own languages and several versions of the common trade language. Eventually, as things quieted down, a particularly rotund Kieshnar-rak-kat-tra stepped forward seeking attention. Seeing the large collection of gold rings in the creature's left ear Billy Ray made a guess as to who he was.

"Yes, Station Trader?"

If the old trader was surprised he didn't show it. He made a surprisingly graceful bow and replied.

"August Captain, are we free to engage in commerce? To trade with each other and any future visitors to this station?"

"Certainly, Honored Trader. We came here looking to trade ourselves."

"And if there are disputes?" asked the some what crotchety haystack creature.

"They will be adjudicated by one of the ship's officers, with myself the final court of appeal. I know this is all a bit disorienting for you, but you'll get used to it. One thing I promise, the Karf will not resume their tyrannical reign over this station."

This prompted shouts of "Kill them! Kill them all!"

Billy Ray raised his hands and motioned for silence. His new subjects figured out what the gesture meant immediately and quieted down.

"We aren't partial to genocide where I come from. So for now we're gonna keep the Karf locked in their spire until I can figure out what to do with them. What I want you folks to do is set about getting your lives in order. Just remember: no stealing, no fighting, no killing, and that includes the whooboo. We will talk again but for now we have things to do, so y'all should mosey on home."

From the Braggitt delegation a deep base voice croaked. "And what if the Others come?"

This time, the assembled creatures were dumbstruck; several physically cringed while others gasped. The Others were a subject never discussed, as though the mere mention of them would summon horrors from the void.

Billy Ray smiled and gestured dismissively. "If they show up I'll have a talk with them. It's our understanding that they brought the Karf here in the first place. Maybe we can convince them to do the right thing and take 'em away."

As one, the Braggitt delegation blinked slowly, then turned to leave. In small groups, talking in lowered voices, the rest of the crowd filtered out of the plaza. Some thought the Earthlings were crazy; others hoped they would deal with the almost mythical Others as they had dealt with the Karf; most didn't know what to think.

Billy Ray switched off his external speakers and commented to his wife on suit-to-suit. "How was that, Number One?"

"Brilliant, dear. My heroes have always been cowboys."

Captain's Quarters, Peggy Sue

Since the town hall meeting, the station's residents started coming out of hiding. The shopkeepers in the Mall reopened their stalls and stores. Slowly at first, creatures began to seek out the ship's officers to settle disputes. Remarkably few violent incidents occurred. A Hisstow attacked a Hoon, prompting a Marine to fling the offending cat-lizard off the second level balcony and into the spire's crystalline wall. The Hoon was thankful and Dr. de Bruin was overjoyed to have an alien patient to work on.

294

The station was settling in to a less terrorized existence as the four partners met in the Captain's in-port cabin to prepare for the arrival of the feared and mysterious Others.

"So where do we stand with our preparations?" the Captain asked his officers.

The First Officer spoke first. "We've checked the other major spires and all the minor ones that showed signs of possible habitation. There are no signs of Karf outside of their own habitat. We've strategically placed battle bots at major intersections and embedded signal repeaters in the tunnels to ensure we have good comms everywhere inside. We have recon drones out among the spires and snakebots and other sensors throughout the interior. Without locking down the residents we are as secure as we can get."

"Very good, and the Tcist is cooperating?"

"Yes, Captain," Bobby answered. "Once we returned its missing parts—and explained what was likely to happen when the Others arrive—it decided to cooperate fully. It was more than happy to give us the fuel containers."

"And the AM containers are OK? They are compatible, not rigged to explode or malfunction in someway at an awkward moment?"

"Hai, Captain. Chief Engineer Baldursson and I checked them over before transporting them to the ship. These standardized antimatter containment devices have been around for millions of years, they even predate the T'aafhal as far as we can tell. We don't know how to make them, and the only time we tried to open one it was a spectacular failure."

That attempt had been several years ago. A team of scientists and engineers tried to slice open an empty type three container using a remote control laser cutter. The result was a vaporized asteroid in Jupiter's Trailing Trojans.

"We know they can be destroyed but nobody knows how to make them? That's just brilliant, the whole galaxy is dependent on technology no one can replicate."

"Least of our current worries, Number One. So Bobby, we are all tanked up on antimatter and ready to rumble?"

"Aye, Captain, that we are. I still wish we had more D, just in case, but we have reserve supplies enough to get us home, though a bit more slowly than we came."

"Speaking of home, has the messenger probe left the system?"

"Yes, Sir. It entered alter-space on the transit line for Aldebaran five hours ago. Still, it will take close to a month for it to get back to Earth."

"Well, at least they will know what became of us if this goes sideways. Have we gotten any new intel on our prospective adversaries, Number One?"

"According to the Tcist and some of the older resident species these 'Others' are about man sized, bipedal and wear armor similar to our own. They came in a fleet of ships and took over the station in a matter of days. Not much to go on I'm afraid."

"Captain, Mizuki and I were talking last night about neutrinos."

"That's the best thing you could find to talk about, alone in your quarters?"

Mizuki smiled at the jest. Once back on board the ship, following the excitement of their abduction and subsequent rescue, she and Bobby had been spending a lot of time in their quarters.

"What Bobby is trying to say is that we were talking about the ship's reactors and how different classes of ship have distinguishable neutrino spectra. As you know there are three types of neutrino: electron neutrinos, muon neutrinos, and tau neutrinos. These can be detected by the way they interact with other forms of matter through the weak nuclear force."

Billy Ray raised his eyebrows questioningly.

"Antimatter annihilation creates a much different neutrino emission spectrum than does, say, fusion in a star. For different reasons, our muon catalyzed fusion reactors also emit a different spectrum, but one that is closer to that of stellar reactions than antimatter reactions."

"OK, and this is leading to what?"

Bobby picked up the explanation.

"What Mizuki told me last night was that—assuming these Others are not familiar with our fusion technology—they might not recognize our ship against the background neutrino flux. Our fusion reactors are well shielded and very efficient. As long as we aren't burning antimatter, it may be possible to hide from the enemy even while underway—as long as it is at low power and with the shields in stealth mode."

Mizuki, ever the scientist, offered helpfully. "I can send you Feynman diagrams of the various reactions if you are interested."

"No, that's quite alright, Mizuki. I'll take your word for it. So what you're saying is we could maneuver for an optimum attack position without tipping them off. That's good information to have. Thank you. What else do we know about our prospective foes?"

Bobby nodded. "We won't know what the enemy looks like until they enter the system and we can get some readings on how much AM they are burning. Like Beth said, from what little we can gather, the last time they came in a fleet of ships, best guess between ten and twenty vessels. How capable these vessels are we can't say."

"All right. Let's get things as prepped as we can. Number One, continue to rotate the Marines out by squad so they can have some down time. And schedule gunnery and damage control drills for the crew."

"Aye, aye, Captain." The First Officer made notations on her arm display.

"Also, let's be extra nice to our polar bears. The earlier we detect the Others' entrance into the system the better, so their keeping a careful watch on the alter-space sensors is critical."

"Roger that, Captain," the Sailing Master agreed. "I just wish we knew more about these 'Others'."

"Remember, pardner, 'the unseen enemy is always the most fearsome.'"

Armory, Peggy Sue

1st Squad had just returned to the ship, replacing 2nd Squad who rotated back to duty on the Starflake. First order of business after

297

getting off the shuttle was to report to the Armory and remove their battle armor. After spending a week in armor, being decanted by the armorers was both a trial and a celebration. The suits' sanitary plumbing retracted, the Marines exited the backs of their armor clad only in skintight inner suits and the fragrance of their week's confinement.

"I don't mind being in armor," commented Grits, pulling himself free of his domicile for the last seven days. "But I sure hate getting out of it."

"Oh man!" exclaimed Vinny. "My suit smells like seven days of BO and ball sweat."

"As long as you keep it to yourself, mate," Brains replied.

"Now you primates know how you smell to me all the time," Inuksuk growled.

"No room for shrinking violets in the Marines," the Gunny bellowed at them, "so quit your bellyaching and get your asses to the showers."

Grumbling, the Marines limped toward the exit. Wearing heavy armor forced bodily positions that required a while to wear off. Brains could not resist teasing his partner.

"So you don't want to wait and talk to your bird? You might catch her in a weak moment."

"With me looking like something the dog drug in? Hell no I don't want to talk to Keti. What I want is a long hot shower, a meal with real food, and then about ten hours of rack time."

Walking behind them Inuksuk rumbled. "You primates constantly complain about being on the hunt." The he-bear looked as misused as the humans, with matted fur and a pronounced limp of his own.

"You'd rather be on the station than here, Bubba-bear?"

"I'd rather be on the pack ice. You monkey boys view the hunt as a chore to get done, so you can go back to lounging around on board. For bears lounging around is the chore. Being out on the ice, free to see what's over the next pressure ridge or across that open lead, that's living. Sitting in our quarters with nothing to do, that is living hell."

298

"If you hate being cooped up on board so much why did you sign on in the first place?" asked Vinny.

"I told you before, it was this or stay locked up in that petting zoo you humans built for us on the Moon. Nothing to hunt, no place to explore, surrounded by females and cubs all the time. That's no way for a male polar bear to live. At least going on this voyage offers a chance to explore, and some prey to hunt."

"And nothing about being back here on the ship appeals to you, mate?"

"I'll enjoy a plunge in properly chilled sea water, and I could eat a nice fat seal, but after that I'd rather get back to looking for things to fight."

"Watch what you wish for, Nanook, you just might get it," Vinny intoned. "See you when we are ready to head back to the Starflake."

Inuksuk made a woofing sound and headed aft to the polar bear quarters, steak knife length claws clicking against the deck as he went. The humans continued forward toward the crew showers.

"I guess we are different, us and the bears," Grits mused.

"I don't know, Grits," Vinny replied. "I've known a lot of bears and Inuksuk seems grumpier than most."

Brains shrugged. "He won't be happy until we are up to our arseholes in space monsters."

"Bite your tongue, Bubba."

Chapter 33

Captain's Quarters

Two days later the Other's arrived at Eudora. Naturally the event took place during Middle Watch, in the middle of the night ship's time. A gentle but insistent tone sounded in the Captain's quarters, causing both Beth and Billy Ray to stir.

Billy Ray was one of those lucky people who could emerge from deep sleep fully awake. He answered the incoming call.

"Captain. Go."

"Captain, Bridge. We have unknown ships emerging in system."

"I'll be right there. Captain, out."

Beth, not being one of the lucky people, stretched sleepily and asked her husband the reason for the disturbance.

"What's happening, dear? And what time is it?"

"It's 0317 hours and our visitors are arriving. I'm headed for the bridge."

Reluctantly, Beth accepted that she needed to arise as well, after all she was the first officer. Throwing off the blanket, she sat up and placed one foot on the floor.

"You realize they won't be here for at least a week, maybe more? We won't even have full drive profiles until the light and particle radiation reaches our sensors."

"Yer right, honey bunch, there's time to grab a shower first. Race you to the bathroom?"

"I was thinking that we could save time if we showered together," she smiled mischievously. "After all, things are probably going to get busy and we won't have much time to ourselves until this is over."

"Have I ever told you I love the way yer mind works, sweetheart?"

She stood up, kissed him, and as she passed him headed for the shower she grabbed his ass.

* * * * *

"Captain on the bridge!" shouted one of the bridge crew.

While OATC ships were not Navy vessels, many of the officers and crew had come from the service. Traditions were observed out of habit, even if their original purpose was obscured. In this case, it was to inform those on the bridge that the Captain was now present and giving the orders, not to make sure no one was caught napping. With the sighting of possible hostiles it was not as though any of the bridge crew were napping. All were paying rapt attention to what was happening.

"Lt. Palmer, status report," Billy Ray barked.

"Sir, PO Siku reports a number of contacts on the alter-space sensors indicating the arrival of a fleet of ships in system."

"Siku, what have you spotted?"

"Captain, I've caught the scent of two waves of ships emerging from the same alter-space transit point. Starting at 0315, the first group consisted of six vessels, which immediately began deceleration. This was followed by another six vessels about fifteen minutes later. They followed the first group's course."

"And where are they now?"

"They have headed for the far side of the primary star. They were assuming some sort of formation before the readings began to washout. I've lost track due to interference from the star's gravity well."

"They are probably going to use a gravitational assist from Eudora to alter their trajectory," added Bobby, who had arrived on the bridge shortly after the Captain and First Officer. "Swing around the star and head for the Starflake."

"A reasonable assumption, Sailing Master. Anything else of note, Siku?"

"None of the scents indicate drives or shields of unusual strength."

"In other words, nothing we should be preparing to run from?"

302

The she-bear grinned. It was not a friendly grin. "Certainly nothing that comes close to the Peggy Sue, Captain."

"Very good. Well done people. Let me know when we have 3-space data to analyze. Number One, Cmdr. Danner, accompany me to the CIC if you would. Lt. Palmer, the deck is yours."

The Officers left the bridge, headed aft. The First Officer called the mess on her collar pip and ordered coffee brought to the CIC, it was going to be a long morning. As they departed Lt. Palmer called out.

"The Captain has left the bridge. I have the deck."

Chief's Lounge, Goat Locker

Steve Hitch and Matt Jacobs had come back to the ship with the rotation of Marine squads. Though light armor was not as taxing for the wearer as the Marine's heavy battle armor, spending extended periods in it was still not a pleasant experience. Glad to be out of their armor, both were in the Goat Locker, chowing down, when Master Chief Hank Zackly entered.

"Well look what the cat drug in," the wizened old sailor said by way of greeting. "Yous finally decided to stop dicking around on the station and return to work?"

"Hey, Master Chief," Hitch replied. "You know we'd rather be on board with you than stomping around dirtside in that uncomfortable armor."

"Stevie, you ain't even any good as an ass kisser," Zackly responded. "Why you hang around with this no load I'll never figure out, Matt." The fact that the Master Chief was using their first names indicated that he really was happy to see them, or at least they were not currently on his shit list.

"So what's the word, Master Chief?" asked Jacobs, hoping to catch up on recent scuttlebutt.

"Looks like there's a fleet of unknown but presumed hostile ships headed our way. The Captain is huddled with the brain trust tryin' to decide how best to handle the situation."

Hitch put down his fork. "Bend over, here it comes again. We just get done with those little gray shits and it's time for act two."

"Are we running or fighting?" asked Jacobs.

"Beats me, that's why they's officers and we ain't. If we are gonna head for the exit we should know soon. If we're gonna engage these new bogies we won't be goin' anywhere. Either way its above our paygrade."

"What do you think will happen?"

"Have yous ever known the Captain to run from a fight?"

CIC, Peggy Sue

"Speaking of our master plan, Captain," the First Officer began. "If they can't find our ship they will probably land troops to takeover the station while standing off to provide cover. The only way I see to limit their incursion on the station is to leave the Marines there as a defense force."

"Can we not intercept them before they reach the station?" Mizuki had joined the discussion late. Not being part of the command structure, she had risen at a more reasonable hour.

"If we go at them they can scatter. No way we can take them all out without some getting past us," Beth answered her friend. "And given what's inside of the Starflake we probably can't prevent them from destroying it."

"I agree, Beth," Bobby concurred. "The only way to keep them bunched up is to get them to commit to a landing."

"And if we do that," Mizuki said, "the station inhabitants would be at the invaders' mercy."

"Yeah, Mizuki-chan. And since these guys left the grays in charge I don't think they have a lot of mercy in them."

"As I said, we are back to leaving the Marines on the station to repel boarders. The only problem with that is we may be hanging the lads out to dry."

"Yer assuming these buzzards won't abandon their landing force if we bloody their noses," Billy Ray added. He was letting the others work through their tactical options while playing devil's advocate.

"From talking with the Tcist it sounds like these Others came with a landing force of several hundred the last time they were here. Armed with plasma weapons and some kind of body armor. Maybe we need to even the odds a bit during the landing."

"That was ten thousand years ago, pardner. Things might have changed a bit since."

"If these are a species of Dark Lord minion, as we suspect, it is improbable that they have been allowed to advance much technically. Masters are always fearful that their subjects will become powerful enough to challenge their rule. Japan almost completely abandoned the development and use of firearms during a period of seclusion known as *Sakoku*. The Samurai class feared the peasants would rise up if they had weapons that could kill them, so they tried to ban firearms completely."

"Yeah, but in the end it didn't work. Never wish away your enemy's capabilities."

"Of course not, Captain. But the policy only failed when more advanced outsiders forced them to adapt."

"Either way, the ship can't be in two places at the same time."

"We do have the two Kestrels," Beth said with a thoughtful look.

"Whoa there Number One, let's not get ahead of ourselves. We don't have good energy use profiles or acceleration data for the hostile ships yet. This may be a fight we don't want to pick."

"And if it looks like we are overmatched?"

"Then we pull the Marines out and slip off quietly. Put enough distance between us and them to be reasonably certain we can make a dash for the transfer point headed home. Then blow the station with the hyperluminal particle cannon."

The others looked at him grim faced. None of them liked the idea of destroying the station and all its inhabitants. Though Beth and Bobby had commands of their own in the past, both were glad that Billy Ray was the captain. In the end, that decision would be his.

"And if it looks like we can take them?" asked Beth.

"All warfare is based on deception. Hence, when we are able to attack, we must seem unable; when using our forces, we must appear inactive; when we are near, we must make the enemy believe we are far away; when far away, we must make him believe we are near."

Mizuki smiled at the quotation. "Sun Tzu."

"Old Sun got a lot of things right. In this case, once we have a bead on these varmints, we will put the Marines on board the station, put the shields in stealth mode, and using only fusion power move off to a position from which we can ambush 'em once they start landing troops"

Station Trader's Bower

"Have you any news from the Earthlings, Shanakta-fek?" demanded the Station Trader. The junior trader had just returned from the Shopping Mall spire where he was sent to observed the invading aliens. For better or worse, he had been the first contact with the outsiders and was now expected to continue as a liaison between the Station Trader and the Earthlings.

"No, Station Trader. But they continue with preparations for battle, installing observation devices and positioning robotic weapons platforms throughout the station's hub."

"They have said nothing regarding the approaching fleet of ships?"

"They have not, though they began moving warriors and supplies from their ship even before the signs of arrival were known. Even the Braggitt did not know of the arrival before the Earthlings activity increased."

"What does that mean? Have they some magic technology others don't know about?"

"I asked the Braggitt that same question, Station Trader. They said that there are records of such technology but it was presumed lost more than a million years ago."

"Unless these Earth creatures have rediscovered it. Interesting, we have been assuming that the oncoming fleet would be more than a match for the Earthlings' single ship. The Others may be in for a surprise."

"Interesting is hardly the word I'd use, Station Trader," commented Master Trader Linoda-tik-toe. "Whatever the outcome we are sure to be in the crossfire."

The Station Trader twitched his bushy tail dismissively. "Regardless, we must make sure that our trade goods are concealed in the maintenance tunnels and all the people safely hidden well before the Others arrive."

"As you command, Faooshda-rik-tik-ta. Preparations are well underway," Linoda-tik-toe replied with an obsequious bow. "We have survived other troubles, we shall survive this as well."

Asserting his dominance, the Station Trader arched his tail over his head like a hooded cobra. He returned his attention to Shanakta-fek, who was trying to remain invisible.

"Junior Trader Shanakta-fek, return to the company of these strange warlike aliens and keep your eyes open. Try to find out when the Others will arrive."

"Yes, Station Trader. By your leave?"

"Yes, yes. Be gone."

Bridge, Uxoreeza Flagship

Seven and a half billion kilometers away, the alien fleet rounded Eudora and settled on an intercept course for the Starflake. Admiral Leezzark preened her neck ruff and stared at the sensor display in front of her. Around the bridge, crewmembers bent to their tasks, aware of their commander's eyes on their necks.

The admiral's kind had patrolled this part of the Orion Arm for time out of mind. Vicious and warlike, the Uxoreeza were well

307

suited to their jobs as Janissaries for the Dark Lords. They were shock troops, sent in whenever a new threat emerged that could not be handled locally. Brutal and effective, this was only the second time in two hundred generations they had needed to visit this system.

The gray vermin must be hard pressed to risk calling us, Leezzark thought. *They are bullies and like all bullies cowards at their core. Whatever this new threat is, it must frighten them more than us—something that I will correct.*

"Your pardon, Admiral," the signals officer said, interrupting the Admiral's thoughts. "You asked for any word from the garrison."

Pushing aside the impulse to kill the officer for disturbing her, the Admiral hissed and made a come on gesture with one clawed forearm.

The signals officer bobbed her head submissively and continued. "The cowardly scum report that a new species has taken over the station. Despite the Karf's best efforts, including the reported deaths of hundreds of the vermin, a race of technically advanced creatures has sealed them in a single spire. The invaders have complete control of the rest of the station."

The Admiral growled deep in her throat. "Did the feckless cowards say anything useful, like the number of invaders or how many ships they have?"

"No, Admiral. Nothing definite. They report at least one-hundred warriors but only one ship, though they are not sure."

"Sensor operator! Can we see their ship?"

"No, Admiral. We are still far away and the alien vessel may be docked at the station."

The admiral's head whipped around and she eyed the signals officer with quick, birdlike movements. "Tell them to send more useful information. Now. These new aliens can't be that fearsome if the gray vermin are still live."

"As you command, Admiral. We are still nearly seven light-hours from the station. It will take close to fifteen hours to receive an answer."

The Admiral's head whipped back around to look at the main display, her clawed forearms sinking into the arms of her couch. The signals officer wisely retreated without another word.

Chapter 34

Karf Spire, The Starflake

With Rick's help, Phil positioned the device so that its long axis was aligned with the central axis of the spire. About two meters long and a half meter in diameter in the middle, the device was obviously not a polished piece of work. Unfolding three spindly collapsible legs, Phil stuck the contraption to the deck with all purpose adhesive. A few minor adjustments and he was satisfied.

Stepping back he motioned to Rick to head back to the airlock where Bud stood watch. They were using hand signals, maintaining total radio silence just in case. The SEALs had worked together for years and were comfortable in silence.

Up two levels and down a side passage, they quickly arrived at Bud's position. They were in the topmost quarter of the spire, only a couple of kilometers from its apex. No Karf were present this far up, no habitat structures, just a collection of devices, wires and antennae stuck to the transparent material of the station itself. All three entered the crystalline airlock that pierced the spire.

Cycling the lock, the SEALs used their maneuvering packs to head for the jet black shuttle floating just off the spire's shear wall. As they approached the rear hatch opened, revealing the small craft's interior illuminated only by infrared light. Slipping inside, the hatch closed behind them and the shuttle sped away into the vacuum.

"Everything copacetic?" asked Pauline Palmer from the pilot's seat.

"Everything's squared away, Lieutenant," Rick responded. "How long, Phil?"

"Another minute and a half, Chief."

"Assuming the grays didn't find it." Bud was always worried about things going wrong on a mission like this.

"I put a trembler switch on it. Any thing tries to move it and it goes off early. Quit worrying."

"I'll give you guys a balcony seat for the event," Pauline said, bringing the pinnace into a nose up drift and turning the top of the passenger compartment transparent. The pinnace was meant as a passenger launch for the Captain and other dignitaries, not a war craft, but sometimes its features could be useful. Staring back at the spire, the SEALs felt as though they were hanging in space.

"Five seconds," Phil called. "...three, two, one."

A bright flash lit up the upper third of the spire. This was followed by secondary flashes, like a lightning storm was trapped inside the crystal structure.

"It didn't blow up," Bud said.

"Wasn't supposed to," answered Rick.

"It was an EMP device," Phil explained. "Super conducting coil with a strong current flowing through it, imploded by an explosive collar. Sent a pulse worthy of a nuclear explosion out both ends when it went off."

Rick nodded. "It should have fried anything electronic in the upper half of the spire, which is where the Karf signals to the approaching enemy fleet were coming from."

"Blowing them up would have stopped the signals too."

"Bitch, bitch, bitch. Some guys are never satisfied."

"You said it, Phil. Lieutenant, let's go back to the barn."

"On our way Chief, and well done."

CIC, *Peggy Sue*

Two weeks after the Karf were silenced, messages from the approaching fleet continued with monotonous regularity. This provided plenty of opportunity for the Peggy Sue's computer to decode and translate the messages. All demanded information regarding the station's invaders but tellingly did not inquire about the Karf's well being. After listening to the latest message the Captain figured it was time to give the enemy a nudge.

"So we're ready to beam this from the remote transmitter the engineers installed, Number One?"

"Aye, Sir. It's located on a spire close to the Karf habitat."

"And you are sure you can translate so they will understand it, Peggy Sue?"

"Yes, Captain. They are using a fairly simple modulation scheme and the underlying language is one of the older galactic common languages. They will understand what you say."

"Great. Well, here goes." Billy Ray collected his thoughts and began to speak:

"Attention, Commander of the approaching fleet. This is Captain Billy Ray Vincent of the OATC starship Peggy Sue. Just wanted to let you know that we found this station abandoned and have decided to keep it. It did have a terrible infestation problem, but we fixed that. You're welcome to take the remaining vermin with you if you'd like. Otherwise, unless you have goods to trade, you may as well just move along. Vincent out."

"Is that it, Captain?"

"Yep, that'll do for an opening gambit. Go ahead and send it. Let's see if they alter their formation or change course in any way."

Bobby was grinning over Billy Ray's message. "That ought to pique their interest."

"I promised to let the Others take the Karf with them. I try to always keep my promises."

"If you boys are through having fun baiting the nasty aliens, the approaching fleet is little more than a day out and decelerating rapidly. I think it time we deploy the Marines and start to move the ship away from the station."

"I reckon so, Number One. I'll send more messages periodically, relayed through the remote transmitter. They should help add to our enemy's confusion."

"I still think we should use the Kestrels to support the Marines."

"Let's see what their landing force looks like first, before we commit any assets."

"Yes, Sir. What about the troop shuttles? Should we leave them docked at the station?"

"Yeah, have the crews in standard armor and armed. And have the SEALs report to Lt. Taylor. They can help hold the Shopping Mall spire if the Marines need to be evacuated."

"This plan is not giving me a warm and fuzzy feeling, Captain."

Billy Ray sighed. "Our priorities are: save the antimatter cache; minimize our own casualties; take out as much of the enemy fleet as possible, leaving no one to regroup for a counter attack; and try to avoid slaughtering the station's inhabitants. We've been over and over this for two weeks and if you have a better plan let's here it, Commander."

The use of her rank was a sign of the Captain's irritation. They had been over this from every angle, but Beth was not one who like to play things by ear. She preferred a detailed plan, even if it did get modified on contact with the enemy.

Nothing for it. She drew herself up almost to attention. "Aye, aye, Sir."

"All right people, let's get ready to kick ET's butt."

1st Squad, Starflake Hub

The two squads of Marines were positioned in the bases of several minor spires, forming a line between the Karf spire and the Shopping Mall spire. They had no firm idea of where the alien landing force would try to board the station, or in what numbers. This put the Gunny and Lt. Taylor in ill humor.

"This goat hump has all the signs of turning into a full on cluster fuck, Army."

"I hear you Gunny. At least our ROEs are simple—whatever shows up, kill it."

"Thank goodness for small favors," Rosey said, sarcastically. "At least you special operator types got our backs, right?"

"I just heard from the XO, the SEALs and Green Berets are to hold the Shopping Mall, just in case ET decides to assault the food court."

The Gunny chuckled. She knew from long experience that when you are about to be slipped the green weenie the best you can do is laugh about it. That didn't mean she had to like it.

"On a serious note, JT. I have a feeling that this time we are going to have to earn our pay."

"Yeah, me too, Rosey. Watch your ass out there."

"Roger that, Army."

* * * * *

Nearby, Grits, Brains, and Beau were also contemplating the coming action. Their concerns were a bit more immediate and personal than their leaders'. While those in command might not provide all the information they wished, grunts had sources of their own.

"I was talking to Chief Hitch, you know, the crazy one?"

"Yeah, mate?"

"He says these critters are a lot nastier than the little gray peckers. About man sized, armed with plasma shooters, and probably some kind of armor."

"And how does he know this?" asked the skeptical Beau.

"Him and the other Chief, Jacobs, are old timers and they chat with the officers a lot. They also know when to keep their traps shut and listen."

"OK, say these new nasties are tougher than the Karf, what's that to us? We hit them as they try to board the station and Bob's your uncle."

"Who?" asked a confused Beau.

"Ignore him, it's just more limey talk." Grits paused and grew wistful. "You know guys, my only regret is that I was unable to convince Keti of my affection for her. I almost talked her into visiting the hydroponic section with me."

"Bloody fabulous. We're about to face hostile space monsters and you have a case of blue balls."

Beau laughed. "That I understood. Come on, *mes amis*, how bad can these space monsters be?"

"Oh hell, don't say that! You want to jinx us all?"

"Get over, mate, and grow a pair. We'll kill these gits and you can go back to the fruitless pursuit of your Georgian amazon."

"If I die with my love for Keti unrequited, one of you polecats make sure there's a song written about it. Something tragically romantic, like Free Bird."

Both his squadmates rolled their eyes, gestures unseen outside their battle armor.

Shopping Mall

"Where do you want us, Lieutenant?" asked Chief Morgan, arriving with his two fellow SEALs in tow. The plaza had a deserted look, with most of the shop fronts already closed. A few aliens headed for the exits glancing furtively at the humans in their armored suits and weapons.

Turning around, JT greeted the three. "Welcome to my little redoubt among the stars, Chief. Why don't you and the boys join the swabbies in moving the civilians out of here. When the balloon goes up I don't want any non-hostile aliens getting in the way."

"Aye, aye, LT. Should we start with that thing coming up behind you?"

JT turned and saw a coffee table sized mollusk advancing on him. It might be the one from the Captain's earlier town hall meeting or not—who could tell with a mollusk? The SEALs subtly moved to either side, clearing their fields of fire. JT looked at the rock-like shell of the approaching alien and thought, *now what?*

"Can I help you?" he asked the creature as it eased to a stop a few feet away from him. He could clearly see a multitude of jewel like crystals that pierced the rough, stone hard shell of the alien. Dr. Krenshaw, the staff xenobiologist, said they were most likely lenses for an array of light sensors. On the surface of the shell there was a small box that was obviously not an organic part of the creature. From the box a mechanical voice replied.

"You should know that the Uxoreeza, the Others as my fellow residents call them, will probably use the docking facilities between the minor spires."

"The what? What docking facilities?"

"There are places to dock large ships between some of the minor spires. That is where they landed the last time."

"Right. And you know this how? Not that I doubt you."

"I was here when it happened."

"Your saying that you were a first hand witness of the invasion over ten thousand years ago?"

"Mine is a long lived species. I was much younger then but I remember the coming of the Uxoreeza. They slaughtered many of the residents, including many of my kind. If you would kill them, I would consider the act most favorably, a kindness to the residents."

"And where are these docking facilities located?"

"They are located near the spire that houses the Karf. Between the first and second rows of minor spires, equally spaced around the major spire. The last time there were several hundred warriors in the landing force. They are much more formidable than the Karf."

"Thank you for the information, this could help us repel the landing force. Why did you decide to come forward and not the others?"

"Most were not alive then, and those that were are pusillanimous cowards. They would rather stay silent and hope the slaughter passes them by."

"Tell the others: 'In the end, we will remember not the words of our enemies, but the silence of our friends.'"

Having said its piece the strange creature turned to leave. Then it paused.

"May the God of all creation be with you, warrior."

With that the mollusk glided away toward the elevators.

"What was that all about, Lieutenant?" asked Phil, as the SEALs relaxed the grip on their weapons.

"It would seem that at least one of the station residents has got some courage."

"Interesting. A religious oyster with a grudge against the—what did it call them—the Uxoreeza."

"Sometimes, help comes from the strangest places, Chief. I'd best call the ship and let the Captain know. We may need to reposition the Marines."

Chapter 35

Bridge, Uxoreeza Flagship

"...where I come from well mannered folk mind their own business. So you see, if you critters insist on sticking your noses into my business you just might find 'em chopped off, if you catch my drift. It's not too late to turn around and go back where you came from. Just a friendly warning. Vincent out."

"Who is this insufferable blatherskite!" the Admiral screeched, her curved talons digging deeply into the arms of the commander's couch. The creature calling itself Captain Vincent had been sending taunting messages to the fleet every few hours, and with each new message the Admiral's rage grew. "I want it taken alive so I can eat its liver in front of its dying eyes."

"Yes, Admiral," replied the flagship's captain, safely outside of talon range. "We are within one thousand kilometers of the station, what are your orders?"

"Send the frigates to surround the station. They are to locate this missing alien vessel and prevent it from escaping. It can't be a very powerful ship or we would have picked up an energy signature by now. Send the fighters and scout carriers out to infiltrate the structure from multiple locations, followed by the assault ships. They are to use the large docking facilities and offload their warriors quickly. We will overrun these annoying aliens before they know what has hit them."

"As you order, Admiral. And the rest of the fleet?"

"The cruisers are to hold four hundred kilometers out, along with the cargo ship. We will stand by in case the assault flushes the insufferable Captain Vincent."

"By your command, Admiral Leezzark." The subordinate officer bowed and turned to pass her orders to the rest of the fleet. The assault on the Starflake was underway.

Bridge, Peggy Sue

Roughly tangent to the Starflake's orbital plane and one hundred kilometers from the station the Peggy Sue was quietly advancing on the alien fleet. Using only its fusion reactors and minimal acceleration, the ship was wrapped in a cloak of invisibility. The advanced T'aafhal shields bent electromagnetic radiation around the vessel, making it all but impossible to pick out from the starry background. Radar and Lidar saw nothing but empty space.

Monitoring sensor readings from recon drones near the station, the Captain and crew watched as a flight of small craft approached the station—scouts and fighters. Behind them were three larger auxiliary craft that had broken away from the large freighter, in-system craft meant to transport troops. As the fighters wove between the station's spires the half dozen larger scout craft disappeared from sight—evidently landing on the station itself.

Aside from the fighters, scouts, and troop carriers, four frigate sized warships spread out around the station. At a distance of thirty kilometers they formed a tetrahedron surrounding their target. The tetrahedron's forward most edge was canted at a forty five degree angle to the Karf's spire.

"Not to be negative or anything," Bobby began. "But these creatures seem to have done this sort of thing before."

"They do seem to know what they are doing, don't they Commander?" the First Officer replied.

Billy Ray sat silently for a few seconds. "Remember when you said we might need to support the Marines with the Kestrels, Number One?"

"Yes, Captain."

"I'm thinkin' you were right."

"Thank you for saying so, Sir."

He beckoned her near so they could whisper. She leaned close and placed one hand on the arm of the commander's chair.

"Who do you want for a wingman?"

"I'll take Lt. Hoenig, if I may."

"You sure he's the best one for the job?"

"The best pilot for the job is Bobby, but you need him on the helm or none of us are going home. Hoenig will do."

He covered her hand with his own and said: "The curves of your lips rewrite history."

"Lovely dear, Oscar Wilde?" Beth smiled at the Captain her husband. "I will be fine. Just take care of those warships for me."

Billy Ray nodded and then called out. "Mr. Hoenig, you will accompany the First Officer and prep the Kestrels. We are going to send the Marines some air support."

"Aye, aye, Sir," Frank said, leaving his chair on the helm console. He and Beth headed aft to board the fighter craft, Beth already issuing instructions.

"Lt. Palmer, report to the bridge." She would take Hoenig place next to Bobby at the ship's helm.

Shopping Mall

"Squads One and Two, we have small craft landing troops in multiple locations. They look like pathfinders for the bigger troop carriers. I'm sending locations. Squad Two, intercept and neutralize."

"Roger that, Ice Castle."

"Squad One, you need to find the major docking areas. That should be where the main push will come. We need to stop them at the docks, if they get loose on the station it'll take forever to hunt them down."

"I copy, Ice Castle. I think we've found what your pet oyster was talking about. I'll report back with confirmation. Squad One out."

The SEALs had returned from sweeping the area for noncombatants. Watching his tactical display, Chief Morgan spoke to JT on suit-to-suit. "These hostiles do not act like a bunch of bush league primitives, my friend."

"You got that right, Rick. I'm thinking we don't have nearly enough Marines to go around."

"You want us to stay here in the plaza?"

"Stick close, you're my rapid response force if someone gets in trouble out there."

Sheltering next to the humans, Shanakta-fek looked around nervously with his bulbous red-orange eyes. He could not hear the Earthlings' conversation but he could tell things were not going well.

* * * * *

Meanwhile, two levels up and on the other side of the spire, Chief Hitch and Kashi Ademola were patrolling the halls of the shopping mall. They paused outside the room that had contained the Tcist when they were first liberated. Though the intelligent moss and the giant flatworms they grew on had been repatriated to the station core, their crystal pond remained.

"Looks like nothing is stirring, Chief," the tall Nigerian sailor said. As he looked out the floor to ceiling window, something dark obstructed the view, eclipsing stars and crystal spires alike. The darkness collided with the station wall. "What the hell!"

"Get back, take cover beside the doorway!" Hitch ordered. As he did likewise he rolled a small observation camera into the room. On it he saw that the dark object was some kind of ship, which clung to the side of the spire with splayed landing pads.

The ship pulled its belly up to the transparent wall and a two by three meter rectangular seal pressed against the crystal. The rounded rectangle glued itself to the station and seconds later there was an explosion. The two sailors jerked back as shards of crystal flew through the doorway between them.

Hitch risked a peek inside, his camera having been taken out by the explosion. There were large, bipedal creatures in space suits, with weapons, exiting the craft.

"Ice Castle, Hitch. We're at the Tcist room. We're being boarded."

"What do we do, Chief?" asked the frightened Kashi.

"Shoot the fuckers!"

Hitch stepped into the doorway and unloaded on the invaders. Kashi followed suit a split second later. More of the bipeds emerged from the landing craft, firing as they ran to either side. Angry orange bolts of plasma splattered off the door frame and the wall behind the sailors as they tried to contain the threat. In growing desperation, Hitch called to his friend Chief Jacobs.

"Matt, Stevie! we're getting our asses kicked out here. Some backup would be real nice about now."

"On our way, Stevie, just hold on!"

As Jacobs replied the wall beyond Kashi erupted in an orange ball of flame and globs of molten metal. Aliens burst from the hole hopping nimbly into the hallway. The first turned to face the defenders as several more ran down the hall away from the battle. The first alien fired, its plasma bolt striking Kashi in the side.

Hitch dove sideways as Kashi fell to the floor. Firing as he fell, he hit the alien in the chest with a 20mm round—the alien exploded but the damage was done. Kashi was down with a smoking hole in his side and Hitch couldn't even reach his body for the fire coming from inside the room. He hugged his railgun and pressed his back against the wall, waiting for the charge that was inevitably coming.

2nd Squad

"The LT said there was a landing near this minor spire, so keep your eyes open." Sgt Aurora and her squad had been tasked with plugging the leaks in the station's perimeter. As they rounded the corner into the zone beneath the spire, Cpl. Kwan, who was on point, held up a fist and backed away from the opening.

There was the normal open area beneath the small spire with the expected glowing elevator shaft in the center. What was unexpected, or at least undesirable, were the dozen or so armed bipeds that were standing around the shaft as more of their kind descended.

"Sarge, we got better than a squad's worth of hostiles on the ground in there."

"Seal shit! Call it in, Kato, and the rest of you spread out. See if we can find covered positions we can fire on them from. We need to try and contain them here."

"What do they look like?" asked one of the squad members.

"Two legs, long neck and tail. Short arms holding plasma weapons. Now quit yapping and spread out."

After telling Ice Castle they had eyes on the hostiles, Kato led his fireteam to the left. The others flanked right. Followed by Haddad, He worked his way down a side tunnel that curved back and forth like a grease trap in a sink. At the other end was a large room, and in that room was a large gray mountain of flesh.

"*Wallah!* isn't that like the creature that knocked out Inuksuk?"

"It is indeed, Assad, a splagg" Kato replied sticking a fiber optic probe around the corner. After a half minute's examination he pulled the probe back and called his sergeant. "Aurora, I think I have an idea."

1st Squad

The Gunny and her squad moved off the familiar pathways of the station's transportation network and walked down side passages, looking for the docking facilities reported by JT. They found a curving hallway that seemed to describe a sizable perimeter around something as yet unknown.

"Bosco, your team left. Inuksuk, your team right."

Both team leaders keyed their comm in acknowledgment. The Gunny motioned Grits and Brains to her left, as Beau followed on her six. In front of them, separated by a bit over ten meters were a pair of tunnels leading inward. The two pairs of Marines stacked at the tunnels. The Gunny motioned them forward and they entered their respective tunnels together.

The tunnels led them into a large amphitheater, a large bowl with tiers of balconies running around a central space. It looked like a crystal opera house except that in the center front, where the stage should be, was a titanic transparent stalactite hanging down from the ceiling. The balconies intercepted the stalactite at multiple levels. As the Marines tried to make sense of the construct before them a dark shadow intruded on the topmost portion of the inverted crystal funnel. Slowly the dark object penetrated the stalactite, filling it with a foreboding shape.

"That has to be the alien troop ship docking," observed Brains.

"Christ on a crutch," the Gunny swore. "Everybody fan out, and find some way up to the other levels. They must be where the passengers disembark."

"On it, Gunny," Bosco replied.

"I don't think I'm going to fit up those ramps," Inuksuk commented.

"So stick where you are, Corporal, and try to find some cover. Everyone turn on active camo. We don't know what frequencies these beasties see in but it can't hurt."

Grits and Brains had already ascended one level and were headed for the next up ramp. Brains glanced over the side and spied the bear attempting to blend in. He commented to his partner on suit-to-suit.

"That bloody bear blends in like a pecker on a poll dancer."

"He does stand out like a hound dog's balls."

"We're all in the shit if we don't find firing positions with some cover."

Farther around the left side, Grits sighted Keti and the rest of Bosco's team spread across three levels of balcony. He was tempted to wave but thought better of it. Over the squad frequency came the Gunny's voice.

"Everyone check your fields of fire. Make sure we got every area in here covered and that the fields overlap. Make sure your tactical computers register the Marines next to you so you can coordinate your fire when the time comes."

There was a deep booming sound, like a giant door being closed, as the alien ship settled into the docking cradle. The crystalline material surrounding its black snout began to shift, growing and sealing the hull from the vacuum outside.

"No homespun saying for this situation, mate?" Brains asked his friend.

"Not for this, Bubba. Other than don't get your ass shot off."

"Roger that."

Chapter 36

Hallway, Shopping Mall

During a lull in the hail of plasma bolts Hitch jumped across the open doorway to the right side where Kashi lay. This prompted a renewed barrage from the invaders that splattered the far wall with angry orange flame and left cherry red hotspots that slowly faded.

Looking at the stricken sailor Hitch could see the wound was serious. Though his suit's nanites were gamely trying to seal the wound, Kashi's side looked like burnt meat. Several ribs were visible through charred flesh. Pulling out a can of spray sealant, Hitch covered the open area with quick hardening foam.

"Hang in their, buddy. Help is on the way." Kashi did not answer, his medical unit having already knocked him out with painkillers. Looking up Hitch saw three sailors coming his way. The one in the lead raised his railgun and fired.

Hitch dropped and tried to become one with the deck as streams of green tracers passed just overhead. The tracers stopped and he looked over his shoulder to see what the new comers were firing at. There was another of the aliens, its neck and head missing and the front of its body chewed to bloody pulp. It toppled over as he watched.

Hitch turned back to the newcomers. "About time you got here, Kashi's messed up bad. We gotta get him to the Doc."

"Good to see you still kicking, Stevie," Chief Jacobs replied. He and the two sailor's with him were stacked up on the left side of the doorway. "What's in there?"

"More like the one you just hosed. Must have been a dozen come out of the landing craft. A bunch of them got away down the hall behind me. That's when Kashi got hit."

A flurry of plasma bolts tore through the jagged hole behind Hitch, as if to emphasize his point. Both Hitch and Jacobs fired bursts of 5mm through the door way and just as quickly pulled back.

"Beans, you need to move beyond Hitch's position and cover that hole. We'll provide suppressing fire on one... three, two, one!"

Again the two chiefs leaned into the doorway and let fly, this time including a couple 20mm explosive rounds. Beans Branford sprinted by the opening as they fired, skidding to a halt just beyond Kashi's inert form. He was just in time.

One of the creatures stuck its head through the hole. Beans hosed it down on full auto, 1200 rounds a minute at a velocity of 1800 meters per second. The alien's head dissolved in a hail of flechettes, spatter flying in all directions.

While Beans was taking out the alien the other sailor, Tamara Wilson, dashed past the doorway. Then Beans hustled past the opening the aliens had blasted in the wall. Now there were sailors on either side of both exits from the room.

"We need to dampen these suckers' enthusiasm. You got any grenades, Matt?"

"Funny you should ask, Stevie." Jacobs pulled a baseball sized object from his backpack. "You want to bet I can put this through the door of that landing craft?"

"No, but do it and I'll buy you a drink in the next bar we come to."

"OK. Some suppressing fire, guys, on one."

The other sailors acknowledged as Jacobs counted down.

"Three, two, one!"

The others fired. Chief Jacobs took a step into the doorway and threw the grenade with an underhanded pitch. It flew straight and true, right through the opening the landing craft had created. He pulled back and bellowed.

"Fire in the hole!"

The four sailors huddled away from the openings with backs against the wall. The grenade went off, the spike of overpressure thumping their chests. A split second later the atmosphere around them began to howl.

"Hold on to your asses, the grenade must have blown a hole in the station!" Hitched yelled.

"Ya think, Stevie?" his friend replied. "Remember, the grenade was your idea."

"You're the one who decided to throw it into the alien ship."

"Everybody's a fucking critic."

2nd *Squad*

Kato hustled past the shuttered opening to the splagg's cage, hoping that his suit's camo worked on big gray alien mutant elephant things. As he went he stuck explosive charges to the shutter. He ran out of charges about midway across the opening and sprinted for the far side.

"Assad. You need to come to me and finish planting charges across the opening."

"I don't remember this in training, Corporal!" the Marine replied. Kato gestured furiously, waving the man on. "I am coming, *in shā' Allāh.*"

Assad scooted across the door opening in a crouch, as if that would help hide him should his suit camo fail. He stuck his two charges to the shutter as he passed and quickly took shelter behind Kato at the other side of the door. Looking back at where they came from they could see the other two members of Kato's fireteam. Kato gave them a thumbs up.

"OK, we're ready. We may have to lure it out into the main chamber."

"Like hell!" one of the others replied. Kato ignored him.

"Sarge, we're set to release the splagg. Over."

"Copy that, Kato. We are in position. Release the beast and try not to get stomped on."

"Roger, I'm blowing the door now."

After one last look to make sure his people were clear, Kato triggered the detonator. There was a loud whomp as the wide crystal door shattered and blew outward. The splagg, which had been contentedly eating some form of leafy fodder from a bin on the back wall of the cage, spun around with impressive quickness for something so large. Then, bugling like a tortured steam calliope, it whirled its way through the opening and into the main chamber where the unsuspecting invaders awaited.

Plaza, Shopping Mall

JT was trying to monitor the progress of both Marine squads remotely when the sailors raised the alarm about hostiles boarding the station. He was about to send Rick and the SEALs to reinforce Hitch and the sailors when Shanakta-fek let out a shriek. He looked down at the lemur-like alien, who was babbling incoherently and pointing across the plaza at the far wall.

As he watched, the dark shape of an alien spacecraft landed on the side of the spire. A docking collar pressed against the transparent station wall and an instant later blew a hole in it.

"Cover! We have hostiles inside the perimeter." JT yelled, but the SEALs were already moving. In the middle of the plaza, atop the raised platform, something else was moving as well, something the aliens did not expect—a battle bot.

Detecting the explosion, the robot weapons platform guarding the plaza correctly assumed it was under attack. In less than a second it's multi-barreled railgun rose and pivoted to cover the point of the explosion. It released a torrent of 15mm explosive shells, six thousand a minute, a rate as high as a half squad of Marines. Before the first alien warrior could set foot on the station the ship and all aboard it disintegrated in a rippling explosion of yellow fire.

Seeing the alien boarding thwarted in such an energetic manner JT could think of only one thing—that wall cannot hold.

"Everybody find something to hang on to!"

Then he remember Shanakta-fek. Grabbing a body bag that was draped over a nearby kiosk, JT sized the Kieshnar-rak-kat-tra by the scruff of the neck and stuffed him into the bag. Shoving the last of the alien's bushy tail into the sack he yelled.

"Don't try to get out until I tell you!"

330

The wall of the spire exploded outward, shards of crystal and debris from the attacking ship blown into space by the station's escaping atmosphere. JT zipped the body bag shut and stuffed it into the kiosk.

Howling like a cat five hurricane, the station's atmosphere tried to equalize pressure with the vacuum out side. The battle bot shook and deployed legs with gravitonic pads to stabilize itself while things not held down were sucked into oblivion. Inside the kiosk, Shanakta-fek's body bag inflated like a balloon due to the drop in air pressure.

"How long is this gale gonna last, Lieutenant?" asked Rick.

"Don't know, Chief. There's a lot of air in this spire."

"Yeah, but that's a damned big hole."

"That it is, but look, it's already getting smaller."

JT was right. The edges of the jagged hole were starting to flow inward as the Starflake's self healing skin tried to plug the leak. After an eternity—which actually lasted only a few minutes—the howling wind diminished and then stopped. The hole was gone.

Phil came jogging up, carrying his assault weapon at the ready. "You OK, Lieutenant? Did any of them get off before our mechanical buddy tried to deflate the spire?"

"From what I saw nothing got off that ship. They probably never knew what hit them."

From the other direction, Rick and Bud approached.

"If I have ever said anything bad about those mechanical dogfaces I take it back."

"Amen, Chief."

"Hey," said Bud. "Where's your little fuzzy weasel buddy?"

"Crap, I almost forgot."

JT leaned over the counter of the kiosk where he had stashed the furry alien and opened the now collapsed body bag. A ball of fur sprang from the bag and wrapped itself around the Green Beret's spherical helmet, hanging on for dear life with all four paws.

"Damn it, get off me you hairball!" JT reached up and tried to get a grip on the frantic alien. "You're OK. The hostiles are all dead. Let go of my helmet or I swear I'm going to space you, fuzz nuts."

With the help of Chief Morgan, JT was relieved of his furry headgear. The trader was deposited on the deck where he continued to glance about frantically, panting and shaking all the while. Eventually he regained his voice.

"We, we are all right? You have defeated the Others?"

"Just the ones on this spire, fuzzy. We won this battle, but the war ain't over yet. Not by a long shot."

1st Squad

Loud creaking noises echoed around the arrival area as the troop carrier settled into its docking slot. Dispersed throughout the four arrival balconies a dozen Marines waited tensely for the balloon to go up, for the invading aliens to begin exiting the ship. On the third level balcony Grits and Brains were spread out at the limit of suit-to-suit comm range.

"So what's keeping them? Do they want an engraved invitation?"

"Cool your beans there, Bubba. This is like deer hunting. We're up in our deer stand waiting for the dear to come to us."

"Great. So tell me, Yank. Do deer often fire back at the hunters?"

"Don't be silly. That's what makes this lots more exciting than deer hunting."

"Will you to clowns quit chattering? You are more annoying than the aliens."

"Hey, is that you Keti?"

"Of course it's me, who else do you like to annoy so much?"

"Where are you?"

"One level down, in between your two positions. Check your tactical display, stupid."

"See, mate? Even Keti thinks you're a bleeding tosser."

"You leave him alone, crumpet-sucker. He's annoying me, I am the one who gets to call him names."

"Now y'all don't fight over me. You'll make me blush. Shit, it's opening up!"

Across the amphitheater curving sections of balcony extended to embrace the crystal dock, sliding out from either side. They stopped moving and the crystal material of the dock melted away, leaving the bow of the alien ship exposed.

"Cheers, mate, I think this is it." Brains brought up the targeting displays inside his helmet, and not an instant too soon.

Hatches opened on the ship, pouring a stream of running aliens out onto the top three levels of balcony. The bottom most level evidently was too narrow to disembark troops from. As they fanned out from the ship the Gunny's voice came over the squad channel.

"Wait for it. Wait for it. Now!"

The amphitheater lit up with crossing streams of green tracers. The lead attackers fell but more poured from the ship. Seeing they were under attack, the boarders came out firing. On the second level they hopped down to the floor and engaged the Marines in the balconies. Soon a wave of invaders was pushing its way across the floor toward the first level exits.

"They are trying to overrun us and escape into the station," Keti shouted. "When we concentrate on the ones below they move around on the balconies."

Grits was positioned farthest to the left on the third level. Marines on the far side of the hall were firing on the aliens trying to advance on his flank. He glanced to the left just in time to see an alien hop over the dead body of one of its comrades and point a weapon in his direction. Instinctively he raised his left arm and shot the alien with a 15mm round, blowing it to pieces.

"Watch your flanks! These critters are coming around the sides."

"Concentrate on your fields of fire!" the Gunny yelled. "Those in the middle target the hostiles coming across the floor."

Grits, Brains, and Keti on the level below fired explosive rounds at the attackers on the right flank. Those aliens were trying to get to the Marines whose fire was keeping the attackers off their left flank. Meanwhile a new wave of hostiles jumped to the floor and raced for the Marines on the first level. Then there was a loud roar and Inuksuk rose up and waded out into the attacking hoard.

Over the squad channel the Gunny's voice was heard.

"Aw shit."

Kestrels

The two jet black fighters drifted away from the Peggy Sue. They were waiting to get clear of the mother ship before announcing their position, which would happen as soon as they fired off their drives. To get maximum acceleration they would also need to burn antimatter, a further tip off to the alien warships.

Her helmet provided Beth with a three dimensional view in all directions, as though the ship around her didn't exist at all. Instruments and targeting information seemed to float in space in front of her eyes. Her hands gripped the controls in a HOTAS configuration—Hands On Throttle-And-Stick. No need to relinquish control to throw a switch.

"OK, Frank. We are going to firewall it and head straight for the station. We need to get between the alien frigates and the station itself so they can't fire on us."

"Roger that, Commander. But what says they can't fire at us then?"

"Unless they want to destroy their prize or cause collateral damage among their own boarding party they won't." *At least I hope they won't.* "I didn't think 15mm was going to get the job done with those big troop carriers, so I had the engineers swap out the lighter railguns for an extra pair of missiles. We are carrying six each. The plan is to go after the farthest out and work our way in."

"What if some of their fighters show up?"

"Use your centerline railgun or wingtip plasma cannon. Save the missiles for the big bogies. Remember, fighting in space is not sport. It is scientific murder."

"Roger that, Ma'am."

"OK, from here on in you're Kestrel Two and I am Kestrel One. Just follow my lead and good hunting."

Beth pointed her nose toward the station nearly one hundred kilometers away and went to full power.

"Tally ho, Kestrel One." Beth didn't know if Frank was using that 'tally ho' stuff because she was a Brit, or if he was just caught up in the moment. It didn't matter in either case, so long as he stuck to her six.

Bridge, Peggy Sue

"Here's the plan, Ms. Palmer. We are going to adjust the ship's attitude to allow railgun shots at these three targets." Bobby highlighted the targets on the main display. "We will hit them in order of decreasing distance: the one on the far side first, the lower front second, and finally the upper front."

"Aye, Sir," the young lieutenant replied. "I thought there were four frigates?"

"The forth is masked by the station, we'll have to come back for it after we handle the big boys."

Pauline nodded as she worked the fire control computer for the main railgun. "Run times are 12.375, 11.25, and 9.56 seconds, respectively."

Bobby's fingers danced across the control panel causing tags and lines to blossom on the main display. He turned to the Captain.

"The fire maneuver is programed and locked in, Captain."

"Thank you, Sailing Master. Engineering, reactors to full power; shields to maximum; execute the attack, Bobby."

The view out the nose of the ship spun in a gut wrenching arc, paused for an instant while the main railgun fired, and swung again. The railgun battery fired three times in the space of two seconds. In space around the Starflake three alien frigates exploded, impacted by 10kg slugs of depleted urainium traveling at thirty-six

335

thousand kilometers per hour. Each delivered as much kinetic energy as the main battery of a WWII battleship.

"Targets destroyed, Sir," Siku reported from the fire control console.

"Good shooting people. Now let's go take care of the rest of these varmints."

The Peggy Sue swung again, pointing its bow toward the alien fleet. The gravitonic drives came to full acceleration and the ship lept toward its new targets.

Chapter 37

Bridge, Uxoreeza Flag Ship

Four hundred kilometers from the Starflake the warships of the Uxoreeza fleet hung in space. All seemed to be going to plan, the scouts and fighters encountered no hostile fire on approach and the pathfinders were landed. The first of the large troop carriers was docked and soon the station would be theirs. Then alarms flashed across the tactical display and the bridge erupted with activity.

"Admiral! Three of the frigates just exploded!"

"What?" There was shock and a bit of panic in the Admiral's voice. "Where is the enemy that fired on them?"

"There is a ship headed for us from the direction of the station. It's accelerating at 30 gravities and has an energy profile higher than anything I've ever seen."

"Captain, signal all ships, shields up and move to attack position. Why didn't we see it before?"

"I don't know, Admiral, it's like it appeared out of the vacuum."

The communication officer interrupted with more bad news. "Two of the scout ships have been destroyed, blasted to pieces soon after landing. And the ground commander on the first troop transport is reporting fierce resistance."

What is happening to us? The Admiral stared at the bridge display in disbelief. *Everything had been going according to plan. Now there is heavy resistance at the landing sites and an impossible ship hurtling our way. We have been ambushed by a single ship and all is undone? The dark masters will never accept such an excuse. I hope our foe realizes this is to the death—better to die than to fail the Dark Lords.*

2ⁿᵈ Squad

The splagg smashed into the party of warriors before they could react. Suited bodies flew in all directions, crashing into walls and the ceiling overhead. A few of the aliens had enough presence of mind to fire on the whirling gray maelstrom that attacked them.

"Somehow this doesn't seem fair, Corporal," said Ahmed.

"If you ever find yourself in a fair fight it means your tactics suck," Kato replied, pleased with the outcome of his plan. The aliens finally mounted a coordinated reaction to the splagg's assault, firing their plasma rifles and moving to surround the spinning death that was in their midst. Their fire was taking its toll on the beast, its spinning slowed and instead of trumpeting in rage it now shrieked in pain.

Sgt. Aurora called over the squad channel. "Looks like the splagg is going down, now's the time to hit them while they are concentrating on finishing the beast off. Open fire."

From a dozen places around the area's perimeter Marines opened fire on the remaining invaders. The few seconds it took them to realize they were under attack from a new threat were enough to be fatal. It was over in less than half a minute.

"Cease fire!" Aurora yelled. "They are all down."

The splagg was an immobile mound of blackened flesh in the middle of the chamber. Around it lay the bodies of twenty-four attackers, half of them killed by the behemoth, the rest turned into alien tartare by the Marines' concentrated fire. The Sergeant called in to report their status.

"Ice Castle, Squad Two. Over."

"Go, Squad Two. What's your status."

"We have just taken out a couple of squads worth of boarders and are securing the area."

"Be advised that they have been boarding the station in small craft that fasten themselves to the station walls. The landing craft are probably still attached to the spire above you."

"Roger that, Ice Castle. Interrogative, how should we proceed?"

"Send a fireteam to find the landing craft and destroy them. Take the rest of the squad and head for the base of the Karf's spire. It looks like a couple of the small craft landed there and may be trying to spring the Karf from containment."

"I copy, Ice Castle. We are on our way." The she-bear changed comm channels. "Kato. Take your fire team up into this spire and find the ships these creatures came in. You are to blow them up. The rest of us are headed for the Karf spire to kill some vermin."

"Aye, aye, Sergeant."

Four recon drones headed for the opening in the ceiling as Kato's team headed for the base of the elevator shaft. The rest of the squad headed for a moving roadway headed north.

Pond Room, Shopping Mall

The roar of escaping atmosphere abated as the station's hull healed itself. The sailors carefully entered the room, alert for any hostiles that had not perished when Chief Jacobs' grenade blew their landing craft away. All the invaders present were indisputably deceased.

"Where's the rest of this goomer?" Hitch asked, nudging a long severed neck with the toe of his boot. The head and neck were still encased in suit armor but there was no sign of the rest of the carcase they belonged to. "Let's see what one of these critters looks like."

Pulling his Woodsman's Pal from its sheath, Hitch placed a foot on the severed neck and began whacking away at the seal between the dead alien's helmet and neck-piece. After a few strokes it opened enough for him to insert his armored gauntlets and pry the helmet off.

"Holly shit! Will you look at that?"

"It looks like one of those dinosaur things," offered Beans.

"But it's covered with feathers," Hitch retorted.

The creature's head featured a long beak-like snout covered with iridescent black feathers. Serrated teeth lined its upper and lower jaw. A feathered crest topped the narrow skull and a malevolent red eye glared from either side.

"Tam, grab the armor while I remove the head and neck," ordered Hitch. He pulled the items in question from the neck-piece.

339

As it emerged more feathers unfurled, an unruly ruff like a feather duster. Holding the grisly trophy by the back of the skull, Hitch lifted the head high giving the sailors their first real look at their foe.

"It looks like a rooster," said Jacobs.

"I tell you it looks like one of those velociraptors," said Beans. "You know, from Jurassic Park."

"We're fighting feathered dinosaurs?" Tamera asked.

"Dinosaur hell. This is a Jurassic chicken," replied Hitch, giving the dead alien a shake.

"Wonderful, Stevie," Jacobs said. "I can't wait to tell the Lieutenant that we're fighting Jurassic chickens. In fact, I'd better tell him that a couple of them got away."

Plaza, Shopping Mall

JT just finished speaking with Sgt. Aurora when he got the call from Chief Jacobs. "...copy, three or four of the 'Jurassic chickens' escaped into the shopping mall. And the rest are dead?"

"Roger, Ice Castle. Mostly body parts. Kashi got hit pretty badly, we need to get him to the Doc."

"Roger, get him to the medical station. I'll handle the escaped hostiles." JT turned to the SEALs. "Chief, I have something right down your alley. How would you like to go after three or four boarders that got away from the sailors?"

"Yes, Sir, we're game."

"Let me check the sensors we spread around... yeah, there they go."

"Where do you think they are headed?"

"Looks like they're headed for the hub." JT shared the video feed showing the escaped hostiles. "I count three of them... what have we here?"

"They got off before exiting the spire, what are they up too?"

340

As the humans watched the aliens made their way to a blank wall on the spire central pillar. A door appeared and they jumped through it. Inside was the familiar glow of a station elevator.

"How did they know where to find that hidden door?" the head SEAL asked.

"Maybe they took notes the last time they were here."

A synthesized voice joined the conversation–the Tcist. "Earth creatures, there are invaders entering the station core. You must stop them."

"They just used an elevator we didn't know about and they are now outside our sensor coverage. Can you track them?"

"Yes. I fear they are headed for the antimatter cache."

Chief Morgan muted the Tcist. "You think they are trying to scuttle the station?"

"Insurance. That's what I would have done if I was planning the attack. Send out several teams of special operators to probe the defenses and be ready to blow the place if the main assault fails." JT switched the station frequency back on. "Tcist, can you guide my men to the Uxoreeza?"

"Yes, I am holding the door to the service elevator open. Come now."

"Roger that, they are on their way."

"Suddenly this ain't so much fun, LT."

"Look at it this way, Rick. If they do light off all that antimatter we won't even know it, we'll just be gone."

Chief Morgan called to his men. "Mount up guys, we got some Jurassic chickens to hunt down."

Kestrel Flight

The two fighters headed toward the station in a twisting spiral, accelerating at nearly two hundred Gs. Inside the pilots wore only skintight pressure suits, their ships were their armor. They were protected from the extreme acceleration by internal gravity compensators. Otherwise they would have been killed by their own acceleration.

Half way there, just over twenty-three seconds after starting their run they stopped accelerating, pivoted, and fired a brace of missiles each at the troop carrier farthest from the Starflake. Then they flipped end over end and continued their erratic, evasive maneuvers as they decelerated.

"When we get close we will drop down among the spires to make it harder to target us. We need to hit the second, undocked transport, then come back and make sure we took out the one we just fired on."

"Roger, Kestrel One."

Maneuvering a fighter in space is not the same as flying a fighter plane in a planetary atmosphere, in a planet's gravity well. Fighter plane engagements are basically an energy management problem. A planet bound combatant enters a fight with his forward velocity, gravitational potential energy from his altitude, and the thrust his engines can provide. In zero G you are on your own. You cannot just pull the nose up to slow down or push over to pick up speed and disengage. Neither can you bank into a curve. There are no aerodynamic forces to modify your path through space—all changes in trajectory come from applying thrust.

To make a turn you not only have to apply thrust in the direction you wish to go, you must also use thrust in the opposite direction of your current course to cancel your velocity in that direction. To describe a smooth turn you must constantly apply thrust in a direction normal to the desired trajectory. The Kestrel pilots were about to engage a superior number of enemies in a dogfight among the spires of the station while maneuvering in three dimensions.

They finished their plunge toward the station and threaded their way between the station's multitude of spires. Behind them the troop carrier they fired on was able to shoot down two of the missiles, but the other two found their mark. The vessel disintegrated from the double blow of twin four kiloton explosions. Beth rounded the Karf's spire and spotted a pair of alien fighters moving to attack.

"Two bogies, three o'clock high," Beth called. "Break left, Kestrel Two. Let's sandwich the buggers between us."

1st Squad

Inuksuk's roars, amplified by his suit's speakers, echoed throughout the amphitheater. Whether this impressed the charging Uxoreeza was unknown, but the bear's slashing stream of 5mm flechettes had a more immediate and physical impact. As those on the theater floor shrank from the withering fire, their comrades in the balconies opened fire on the polar bear. One of the plasma bolts struck him in the arm, silencing his flechette weapon.

"Give him cover fire!" the Gunny shouted over the squad frequency. *Damn undisciplined hairball! If he lives I will skin him alive.*

Having lost one of his weapons, Inuksuk switched to the other—the 30mm on his left arm. He began spraying everything in sight with a stream of explosive shells, each the equivalent of an old-fashioned 155mm artillery shell. The balcony tiers came apart, shattered by explosions. Aliens and alien body parts flew through the air as the rampaging bear pounded the attackers. It then became clear why there were no troop hatches on the lowest level.

Shielding panels retracted, revealing a turret and the twin barrels of a pair of heavy plasma cannon. They quickly turned to target the armored giant that was demolishing the docking bay.

"Inuksuk! The ship!" yelled Zippy, trying to warn her team leader.

Inuksuk brought the ship under fire but he was too late. The first salvo from the ship's guns struck him full on. A nimbus of orange fire surrounded the upright bear. The force of the blast spun him around. In that instant, the Gunny could see the plasma had burned through his armor and most of the bear's body cavity. Inuksuk was a dead bear standing. Then came the second salvo.

The ship's cannon fired twin blasts into the bear's back. That was a mistake. The plasma burned through Inuksuk's back armor as it had in the front. Marine armor was tough but it was never meant to take direct fire from heavy shipboard weapons. After burning its

343

way through the refractive outer armor the hot plasma reached the magazines on the bear's back. The magazine containing unexpended 5mm flechettes, which were inert, and the magazine half filled with 30mm explosive rounds, which were most definitely not.

Inuksuk vanished in a gigantic explosion that shattered the docking structure surrounding the ship. The balcony sections the Marines were firing from were also damaged, sections collapsing, the Marines knocked from their feet by the concussion. Fortunately none of them were severely wounded, just shaken and bruised. Once the impact distributing layers in their suits unstiffened they began moving again.

The amphitheater was a shambles, the nose of the alien ship battered and bent. No invaders came from the still open hatches and none remained alive inside the docking area. Then it became clear that the troop carrier was moving, withdrawing from the docking cradle. Slivers of black space could be seen around the edges of the damaged ship. Through those cracks the local atmosphere was streaming, its escape creating vortices that sucked rubble and dead Uxoreeza out into the vacuum.

Staring out across the desolation, Grits saw a lone figure making its way across the rubble strewn floor. "Hey, what's Zippy doing down there?"

"Ben-Ezra, get your ass back here!" the Gunny ordered, but Zippy ignored her.

As they watched, Ben-Ezra knelt at the bottom of the docking cradle and drew a tubular object from her backpack. It was a Shoulder-launched Multipurpose Assault Weapon, a shoulder-launched rocket whose primary purpose was as a bunker buster. In its warhead was two hundredths of a gram of antimatter, the equivalent of a kiloton of TNT. On this deployment a Marine in each fireteam carried one just in case. In Inuksuk's team Zippy was the designated rocketeer. As she made ready to fire the implication of her actions dawned on the other squad members.

"Everybody get out!" screamed the Gunny. "Get some solid wall between you and the chamber. Now!" The Marines fled for their lives.

Chapter 38

Bridge, Peggy Sue

"Range to targets one-hundred kilometers, rate of closure is thirteen point three kilometers per second," called Mizuki from the 3-space sensor console.

"Weapons control, I want a spread of four torpedoes, X-ray warheads. Concentrate fire on the four cruisers." Four bright dots sped toward the enemy ships—the four that were beginning to move away from the huge freighter.

"Sailing Master, I want a volley of railgun slugs down the throat of that big bogey."

"Aye, Captain." The ship's attitude shifted slightly as Bobby sighted the main railgun cannon on the enemy freighter. The ship shuddered perceptibly as the railguns fired.

On the forward display four miniature suns blazed simultaneously and as quickly faded to black. The shields and hulls of the Uxoreeza ships flared under the fearsome light of X-ray laser beams. Beams generated by the annihilation of antimatter in the torpedo warheads, hellish radiation pumping rods of lasing material to unimaginably energetic levels in the instant before they vaporized.

"We have hits on all enemy vessels," Mizuki reported. "Multiple flares on one of the cruisers. That ship is no longer accelerating. The other three are moving to attack."

An instant after she finished her report warnings sounded across the bridge, an indication that enemy fire was striking the Peggy Sue's shields. At the same time two ten kilo slugs of depleted uranium struck the alien freighter. A miss would have been embarrassing, since the freighter was a roughly spherical blob, as big in diameter as the Peggy Sue was long. Strangely, the freighter did not explode. The slugs must have missed its antimatter fuel stores.

"Aput, Siku. Target the alien cruisers with the main battery, nearest first. Fire at will. Helm, evasive maneuvers."

The two bears raced to fire their hyperluminal particle cannon first. It was effectively a tie, twin red lines lancing from port and starboard. The visible lines were computer generated, the actual particle bursts traveling invisibly through the edge of alter-space. The blue-white explosions that announced the end of the two ships were fully visible in 3-space.

As the polar bears were picking off alien cruisers, Bobby threw the eighteen thousand metric ton ship into an intricate pirouette, reversing its attitude while dancing past the alien warships.

* * * * *

Alarms screamed on the flagship's bridge as the crew gamely struggled to strike back at their attacker. Multiple beams of coherent X-ray radiation had blasted their shields and severely degraded the ship's capacity to maneuver.

"They employed some kind of explosion pumped X-ray lasers, Admiral. Shields are down and we cannot move to the attack," the ship's captain reported.

"The freighter has been struck by some kind of kinetic energy weapon!" a sensor operator added.

X-ray laser warheads, kinetic energy weapons? Weapons not unknown but not used by other species. What are these creatures? the Admiral thought. "Fire on that ship! Whatever we have left."

"Cruisers two and three just exploded." The Uxoreeza were not sentimental creatures—they did not name their ships, they numbered them.

"What type of weapon?" the Admiral demanded.

"Unknown, Admiral."

Spirits of the Void, have you forsaken us?

That was the Admiral's last thought.

* * * * *

The Peggy Sue was now beyond the alien fleet, thirty kilometers to sunward and decelerating rapidly. Red lines appeared from port and starboard and two more star-bright flares blossomed on the main display.

346

"The targets are destroyed, Captain," reported Mizuki. "The only alien vessel left is the freighter and it is dead in space."

"We can't let it stay like that, it would create a hazard to navigation. Weapons control, a single torpedo with a one kilo warhead, if you please. Fire as she bears."

"Weapon away, Sir. Run time 7.2 seconds."

There was silence on the bridge as the bright dot representing the torpedo converged on the alien hulk. When time expired a massive explosion flared, the equivalent of a 43 megaton nuclear explosion. When the dreadful brightness faded nothing remained of the freighter, the course back to the space station was clear.

"Engineering, damage report."

"No damage, Captain. The shields barely dropped under fire and nothing penetrated."

"Very good, Mr. Gunderson."

"Captain, I am detecting the drive signature of a small ship heading toward the system center, possibly a messenger ship intent on leaving the system."

"A packet boat carrying word of the Uxoreeza's defeat back to their masters? Well this just won't do. Mr. Aput, do you think you can take that ship out with the starboard main gun?"

"Aye, Captain, like snagging a seal at an air-hole."

"Helmsman, bring the ship around. You may fire when ready, Mr. Aput."

Again a red line marked the effective trajectory of a hyperluminal particle burst. Again a blue-white flash marked the death of a ship, this one much smaller than those that marked the passing of the enemy cruisers.

"Good shooting, Mr. Aput. Sailing Master, take us back to the Starflake. We still have that frigate to take care of, the one that was hiding behind the station when we took out its companions."

"Aye, Captain. We are now on course for the Starflake."

347

1ˢᵗ Squad

Around what was left of the amphitheater Marines pulled themselves from the wreckage. Inuksuk's detonation collapsed the Balcony between Grits and Brains making the path between them impassable.

"Go, mate. I'll see you back in the perimeter hallway."

"Roger, Bubba. I'm already gone."

As Grits started to turn away he heard another voice over suit-to-suit. It was Keti. She was trapped on the balcony below.

"Anybody, I'm trapped on the second balcony, the exit hallway is collapsed."

"Keti, this is Grits. I'm on the level above you. Can you make it to where the third level is busted?"

"Yes, I'm under the edge now."

Grits leaned over the edge of the collapsed section and saw the armored bulk of another Marine. He reached down and said, "Grab my hand, and I'll pull you up."

Keti jumped up and clasped hands with him. With the superhuman strength of his suit's electroreactive muscles he lifted her four-hundred kilos of dead weight up onto his level. For a moment they stood, holding each other. It might have been a tender, even romantic moment had they not both been encased in seven foot, faceless armored suits.

"Thank you, I was trapped," she began.

"No time, darlin', we gotta make tracks."

As they ran to the ramp leading down to the perimeter hallway, Zippy finished aiming her weapon. She sighted carefully upward, through the largest of the still open hatchways on the alien ship. The missile flashed from its tube and flew into the alien vessel. Zippy stood and spread her arms wide, as if in supplication.

The amphitheater lit with an impossibly bright light and the Universe exploded.

* * * * *

Entering the perimeter hallway Grits turned and stepped to the side. As Keti reached him he grabbed her arm and swung her clear of the door way. A split-second later the shockwave hit knocking both of them from their feet. Radiation alarms sounded in their ears as chunks of crystal fell from the walls and ceiling. Then silence.

"You OK, Keti?" Grits asked, concern in his voice.

"Yes, I am fine, thank you."

"Good, I was afraid we might not make it."

Keti paused for a second.

"You remember, back on the ship, when you wanted me to go to the hydroponics section with you?"

"Well yeah, but don't misunderstand..."

"You wanted to go and have sex, right?"

"Well, yeah," the embarrassed Marine stammered.

"When we get back, we will go and have sex."

"Sex?" Disbelief fought with elation in his voice.

"Steamy hot monkey sex, assuming we both live. Now let's go find the others."

Kestrels

The harsh light of an antimatter explosion reflected off the station's spires. For an instant the Starflake was as bright as a star.

"Did you see that, Kestrel One? I bet that left a mark. It must have come from the docked troop ship."

"Keep your mind on the business at hand, Kestrel Two. Stay low amongst the spires."

Between them they had taken down five enemy fighters in a twisting, turning furball among the spiky towers of the station. The enemy fighters were not nearly as fast or as well armed as the Kestrels, but they were numerous and persistent.

"We need to stop playing tag with enemy fighters and get to that other troop carrier."

"Roger that, Kestrel One."

The pair of Earth fighters slalomed between minor spires and emerged on the far side of the station. There, hanging in space and maneuvering slowly to align with the docking slip, was the last remaining troop carrier.

"Stay close, Kestrel Two," Beth ordered as she threw her fighter into a hard right, passing between two minor spires. Immediately she turned left and dove. Rounding the spire on her portside she pulled up with the troop carrier directly in front of her.

As the nose of her Kestrel pitched up Beth fired her centerline railgun three times. Then she pulled through into an Immelmann. Once headed away from the troop carrier she again dove for the deck. Behind her Frank mimicked her maneuver, also firing three slugs at the enemy ship. One of his shots missed, but in all they pumped five rounds into their target.

The slugs used in the Kestrels' railguns were smaller than those in the Peggy Sue, five kilograms verses ten. They also traveled more slowly, only twenty-five thousand kph instead of thirty plus. This meant that they did not pack the same punch as the mother-ship's big kinetic weapons. Five times less massive but traveling ten times as fast, each Kestrel slug carried twenty times the kinetic energy of a main battle tank's 120mm cannon. In effect, the alien troop carrier had just taken the equivalent of a broadside of 16" naval shells.

The depleted uranium slugs did not carry a bursting charge but at those impact velocities none was needed. Vaporizing at the point of impact uranium burns away around the edges so the projectile doesn't mushroom. In an oxygen atmosphere Uranium is "pyrophoric," capable of igniting spontaneously. When a slug penetrates its target the burning DU turns the target's inside into an inferno of white-hot gas and burning metal.

Though the Uxoreeza wore space suits the troop carrier maintained a nitrogen-oxygen atmosphere. Once the railgun rounds penetrated the ship's hull they transformed its interior spaces into a flaming hell. Over half of the Uxoreeza on board died immediately—

350

they were the lucky ones. The rest cooked more slowly. While the ship's fuel supply did not detonate, the flight deck, hidden amidships for greater survivability, was taken out by a near direct hit. As a result, the ship was now out of control, drifting away from the Starflake, leaking incandescent gas while describing a slow pinwheel in space.

Beth did not have time to contemplate the fate of those aboard the enemy troop carrier, she had other concerns. Pulling hard into a downward spiral around a spire she managed to shake the enemy fighter that had tried to follow her course. Frank was not as lucky.

He managed to shake one and turn left into a tight upward spiral. As he looped around a spire Frank sighted a pair of enemy fighters above him. Pulling vertical with respect to the spire he blasted one bogey then the other.

"Splash two!" he shouted with exuberance.

"Kestrel Two, push over and head for the deck," Beth yelled in reply. "Do not get any farther from the station!"

Caught up in the moment, Frank did a victory roll, a full 360° revolution around his fighter's longitudinal axis. Pilots have long used the maneuver as a celebration of victory over an opponent. When executed properly, the craft exits the maneuver on the same heading as it entered, so Frank continued traveling away from the station. That properly executed victory roll is what killed him.

Frank's upward course exposed his Kestrel to the guns of the surviving enemy frigate, which had been loitering off the station hoping to get a clear shot at the attacking Earth fighters. As he came out of the roll a streak of orange plasma hit. The Kestrel flared bright orange and then brighter blue white as its AM supply detonated. All that was left was hot, drifting gas.

"Damn it Frank!," Beth cursed, putting her fighter into another violent maneuver. "Why didn't you listen?"

SEALs, Station Core

To the SEALs descending in the hidden elevator shaft it seemed like they had fallen many kilometers before they were ejected into the dimly glowing warren of passages that filled the core of the station hub. The three special operators looked around and found they had no clue as to which direction to head.

"Ice Castle, Ducklings. Come in."

No answer.

"Ice Castle, Ice Castle, Ducklings, over."

Still no answer.

"Well shit. The station material is blocking radio contact and we never spread any repeaters down here. Anyone got an idea which way we should go?"

"Don't know, Chief. I've got nothing on IR, no tracks to follow."

"Me either," added Bud. "Have you tried talking to the station?"

"I guess it's worth a shot." Rick activated the channel that communicated with the Tcist. "Station, we are somewhere in the core and have no idea where the hostiles have gone, please advise."

A synthetic voice, devoid of emotion replied. "Follow the whooboo. Proceed quickly."

"What?" Phil said to his companions.

"There," said Bud, pointing down one of the passageways. Standing in the distance was a squat yellow figure. It waved and disappeared around a corner.

"You heard the talking moss," Rick said, breaking into a run. "Follow the little yellow bastard."

Chapter 39

Kestrel Flight

Beth flew a tortuous course, threading her fighter between spires and strange objects that formed part of the Starflake's surface. The swarm of enemy fighters was severely depleted and she quickly lost the remaining few in the crystalline canyons close to the station's hub. Having lost her wingman she needed to be extra vigilant about picking up hostiles.

Coming to the base of a minor spire she pulled up into a climb, hugging the side of the station. Almost at the spire's pinnacle she veered off and headed for the out of control troop carrier. Carefully sighting on the aft of the alien ship she put her last two solid railgun slugs into the damaged hulk. This time one of the projectiles found the transport's antimatter store and the alien ship exploded.

Beth had chosen her course of attack carefully, making sure that the troop carrier's bulk masked her from the enemy frigate hanging ten kilometers off the Starflake's perimeter. As her target disappeared in an expanding sphere of hot gas and debris, Beth felt a flash of anger. *Kill my wingman will you, you alien bastards?*

Without further thought, she flew her Kestrel through the heart of the debris field. She was out of solid railgun slugs but she had three beehive rounds—shells that fragmented into a score of smaller projectiles after launch. She also still had four missiles like the ones that destroyed the first troop carrier.

Exiting the farside of the debris field Beth fired the three beehive rounds with minimum delay between shots. Her intention was not to damage the frigate with the railgun rounds but to mask her true intent. A second after firing the last railgun shot she released her last four missiles.

Her plan worked perfectly. Sensors confused by the cloud of shot fragments, the frigate had no time to target the incoming missiles. They flashed across the gulf between fighter and frigate in just under two seconds. But the frigate crew was good; they detected her Kestrel coming through the blast debris and managed to fire a salvo an instant before Beth's missiles blew the ship to hell.

Being an experienced combat pilot, Beth did not fly straight and level after firing on the frigate. She pulled a high G turn as the missiles separated. The heavy plasma bolts grazed the aft end of her Kestrel. The impact sent the fighter tumbling off into space.

Marines, Base of the Karf Spire

Keti and Grits ran into Brains as they headed toward the Karf spire. Over the comm they discovered that Sgt. Aurora and most of 2nd squad were already at the target zone. The had moved around to the far side of the base chamber to keep Karf and any new comers from escaping that way. Ahead of the trio, the Gunny arrived with Vinny, Beau, and John. Right behind them was Bosco with Fanni and Simba.

"Bosco, take the left flank," the Gunny barked. "We're going right."

"Roger that," Bosco replied.

"Brains, where the hell are you?"

"Coming up on the chamber now, Gunny."

"You three will hold this side of the chamber. Let nothing down the roadways into the rest of the station, you got that?"

"Aye, aye, Gunny. We hold the roadways south."

The trio of Marines emerged into the chamber and stepped off onto an unmoving part of the floor. Looking around they discovered that this spire's base was configured differently than the one beneath the Shopping Mall spire. Instead of two separate chambers, one for freight and one for passenger traffic, this one was configured as one big interchange with a multitude of ramps and bridges leading from the central column elevators to the chamber walls.

On suit-to-suit Grits addressed his two companions. "Holy crap, how are we supposed to cover this whole side?"

"We're going to have to spread out," Keti replied. "Who has the most ammo left?"

Checking their suits' tactical readouts it was found that Keti had the biggest 5mm reserve. They were all about equal in terms of 15mm.

"OK, I will stay on the first level and defend the entrance to the main roadway. You two need to go high and close the secondary exits."

"How do you propose we do that, luv?"

"Use your grenades and blow them up."

"That'll work."

As they were talking a torrent of gray bodies descended the elevators into the chamber and began swarming toward the perimeter exits. Streams of green tracers could already be seen coming from the rest of the Marines spread around the chamber's edge.

"We have movement. Go you two!"

"Damn, Bubba, how are the two of us gonna cover this side before the grey horde gets here?"

"We have to move like tigers on Vaseline, mate."

"What?"

"You know, Bowie? Ziggy Stardust, Spiders from Mars? That's the trouble with you Yanks, no bloody sense of culture. Haul ass!"

"Haul ass I understand," Grits answered. "Going left."

"Going right." The two friends split and headed up nearby ramps to the upper level.

"Just blow the small exits and get back here, you two clowns." But Grits and Brains were already out of suit-to-suit range. Keti swallowed and began sending short aimed bursts into the approaching wave of aliens.

* * * * *

Grits ran along the unmoving apron of the upper round-a-bout. The Karf racing outward from the chamber's center had not yet drawn a bead on him, a flickering phantom with his active camouflage on. He passed the first exit and continued to the second before crossing the moving roadway.

355

Stopping himself at the entrance he set ten seconds on the grenade's timer and stuck it to the tunnel wall a couple meters inside the opening. Scrambling against the moving surface he worked his way to the perimeter roadway, which carried him back to the entrance he skipped.

As he arrived at the open entrance the first grenade went off. The Marines' grenades were variable yield and Grits had dialed his up to maximum. The blast sent a tongue of flame and shards of crystal flying from the tunnel entrance before its ceiling collapsed. This also had the side effect of stopping the round-a-bout's flowing surface, at least locally.

Grits mined the second tunnel and headed back toward Keti and the main exit on the level below. The second tunnel erupted much like the first. Halting seven meters to Keti's left he knelt and added his fire to hers. To the right he saw the two exits assigned to Brains erupt simultaneously. Brains came jogging up and took up a similar position on Keti's right.

Back in suit-to-suit range Grits commented, "Show off."

"I have certain standards to maintain, mate."

"You two shut the fuck up and kill the aliens."

SEALs, Station Core

The three SEALs pounded down the hallway, not noticing the softly glowing crystal walls or the flashes of light that moved like living things within. Up ahead another mustard yellow troll awaited impassively for them to draw closer.

"Where are these little troglodytes leading us, Chief?"

"I guess we'll know when we get there. Now shut up and run."

The voice of the Tcist sounded inside their helmets.

"Hurry Earthlings. The Uxoreeza warriors are almost to the antimatter storage chambers."

"Can't you do something to slow them down?" Rick asked plaintively.

356

"I have closed off several tunnels and tried to mislead them but I cannot prevent them from gaining access. I have only limited control over the station's material configuration. Most of its growth function is an automatic response to damage."

"So how did you seal the tunnels?"

"I had the whooboo damage some of the passageways."

"Great, we got team yellow running interference for us," Bud said sarcastically.

"Hey, short yellow help is better than no help," Phil quipped.

Up ahead one of the aforementioned whooboo disappeared down yet another hallway. The SEALs had lost track of the number of twists and turns they had taken so far. The little yellow guides always seemed to lead them around yet another corner to yet another hallway.

"Come on boys, faster. We don't stop these chicken bastards all this is for nothing."

This time the light at the end of the hallway looked different from the passages they had been racing through. They were within a hundred meters of their destination. Now all they had to do was find the Uxoreeza and keep them from blowing the station and everyone on board it into their constituent atoms.

Bridge, Peggy Sue

"Swing wide to port, helmsman. I want to see what damage was done by that explosion we saw on approach."

"Aye, aye, Captain."

The ship passed to the left of the crater that had been the docking port where the Uxoreeza landed. The station's hull material had quickly sealed off the area, preventing further loss of atmosphere, but the crater was impressive and the surrounding minor spires all showed significant damage.

"Did the aliens do that or did the Marines?" Billy Ray pondered the meaning of the destruction below. "Ice Castle, Peggy Sue. Give me a situation report."

"Roger, Peggy Sue. We've managed to close all the breaches in the station perimeter. One larger troop ship docked, but 1st squad repelled the boarders and took it out. Now 1st and 2nd squads are at the base of the Karf spire where the remaining Uxoreeza are trying to spring the gray hostiles and breakout into the station proper."

"But the Marines are holding?"

"Roger, the Marines are holding so far. But there's some bad news. Three of the Jurassic chickens got lose and are somewhere in the station core. I sent the SEALs after them."

"Jurassic chickens?"

"That's what the sailors named them. We had a breach in the Shopping Mall."

"Have the SEALs run down the escapees?"

"I don't know, Sir. I lost communications with them when they entered the station core. The Tcist is helping them hunt the hostiles down but it's not very good at keeping me updated."

"Casualties?"

"The Marines have lost two, missing and assumed KIA. One of the sailors was wounded."

Damn, the Captain swore to himself. "The status of the other enemy troop carriers?"

"The Kestrels took out one on this side of the station, along with a bunch of enemy fighters. Then they moved to the far side and I lost contact. Sensors haven't detected anymore ships docking so they must have gotten the rest of them."

"Roger that, Ice Castle. I am moving to the far side of the station to make sure there are no more surprises left."

"Interrogative, the status of the enemy fleet?"

"We have met the enemy and they are ours. Peggy Sue, out."

The ship passed by the Karf spire, which gave no sign of the battle raging at its base. Swinging around in a wide arc there were no enemy ships to be seen. Two small craft, enemy fighters, rose toward the Peggy Sue in a forlorn hope.

"Enemy fighter craft approaching, Captain."

"Secondary battery, take them out."

"Aye, aye, Sir."

X-ray lasers target the two fighters. They flared briefly and were gone. From her sensor station Mizuki called out.

"Captain, I am detecting the remains of at least one large vessel. Perhaps two given the pattern of debris dispersal."

"The missing enemy frigate perhaps?"

"Readings are consistent with a ship's antimatter store detonating. I cannot tell for sure."

"And where are the Kestrels?"

"I have been hailing them, Captain. There is no reply."

The Captain said nothing. His only reaction was the tightening of his grip on the arms of the commander's chair. But underneath his calm demeanor he thought, *God in heaven, please don't let her be dead.*

Chapter 40

Marines, Karf Spire

Grits looked up and saw a string of large explosions run down the length of the left hand bridge from the central column to the second level round-a-bout. Too big to be 15mm, it could only be fire from Sgt. Aurora's 30mm—hers was the only heavy railgun left since the demise of Inuksuk. The bridge collapsed, showering the chamber floor with crystalline rubble.

A new wave of Karf swept toward his position, trying to force the way into the main roadway below. In front of the tunnel entrance, like Horatius at the Sublician bridge, stood Keti. That tale was one of the few Grits remembered from school. He even recalled a snippet of verse:

> To every man upon this earth
> Death cometh soon or late.
> And how can man die better
> Than facing fearful odds,
> For the ashes of his fathers,
> And the temples of his Gods.

Seeing the approaching gray tide he suddenly felt very much like one of Horatius' companions, trapped on the wrong side of the Tiber. From the right Brains called out.

"We need a barrage of air-burst above the hostiles. Link your tactical comps to coordinate the pattern."

Both Keti and Grits complied, their suit computers mapping out a pattern of shell burst locations covering the approach to their shared position. Each of the three Marines received a fire mission, their part of the pattern of destruction. Beeping tones counted down. They raised their left arms and fired.

The air above the approaching horde of Karf erupted with angry yellow blossoms, four meters above the deck. The exploding 15mm shells sent a hailstorm of shrapnel onto the teeming aliens. The interlocked patterns covered the entire area facing the trio of Marines. Karf died by the score.

"I'll be buggered," Brains exclaimed. "That worked just like it did in the training simulations."

"Don't feel too smug," Keti added. "It looks like they are forming up near the elevators to try another charge."

"Is this what you'd call an inhuman wave attack?"

As they watched, the right-hand causeway exploded and collapsed. The Marines' hold on the upper level round-a-bout was now fairly secure, but the situation on the lower level was far from decided.

"Looks like Aurora is still at it." Keti stood and surveyed the scene before her. "The gray bastards keep coming down from the spire."

While she was talking, Grits looked over the edge of the upper round-a-bout and spotted two of the alien invaders. Under cover of the Karf attack they had worked their way around the edge of the chamber and were now in position to strike at Keti. With out a second thought, Grits jumped off the upper level while shouting a warning.

"Hostiles attacking from the left flank!"

He landed on the back of the first Uxoreeza sending the raptor like creature sprawling, its weapon flying from its grasp. Grits turned and came off the floor. His left arm knocked the second alien's weapon aside just as it fired. The plasma bolt went wide, impacting on the lip of the roadway opening.

Too close to use his railguns effectively, Grits acted out of instinct and punched the alien in the head while yanking the plasma rifle out of its hands. The alien fell backward but used its long muscular tail to keep from falling to the floor. Bouncing back it lept at the Marine lashing out with both its legs. Like a rooster in a cockfight, there were long sharp spurs on the inside of each leg just above the ankles.

The twin spurs scraped across Grits' midsection, leaving visible grooves in the metal-ceramic armor. With the alien literally up in his face, Grits struck back with a right uppercut. While polar bears had long mounted mechanical claws on the gauntlets of their battle armor, there was not as much room on the arms of human Marines.

362

They settled for a single extensible blade—a half meter in length, double edged with a sharp triangular point.

As Grits delivered the punch to the underside of his opponent's jaw he triggered the blade. It shot forward and locked in position an instant before the power of the blow drove the blade through the alien's armor. It went clear through the alien's skull, its tip just emerging from the top of the Uxoreeza's helmet.

The impaled Uxoreeza hung from Grits' extended right arm, its legs still kicking, twitching in death. He turned around, trying to fling the dead alien from his blade but the creature would not dislodge. Finally he had to place a foot on his vanquished foe's neck so he could extract the impaling spike. Looking up he saw the second of the two attackers being swung through the air by Keti.

Finding itself disarmed, the lead Uxoreeza had made a similar leaping attack on Keti, who feinted right and knocked the raptor to the ground. Lying on its back it kicked out again, but the Marine grabbed the offending leg by the ankle. Using both hands, Keti swung the alien around in a circle, leaning back to counterbalance its weight like a hammer thrower at the Scottish Highland Games.

On the second complete revolution Keti released her attacker, throwing it in a high arc through the air. At the apex of its trajectory it exploded in a bright yellow flash leaving a splatter of flesh, pink mist, and drifting feathers.

"Wait 'till I say 'pull' next time, luv," Brains said, standing on the upper level.

"I think you should come down here, it looks like they are forming up for another charge."

"Right you are." He lept nimbly down to the main floor, joining his comrades. "I don't know about you two, but I'm running short on ammunition."

"Yeah, Bubba. I got only a couple hundred flechettes left and a half dozen 15mm."

"I have about the same, plus a couple of grenades," Keti replied. "I don't think that will be enough to stop the next wave."

"I think you're right. Looks like we're bloody well fucked."

363

The trio stared at the wave of screaming gray savages converging on their position. Keti broke the silence. "When we are out of ammo back into the mouth of the tunnel, limit the front they can attack us on."

More out of helplessness than expectation, Grits called out on the common channel. "This is Grits at the entrance to the main roadway south. We are almost out of ammo and about to be overrun. If y'all got any suggestions we're all ears."

"Clear the mouth of the tunnel," a new voice answered.

The trio did as they were ordered. An instant later, tracer fire streamed from the roadway entrance slaughtering the approaching Karf.

"Is that you, LT?" Brains asked.

"You called for the cavalry, Marine?"

Railguns blazing, a battle-bot emerged from the entrance. Its heavy railgun sent a torrent of explosive shells into the mass of hostiles at the base of the central column. A string of explosions rose up the glowing shaft of the large freight elevator, blasting the bodies of descending Karf to pieces.

"Yee-haw! Now that's what I call reinforcements."

"Right, mate," Brains said, "and what do we do when robo-boy runs out of ammo?"

Bridge, Peggy Sue

"Peggy Sue, Ice Castle. The Marine's are reporting that they are almost out of ammunition and there are still Karf coming from the spire. I have no way of resupplying them effectively. There could be thousands more of those gray bastards in that spire for all we know."

"And the Uxoreeza?" the Captain replied.

"Maybe a dozen accounted for, its hard to tell. That place is a slaughter house. In a couple of places it has come down to close combat—hand-to-hand with the Jurassic chickens."

Billy Ray thought for a few seconds, arriving at a decision. "Ice Castle, tell the Marines to take shelter. We are going to take out the spire."

"Aye, aye, Sir. Ice Castle standing by."

"Cmdr. Danner, could you please position the ship so we have a clear field of fire on the Karf spire."

"Aye, aye, Captain." Bobby already had the ship in motion. In fewer than twenty seconds the Peggy Sue stood off the top spire with no obstructions in the ship's line of fire. "The ship is positioned, Sir."

"I want you to walk a line of railgun slugs up the spire, from as close to the base you can get."

"Are we trying to demolish it or just kill everything inside of it?" Mizuki asked.

"You think we can exterminate the inhabitants without totally destroying the structure, Dr. Ogawa?"

"Hai, Captain. The spire is essentially a tube filled with air. The shockwave from a railgun projectile striking it should kill everything within half a kilometer of the impact point."

"OK, so spread the impact points out one every klick or so. Any thing else?"

"From the SEALs' reconnaissance of the structure we know the top one third contains no inhabited spaces. We need to only target the lower ten kilometers."

"Understood, thank you, Mizuki. Bobby, take the bastards out."

"Aye, aye, Captain."

The ship quivered, rose slightly and quivered again. Nine times the firing cycle repeated. The impacts were plainly visible on the side of the spire, shattered crystal splashing outward. The momentum of each round was sufficient to blast corresponding holes on the opposite side of the spire. Inside the transparent spire walls bright angry flames could be seen as the immense kinetic energy of each slug was dispersed in a shockwave of superheated air and vaporized metal.

365

A minute later and the Karf were no more, nor were any Uxoreeza who remained in the spire with their underlings. What was left of the spire's atmosphere escaped, carrying with it debris and mutilated dead bodies. The struggle for the Starflake was all but over.

SEALs, Station Core

"They approach from the center hallway," the Tcist informed the three SEALs. The humans stood on a wide balcony from which the station's cache of antimatter eggs could be seen. They were all that stood between the approaching Uxoreeza and the Starflake's destruction.

"We're playing this kinda close, don't you think?" asked Bud.

"So don't fuck it up," Rick replied.

"How we going to handle this?" asked Phil.

"Take cover on either side of the doorway. We can't just shoot the hostiles, that might set off whatever explosives they are carrying—and if they are carrying antimatter they're probably already close enough to set the whole place off."

"Wait till they emerge and take them out?"

"Yeah, simultaneous head shots. We have to assume that a head shot can prevent an involuntary trigger squeeze in these birds, just like with humans."

"Right, let's do this." Bud and Phil moved to opposite sides of the hallway opening. Rick took the same side as Bud, farther in from the opening. All three activated their suit camo, becoming almost invisible. They didn't have long to wait.

The sound of claws running on hard flooring approached. The first Uxoreeza burst from the doorway and headed straight for the balcony railing twelve meters away. It was immediately followed by a second. When the head of the third alien emerged the SEALs fired.

Each fired a three round burst, the 5mm flechettes emerging in such rapid succession that the muzzles of their weapons didn't have time to rise from recoil. From less than three meters away and traveling at 4,000 fps, the flechettes cut through the aliens' helmets and shattered their skulls, killing the Uxoreeza instantly.

Their bodies fell to the floor, forward momentum carrying them toward the balcony. The lead warrior slid to a stop only two meters from the edge.

"Clear!" each SEAL cried in turn.

"Search the bodies for explosives," Rick ordered. Bud and Phil were already moving to check their targets. Phil, who had taken out the middle alien yelled, "I think I got something."

Strapped to the dead alien's chest was a bundle. Inside the bundle was a silver container with a glowing display on its side. The symbols on the display were changing.

"I think this thing is counting down," Phil said.

"We need to get it out of here, ASAP!" Bud said.

"Station. How do we get this bomb out of here?" Rick demanded.

"Give it to the whooboo," came the Tcist's reply.

"What whooboo?" Bud asked, looking around as Phil cut the demolition charge free of the dead Uxoreeza.

"There!" said Rick, pointing to a yellow troll that appeared seemingly out of nowhere.

Phil handed the pack to the mustard colored creature and it ran off, clasping the bundle to its chest. It rounded a corner and disappeared.

"I sure hope that little guy makes it," Bud said, gazing after the vanished maintenance troll.

"Amen to that, brother," Rick said. The problem was now beyond their control.

Plaza, Shopping Mall

Hitch and Jacobs had dropped Kashi off at Dr. de Bruin's makeshift medical station, just off the main plaza. The Doc didn't say much but the chiefs could tell Kashi's condition was serious. He put the wounded sailor into a drug induced coma and flooded his system with nanites, saying only that he needed immediate medivac to the ship.

Since there was nothing else they could do, the two old shipmates went out into the plaza to see the Lieutenant. They had listened in to the conversation between JT and the Captain, hearing the Captain's decision to take out the Karf's spire.

"I figure this dust up is about over, Stevie."

"Yeah, Matt, this was a tough one. Can't remember a bigger pooch screw in years."

"We won."

"Yeah, but it cost us, man. I heard the Marine's lost a couple KIA."

"I just hope that Kashi didn't buy the farm ...hey, what's that?" Jacobs pointed toward the transparent wall of the spire.

"It looks like one of those little yellow guys, what's it doing outside the station without a suit?" They watched the whooboo rising, moving away from the station.

A blinding flash illuminated the Starflake. The sailors' helmets darkened to save their eyesight, then slowly regained transparency. Outside the spire, the whooboo was gone.

Chapter 41

Pinnace, 4,000 km from the Starflake

The object of their search was barely visible ahead of them, its pitch black exterior more noticeable by the stars it occluded than by the light reflecting off it. On the flight deck of the Captain's pinnace Lt. Pauline Palmer was at the controls with Master Chief Frank Zackly riding right seat. The Chief worked the comm.

"Ahoy the ship."

After a brief silence there came a reply.

"It's about bloody time, Master Chief."

The old Chief smiled widely, an unusual occurrence.

"Sorry, Commander. Took us a bit to figure out which way you were headed."

Inside the all but dead Kestrel, Cmdr. Beth Melaku stirred and peered out through the fighter's small windscreen. She could almost make out the outline of Peggy Sue's smallest shuttle.

"You want us to come and get you out of that bird?"

"No, thank you. I've enough reserve power to get back to the ship, if you would be so kind as to give me a tow." The fighter had lost power when it was hit by fire from the alien frigate some five hours ago. Using the Kestrel's attitude gyros she had managed to stabilize the fighter and had been tapping the gyros for power to keep the cabin heat on since. Another six hours and she would have frozen to death inside her already dead fighter.

"Aye, aye, Ma'am. Give us a few minutes to rig a tow line and we'll head back to the ship."

"Roger that, Master Chief. Wake me when we get there."

Sickbay, Peggy Sue

Dr. Belinda White surveyed the controlled chaos of her normally empty medical section. The arrival of shuttles from the nearby space station changed her usually quiet routine as casualties from the battle streamed in. She had already operated on one of the sailors with a bad plasma weapon wound, but most of the casualties were Marines.

The entire 1st squad, at least those who survived, had received a potentially fatal dose of radiation from an antimatter explosion. All had been stripped and washed before being moved into the sickbay. Since the Marines had all been wearing armor there was no threat of surface contaminants, but there were other reasons to wash the victims. Since even high-dose radiation exposure is generally not lethal within the initial two weeks, emergent medical care took precedence over assessment of the degree of exposure. Several were treated for bruising and trauma, but thankfully there were no other wounds.

It had been more than eight hours since they were exposed and symptoms were starting to present themselves. Though varying from patient to patient, nausea, vomiting, diarrhea, abdominal cramping and/or bleeding, fatigue, and fever were observed. Betty didn't think that the amount of exposure recorded by the Marines' suit instruments was invariably fatal, but she had the medical staff monitoring for signs of lymphopenia or decline of absolute lymphocyte count to dangerous levels. As a precaution they were in the process of transfusing all of the stricken Marines with synthetic blood and administering enhanced nanite injections.

Betty looked across the ward and saw the Captain walking toward her. Puting on her best professional doctor's face she greeted her friend and commanding officer. "Hello, Captain."

"Is it that bad, Doctor?"

"I didn't say anything yet."

"You never call me 'captain' unless there's bad news."

"It could be better, but it could have been much worse. The crewman that was wounded should make a complete recovery. I replaced his damaged ribs with demineralized bone matrix and, after removing all the necrotic tissue, reprinted muscle and dermis layers using cultures from his own body. He should fully recover in five days to a week."

"And the Marines?"

"According to their suits they took between two and three grays of radiation. At that level of exposure radiation-induced damage to hematopoietic stem and progenitor cells is reversible. With judicious used of transfusions, regeneration should result in the production of adequate numbers of functionally normal neutrophils and platelets within a few days to a week. Non-hematopoietic stem cell transplant scenarios are dependent on other injuries: cerebrovascular, gastrointestinal, and cutaneous syndromes, as well as radiation-induced lung injury and other trauma."

"You lost me at 'three grays', Doc."

"Sorry, doctor speak. A gray unit is the international measure of radiation exposure, the same as a hundred rads old school. Blood and the tissues that produce red and white blood cells are most susceptible to exposure. We will use transfusions and stem cell treatments to restore healthy blood composition in each patient. If there are other damaged organs we'll fix them along the way as well. Barring any complications, they should be ready for discharge within two weeks."

"Thank you, Doctor. I'll leave you and your people to it then."

As the Captain left the ward he could swear he heard one of the stricken Marines mumble something about 'monkey sex'. He passed it off as delirium.

Captain's Quarters

Two days after the end of hostilities, the four principle partners gathered in the sitting room of the Captain's quarters. The ship was no longer at general quarters and the officers were enjoying a well deserved libation. Billy Ray and Bobby were drinking Wild Turkey, Beth Hendrick's Gin, and Mizuki some concoction made with rum and tropical fruit juices.

"Here's to absent comrades," the Captain intoned, raising his glass.

"Absent comrades," the others repeated. They all drank. Tradition observed they got down to the business at hand.

"What's the status of the crew and Marines, Number One?"

"All present or accounted for. We have three killed in action and eleven in hospital. JT is still down on the station, dealing with the natives—you know how those Green Beret types love to work with indigenous peoples. 2nd Squad is also on the Starflake continuing to patrol and search for any surviving hostiles."

The Captain nodded, acknowledging the report.

"You've been to sick bay most recently, what is the prognosis for the Marines, Dear?" Beth asked her husband.

"I talked to Betty and she says all the wounded will recover. The wounded sailor, Kashimawo Ademola, in a week and the Marines will be fit for limited duty in two. Dr. de Bruin has asked to return to the station so he can treat any wounded among the residents. What about material losses?"

"Other than munitions expended we lost one Kestrel to enemy action."

"I see. We were fortunate to get off so lightly."

"I wouldn't call it lightly," Beth said with a frown. "Three KIA and eleven wounded is a pretty stiff butcher's bill."

"When you consider that every engagement the Marines fought they were outnumbered by at least two to one, I think we got off lucky," Bobby observed. "Even the sailors acquitted themselves well."

Beth sat stiffly, staring at the drink in her hands. "You forget that I managed to lose half of my unit and rendered it 100% combat ineffective by the end of the engagement."

"Sweetheart, two of you took on a score of enemy fighters and still managed to take out the troop carriers they were protecting. Hell, you took out an enemy frigate single handed. I'd say that ranks more as brilliant success than tragic failure."

"I lost my wingman. I've never lost a wingman before."

"I was in command. In addition to Lt. Hoenig, I also lost two Marines: Private Ben-Ezra and Corporal Inuksuk. I don't think anyone's ever lost a polar bear in combat before. Every death, every casualty is on me—it was my decision to fight instead of running."

372

In a quiet voice Mizuki spoke. "You are being too hard on yourselves. Exploring the galaxy is a risky business; people die, often by accident. In this case we fought and died for a purpose."

"It doesn't change the fact that under my command we shot up half the station while wiping out the Uxoreeza fleet and exterminating the Karf. Like Agricola said, we make a desolation and call it peace."

"I prefer Saint Matthew," said Bobby. "'Blessed are the peacemakers for they shall be called children of God.' If we'd have abandoned the station its inhabitants would have been slaughtered and the Uxoreeza would have regained control of the antimatter cache. Who knows how many deaths on how many worlds that would have contributed to. The way I see it, Frank and the others died warriors' deaths fighting for a just cause, fighting ultimately for peace."

"Perhaps yer right, pardner. I guess we should be thankful for our victory."

Beth sighed. "I suppose Bobby's right, but I'm still going to get totally pissed once this meeting is over."

"I think we all deserve to tie one on, honey bunch. But before we get too drunk to think we need to decide what we're gonna do next."

Beth forced a smile and looked at her friends. "We bloody well paid for this place, I say we keep it."

Relieved that the conversation had taken a turn for the hopeful, Mizuki seized on Beth's thought. "There is certainly much to be learned studying the Starflake. Such an old entity can not only fill in important historical information, the station's technology is highly advanced in many areas."

"You're right, Mizuki-chan. I say we set up a permanent station here. After all, there's plenty of empty space, particularly once the ex-Karf spire gets repaired."

"Well that's three in favor of staying. I make it unanimous. This is going to take a lot of planning, people."

"Hai, we should plant Earth crops in the agricultural section above the Shopping Mall. And we can convert the condominium apartments into quarters."

"What's more, the ship has enough fabrication units and manufacturing capability we can crank out anything we need." As Bobby spoke he became more animated. "All we need is raw material and energy, both of which the station has in spades. Given time we could probably make a second ship!"

"Whoa there pardner. Let's not get too carried away. I still need to send a report back to TK and the company board."

"I've always wanted a condo in outerspace, dear." Beth smiled demurely.

Billy Ray sighed and looked around at the faces of the people he loved most in the Universe.

"Hell, it'll take 'em months to get back to us. We may as well be comfortable while we wait. Bobby, pour us another round."

Epilogue

Shopping Mall Plaza, Starflake

Three and a half months after dispatching the messenger drone to OATC headquarters several ships popped into existence from alter-space. Earth ships by their drive signatures and confirmed by radio seven hours after emergence. It took another fifteen days for the three ships to arrive: the *Rosa Amarilla*; the *Fortitude*, a sister ship to the *Peggy Sue II*; and the freighter *Halifax*. While the Fortitude stood off as a picket, the others docked with the Starflake.

The Halifax carried a hold full of military material: weapons, suits of armor, and three new Kestrels. Also, the hard to manufacture pieces for shield generators and particle cannon. Everything the Earthlings would need to fortify the station and prevent future hostile invasions. New engineers and technicians joined those from the Peggy Sue's crew in the work while fresh recruits were put through their paces by the Gunny.

As the representatives of the Honorable Orion Arm Trading Company arrived in the main plaza they were met by the Peggy Sue's senior officers. Led by Captain Vincent, the four walked among the other inhabitants of the station without armor, though they wore swords and handguns on their waists. The lack of armor was both a sign of trust and a statement that said no sane creature would attack an Earthling on board the Starflake.

"Billy Ray! It's good to see you alive and kicking, son," shouted TK Parker from halfway across the plaza. Striding up to the four, the former Texas oil man and current merchant prince greeted them all in turn. "Beth, you look radiant! Mizuki, Dr. Saito sends his love; and Bobby, yer a sight for sore eyes."

As her husband pumped the men's hands and kissed the women's cheeks, TK's wife, Maria, made a more dignified approach, trailed by several aides and attendants. "Hola, everyone. TK, stop making a spectacle of yourself in front of all the aliens."

"Welcome, Maria," Beth said, stepping up to embrace her. She might harbor some reservations when it came to TK and his schemes but Beth genuinely loved his wife. Mizuki joined the other two women, accompanied by a swarm of excited butterflies flashing festive colors. The *aoi chō* reflected their mistress' emotions and Mizuki was very happy to see old friends from Earth.

"When I sent my report I was hardly expecting a reply in person, TK," Billy Ray began.

"What? And miss humanity's biggest discovery since the M'tak Ka'fek? Ain't no way I was gonna sit at home and miss coming to take a gander at this Starflake of yours."

"Well this is it," Billy Ray gestured with a sweep of his arm. "What do you think?"

"It's even more impressive than the holograms you sent. That moving roadway system is something else, I can see a thousand uses for that technology alone. And you say this place is more than a million years old?"

"That's what the entity that maintains it says."

"Right, that would be the intelligent moss you found."

"Actually, Bobby and Mizuki found the Tcist. It was only later that a couple of lost Marines found the treasure at the heart of the Starflake."

"You and that wife of yours, Bobby, always finding treasure where no one else can. Way to go, son. You realize that you are now all rich enough to retire a hundred times over?"

"Thanks, TK, but the payoff was not why we came. And winning the station was not without cost."

"Yeah, I read about that too. Damn shame those brave Marines and sailors died fightin' them alien varmints." TK looked out across the plaza as the conversation fell silent for a moment. There he spotted a strange statue.

"What in the Sam Hill is that?"

The others turned. There, in the middle of the plaza was a more than life-sized statue of an alien. Squat and muscular, clutching a package to its chest, it was a sculpture of a whooboo. TK led the group of humans over to the monument. A bronze plaque was affixed to the two meter tall plinth. On it were the words: "The Unknown Whooboo."

"What in tarnation is a whooboo?"

"It's one of the maintenance workers that fix things around the station. At the very end of the battle against the Uxoreeza, our SEALs intercepted a detail of hostiles who were intent on blowing the station up. They stopped the aliens but the timer on their demolition charge was already activated—an antimatter bomb that would have set off the entire cache at the station's core.

"To make a long story short, one of the whooboo took the bomb and got it off the station just in time to save the lives of everyone on board. It ejected itself into space with the bomb, giving its life for the rest of ours."

"So this whooboo critter is the hero of the battle of the Starflake?"

"Hai, TK," Mizuki said, as the women joined the three men at the base of the stature. "We still do not know if the whooboo are sentient, biological constructs, or just very smart animals, but we do know that one of them gave its life to save the station. We thought the least we could do was erect a statue in memoriam."

"Amazing," the old Texan said, looking up at the ugly yet somehow heroic figure above them. "I guess heroes come in all shapes and sizes."

"Yep," Billy Ray added. "Some even come in mustard yellow."

Beth took the moment as an opportunity to move the party along. They had a lot of business to take care of and she was anxious to get to it. "Let us show you our temporary company offices. They have a great view of the plaza. We can relax, catch up and have a drink."

"A drink? Now yer talking sweetheart." TK Parker was a man who enjoyed his whiskey, particularly when it was consumed with friends while telling tales of adventure. Beth exchanged a secret smile with her husband, as if to say, *I knew that would get him moving.*

As the party moved toward an elevator shaft, Maria asked, "Now that you have found this magnificent palace among the stars, what are you going to do next?"

377

"We figure we need to stick around here until we get things squared away," Billy Ray answered. "But we still have some unfinished business."

"Oh? How is that?"

"We didn't come here looking for the Starflake. As marvelous as it is, its discovery was pure serendipity." Billy Ray paused and Mizuki completed the answer.

"You see, Maria, we came this way looking for the Lost Pleiad. She is still out there among the stars, waiting for us to find her. The Pleiades are calling, and curiosity compels us to answer."

www.ingramcontent.com/pod-product-compliance
Lightning Source LLC
Chambersburg PA
CBHW071223250626
47163CB00001B/84